Karen Mac

*He was gazing*
*sity that sent shivers of excitement*
*racing through her veins . . .*

He leaned towards her and she was vividly
aware of the strong line of his cheekbone, the
thrust of his smooth-shaven jaw, the sensuous
curve of his lips, and suddenly she wanted to feel
his cheek against her cheek, his lips against her
lips, his body against hers. She reached up and
touched his face with her fingertips. He gave a
small groan and then she was in his arms. He
kissed her, hungrily, urgently, and she returned
his kisses with equal fervor, both consumed with
a passion they had never known before . . .

# SILK

## EILEEN VAN KIRK

DIAMOND BOOKS, NEW YORK

SILK

A Diamond Book / published by arrangement with
the author

PRINTING HISTORY
Diamond edition / October 1991

ISBN: 1-55773-594-8

Diamond Books are published by The Berkley Publishing Group,
200 Madison Avenue, New York, New York 10016.
The name "DIAMOND" and its logo are trademarks
belonging to Charter Communications, Inc.

PRINTED IN THE UNITED STATES OF AMERICA

10  9  8  7  6  5  4  3  2  1

# CHAPTER

## ❧ 1 ❧

## 1910

THE air was still as the great ship, smoke trailing from her fat smokestack, edged her way slowly into the harbor. A faint mist lay in pale swirls along the water. Later, it would burn off under the relentless power of the hot August sun.

Grace leaned on the ship's railing, straining eagerly to catch her first glimpse of the city. New York—with its skyscrapers, its mansions, its traffic, shops and people—represented everything she yearned for. She pictured herself driving a fashionable carriage, wearing silk dresses and elegant kidskin gloves, dining in expensive restaurants. One day, she promised herself, one day.

More and more people were drifting up on deck. Men in their best black wool suits, suits creased from days of being packed in cheap cardboard suitcases; gaunt, bony women, their heads wrapped in kerchiefs, many wearing black woollen shawls and carrying, fat, pink-cheeked babies, stood quietly alongside their men. The babies, already warm in their hand-knit bonnets and jackets, squirmed in their mothers' arms.

Grace ignored the milling crowd, knowing that she stood apart in her pale gray traveling outfit. No shawls and kerchiefs in her wardrobe. She felt a faint twinge of guilt as she wondered how Maggie and Jeannie were getting on.

She should probably go below and see if they needed help, but the thought of facing those cramped and smelly quarters once more was more than she could stomach. She took several breaths of the fresh morning air.

"Up early today, Miss Cameron." A young man in the neat uniform of a steward was beside her holding a cup and saucer. "Would you like a cup of coffee? I have an extra." He handed it to her. He had been a kind friend throughout the journey and had made a point of slipping her a few delicacies from the first-class cabins. It had helped a lot; the food below was awful.

"Do you think they mind?" she whispered, glancing around at the people on deck.

"That lot," said the steward scornfully, "probably wouldn't know what to do with a cup of coffee if they got one. They'd drink it out of the saucer, like as not." She laughed. The coffee was hot and good, and she drank it down quickly.

"Thanks Ted, that was delicious." She gave him back the cup. "When will we dock?"

"Not for hours yet. The first-class passengers get off first. Then it's Ellis Island for the immigrants."

*I'm an immigrant,* thought Grace, *lumped together with all these poor and ignorant peasants. But I'm not one of them, I'm not,* she thought fiercely.

Ted was pointing out the sights coming into view. "New Jersey's on the left. On your right is little old New York. That's the place for yours truly. And coming up is what they're all up on deck waiting to see: the Statue of Liberty. Don't know what it is about the old girl, but there's certainly something. Gets to you every time you come here."

"It's New York I want to see," said Grace, "but Aunt Flora lives in New Jersey, so that's where we're going. Paterson, I think."

"You a silk worker?"

"What makes you ask that?"

"That's where all the silk workers go. The Scots, the Limies, the Italians, all of 'em flock to Paterson. Silk City they call it."

"Maggie's a silk worker, and I guess Jeannie's going to be one too, but I don't know what I'm going to do yet." What would she be able to do? She wasn't trained for anything, unless you counted reading Sir Walter Scott's novels to old Lady McLeod.

"Well I've got a busy day ahead of me, Miss Cameron. Good luck. Maybe I'll see you sometime when we're in port."

"That would be nice, Ted," said Grace, although they both knew it would never happen. She resumed her stance at the rail. The mist was lifting, and she could make out trees and buildings and roads. Now and then she glimpsed a smart carriage behind a high-stepping horse. Behind her was a babel of voices as people began crowding the decks. She was aware of the smell of humanity mingled with the smell of garlic, and she made a vow. Never again would she travel steerage. Never again would she put up with the noise and the stink and the degradation. Next time she traveled she would go first class.

Below decks the noise and the smell were considerably stronger. Maggie was aching to get out into the fresh air. She wanted more than anything to see the Statue of Liberty. She'd read all about it in her geography book, and now she was going to see it. She, Maggie McHugh, who'd never traveled farther than a trip to Glasgow. She glanced along the rows of cramped and crowded bunks they'd shared with the other women and children making this fateful and fearful journey. She remembered the first night when they hadn't been able to sleep for the weeping and sobbing. Then as the ship began to pitch and roll, the crying gave way to groaning and the stench of sickness filled the air. But now it was different. There was laughter and talk, even if much of it was high pitched and slightly hysterical as hope mingled with fear. But the journey was over. They'd arrived. For better or worse they were entering a new country, a new world, a new life.

All except Jeannie, who stubbornly refused to leave her bunk and get dressed. Maggie was pleading with her.

"Jeannie, please get up, we're nigh to New York. Don't ye want tae see the Statue o' Liberty? Och, they say she's a bonnie sight wi' her lamp shinin' all over the harbor."

"No. I dinna give a hoot for your old statue, nor New York, nor America. I want tae go home. I want tae go back to Scotland and see mae friends. I want tae play hopscotch wi' Mary and 'Em.'' Jeannie buried her face in her pillow and began to sob.

"Jeannie, ye canna go back. You're here in America."

"The ship goes back. I'll stay aboard and go back wi' her."

"But there's no one tae go back to. I'm here, Grace is here, and Aunt Flora's meeting us."

"I dinna want tae go and live wi' Aunt Flora. I dinna ken Aunt Flora."

"Ye dinna remember her," said Maggie, "but she's Mama's sister, so you're bound tae like her." Jeannie continued to cry and Maggie looked around in despair.

"What's the matter wi' your sister? She sick? They won't let her in if she's sick." The speaker was a tall, untidy woman who was struggling to anchor a battered straw hat onto a mass of gray, straggly hair.

"She's a wee bit homesick, Mrs. Green, there's naught else the matter wi' her," said Maggie.

"Well she'd better get over that. We're here. She can't swim back, now can she?" The woman laughed harshly. "She'd best get up, too, they want everything cleared out of here before we get to Ellis Island." She looked around sharply. "Where's your high and mighty friend this morning? Off flirting with the steward again, I suppose, when she should be here helping you young 'uns.''

"I'm sixteen, Mrs. Green, and I can manage fine," said

Maggie firmly. She, too, had been hoping Grace would come below and give her a hand, but she wouldn't admit that to Mrs. Green. But it was Jeannie who flew to Grace's defense. She lifted her head from the pillow and glared at the woman.

"Grace is our cousin and she's not high and mighty." Jeannie sat up and swung her legs over the side of the bunk. She detested Mrs. Green, the interfering old busybody, and she wasn't going to let her talk about Grace like that.

"Hmph," Mrs. Green sniffed. "Just because she's got fancy clothes and talks all la-di-da, she thinks she's better than the rest of us."

"She makes her own clothes and she talks like that because she lived wi' Lady McLeod after our Aunt Mattie died, and Lady McLeod taught her to speak fancy."

"If she's a lady's maid, what's she going to Paterson for? I thought you girls were all going to work in the mills."

"She's nae a lady's maid," said Jeannie, jumping off the bunk. "And what does it matter to ye where we work? Come on, Maggie, we maun hurry if we want tae see yon statue."

When the girls did finally get up on deck, it was jam-packed with people. Families clung together. Nervous mothers and fathers, clutching bundles of precious possessions, tried to keep track of their children, who tugged at skirts or darted off between the legs of other passengers. But overall there was a festive air to the crowd. Men laughed and joked with one another, exchanged names and the names of the towns where they hoped friends and relatives awaited them, and promised to send postcards.

The girls could feel the excitement growing as they worked their way towards the rail. A murmur ran through the throng, "Look! Look! There she is, over there, look! Look!"

"Here, Jeannie, get in front of me. Now you can see."

A hush descended on the crowd as the ship slowly steamed up the river and a sea of upturned faces gazed at the tall, powerful figure with the raised torch, bidding them welcome, lighting the way. With a mighty roar a great cheer burst spontaneously from every throat. The men waved their hats in the air, women their kerchiefs, children were lifted high on shoulders and waved too, babies had their hands held in the air as everyone laughed, cried and shouted, ''America, America, America,'' over and over again. Maggie felt tears streaming down her face. She wasn't sure why she was crying, but she was not the only one. She saw both men and women wiping their eyes, and she remembered the words she had read in her book, ''I lift my lamp beside the golden door.''

The golden door to America was swinging wide to greet hundreds of thousands of men, women, and children as they poured in from across the ocean, speaking a babble of languages, bringing with them their own foods, customs, prayers, politics, hopes and dreams. And she, Maggie, was one of them.

The joyful atmosphere on board lasted while the ship, pulled and pushed by squat tug boats, slid into her pier at Battery Park. Here they waited while the wealthier passengers disembarked. Grace, who had finally joined the two girls, gazed at them enviously.

''Look at the beautiful coat that woman is wearing. It looks like linen, but not a wrinkle. One day, Maggie, I'm going to have clothes like that. A carriage too, just like the one she's getting into. Oh, isn't this the most exciting place in the world?'' She leaned over the rail trying to absorb the atmosphere of the city that lay before her. A great mass of buildings reached high into the sky—tall, gray, splendid buildings. She tried to imagine what went on inside of them. There would be shops selling furs, jewels and perfumes, and there would be offices where handsome men made and lost fortunes, and there would be thick carpets and all sorts of rich and wonderful things . . .

"Where's Aunt Flora?" wailed Jeannie. "I dinna see Aunt Flora."

"She's nae here, Jeannie," said Maggie. "She's tae meet us at Ellis Island."

"Isn't this Ellis Island?"

"No, this is Manhattan," said Grace. "They'll ferry us over to the island." She sighed. If only she were getting off now.

"Suppose she doesna' come. Suppose she's gone home already. Suppose she doesna' know us, and we'll nae know her." Jeannie was getting thoroughly worked up.

"She'll be there," said Maggie soothingly. "I have her letter in mae handbag, and she'll remember Grace."

"I don't know that she'll remember me," said Grace, annoyed at being brought so abruptly back to reality. "I was only eight years old when she left for America. But I remember her—she's tall and thin, with reddish hair, a long nose, and horsey looking teeth."

"Grace!" Maggie was shocked. "That's nae way to describe your aunt."

"I dinna care what she looks like as long as she comes," said Jeannie. The girls watched as porters hurried up and down the pier with suitcases and trunks.

"Why do we have to go to Ellis Island? Why can't we get off here?" asked Jeannie.

"Because we're immigrants. We have to be checked tae see if we're healthy."

"You mean by a doctor. I'm nae going to be looked at by nae doctor." Jeannie sat down on her suitcase and set her mouth in an obstinate line, but when the call went up, "All for Ellis Island at the front gangplank," Maggie grabbed her sister and the three girls were swept along with the surging crowd. Down the steep wooden gangplank they stumbled, into a straggling line on the pier, where they were again carried along, pushed, shoved and finally herded into waiting barges. And there they sat.

The sun climbed higher and higher, the day grew hotter,

babies cried, children wailed, those who could find a seat sat, others shifted from foot to foot. Some of the younger men shed their jackets, but most of them just sweated in their heavy wool clothing, mopping their faces with huge handkerchiefs, until, hours later, the barge slowly inched its way to the shore and disgorged its weary crowd into a huge cavernous room with a warren of wooden stalls that would be forever remembered by all who passed through it.

The noise broke over them in waves. In this great echoing hall everything was magnified: children suddenly released from captivity were yelling, screaming, climbing on and off benches, babies cried, and parents—tempers worn to a frazzle by the heat, thirst, and sheer exhaustion—shouted and grumbled. Over all this din, directions were boomed at them through megaphones in what seemed to be a hundred different languages.

*It's like a cattle market,* thought Grace with a shudder, *and we're the cattle.*

But to Maggie it was magnificent. She had never been in such an enormous room, and her eyes ranged from the fine balcony that surrounded it, to the great windows and the fancy domed ceiling with its rows of beautiful hanging lamps. She felt a tug at her sleeve.

"I'm hungry," said Jeannie, "I want something to eat."

"Please, let's not eat here," said Grace. "I want to get out of this awful place." She caught the eye of a young, harried official, and after a few minutes of pleading for her two young cousins, she convinced him to push them through the line. A cursory examination by a weary looking doctor, a quick eye check, a couple of signatures, and the next thing they knew a kindly official took their papers and stamped them ADMITTED.

"Welcome to America," he said, "Your aunt should be waiting for you in the next room." Maggie clutched her immigration papers tightly, her heart was pounding as they made their way to the other waiting room. She hadn't admitted even to herself how frightened she'd been—frightened that they wouldn't get accepted, that they'd be sent back to Scotland, or that Aunt Flora wouldn't come for them.

"There she is," cried Jeannie, pointing to a tall red-haired woman wearing a dark gray cotton dress and a black straw hat. "She looks just like you said, Grace. Tall and thin with . . ." A sharp kick in the ankle from Maggie cut her short just as Aunt Flora reached their sides.

"Och, you're here at last." She gave them each a quick kiss on the cheek. "What took ye so long? I've been waiting here since nine o'clock this morning."

"We've been waiting, too, Aunt Flora," said Grace.

"Aye, and we've had naught tae eat since breakfast," said Jeannie.

Aunt Flora looked from Grace in her smart traveling suit to the two girls in their white cotton shirtwaists and black skirts.

"Which is Maggie and which is Jeannie?" she asked.

"I'm Maggie."

"Aye, ye look like your mother. I couldna' believe it when ye wrote that she had died so sudden."

"We could hardly believe it ourselves," said Maggie softly. Aunt Flora produced a large white handkerchief and blew her nose.

"We'll eat when we get home," she said firmly. "Come on girls, follow me." And they stepped outside into the bright, hot sunlight. *America,* thought Maggie, *I'm in America.*

# CHAPTER

## ❧ 2 ❧

"THAT was delicious, Aunt Flora," said Maggie as she mopped up the last drop of gravy with a slice of bread.

"There's nothing like a good plate o' mutton stew when you're hungry," said Aunt Flora. "I made it yesterday and kept it in the icebox." She pointed with pride to the large wooden chest that stood on four legs in the corner of the room. "Ye've nae seen the like o' that in Scotland, I'll be bound."

"What does it do?" asked Maggie.

"It keeps the food cool and fresh in this hot weather, see." She opened the door to the chest revealing shelves filled with milk, butter, meat, and eggs. Then she showed them the big block of ice that slowly dripped into the pan below.

"What happens when the ice is all melted?" asked Jeannie.

"The iceman comes and brings another block of ice. I put a sign up in the window so he knows when to stop."

Maggie shook her head. "I never heard of an iceman," she said.

"Well, you really don't need them in Scotland. It never gets this hot," said Grace, fanning herself with her handkerchief.

Aunt Flora looked annoyed. Grace was not what she had expected. The other two girls were fine, exclaiming excitedly about everything they saw; but Grace kept herself apart, and when she did say something it was some slighting remark like the one just previous, or like on the way home when Aunt Flora pointed out the trolley cars and Grace had said, "We do have trams in Glasgow, you know, we're not that backward." *She really gives herself airs, that one,* thought Aunt Flora. *She needs to be taken down a peg or two.* But Maggie made up for Grace in her enthusiasm, and even Jeannie, now that she was no longer hungry and thirsty, began to warm up.

" 'Tis a bonnie kitchen ye have, Aunt Flora, and such a big house." *Even if it is made of wood,* she thought. She had never seen so many wooden buildings before, and all with verandas. "Porches," Aunt Flora called them—and those funny doors and windows that let the air in.

"They're called screens," Aunt Flora explained.

"But why do ye need them?" asked Jeannie. "At home when we want to let the air in we just open the windows and doors."

"When ye meet your first New Jersey mosquito ye'll know why we have screens. There's a million bugs out there in the summer, all trying to get in the house." She looked pointedly at Grace. "Ye'll hear them tonight."

"Hear them?" asked Grace with a shudder.

"Aye, they sing a regular chorus. Wait till it gets dark, ye'll hear them. But speaking o' tonight, I've asked a few friends and neighbors in tae meet ye. All folks from the old country."

"Old country," echoed Grace.

"Aye, you're in your new country now," said Aunt Flora, "Scotland's the old country." It was an expression Grace would hear over and over, and for some reason it always annoyed her. It made her feel like an immigrant— one of those gaunt, bony women with the black woollen shawls. And she'd look in the mirror for assurance that she really was Grace Cameron—tall, slender, with red-gold hair, blue eyes, and fair smooth skin—and she'd give a quick sigh of relief.

The party was held in the small front parlor, crowded with heavy, overstuffed furniture. Grace thought she was back in Scotland the burr was so thick on everyone's tongue. As more people crowded in, the heat grew intense and she longed to escape to the coolness of the outside.

"And tell me, lass, are the McTavishes still running the Crown and Thistle? Och, 'tis many a dram I had there," said a wizened little man with a thin sprouting of bristly gray hair, whom everyone addressed as Jock.

"Sit down, Jock, ye auld fool. Why would these young lasses be acquainted wi' the Crown and Thistle?" said a heavy-set woman who took up a large portion of the sofa as she sat fanning herself with a newspaper. "Besides, ye'll be shocking Flora wi' your talk o' strong spirits. What kind of a churchman are ye anyway?" Grace noticed that Aunt Flora was serving lemonade to men and women alike, and she remembered her aunt's strong objection to drink—brought on no doubt by her late husband, who, if Grace remembered rightly, liked to take a drop or two or three.

"Quite right, Dora, me love," said Jock. The woman was apparently his wife. "And beggin' your pardon Flora, I was just anxious to hear about the old country." He made a mock bow. "What about Old Angus, now, is he still runnin' the greengrocers?"

"Auld Angus died last January," said Maggie. " 'Tis young Angus has taken over, and he's fixin' the place up fine. Addin' a whole new counter for tinned fruits."

"Tinned fruits at the greengrocers," exclaimed Jock, shaking his head. And so the conversation flowed back and forth as the friends and neighbors, all hungry for news of Scotland, plied the girls with questions.

"What happened to Lady McLeod?" asked someone.

"She died in the spring," said Grace. *And that's why I'm here,* she thought. *If Lady McLeod hadn't left me those few pounds . . .*

"She was near eighty," Grace finished.

"Who'll be living in the manor house now?"

"There are no heirs. I think it's going to be made into a private school for girls."

"A school for girls," said Jock in disgust. "What need is there for sending girls to school?"

"No need," said his wife. "Everyone knows girls are smarter than men, e'en without schooling."

"I'd like tae go to school," said Jeannie softly.

"Whatever for?" exclaimed her aunt. "You're nigh to thirteen, too old tae be going to school. 'Tis time ye got started at the mill."

"Thirteen," repeated Jock. "When I was thirteen, I was a carder already. I started in the mill when I was eight years old, as a runner. My mother used tae make me wear two pairs o' long woollen stockings, the floors were so cold and damp."

Grace slipped quietly out of the room onto the porch. All the excitement of the morning seemed to have drained away. *I've exchanged one dreary mill town for another,* she thought. *Is there no escape?* She sat down on a wooden bench and discovered that it was a swing, and as she pushed the ground with her foot the swing moved back and forth. With a faint squeak and creaking of springs she rocked slowly and steadily and looked out into the warm darkness. Faint lights glimmered here and there along the quiet street. The tall, narrow houses were separated only by small alleyways. In the backyards, as they called them, she had seen a few straggly vegetables, some makeshift chicken coops, and even a goat tethered to a stake and nibbling on the grass. She sighed. Somewhere out there, across the river, was a great and glittering city, bursting with energy, people, and excitement, but for her it was

just as far away as if she were back in Scotland. She wondered if she would ever be able to find her way there.

She closed her eyes and gradually became aware that
beyond the squeaking of the swing there was another
sound—a low, insistent, throbbing hum; an unspoken
chorus that rose and fell in a strong, steady rhythm, and
suddenly it seemed as if all the strange, aching longings
hidden in the heart of this hot summer night were con-
tained in that low, steady, insistent throb. It spoke to her,
softly, surely, over and over again: "Yes, you can," it
whispered. "Yes, you can."

A footstep on the stair and the light slam of the screen
door made her jump.

"Sorry, I didn't mean to scare you. I didn't know anyone was on the porch." The voice was low and pleasant,
and in the darkness she could make out the silhouette of
a tall, broad-shouldered man. "You must be Maggie, or
is it Jeannie?"

"Neither. I'm Grace," she said. "I'm their cousin."

"Welcome to the States, Grace." He extended a hand
and clasped hers in a warm, strong handshake. "I'm Ian
Campbell. I guess your Aunt Flora mentioned me."

"Yes, you're the . . . the young man who stays here."
She didn't want to say "boarder," although that's what he
was. She caught a gleam of white teeth and there was
amusement in his voice when he spoke again.

"Is the party still going on? I thought it might be over
by now. You must all be very tired after your first day."

Grace suddenly realized that she was very tired. It
seemed years ago that she had stood on deck and watched
New York materialize out of the morning mist.

"It's very hot in there. I came out here to get cool,"
she said.

"Smart girl." He had an easy way of speaking that was
quite new to her. "Have they started singing yet?" Then
he laughed. "They always start singing the old songs.

That's usually a sign the party's about to break up. Are you going back in?''

"Yes, I'd better, or Aunt Flora will get upset." He held the door open for her and they both stepped into the hot, crowded room. As the light struck her, Grace stood blinking for a moment, then she turned to look at Ian and caught her breath. He was the handsomest man she had ever seen. His face was bony but well shaped. He had light brown hair, straight dark eyebrows over deepset gray-green eyes, and a lean and muscular physique. Beside him, all the other men in the room seemed thin and workworn. She made a motion to speak, but Aunt Flora shushed her with her finger to her lips, and Jeannie began to sing in a clear, sweet-sad voice, the old song:

"Speed bonnie boat like a bird on the wing,
'Onward' the sailors cry;
Carry the lad that's born to be king
Over the sea to Skye.''

It was Aunt Flora's favorite, and when Jeannie finished there was a momentary hush. Then a small gray-haired woman in the corner burst into tears.

"Och, but I wish I were back in the old country," she said in a choking voice. "Watchin' the sheep, listening to the cool waters 'o the burn splashin' over the stones, the air filled wi' the sweet scent o' the heather. Och, why did I ever come tae this heathen place?''

"Ye came because ye were sick o' eatin' naught but oatmeal mornin', noon, and night," said a small, bald-headed man fiercely. "Don't start awailing o'er Scotland my lass. Remember how ye slaved sixteen hours a day for a few pennies, when ye could get work at all. Be glad for what ye've got here.''

"Aye, 'tis true," said Jock. "Here we've got work, at least. And that means we ha'e to get up early tomorrow morning. Best be gettin' home." There was a bustle of movement as everyone made ready to leave. Grace found herself shaking hands with several men and women and being wished good luck, until at last they were all gone, their faint goodbyes echoing up and down the street.

She sank down on the sofa, feeling as if she might never get up again she was so tired. But then Aunt Flora was back, leading them up the narrow stairway. Maggie and Jeannie were to share the big double bed in the front bedroom, but Grace had her own little room in the back, directly across from Aunt Flora. Between them was the bathroom, boasting a toilet, sink, and small bathtub, but no hot water. Ian, apparently, slept in the attic, up another flight of steep stairs.

As Grace opened her bedroom door a blast of hot, stale air met her, and she was appalled to discover that her window was shut fast.

"Can't we open the window?" she asked Aunt Flora.

"No, there's nae screen for that window. I'll see if I can find one for ye tomorrow," said her aunt impatiently. Ian paused on his way up the stairs.

"There's some half screens up here. Wait a minute and I'll find one for you." He disappeared, returning in a few minutes with a small wooden frame. Aunt Flora stood tapping her foot, and the girls watched curiously while he fitted it into Grace's window. The curtain lifted lightly as a faint stirring of air drifted in.

"Thank you, Ian," said Grace. "That makes all the difference. I'll be able to sleep now."

"What about you two girls?" he said to Maggie and Jeannie. "Are your windows open?" Maggie peeked into her room.

"Yes, thank ye," she said.

"Then you can all go to sleep listening to the katydids. Hear them?" The long steady chorus of insects filled the room. "They're saying 'Katy did, Katy did.' That means six weeks till frost, they say."

"Ye mean 'tis not always this hot?" asked Jeannie.

"Only in the summertime," Ian said with a laugh. "Well goodnight girls, goodnight Mrs. McDonald."

"Wasna' that kind of him?" said Jeannie when they were alone. "Don't ye think Ian is the bonniest braw man ye've ever seen?" Grace noticed the hot blush that rushed into Maggie's cheeks, and she answered lightly so as not to betray her own feelings.

"He's bonnie enough, I dare say." She waited while the two girls lay down on the bed in their petticoats, too tired, they declared, to search for their nightclothes.

Back in her own room she stood for a few minutes looking out into the darkness, grateful for the slight breeze that freshened the staleness of the air. Her depression had vanished. Imagine meeting someone like Ian right here in Aunt Flora's house! She smiled at Maggie's description of him, "the bonniest braw man" she'd ever seen. Oh, he was that all right, and he'd noticed her. She'd seen his expression when they walked into the lighted parlor. Just for a moment their eyes had locked, and his had been filled with astonishment and pleasure. She'd felt the tug of excitement that had raced between them.

She was aware once more of the insistent chorus of insects. *But it's not Katy they're talking to,* she thought, with a shiver of anticipation. *It's me.* "Yes you can, yes you can," they sang. *And I will,* she thought as she climbed into the narrow iron bedstead, *tomorrow Grace Cameron is going to set out and conquer America.*

# CHAPTER
## ❧ 3 ❧

"So this is Paterson." It was Grace who spoke. They had walked several blocks from Aunt Flora's house to the center of town. Now they were surrounded by tall, red brick buildings. These were the mills where rows of machines were constantly in motion as they carded, spun, threaded, and wove the silk. Silk—that sensuous, luxurious, soft, shimmering fabric that clothed the wealthy and furnished their houses. It came from here, from these great noisy buildings where the sound of the machinery humming, grinding, rolling, clicking, and clacking drifted through the high open windows and reverberated on the pavement. They would soon learn that the steady clickety-clack of the looms was the music of Paterson by day, just as the scratch of insects was the music of the night.

"How nice and bright they are," exclaimed Maggie as she peeked through the windows. If she stood on her toes she could just glimpse a young woman, looking neat in her snowy white blouse and black twill skirt, who tended the loom. "Soon," she murmured, "I shall be doing that," and the thought filled her with pride.

"Ye'll be working at Potter's Mill. It's just around the corner," said Aunt Flora. "Ye'll report to Mrs. Anderson at seven o'clock on Monday morning, and she'll tell ye what jobs ye have. Mrs. Anderson's a member o' my church, which is lucky for you girls with you havin' no experience."

"Maggie's experienced," said Jeannie.

"I wasna' thinking o' Maggie, it's ye two that are the problem. So Grace, ye'd better not act like you're too grand for the job, but take what's given to ye and be grateful."

"How much will they pay us?" asked Grace.

"Well now, Maggie could make up to five dollars a week, but ye two will earn less. Remember, it's a chance to learn." Grace wasn't sure she wanted to learn mill work, but she was wise enough to say nothing.

"Jeannie, come over here. If ye stand on your toes, ye can look in and see the looms," said Maggie.

"I dinna want tae see the looms," said Jeannie. "I want tae see the Great Falls. Aunt Flora, ye said we would see the Great Falls."

"Come along then," and they followed her down to a small promontory where they could look down at the falls. Here the rushing waters of the Passaic River plunged over a cliff, which was curved like a giant crescent, and tumbled into the chasm below, tossing up clouds of spray.

"Can't we go down there and get closer?" asked Jeannie.

"Nae, I don't want ye slipping and falling in." The girls looked down at the eddies and whirlpools of gray-green waters and listened to the thunderous roar.

"I think we'd better stay where we are," said Maggie nervously. "I canna' swim."

"I dinna think it would make much difference if ye could swim or not," said Jeannie, "but further down it's nice and peaceful." Beyond the falls the river meandered on, the growth on either was lush and green and the air was cool.

"These are the finest falls ye'll ever see, outside of Niagara," said Aunt Flora.

"They are pretty," said Grace. "It's a pity they're right in the middle of Paterson."

"What do ye mean, a pity? 'Tis the falls that make Paterson possible. Where do ye think they get the power to run all that machinery? See all the mill races that run alongside the mills—that's what keeps them going. And it was all thought up by Alexander Hamilton."

"Who's he?" asked Jeannie.

"He was a great man, from the Revolution," replied Aunt Flora, with a vague wave of her hand. They stood looking down and listening to the boom of the falls and drinking in the cool, watery smell that rose from the turbulent river below.

"What's up yon hill?" asked Maggie.

"That's Lambert Castle," replied Aunt Flora.

"A castle in America!" exclaimed Jeannie. "I didna' think they had castles in America."

"Well 'tis not a true castle, like they have in Scotland, but 'tis just as fine. They say 'tis the grandest home of all the mill owners. It belongs to Catholina Lambert—that's his mill down yonder."

"He must make a lot of money if he can live in a castle," remarked Jeannie.

"Aye, the mills here make a rare profit." Grace looked curiously up at the castle, but there was little to be seen through the thick foliage of the trees. *I'd like to go up there one day and take a good look*, she thought. *But not with Aunt Flora.* She glanced back at the rows of factories.

"Where are the shops?" Grace asked.

"I'll show you on the way home. Roses' Dry Goods store has everything ye could need."

"I mean the real shops, where they sell fine things like they have in Glasgow. Even Paterson must have some decent shops."

"If ye mean the big stores where the mill owners and their families go, they're on Market Street, but Roses' is much cheaper."

"Just the same I'd like to go and see for myself," said Grace. "But you don't have to come with me, Aunt Flora. You can take Maggie and Jeannie home, I'll be back later."

Grace swung away and walked swiftly down the street.

"Well I never," exclaimed Aunt Flora. "That young woman had better mind her manners, or I'm going to send her back to Scotland."

Jeannie watched Grace enviously. How wonderful to be able to do as you pleased and not have to follow Aunt Flora around. And as for sending Grace back to Scotland, Jeannie didn't think her aunt could do that. After all, it was Grace's money that had paid for both her fare and Maggie's. If old Lady McLeod hadn't left Grace those few pounds, they'd never have been able to come to America at all.

America! Even though she was walking around with her feet firmly on the pavement, "sidewalk," Aunt Flora called it, Jeannie still didn't really believe she was here. Even though people talked funny, and said things like "Yes Ma'am" to Aunt Flora and told her that she and Maggie were "cute," even though they drank coffee instead of tea and said it tasted "swell," she still didn't believe it.

Maggie looked around in bewilderment. At home there had been only one mill in the little town she had lived in, but now she was surrounded by them. Great red brick buildings that all looked alike. Rows and rows of streets that all looked the same. It was like Glasgow, only brighter and sunnier. How would she ever find her way in on Monday morning? Or, even worse, how would she get home at night? She could picture herself lost and running up and down street after street, Jeannie crying, and Aunt Flora angry.

"How are we going to get here on Monday morning?" she asked. "I'm lost already. I canna' remember which mill it is we're to be working in."

"Dinna worry on that, Maggie. Ian will bring ye girls

in wi' him on Monday. He'll no be working at the same place, but he'll take care of ye, and see that ye get home safe at night.''

Maggie sighed with relief. If Ian was going to take care of them, everything would be fine. Suddenly she felt happy, very happy, giddily happy. She wanted to run and jump and laugh and sing. As usual it was Aunt Flora who brought her back down to earth.

'' 'Tis time we got back, girls. I have to buy some groceries and then we have supper to cook. 'Tis not too far a walk if we stay on the shady side of the street.''

They'd been home several hours before Grace arrived. Maggie was scraping carrots and Jeannie slicing green beans when Grace burst into the kitchen, her arms laden with packages, her face glowing from both the heat and excitement.

"Well, miss, 'tis aboot time ye got here," said Aunt Flora. "Where've ye been?"

"I've been having the most wonderful time," exclaimed Grace, pushing the vegetables aside as she piled her bundles on the table. Both girls immediately abandoned their jobs and eagerly crowded round her. "I found the most wonderful shops. 'Stores,' they call them here, finer than anything you'll see on Argyle Street. Oh, Maggie, when you go in they have bottles and bottles of perfume, and you can actually try them. Here, smell my arm." She extended a slender, pale wrist and Maggie sniffed. Her eyes popped wide with astonishment. Grace's wrist smelled as fragrant as apple blossom.

"They have beautiful glass cases filled with brooches and necklaces, all made of gold and silver and pearls. But they were very expensive. I tell you, they have everything you could ever want in those stores.''

"What did ye buy, Grace? What's in all these packages?" Jeannie was bursting with curiosity.

"Let's see. First of all I bought some cool dresses for

this hot weather. Look at this, it's called chambray.'' She unwrapped a package and laid out a pale lavender dress made of a soft, lightweight cotton. "And I bought some cool underwear, too. No more of those stiff heavy petticoats for me." She heard a gasp of shock from Aunt Flora, but continued. "Here, Maggie and Jeannie, I bought you each a blouse. See how fine they are, they even have lace at the wrists." Jeannie stared at the blouse in astonishment.

"Och, 'tis beautiful Grace," said Maggie, "but ye shouldna' have spent all this money on us."

"Indeed ye shouldna' have spent all this money at all," exclaimed Aunt Flora. "You're a wicked girl, Grace, buying all these sinful clothes. These are things the mill owners wives buy, not the likes o' you."

"And why not me?" exclaimed Grace quickly. "I'm just as good as a mill owner's wife. And if it's not sinful for them to wear nice things, then it's not sinful for me, either." Grace tossed her head and her eyes shone with excitement. "But here, Aunt Flora, I bought a present for you." She handed a small package to her aunt and stood watching while she unwrapped it. A small, shimmering scarf of cool delicate green was revealed.

"But it's silk," murmured a dazed Aunt Flora as she fingered the soft smooth material.

"Of course it's silk! This is Silk City, isn't it?"

"But the workers don't wear silk, that's only for the fine ladies and gentlemen."

"I thought this was America, where there are no more fine ladies and gentlemen. I tell you I intend to wear silk whenever I can, and enjoy it too." With that, Grace swept her things up into her arms and carried them to her room.

Monday morning Grace dressed with care. She realized it would not help her if she looked different, so she found an old black skirt and a plain white blouse. No lace, no ruffles. She struggled to pin her wayward hair into a neat coil at the back of her neck, but wisps and tendrils still escaped into curls that shone like bright copper pennies. She found a pair of plain black boots and laced them up over her ankles.

Maggie and Jeannie were already at the breakfast table, where Aunt Flora, ladling out porridge and cups of hot, strong tea, was offering them advice.

"Now girls, remember that Mrs. Anderson knows the mill inside and out, so dinna pretend you know a job that ye don't know, because she'll find ye out in two minutes." She looked sharply at Grace. "Ye'd best be honest with her and take whatever job she offers ye, without complaint."

"We all have to start somewhere, I suppose," said Grace, pushing away the porridge but drinking her tea.

"You'll have nothing to worry about," said Ian. "You'll soon learn the ropes. But we'd better get going, I don't want to be late."

Maggie wondered if Ian would walk with Grace and leave herself and Jeannie to follow, but instead he took Jeannie's arm and led her along, chatting cheerfully and pointing out the sights while she and Grace walked behind them. *How kind he is,* she thought. *He knows how scared Jeannie is and he's putting her at her ease.* To her annoyance, once more Maggie found herself blushing, but luckily no one noticed it. Grace seemed to be a thousand miles away.

But Grace, too, was noticing how thoughtful Ian was. She'd been so wrapped up in herself that she hadn't paid any attention to Jeannie. *Poor child,* she thought. *And she is only a child, younger than I was when my mother died and I went to work for Lady McLeod.* She recalled that odd remark Jeannie had made the other night when she talked about wanting to go to school. *How lucky I've been,* thought Grace. Living with Lady McLeod had been as good as going to school. The books, music and poetry she had introduced her to had changed her life forever. *I must do something for Jeannie,* she thought. *I must.*

"Here we are," said Ian as they stopped in front of a tall, narrow building. "Now you go in this door and on your right you'll find a small waiting room. Go in there and Mrs. Anderson will find you." He smiled at Grace. "I wish I were coming with you," he said, and she felt a tremor run through her. *Oh, I wish you were too, Ian,* she thought.

"Where will ye be?" asked Jeannie a little tremulously.

He forced his gaze away from Grace. "See that fine building down the street, with all the arches." He waved his arm. "That's where I work. But I'll be here at six o'clock to walk you home. Good luck." He left them standing in a little group on the corner. The streets were swarming with men and women, girls and boys, many carrying lunch pails, all swirling along until they were swallowed up by the great brick buildings. It was as if a giant vacuum was sucking them inside, dozens at a time, until only a few stragglers remained. Soon the streets would be deserted until they all came spilling out again at the end of the day.

"Come on," said Grace. "We might as well get this over with." She opened the door and they walked into the waiting room. To their surprise the room was crowded with an assortment of men and women, both young and old. There were no seats left, so the three of them stood together just inside the door. In a few minutes a tall, grim-faced woman walked in. She glanced around and spoke one word in a loud, harsh voice.

"Weavers," she said. About half a dozen people stood up. "Follow me," was her next command, and they obediently trooped out of the room allowing the others to spread out a little. They could hear footsteps going down the hall and a murmur of voices. Then suddenly at the stroke of seven, the whole factory exploded with noise. Grace grasped and Jeannie clung to her as their ears were assaulted by the racket of the looms. Clickety-clack, clickety-clack, it sounded like a hundred thousand sticks being clapped together in some sort of crazy rhythm. Grace put her hands over her ears, but Maggie just laughed.

"You'll get used to it," she shouted.

"Never," said Grace. "Never."

The woman returned, grim-faced as ever, and this time shouted at the top of her lungs.

"Winders." Maggie hesitated for a minute then stood up. She turned back to Jeannie, but Grace mouthed, "Go, I'll stay with Jeannie."

Maggie disappeared into the depth of the racket. The procedure was repeated through "Warpers," "Spinners," "Reelers," and "Lacers" until only Grace and Jeannie remained. The woman looked at them, then closed the door. The noise slackened a little.

"Well, what can you two do?"

"I'm afraid we've no experience working in a mill," said Grace.

"Oh, you've no experience," mimicked the woman in her harsh voice. "Just off the boat I suppose." Grace felt herself flush in anger, but at that moment the door opened and a man stepped inside. He was dressed in a business suit and carried a sheaf of papers in his hand.

"Oh, there you are, Mrs. Anderson, I've got these figures ready to be checked when you have time."

"Certainly, Mr. Whitehead," she replied.

"I'm good at figures," exclaimed Grace and realized immediately that she'd made a terrible mistake. Not that the man objected. He took off his gold-rimmed glasses and looked at her with interest, but Mrs. Anderson gave her a viperish glance.

"You're here to work in the factory," she said. "If I need help with the figures, my niece is a trained book-keeper."

"Ah, yes," murmured Mr. Whitehead, "I'll see you later, Mrs. Anderson." He left the room, but Mrs. Anderson continued to glare at Grace, who returned her stare as coolly as she could.

"Who sent you here?"

"Our aunt, Mrs. Flora McDonald," she said. The woman gave an elaborate sigh.

"Then I suppose I'll have to find something for you to do. Throwing, there's always need of help there. Come on."

They followed her into the mill where the throb of machinery made talking impossible. She led them through rows and rows of looms, all click-clacking to a steady beat, then down a steep iron staircase to the basement. A wave of dampness enveloped them as they entered a long dreary room, lit by a couple of small grimy windows near the ceiling. A few tired looking men were bent over great vats of greasy water.

"Ugh, what's that awful smell?" asked Grace.

"You'll get used to it," said Mrs. Anderson briefly. "Where's Big Nellie?" She spoke to one of the men who pointed to the other side of the room. A woman was standing by a row of silent machines. She was the biggest, fattest, and possibly the ugliest person Grace had ever seen.

"I've brought you a couple of helpers, Nellie," said Mrs. Anderson. "Now get these machines going, you're holding up the works." She looked at Grace and Jeannie. "You do what Nellie tells you," she said, and walked away shaking her head and muttering. Grace overheard the word, "Greenhorns," and felt an overwhelming desire to kick Mrs. Anderson in her bony shins.

"Don't pay no attention to the old cow, we don't give her no mind, do we boys?" said the big woman. One of the men spat a long stream of dark brown liquid onto the floor.

"Hey, you get fined for spitting the floor," said another of the men.

"If I aimed it where I'd like to I'd get fired," he replied.
Nellie slapped her sides and roared with laughter.

"I'm going to be sick," said Grace. "I just know I'm
going to be sick."

"Oh, please dinna get sick, Grace," whispered Jeannie. "Dinna leave me here alone."

Nellie put her hands on her hips and surveyed the two
girls.

"Wots yer names?" she asked and they told her.
"Where yer from? As if I didn't know, yer from the other
side."

"Scotland," said Jeannie proudly.

"Well yer in America now, land of opportunity," she
let out another roar of laughter. "Fat lot of opportunity
you'll find here, most backward mill in Paterson."

"What's that awful smell?" asked Grace again.

"It's the neatsfoot oil. They puts in the water when they
soak the silk skeins. They hafta soak it good to get all the
gum out. D'yer know where silk comes from? It comes
from a worm." Another bellow of laughter. "Fancy that,
all these fine ladies walking around in something made by
a worm."

"It's really more like a caterpillar," said Grace. Nellie
looked at her sharply.

"Have it yer own way, but it's a worm to me. Anyways,
they soaks it and hangs it up to dry." She pointed to the
heavy skeins hanging in rows from the ceiling. "Our job
is to put it on these here swifts." She pointed to a row of
reels with long spindles sticking out of them. "Come on,
I'll show you."

For all her bulk Nellie moved swiftly and dextrously.
She took each skein of raw silk, and draped it over the
hexagonal reel. The two girls tried to help, but kept getting scraped and scratched by the spindles. Grace looked
along the long frame and counted about eighty swifts. She
groaned inwardly. Nellie's hands were red and raw but she

didn't seem to care. They worked through the morning filling the long row of swifts.

"Now," said Nellie. "Yer've gotta find the ends and bring them over and tie them to the bobbin here, an' yer keeps doin' that 'til all the bobbins is full."

"Find the end, but that's impossible," said Grace, looking at the spiderweb-thin mass of threads.

"Yer'll soon get the hang of it," said Nellie, and she ran her rough, red fingers over the seemingly tangled skeins until she picked out one slender thread. "See," she said. "Nothin' to it." She pulled the hair-like thread and fastened it to the bobbin. Suddenly a great clanging bell sounded throughout the mill and one by one the machines stopped. It was only when the clamor and vibration ceased did Grace realize just how loud was the noise that had been assailing their ears all morning.

"Lunch time," said Nellie. "D'jer bring yer lunch?" They nodded. "We got a gas ring over here where we boils up water and makes our tea. Come on."

"You mean we have to eat our lunch here?" asked Grace.

"That's right. Each group gets to eat in one place, the winders and soakers eats here." She led them over to a corner where several buckets were hanging on the wall. She reached up and took down three of them.

"Have a seat girls," she said, and turning over the largest bucket she sat down. Grace and Jeannie looked at each other. Grace shrugged and sat down on the upturned bucket. It was very uncomfortable. Nellie laughed.

"Yer needs some more fat on yer behinds," she said. "Like me." And she once again slapped her ample proportions with pride.

"Stop bragging, Nellie," said one of the men. "You've got enough there for three women." He sat on the floor with his back to the wall, and gradually the other men who worked at the vats came over to join them. Nellie introduced them.

"This here's Ed, this is Harry, Will, and Old Ebe-neezer—we calls him Sneezer—he's making the tea. He's a proper Limey. We're all bloody Limeys, that's why we drinks so much tea. Fellers, these here girls are from Scotland." They nodded hello. Grace noted they were all pale and thin and their hands were cracked and sore.

"Are ye from Glasgow?" asked the one called Will. "I'm from Glasgow, but I've been here for years now, scarce remember wot it's like anymore."

" 'Tis a bonnie city," said Jeannie, "but Paterson's a bonnie city, too."

"Aye, Paterson's all right, at least there's work here."

"Tea's up." A small bent man walked over carrying a tin tray with several thick white cups on it.

"Two new lassies today, Sneezer," said Will.

"I knows it, I ain't blind yer know," he said. " 'Ow d'yer like your tea, ladies?"

"Ladies," snorted Big Nellie. "Yer don't call me that."

"Aw, you're just one of the boys, Nellie."

Grace had grown quiet while all this bantering went on and she looked around the dreary workroom.

"Why is none of the silk colored?" she asked. It was all a plain beige. "It's all so drab."

"That's because this here's the raw silk," said Sneezer. He was, she noticed, the oldest man in the room. "This is the throwing part of the mill, here's where it gets soaked, sorted, spun, and reeled back into skeins, then it goes to the dye shop where it gets dyed all the fine colors. After that it gets worked on upstairs."

"Maggie works upstairs," said Jeannie. "She's a winder."

"Nellie's a winder too," said Sneezer with a chuckle. "Or would be if she weren't so fat."

"Now see here, Sneezer, I'm the best winder they ever had."

"So the actual weaving all goes on upstairs," said Grace.

"Aye. Most mills around here don't do their own throwing, it's done in Pennsylvania."

"I told yer this was the most backward mill in Paterson," said Nellie. "And the cheapest. Don't even give yer a bench to sit on." The shattering clang of the bell told them it was time to go back to work. "Bring yer buckets with yer," whispered Nellie, "so's yer can sneak a sit down once in a while, but don't let that old cow Anderson catch yer or it'll be a fine. She likes to fine us for everything. If she had her way we'd wind up with an empty pay envelope."

After lunch a few women came in to work the throwing frames that Nellie had set up. They spoke no English, but smiled shyly at the two girls. Jeannie learned later that they were sisters, part of the big Simonetti family, all silk workers. They had no difficulty finding the threads and soon the swifts were all spinning as the silk was transferred to the bobbins. The women moved up and down between the frames, catching any broken threads or knots. They were on the move every minute.

"Seems daft, don't it," said Nellie. "They do all this now, then they dye it and they 'as to do it all over again."

"Why don't you work the frames?" asked Jeannie. Nellie laughed again.

"Because this is a cheap mill and they've got them too close together. I can't walk between 'em when the swifts are spinnin', I keep getting caught on the spindles, and when they catch on me they breaks. But you girls are both skinny, you'll have no trouble. I bet after a while yer'll even get moved upstairs, as long as yer don't get on the wrong side of the old cow." Grace was pretty sure she was already on the wrong side of Mrs. Anderson, but it was too late to worry about that.

The afternoon seemed endless. There was very little chance to sit, and even when they did they had to bend and stretch. Grace found herself praying for six o'clock to come, and when it finally did she grabbed Jeannie and ran out of the building.

"Thank God for some fresh air," she gasped, "I thought the day would never end."

"Me, too," said Jeannie with a sigh. "But I suppose we'll get used to it." They were soon joined by Maggie. She too looked tired.

"I'm out of practice," she said, "but it felt good to be back at work." Grace looked at her in amazement. In a few minutes Ian appeared, looking as fresh and cheerful as he had ten hours ago, but even the sight of Ian did not raise Grace's spirits.

"Well girls, how did it go?" he asked. Maggie's beaming smile and Grace's groan answered his question. "You all look tired, so maybe we'd better take the trolley car home."

"A walk in the fresh air might do us good," said Maggie, but Grace firmly interrupted her.

"I'm not walking a step more than I have to. If I can't take a trolley I'll take a cab."

"Grace, ye wouldna'!" Maggie was shocked. Ian laughed.

"No need for such extravagance, the trolley stops at this corner. Looks like I might have to carry young Jeannie, she's falling asleep standing up."

Jeannie was leaning against the lamppost, her face pale, her eyes closed. Grace could see she was trembling with exhaustion, and no wonder, Grace herself ached from the top of her head to the soles of her feet. Her back and shoulders had progressed from a dull ache to fiery stabs of red hot pain as she bent over her work, reaching, lifting, turning, not a minute to rest, hour after hour after hour. *Is this what life in America is all about?* she wondered.

# CHAPTER

## ❦ 4 ❧

As the days went by they began to get more used to the work. While Grace was still dog tired at the end of the day, she noticed that the terrible burning pains in her back and shoulders had eased. Jeannie, too, was gradually adjusting to the long hours. But Maggie, like Ian, seemed to thrive on it. *I guess it's because they like their work,* thought Grace. She still hated it. Hated the noise, the smell, the dampness, but most of all she hated Mrs. Anderson.

Surprisingly enough she had grown to like Big Nellie. For all her crudeness she was kind. She took the two girls under her wing, and Grace noticed she did the really heavy work herself. She was especially watchful of Jeannie. She also extended her huge mantle of protection to young Albert, a sickly looking boy whose job was bobbin carrier. He'd been out sick the first few days, and when he returned he still had a wracking cough. Grace remarked on it one day.

"Is Albert going to cough like that all year? Can't the doctor give him something for it?"

"Not much can be done for Albert, poor kid," said Nellie. "He's got the consumption, I reckon."

"Then he shouldn't be working here where it's so cold and damp." Grace was horrified.

"Wot else can he do? He's too young to be working at all, but his Ma's a widow with six more to feed." Nellie shrugged. "His coupla dollars helps some, I guess." After that Grace noticed that Nellie, and the men too, often shared their lunches with Albert.

" 'Ere, kid, I can't eat all this, want a piece?" And whatever it was, Albert would wolf it down without pausing to chew it.

"That Albert," said Jeannie in disgust, "I suppose no one taught him any table manners."

"I doubt it," said Grace. "Probably lucky if he gets anything to eat half the time."

"Poor kid," said Nellie. "It's not his ma's fault. His dad used to work here. Got his hand caught in one of these here machines. Smashed it up proper. Got blood poisoning and died of it. Not a penny insurance either, but a lot they care." She rolled her eyes up in her head.

"That's not right," said Jeannie. "The mill should have paid something to the family."

"Ha! Can you see the old cow, or that skinflint Potter paying out money? All they wants to do is take it from yer. So ye'd better not get yourselves mashed up while yer working 'ere."

Grace looked at the whirling spindles she and Jeannie tended. Both girls had started scragging back their hair and wearing a net. She shuddered to think what could happen if a lock of hair got caught in those flying reels. *I wish I could get out of this awful place,* she thought, *but where else could I find a job?* She worked such long hours that she had no time left over to even look for something else. Besides, Nellie had told them that if you got caught looking for another job you'd get fined, and she needed all of her meager salary.

But Jeannie was still concerned about Albert.

"It's not right," she said hotly.

"There's lots o' things is not right," said Nellie, "but

they happens. And one o' the things that's going to happen here is that the inspectors is coming soon."

"Who are the inspectors?" the girls wanted to know.

"They's men from the state, and they comes here to see if the workers are being treated right—bunch o' baloney that is—course everyone acts like we're one big 'appy family. Ain't that right Sneezer." Sneezer spat into the vat of greasy water.

"Yeh, we all pretends we're 'aving a loverly time working here." He spat again. "But 'ow d'yer know they're coming, Nellie?"

She slapped her sides and gave a hoot of laughter. "They're cleaning up the toilets," she said.

The toilets were a great hardship for Grace, but since they spent over ten hours a day at the mill she had to use them. The washroom was small and dirty, with a chipped sink, old greasy towels, leaky pipes, and a smell of disinfectant that failed to cover the overpowering reek of urine. But to her astonishment, on Wednesday morning, they arrived to find the washroom scrubbed down, a new bar of soap in the sink, and freshly laundered towels.

"Today's the day the inspectors are coming," said Nellie. "Bet your bottom dollar." Her prophesy was fulfilled a few minutes later when Mrs. Anderson appeared, her usual black dress set off by a lace collar, but her face as grim as ever.

"The inspectors are coming today," she said. "So you all better toe the mark. Nellie, you get these machines in working order. They'll be off when the inspectors arrive, but ready to go if they want to see them running." She looked closely at Jeannie. "How old are you, girl?"

"I'm thirteen," said Jeannie.

"If anyone asks tell them you're fourteen, understand."

"What about Albert?" said Grace. "He's barely eleven." A flash of anger swept over Mrs. Anderson's face and she glared at Grace.

"That's no concern of yours, Miss Smart Aleck. You

speak only if you're spoken to.'' And Mrs. Anderson was going to make sure no one did speak to her. "As for you, Nellie, if any mention is made of a bench, you tell them it's out for repair. They'll be here right after lunch so don't leave a mess.'' She turned on her heel and walked away. Nellie stuck her tongue out at the receding black-clad back.

"I'd like to strangle her,'' whispered Grace.

"Strangling would be too good for her,'' said Nellie. "She oughta drown in one o' these greasy vats.''

They worked steadily all morning until the bell rang for lunch, and they gathered in their usual corner while Sneezer made the tea. Jeannie and Grace had brought in two small cushions which they placed on top of the buckets, but Nellie had scoffed at the idea.

"Got me own cushions right on me arse,'' she said with a hoot of laughter. The men, as usual, sat on the floor.

"Here, Albert, want some baloney?'' said Will.

"Naw, I ain't hungry,'' said Albert, wiping his nose on his sleeve.

"Not hungry,'' exclaimed Jeannie. "Are ye sick Albert? Ye look awful pale.''

"Naw, I ain't sick.'' But he looked sick. His thin face was a pasty white, nose pinched, eyes red and watery. He looked anxiously at Nellie. "Nell, you won't forget to let me out when they're gone, will you?''

"No, I won't forget. Stop worrying and eat your baloney.''

"What d'you mean, let you out?'' asked Jeannie.

"They locks me in the closet when the inspectors come,'' said Albert. " 'Cause I'm too young to be working here, see.''

"Lock you in the closet!'' exclaimed Jeannie in horror. "But that's terrible.''

"It's better than getting fired, I reckon,'' said Albert, but she could see he was shivering. "Nellie gives me some horehound drops to suck on so's I won't cough and give meself away.''

"What do the inspectors do when they come here?" asked Grace.

"Not much," said Nellie. "They comes down here first to get it over with, Potter himself, that wishy-washy Whitehead, the old cow and a couple o' inspectors. They looks around a bit but they never stay long. See, you don't have to worry, Albert; they don't like the smell." She held her nose with one hand and made a coarse gesture with the other.

"What did Mrs. Anderson mean when she said the benches were out being repaired?" asked Grace. Everyone burst out laughing.

"Them benches been out for repair for all the years I been here," said Sneezer. "Good an excuse as any. See, we're supposed to 'ave somewhere to sit when we eats our lunch, not on this bleedin' cold floor. Beggin' yer pardon, ladies."

"You watch yer language in front o' these young girls," said Nellie as she heaved herself to her feet. "No sense worrying about the benches, they never asks. But we won't be able to take our buckets with us today, girls. Here, Albert, you can sit on it while you're in the closet."

"Take the cushions with you, too," said Jeannie. "Might as well try to be comfortable."

When the bell clamored to let them know lunch time was over, Joe, the foreman from upstairs, came down and made them all line up alongside their workstations. Then he marched poor Albert off to the closet.

"Like the bloody army," muttered Will.

In a few moments they heard the heavy clomping of footsteps on the metal stairs and the whole party trooped into the room. Mr. Potter was just as Grace had imagined him. Small, hunched over, wearing a long old-fashioned frock coat, a pince-nez clipped to his thin nose, Mr. Whitehead looked positively handsome by comparison. Mrs. Anderson, a simpering smile on her face, walked behind them, followed by the two inspectors—one heavy-set, the other thin, both suitably expressionless. They stopped to study the hanging skeins of silk and Grace heard one of them ask how many were handled during a day. Then they came to the spinning machines.

"All set ready to go, I see," said Mr. Potter.

"Yes, sir," said Nellie. It was barely a whisper, nothing like her usual booming voice. *Why are we all so afraid?* thought Grace. *What can they do to us after all?*

The two inspectors walked up and down checking the swifts and the reels, then they returned to the end of the row.

"Everything satisfactory here, girls?" asked the heavy-set one. It was obviously a rhetorical question and everyone smiled and nodded in agreement. Except Grace. She stepped forward and spoke directly to Mr. Potter.

"Sir. Mrs. Anderson asked me to point out that our benches, which were sent out for repair, have not returned. We are forced to sit on the floor to eat our lunch." She heard a gasp from Nellie and a snake-like hiss from Mrs. Anderson, who turned bright red and began to sputter. She was silenced by the thin-faced inspector who held up his hand.

"Is this true? Are there no benches for these employees to sit on when they eat their lunch?" he asked. Mr. Potter turned angrily to Mr. Whitehead, who blanched visibly.

"What about this, Whitehead?"

"I'll see to it that we get benches down here right away, sir," he said. "I didn't realize they were . . ." his voice trailed off and he watched in dismay as the inspectors both wrote something in their notebooks.

"We'll be back in two weeks to see that benches are provided," said the thin one as he pocketed his notebook. "These women should not have to sit on this cold floor." After a brief look around they all trooped upstairs, but not before Mrs. Anderson favored Grace with a venomous glare that boded no good. Everyone remained stock still for a few minutes, then Big Nellie grabbed her stomach and doubled over.

"Oh, my God, Grace, you'll get us all fired for sure. But it'd be worth it," she said, her great frame shaking with laughter as she wiped the tears from her face. "Did you see her face? I thought smoke was going to come outa her ears she was so hot. She'll have it in for you now, Grace."

"Yeh, she will too," said Will. "But d'yer think we'll get the bloomin' benches?"

"Oh, we'll get them all right," said Sneezer. "Whitehead's more scared o' Potter and them inspectors than he is of old Anderson. We'll get them. And when we does I think we should 'ave Grace's name carved on 'em. I gotta 'and it to yer, me girl, yer spoke up at the right time."

"Back to work, back to work. No more standing round yapping." It was Joe, the foreman.

"Are you going to let Albert out now?" asked Jeannie.

"Not yet, he has to stay until they leave the mill. I'll be back."

Another couple of hours went by before Albert was finally let out of the closet. He looked even more sickly, and Sneezer risked the wrath of the powers that be by boiling some water and making him a cup of tea.

"Cheer up, Albert," said Nellie. "They probably won't be back for months."

All afternoon Grace expected Mrs. Anderson to come storming down the iron staircase, but it was almost six before she did appear. She singled Grace out immediately.

"You smart-mouthed hussy," she hissed. "I told you not to speak unless you were spoken to. You had no right, no right at all to use my name in your lying claims." She was shaking with anger and her face was a splotchy red.

"But Mrs. Anderson . . . I only told them what you told us to tell them. I didn't know it was a lie." Grace was the picture of innocence.

"Are you calling me a liar? That does it. A two dollar fine out of your pay this week for insolence."

"But Mrs. Anderson . . ."

"You 'Mrs. Anderson' me one more time and it'll be a three dollar fine, understand." The clanging of bells signalling the end of the shift ended the conversation. Grace shrugged resignedly as she walked over to get her coat.

"We'd better get out of here, Jeannie, while I've still got some wages left."

The benches came the following day. Joe the foreman supervised their installation.

"Don't know what you did to deserve these," he said. "But it's orders from Mr. Whitehead."

"Well ain't this something," said Will when they all assembled for lunch. "Let's put them over there so's we can rest our backs against the wall. Come on young Albert, sit alongside me." The men sat on one bench and Grace, Jeannie, and Big Nellie on the other.

"I'd best sit in the middle," said Nellie, "else I'll upend it for sure. Hey, Sneezer, 'ows the tea comin'?"

"Keep yer shirt on, Nell. Grace gets 'ers first. If she hadn't spoke up we'd still be sittin' on this bloomin' cold floor and me piles been actin' up all week as it is."

"Mrs. Anderson is fining Grace two dollars for asking for these benches," said Jeannie.

"That ain't fair," said Big Nellie. "We'll all chip in and 'elp pay it. 'Ow about it, folks?"

"No, that's all right," said Grace. She knew they needed their few dollars even more than she did. Besides, it was worth the fine just to get even with Mrs. Anderson.

# CHAPTER

## ❧ 5 ❧

"THANK God for Ian." Grace offered up her somewhat irreverent prayer on a warm Sunday in September. Her gratitude stemmed from the fact that Ian was rescuing her from at least four hours of church, consisting of deadly dull hymn-singing and sermons, which was Aunt Flora's idea of a suitable way to spend Sunday. But today they were going to the Clansmen's Picnic. Ian had got tickets for all of them, even Aunt Flora.

She put on her pale blue chambray dress and took out her wide-brimmed straw hat trimmed with blue ribbons. It would help keep the sun off her nose. She pinned up her red-gold curls, splashed herself with cologne she'd smuggled in past Aunt Flora's disapproving nose, and tucked a clean lace handkerchief into her sleeve. She was ready—ready for whatever this day might bring. She'd dreamed so often of a whole day spent with Ian, and now her dreams were coming true. If only they could escape the ever-watchful eye of Aunt Flora, the day would be perfect.

They were all waiting for her at the foot of the stairs.

"It's aboot time, miss," said Aunt Flora. "Come on, let's get going, we have tae catch the trolley."

"Och, ye look sae bonnie, Grace. Ye'll be the bonniest girl at the picnic," said Jeannie.

43

"Aye, 'tis true," said Maggie, with a little sigh of envy. Ian said nothing, but Grace could see the admiration in his face as his eyes swept over her, and she felt her heart skip.

"Dinna stand there like a bump on a log," said Aunt Flora crossly. "Make yourself useful for a change. Here." She deliberately handed Grace the heaviest of the baskets she had packed with meat pies, hard-boiled eggs, oat cakes, and enough knives and forks to set a table for ten.

When they arrived at the picnic grove, the men were already setting up long tables under the trees. The tables were soon groaning under the weight of the food as each family contributed one or two of their favorite dishes. Maggie and Grace were quickly put to work, but Jeannie escaped to explore the grove.

Under a big maple tree she saw great tubs of ice used to cool the bottles of ale and beer for the men (and a few strong-minded women who didn't worry about the disapproval of their church elders). For the more proper ladies there were jugs of fresh-squeezed lemonade and a few bottles of milk.

"What's the milk for?" asked Jeannie.

"For the tea, lassie," said a red-haired man wearing a McDonald tartan kilt. "The ladies have tae have their cup o' tea, nae matter how hot the weather. The kettles are boiling already."

A large fire had been built in a makeshift fireplace made of stones. Several kettles and two big black pots were suspended over it, tended by a little man also wearing the McDonald tartan. She recognized him as Aunt Flora's friend, Jock.

"Well, if it isn't young Jeannie McHugh! And how d'ye like America now, young Jeannie?"

"I like it fine," said Jeannie. "What are ye cooking in the pot?"

"Boiling up water for the corn. Have ye ever tasted corn on the cob?"

Jeannie looked puzzled. "Corn doesna' grow on a cob, and ye canna boil it like oats. What are ye talking about?"

Jock let out a bellow of laughter. "Och, I clean forgot. What ye call corn, Americans call wheat. American corn is what the Scots call maize. Maize on the cob, that's what it is. But 'tis not tough like Scottish maize. Wait till ye taste it, lass—young, sweet as sugar, and drippin' wi' butter. Fit for a laird."

Jeannie had her doubts. In Scotland they fed maize to the cattle. Well, she'd give it a try when the time came.

She left Jock to his fire and skirted the broad meadow where the men were practicing throwing the heavy logs known as cabers, and where the Highland pipers were to give their performance in the afternoon. Beyond the meadow lay the river. A few children had taken off their boots and stockings and were wading in the cool, greenish water. Jeannie longed to take off her boots and cool off in the water, but she dared not—Aunt Flora would be disgraced. She noticed a dozen or so canoes tied up alongside a small docking area. Aunt Flora couldn't object to a canoe ride. She'd ask Ian.

Ian, who'd escaped from the group of muscular Scots heaving the caber also had his eye on the canoes. He was planning the best time to steal Grace away from the ever-present crowd. The whole reason for this picnic, as far as Ian was concerned, was to give him a chance to be with Grace. His pulse raced at the thought. She was the most beautiful, wonderful girl he'd ever met. And she liked him—he could tell. Whenever their eyes met there was an unspoken message in hers, a promise of endless enchantment that made him tremble with anticipation.

"Ian, Ian," Jeannie ran up to him. "Will ye take us for a ride in the canoe, please, please?"

"Sure, Jeannie. Why don't you find Maggie and I'll take you both."

"What about Grace?"

"There won't be room for four. Just find Maggie." He'd

take the two girls first, then he'd ask Grace. He felt a tremor of excitement run through him as he watched Jeannie, pigtails flying, race back to the picnic tables.

"Maggie, Maggie, come quick. Ian wants to take us for a canoe ride." Maggie's face was already flushed with the heat, so no one noticed the blush that swept up to her forehead.

"But I canna go now. I'm tae help wi' the serving."

"Nonsense," said Grace. "There's plenty of women here to serve. Go and have some fun. When you get back lunch will be ready." Maggie gave Grace a grateful look and the two girls picked up their skirts and ran back to the dock where Ian was already holding a canoe for them. Aunt Flora frowned at her niece.

"You'd better not go skippin' off, miss," she said. "Someone has to do the work."

"Och, stop fussin' Flora," said Jock's wife. "You're only young once."

When Maggie and Jeannie returned, with Ian in tow, faces flushed with pleasure, everyone was sitting down to lunch.

" 'Tis a bonnie river, Grace," said Jeannie. "You'll have tae get Ian to take you in the canoe."

"I'll be happy to take Grace for a canoe ride, if she'll come with me," said Ian, trying to keep the tremor out of his voice.

"Of course she'll go with you," said Maggie hotly. "Why wouldna' she?"

"Perhaps she already has a fine lad to go with," said Ian. Both Maggie and Jeannie stared at Grace accusingly and she broke into a peal of laughter.

"Stop teasing, Ian. I'd love to go for a canoe ride after lunch." Ian silently released the breath he had been holding.

"There's an island in the middle of the river," said Jeannie. "Just like in 'The Lady of Shalott.' "

"Who's the Lady of Shalott?" asked Maggie.

"Och, she was a beautiful lady who was cursed if she should look down to Camelot."

"And did she?" asked Ian.

"Aye, she left her loom and looked out the tower window."

"And then what happened?" asked Maggie.

"Och, 'twas terrible:

> "Out flew the web and floated wide;
> The mirror cracked from side to side;
> 'The curse has come upon me,' cried
> The Lady of Shalott."

Jeannie's rendition was very dramatic and they all laughed. But Grace felt a slight shiver. New York was her Camelot—what would happen if she, too, left her loom?

"I don't know about anyone else," said Jeannie, "but I'm hungry."

"My goodness," said Maggie, "look at all this food." They sat down, and with the hearty appetites of the young, made short work of the meat pies, potato salads, cakes, and tea. Ian and Grace slipped away just as Jock appeared with a platter of hot, golden corn.

"Now, Miss Jeannie, you're in for the treat of your young life," he said, setting it down with a flourish.

It was cooler down by the river. The canoes had all been abandoned in favor of lunch so they had their choice. Ian picked a sturdy green one with a good paddle, which he used with skill, and they were already skimming downstream when the first skirl of the bagpipes came over the hill.

"Whew! We got away just in time," he said with a laugh. "Let's go and explore Jeannie's island."

Grace lay back and trailed her fingers in the cool, green water. It was wonderful to be alone with Ian. She watched him dreamily. He wore a white shirt open at the neck, sleeves rolled up. His face and arms were brown from the

sun, his hair sunstreaked and windblown. He smiled at
her and she sat up a little straighter. Ian's smile disturbed
her more than she cared to admit. It was as if it were
for her alone, drawing her into a warm and secret circle
of happiness shared exclusively by the two of them.

He edged the canoe into shore and tied it to a tree. They
climbed out and looked around. The island was a tiny
patch of land overgrown with wild laurel, pine trees, and
honeysuckle. A narrow path led through the trees and they
took it, Ian leading the way. The only sounds were the
long sweet notes of the woodthrush and the occasional
sharp snap of twigs beneath their feet. When they reached
a small clearing they stopped. Long shafts of sunlight
streamed through the trees making small pools of gold at
their feet.

"Oh, Ian, it's beautiful."

"Not as beautiful as you are." She looked up. He was
gazing at her with an intensity that sent shivers of excitement racing through her veins. He leaned towards her and
she was vividly aware of the strong line of his cheekbone,
the thrust of his smooth-shaven jaw, the sensuous curve of
his lips, and suddenly she wanted to feel his cheek against
her cheek, his lips against her lips, his body against hers.
She reached up and touched his face with her fingertips.
He gave a small groan and then she was in his arms. He
kissed her, hungrily, urgently, and she returned his kisses
with equal fervor, both consumed with a passion they had
never known before.

"Grace, Grace," he murmured, as he kissed her face,
her neck, her throat. Then he held her away from him and
swept her with a look that made her dissolve inside. His
eyes were filled with desire, and a pulse in his neck
throbbed steadily. "Let down your hair," he whispered in
a hoarse voice. "Please, let down your hair." Slowly she
raised her hands and unloosed the pins that held her shimmering red-gold tresses in check, then she shook her head
and her glorious hair cascaded down her back and around

her shoulders. Ian caught his breath. He moved towards
her, but as he did so a small twig snapped under his foot,
echoing like a rifle shot through the glade. They both
jumped. Shocked. He looked around as if in a daze. They
were alone. All alone in the fragrant shelter of the pine
trees.

"Oh, my God," he exclaimed. "We can't stay here."
He took her arm and all but dragged her over the rough
ground back to the shore. When he reached the canoe
he stopped, and turned once more to look at her as she
quickly rebraided and pinned up her wayward locks. He
touched her cheek softly.

"I love you, Grace, and I would never do anything to
hurt you. I think I fell in love with you the first night I
met you on the porch, before I even knew how beautiful
you were." He took both her hands and kissed them
gently. "I want to marry you. I want you to be my wife,
if you think you could love me, too." A faint breeze shook
the branches of the trees and Grace shivered slightly.

"Oh, Ian, I need a little time . . . I need to get used to
this."

"There's no one else, is there?" His voice was anxious.

"No, there's no one else." *How could there be?* she
thought. Ian was the handsomest, finest, most desirable
man she'd ever met. And he was in love with her!

He relaxed then, and even managed a laugh. "Then you
can have all the time in the world, my darling," he said
gallantly, not knowing how he would regret those words
in the days to come. They kissed again, a long, exploring
kiss that left them both breathless. "Oh, God, Grace," he
murmured, burying his face in her hair, "I'm the luckiest
man in the world."

When they got back Maggie saw at once that something
had happened between them. There was a glow about
them, their faces shone and their smiles were radiant. Aunt
Flora pursed her lips with disapproval. *No good can come
of this*, she thought. But Jeannie was ecstatic.

"D'ye think Grace and Ian will be getting married?" Jeannie whispered to Maggie. "Wouldna' that be grand?"

"Aye," said Maggie, " 'twould be grand, I guess. For Grace."

For Ian the weeks that followed remained forever tinged with a golden glow. She was his! This beautiful, golden girl was his. All his years of loneliness were over. Ian barely remembered his mother, she had died when he was a little boy, and from then on he and his father had lived in a series of boarding houses while his father worked the mills in Pennsylvania. A dark, taciturn man, he had provided food and shelter for his son but little else. Ian had grown up in the mills. The clickety-clack of the looms had been his music, the hard-working mill workers his surrogate mothers and fathers. And he had worked, too. They were long, hard hours, but he had learned. He was smart and intelligent. He had worked his way up from winder to warper to weaver, and now he was going to be a loom fixer, the most important job in the mill.

He had come to Paterson after his father died. Paterson—Silk City—where the finest silks in all America were made. And here he had met Grace. The future stretched before him like a bright, shining road. He pictured their little apartment, scrubbed and clean, the sun streaming in through the windows. He could see Grace in a gingham dress sitting across from him at the breakfast table, smiling at him, reaching across the table for a kiss. He wanted to shout for joy. Life had never been more wonderful.

They were not yet formally engaged, he was saving up to buy a ring, but everyone knew they were going together. He walked to work with her in the mornings while the air was as fresh and cool as Grace herself. His heart would leap at the sight of her red-gold curls shining in the sunlight, the clear pale color of her skin, and the fragrance that always surrounded her.

The last lingering days of summer they spent on the

river, Grace idly trailing her fingers in the water while he guided the canoe with long clean strokes, gently feathering the paddle to keep them on course. They didn't revisit their island, which had been taken over by a group of young boys. Just as well, thought Ian, he didn't know if he could trust himself alone with Grace in that green silent arbor. But they did pull ashore where, in full view of passing boats, they enjoyed a simple picnic, and where Ian shared with her his hopes and dreams for the future.

"Pretty soon I'll qualify as a loom fixer. It's the best job in the mill. They already call on me for small breakdowns, and I've been working with MacPherson to learn the trade." He grinned. "Most of it's common sense and not being afraid to get your hands dirty. One of these days, Grace, I intend to open my own shop."

Ian's eyes took on a distant look and Grace noted with pleasure how handsome he was. His light brown skin glowed with health, making his eyes a deeper green and his white teeth even whiter. His hands, the hands he was not afraid of getting dirty, were strong and brown and capable. Just looking at Ian's hands sent a disturbing thrill through her.

"Of course, it's going to mean working extra hours . . ."

She frowned. What was he saying? She hadn't been paying attention.

"I know, I hate the thought too, but the more money I can save the sooner we can become properly engaged. Oh, Grace, I can hardly wait. I want you all to myself. We won't need a fancy apartment. One room will do, as long as we're together."

Grace suppressed a slight shiver. She didn't want to think about living in one room, or about settling down and becoming a housewife.

"That would be wonderful," she said softly, wishing she could feel more enthusiastic, but Ian didn't seem to notice and he gave her a smile that warmed her all over.

"Oh, Ian," she said with a sigh, "why can't it always

be like this? Summertime and drifting on the river, just the two of us.'' He kissed her then, long and passionately, and she returned his kiss with equal passion. But she felt guilty. He had bared his heart to her while she still held back. Why? What was wrong with her? Her whole being cried out for Ian, and yet she always held back.

The warm golden days of September gave way to the crisp coolness of October and the surrounding countryside burst into a blaze of glory.

''Och, Maggie, did ye ever see such colors?'' exclaimed Jeannie. ''Look at that red against the blue sky. It's as if it were afire. Ye never did see the likes o' that in Scotland.'' Maggie, too, was entranced by the brilliant reds and golds of the maples, by the big orange pumpkins and piles of huge red apples being sold in baskets along the roadsides. It was as if all the richness of America were being spread at her feet, and when a sudden breeze sent a shower of golden leaves tumbling to the ground, she laughed aloud for the sheer joy of it. *What a wonderful, magnificent country this is,* she thought, *and now I'm part of it.*

Grace alone was the least moved by the beauty that was around her. Instead she felt more and more closed in, dreading the moment each day when she and Jeannie descended the black iron staircase into the dank and smelly basement of the mill. Her attention wandered during the endless conversations of the men about ball games and beer parties. She failed to laugh at Nellie's crude jokes, and even the sight of Mrs. Anderson left her indifferent. But they all made allowances for her and teased her about being in love.

*Am I in love?* she wondered. True, the sight of Ian still gave her a deep thrill, but nothing seemed to dispel her sense of melancholy. Perhaps it was the dying of the year, but more than that it was a sense of being trapped in a dead end.

*Dead end,* the words sent a chill through her. She listened to Albert's endless wracking cough, smelled the greasy vats of water, and watched her hands grow red and raw from the damp skeins of silk. Perhaps it would have helped if she and Ian were together more, but he was now practically working two jobs, and when he was home Aunt Flora made every effort to see they were never alone. She made little secret of her disapproval of Grace, and was certainly not going to open the parlor so they could have a little privacy for courting.

The days slipped by, the leaves fell, and soon the surrounding hills were a dull, drab gray.

# CHAPTER
## ❦ 6 ❦

THE flu, or grippe as it was called, was taking its toll. Both Maggie and Jeannie were still too sick to work. Looms stood idle, carders had to double up, and even the throwers found themselves shifted from job to job. By Thursday even the indomitable Mrs. Anderson had succumbed. Joe, the foreman, had been forced to bring Grace upstairs where she tended the long, long rows of wheel-like skein holders as they spun around winding the silk onto bobbins.

The advantage of this job over the same one in the throwing department, at least to Grace, was that the silk had now been dyed. Silk was particularly amenable to dye and could be found in colors ranging from the most delicate pastels to rich jewel-like reds and blues, although it depressed her to see how much of it was dyed black. But her particular skeins were a pale but lustrous yellow, the color of winter sunshine, and she rejoiced in them.

Beyond her she could see the warping machines. Here the bobbins were set on a creel and lined up by color according to the design. Each slender, delicately twisted thread was stretched from the creel to the warping machine over an area of about five feet, spreading out in a fan shape and creating a shimmer of color so faint and transparent as to be almost invisible. To Grace it was as

if a series of pale moonbeams had been captured, tinted a
rainbow of colors, and scattered across the breadth of the
mill.

As she tended her bobbins she noticed Mr. Whitehead
in and out of his office, which was visible from where she
stood. He consulted with Joe, shook his head, and muttered to himself. He must be lost without Mrs. Anderson,
she thought, and not even Jessie, her precious niece, was
around to help out. But what impressed Grace the most
was the fact that whenever Mr. Whitehead went back into
his office he sat down. Grace longed to sit down. Her legs,
her back, her shoulders all cried out for a rest, but the
workers never sat down—they stood for hours on end, and
while the machines were running they couldn't leave them.

When at last the whistle blew and everything stopped
she was aware again of the strange, eerie silence. The mill
was alive only when the machines were rattling, banging,
and clacking. When they stopped it was as if life was held
in suspension, the only sounds being the shuffling of feet
as the workers gathered up their belongings and hurried to
the rear doors, spilling onto the street and calling faint
goodnights to each other.

She took her time, she was not in any particular hurry
to get back home to an irritable Aunt Flora and her two
patients. Ian was working at MacPherson's, so she was on
her own. She overheard Mr. Whitehead asking hopefully
if Mrs. Anderson were coming in tomorrow, but no one
seemed to know.

Looking back on it afterwards, Grace never fully understood what prompted her to do what she then did. Perhaps it was a latent desire to get even with Mrs. Anderson,
or again perhaps it was simply a need to sit down for a
while, but when Mr. Whitehead disappeared once again
into his office, shaking his head sadly as he did so, she
followed him and tapped on the door.

"Excuse me, Mr. Whitehead, but I wonder if I could

be of some assistance? With Mrs. Anderson and Jessie both out I thought you might need someone.''

He looked up at her with mild astonishment.

"Do you understand percentages?'' he asked quickly.

"Yes. I used to take care of Lady McLeod's books before she died,'' replied Grace. "I understand debit and credit, discounts, percentages, simple and compound interest . . .''

"Then come in, come in, Miss . . . ?''

"Miss Cameron,'' she said.

"Can you stay this evening, Miss Cameron? I have the auditors coming in tomorrow.''

"I can stay,'' she said.

"Good, good. First check over these figures for me, first column is net total, then discounted at six percent. You may sit here.'' He pulled a chair up to a small desk and switched on a lamp. Grace sank happily into the chair and began quickly adding up columns of figures. She had a natural aptitude for mathematics and felt a surge of simple pleasure at once again doing a job she felt suited for.

As Grace worked she gained a new respect for Mr. Whitehead. He might be a milquetoast when it came to dealing with the workers, completely dominated by the overpowering Mrs. Anderson, but he was a first-rate, meticulous accountant. His figures, written in a round, firm hand, were clear and accurate. Grace discovered a few minor discrepancies, probably made by Jessica, she thought, but for the most part everything looked good. The mill, though not as up-to-date or efficient as many of its neighbors, was turning a fair profit—a very fair profit. Grace was impressed.

They worked quietly, heads bent over their books, the light shining softly on Mr. Whitehead's gleaming bald spot and on Grace's coppery curls. She became so caught up in the work she barely noticed the darkening of the mill as the sweepers left and the lights went out one by one until the office was a small bright oasis in a vast shadowy world. Finally she glanced up from her books and looked out of the window into the deserted street. Blank-faced brick buildings, lit only by the faint gleam of the street-light, brooded over the silence.

"My word, Miss Cameron, just look at the time. It's past nine o'clock. I must apologize for keeping you so late." Mr. Whitehead consulted his watch, clucking slightly and shaking his head as he pocketed it.

"It's quite all right," said Grace. "I really enjoyed doing this."

"You've been a great help, believe me. I think I'm now sufficiently organized to face the auditors." He stood up. "We'll leave the lights on in here—Jim can switch them off later. Come, I'll walk with you to your coat." She followed him down the long, shadowy rows of idle looms, their footsteps reverberating loudly, to where her coat was hanging on a peg. He assisted her with old world courtesy, then called to the nightwatchman.

"We're leaving now, Jim. See that the lights are put out."

"Yessir, Mr. Whitehead, sir. I'll take care of it."

Mr. Whitehead took her elbow and steered her to the street.

"I must insist, Miss Cameron, that you allow me to buy you something to eat before you go home. Otherwise you may faint from hunger on the way." He laughed a little nervously. Grace was startled.

"There's no need for you to worry about me," she said. "I'll get supper when I get home."

"No, I insist," he said. "I'm sure Strubles will have a table for us."

*What will Aunt Flora say?* wondered Grace. *Oh, well, I'm late now, might as well be hung for a sheep as a lamb.* Besides, she was starving and Strubles was considered one of the best restaurants in town.

It wasn't far, so they walked together through the cold, damp streets where the tall mills rose like steep cliffs on either side and the only sound, other than their footsteps, was the rushing waters of the millrace. But once they entered through the restaurant's heavy glass doors, they were enveloped in warmth, the delicious smell of good food, and the soft hum of conversation. The room was only partially filled, mostly older couples she noticed. Some of them nodded to Mr. Whitehead, and she felt a few surreptitious glances in her direction. Mr. Whitehead was obviously a regular patron and they were quickly escorted to a small, elegantly appointed table.

Grace excused herself and made her way to the ladies' room where she washed her face and tidied her hair. She looked with dismay at her shabby black coat and even drearier black skirt and boots. Her shirtwaist was serviceable, but hardly fashionable. If only she'd worn her grey suit and lace blouse, but that would have been absurd. She was a mill worker and she dressed like a mill worker. She shrugged. There was nothing she could do about her clothes now, so she might as well relax and enjoy herself. A glance in the mirror should have reassured her—even in her old working dress she managed to look more beautiful than most women in their finest silks.

When she returned to the table, she found Mr. Whitehead had ordered a bottle of wine.

"Would you care for a glass, Miss Cameron, or are you one of the strict Presbyterian Scots?"

"No, and I'd love a glass of wine, thank you." Grace envisioned Aunt Flora fainting away with an outraged gasp, but she didn't care. Wine was one more civilized aspect of living she had acquired from old Lady McLeod. *God bless her soul,* thought Grace with a sudden fervent burst of gratitude.

The dinner was excellent—roast tender breast of chicken, tiny baked potatoes, buttered carrots—and Mr. Whitehead, once away from the dour shadow of Mrs. Anderson, proved a pleasant conversationalist.

"Paterson is a unique city, you know. The Lyons of

America some say. Our silk is the finest in the land. We don't handle any really intricate designs at Potter's mill, but there are some—the ribbons for example—that are a work of art.'' He took off his glasses and began to polish them vigorously. ''And it all started with a man named Alexander Hamilton. A man of vision, Miss Cameron, a man of vision.'' His eyes, a rather washed-out blue, gazed into the distance as if seeking visions of his own. ''Perhaps some afternoon when the mill is closed, you would allow me to show you how the waterways are laid out. They were originally designed by Pierre L'Enfant, the man who planned our capital, Washington, D.C.''

''That would be very interesting, Mr. Whitehead,'' said Grace, somewhat surprised.

''But now I must not keep you any later. Tomorrow is another day of labor. Whereabouts do you live, Miss Cameron?'' She gave him her address. He summoned the waiter for the check, and instructed him to call a cab for the young lady. ''My destination is in the opposite direction, but you will be quite safe. The cabbies in this area are completely reliable.'' Grace protested that she really didn't need a cab, but she was grateful when he finally helped her up the high step, bade her a courteous goodnight, paid the cabbie, and directed her on her way. She leaned back against the black cushions. *This is the life for me,* she thought, *a good meal, pleasant surroundings* . . . It would be quite a comedown to go back to the dreary job in the basement of the mill. She waited on the porch until the cabbie had disappeared down the street and the faint clip-clop of his horse had faded, then she opened the front door. Aunt Flora was poised on the stairs, ready to pounce.

''So there you are. And what do you have to say for yourself, miss? Staying out until all hours, worrying your aunt to death.''

''It's not eleven o'clock yet,'' protested Grace.

''Not eleven o'clock! Is that any time to be coming home, and in a cab too? Dinna think I didn't see. Where are you getting money for cabs, pray tell? Is this any way for an engaged young woman to behave? I always knew . . .'' But Grace refused to hear any more.

"I had to work late. It was an emergency, and I'm very tired, so goodnight Aunt Flora. I'm sorry if I kept you up." And before her aunt could say another word, Grace ran swiftly up the stairs and into her room.

The next morning Grace lingered in bed. She would be late for work, but the longer she waited the less time she would have to listen to Aunt Flora's wrath. But the real reason for her delay was that she didn't want to see Ian. She didn't want to see the hurt look in his eyes. Aunt Flora had touched a nerve last night. While she knew Ian wouldn't join with Aunt Flora in condemning her, he would be unhappy. She sighed. Ian was the most attractive man she'd ever met. When he touched her arm or looked across the room and smiled at her in that special private way of his, she could feel her senses tingle.

If only Ian would look beyond Paterson, she thought, beyond the mills and the small, narrow life of a mill worker. But he felt no need for the things she longed for— vain, foolish things like beautiful clothes, nice restaurants, concerts, or parties. It took very little to please him, "A loaf of bread beneath the bough, a jug of wine, a book of verse, and thou . . ." She sighed once more. Ian wouldn't even need the wine or the poetry. But she did. She needed them desperately.

She waited until she heard the front door close, then quickly slipped out of bed, washed, and dressed hurriedly. Aunt Flora was in the kitchen stirring the porridge.

"Och, you're sae fine now ye don't need tae get tae work on time. Ye can stroll in late like ye own the place, I suppose. Ye two cousins, just getting over the grippe, managed to get off on time."

"Did Maggie and Jeannie go to work today?" Grace was surprised.

"Aye, they're conscientious, they don't lay about unless they're real sick."

Grace said nothing, but quickly drank her tea. "I don't have time for breakfast, I've got to run."

"Will ye be home for supper at least?"

"I don't know," said Grace, slamming the door as she went out.

When she got downtown it was deserted, but the throb and hum of machinery vibrating through the streets told her the mills were alive. She slipped quickly through the side door hoping to escape notice, and hurried through the rows of looms aware of the scrutiny of the operators. Some nodded sympathetically, some stared at her accusingly. She saw Maggie in the distance absorbed in her work. She ran down the black iron staircase and hung her coat on a peg. Big Nellie mouthed a message to her as she went by.

"Watch out for the old cow, she's on the warpath." *I'm in for it now,* thought Grace. She arrived at the dark, damp corner of the mill where the soakers were crouched over their vats. Jeannie, who was filling a winding frame, looked up anxiously, her eyes wide and scared, her face white. *She should be home,* thought Grace, *sitting in a nice warm kitchen, not crouched here in this cold, damp hole.*

"Sorry I'm late, Jeannie," she said, "I overslept." She felt rather than saw the shadow that fell between them. It was Mrs. Anderson, risen from her sick bed like an avenging angel to defend her small patch of authority. Her face was grimmer, her voice harsher, her anger more bitter than Grace had ever seen it.

"So you overslept, just like other low and evil women who spend their nights shaming themselves." Grace was staggered. She'd expected Mrs. Anderson to resent her working on her precious books, but this was naked female jealousy that had nothing to do with bookkeeping. So that was it. She'd had her eye on Mr. Whitehead herself.

"Mrs. Anderson, all I did was help with the books. The auditors are coming in today . . ."

"Oh, sure you did. And you worked on the books in Strubles restaurant, I suppose. Drinking and making an exhibition of yourself." By this time anyone who was within earshot had given up all pretense of work. Jeannie looked frozen with fear.

"I did not make an exhibition of myself," said Grace, her good intentions of not fighting with Mrs. Anderson fast disappearing.

"Oh, no. You were seen—you can't deny it—drinking wine, behaving like a—a—chorus girl, taking money."

"That's not true," said Grace hotly. She stared at the woman in front of her who seemed to be choking with rage.

"A slut, that's what you are, nothing but a slut." She had barely spat out the words when Grace, in a reflex action, slapped her hard across the face. Mrs. Anderson gasped in shock. The room suddenly grew very quiet. Jeannie began to cry. Grace, her hair shimmering like fire, advanced towards her enemy.

"No one calls me names like that, no one," she said softly. "You apologize."

"Apologize?" spluttered Mrs. Anderson. "To you?"

"Yes, apologize."

"You were seen—"

Suddenly Grace reached out and gave the woman a shove that sent her staggering backwards. Then Grace pushed her hard until she went down onto the bench where she clutched the side and stared blankly, the bright mark of Grace's slap blotching her sallow face. Grace stood over her. Once more she spoke very softly and slowly.

"Now apologize for calling me that disgusting name." The other woman looked around wildly but the crowd that had gathered stood motionless. "I am not a slut, Mrs. Anderson."

"But you were seen . . ."

"Having dinner with a gentleman," said Grace. The only sound was Mrs. Anderson's harsh breathing.

"All right," she muttered, "I'm sorry." She looked up. "But you're fired."

"Oh, no I'm not," said Grace. "I quit."

"I'll see to it that you never get another job in any mill in Paterson."

"That's fine with me," said Grace. "I'm never going to work in a mill again as long as I live." She turned her back on the defeated woman and took her coat back off the peg. She put her arms around Jeannie. "Don't worry, dear, everything's going to be all right." Then, head high, eyes straight ahead, hair flaming, she walked slowly and deliberately through the aisles, past Nellie who gave her a thumbs up sign, past the men who stared at her with open admiration, up the stairs, down the long rows of looms, and out the main entrance into the cold, bright sunshine.

For a while she walked aimlessly through the streets, still simmering over the insults, but gradually a lightness of heart gave a lightness to her step. She was finished with Mrs. Anderson. Never again would she have to see that sour face or listen to that harsh voice. Never again would she have to smell those vats of greasy water, or hear the drip, drip, drip of the hanging skeins of raw silk. She was free. She had a whole day to herself. A day to browse in the shops, to eat lunch in one of the cafes instead of their usual dank basement corner. Her only regret was that she was wearing her old working clothes and boots—but no matter. After today she would throw them away.

By afternoon Grace was still filled with the energy that comes from a confrontation. She set off in the direction of Garrett Mountain, finally climbing the grassy slope that led to the large mansion she had seen that first day at the Falls. Belle-Vista, known to everyone as Lambert Castle, towered over Paterson like some medieval fort.

*It's not as graceful as Lady McLeod's manor,* thought Grace as she stared up at the brooding pile of sandstone with its odd turrets, one round and one square, *but it is powerful*. Powerful like the man who built it, who'd come to America as a penniless immigrant and now owned the great Dexter-Lambert Company. She peered through the gate at the grounds. Most of the flowers had already been nipped by the frost, the last few straggly leaves clung to the trees, and the lawns were fading to a wintry brown. But the elegant walks and terraces remained, awaiting once more the bright green flowering of spring.

"It's not open today, miss." Grace turned to discover an elderly man at her side. He was wearing a heavy tweed suit and thick boots. "The art gallery's not open today. Saturdays it's open. Mr. Lambert lets folks come in on Saturdays to see all his paintings and statues."

"I'll have to come back, then," she said.

"If you'd like to come in and see the grounds, I can show them to you." He took out a heavy bundle of keys and began unlocking the gate. "I'm one o' the gardeners. Family's away right now, but I can show you the gardens." She thanked him and followed him through the gate. A small cluster of sparrows flew chattering to the safety of the trees as they walked along the path.

"This here's the main house, all built of local stone." They walked along the terrace, past the two turrets. "This part's the art gallery, and at the end of that we comes to the arcade." They entered a charming, open-arched covered walkway—spacious but airy. It was built of white stone, a marked contrast to the heavy, ponderous construction of the main house. "And through here," he added, "is the Eyetalian garden." Again, a dramatic change of scene, statuary, and archways reminiscent of the sunny gardens of Italy. "See them fountains. They're not going now, but in the summer they're splashing with water, and when Mr. Lambert has a party this here garden's all lit up with electric lights. The ladies and gentlemen wanders around in their fine clothes; it's some sight, let me tell you.'' There was pride in his voice as he described the scene, and Grace pictured it with a pang of envy.

"Now, miss, look over there, see them arches. Looks like you could walk right through 'em, don't it? But that there's a painting on a wall. You try to walk through there and you'll walk smack dab into the wall. They call it 'trump' something or other—means fool-the-eye. I think it's better than anything Mr. Lambert's got in his gallery.''

They continued to wander around and Grace admired everything from the greenhouses to the observation tower on top of the mountain, returning at last to lean on the wall that fronted the estate. Below them lay Paterson, where the mills hummed steadily making money, money, money for Mr. Catholina Lambert. *I've been on the wrong side of the fence*, thought Grace. *Maybe it's the fault of Lady McLeod, who gave me a taste of luxury. Maybe it's my own nature, but I can't go through life being poor, struggling to make ends meet. Not even for Ian.*

There, now she'd said it. She'd finally faced the reason for her melancholy. She knew now why she always held back. She loved Ian. Ached for him. But she couldn't marry him. He was a proud man, and she would destroy him with her discontent. She had to be free to test her wings. To discover what life in America was really all about.

She lifted her gaze to the far horizon, beyond Paterson to New York. *That's where my chances are*, she thought, *and that's where I'm going. I won't tell anyone, I'll just pack up and leave.* She thanked the old man for his courtesy and made her way back down the mountain towards home.

# CHAPTER
## ❧ 7 ❧

GRACE slid out of bed as the first faint streaks of light appeared in the sky. Her little room was icy cold and she shivered as she pulled on her stockings and heavy petticoat. She dressed rapidly, putting on everything except her boots. Her valise was already packed, and all that remained were a few possessions—her books, her music box. She'd leave them to the girls. She sat down at the dresser and wrote a quick note.

Dear Maggie and Jeannie,
   I'm going to New York. Paterson is just not for me. Maggie, you may keep my music box, and Jeannie, I want you to have my books. Don't worry about me, I'll be fine. Tell Aunt Flora I'm sorry, and she's to have any wages coming to me from the mill.

Love,
Grace

P.S. Say goodbye to Ian for me.

She knew that was cruel, but there was no way she could explain herself to Ian. She tip-toed down the stairs in her stockinged feet until she reached the hallway where she sat down on the bottom steps and put on her boots. It was dark but she was keenly aware of her surroundings.

67

She could almost feel the densely patterned wallpaper, as if the roses themselves were pressing against her, and she smelled the faint scent of furniture wax, mingled with the lingering echoes of mutton stew and cabbage, that permeated the house. The only sounds were the slight creaking of bedsprings and the faint whisper of a sigh, but perhaps that was her imagination. Soon Aunt Flora would be down, wearing her old flannel wrapper, her hair done up in a hairnet, to light the stove and put the porridge on to cook. Maggie and Jeannie would be stirring, rubbing the sleep from their eyes. Then Ian would come bounding down the stairs. She squeezed her eyes shut. She would not think of Ian. She dared not think of Ian or her resolve would melt away.

She stood up, picked up her valise, slipped her purse over her shoulder and approached the front door. Cautiously she slid the bolt from the lock, grasped the doorknob and turned it slowly until she felt the door yield to her touch. It opened a crack and she slid through, scarcely daring to breathe. Then she closed it behind her, releasing the knob slowly until a soft click told her it was in place. She took a deep breath of the cold, damp air. She was free.

The first light of morning glimmered behind the rooftops, but the streets were still dark. Cocks were beginning to crow in ramshackle backyard chicken coops, and occasionally a dog barked. In the distance she heard the clop-clop of a slow moving horse that could only be the milkwagon. Shapeless gray shadows were now beginning to solidify into tall brick factories as she hurried along, until the rushing waters of the raceways told her she had reached the heart of Paterson.

At the railroad station a welcome blast of warm musty air greeted her as she entered the waiting room, where a few faded posters on the yellow-brown walls advertised the Phoebe Snow, the pride of the Erie-Lackawanna. A loud bang and rattle announced that the ticket window was open for business. Grace waited while a couple of shabby looking men, unshaven and weary, bought tickets, also an old woman carrying a basket of eggs. Then she walked up to the window.

"New York, one way," she said.

"Hoboken's far as we go. Then you gotta get the ferry." Grace pocketed her ticket. She hadn't thought about the ferry. Where would she get it? And where would it let her off? But it didn't matter. Wherever it was, it wouldn't be Paterson.

When it arrived, the train was almost empty, and she sat alone on the stiff, straw seat and watched the red-brick mills and huddled clapboard houses fade into the distance. Soon they were speeding across long flat stretches of tall, waving grassland, where an occasional flock of birds rose up, circled, and dropped back down. The train clickety-clacked steadily over the rails, every mile taking her further and further from weary days of picking, sorting, and winding, until she saw the outline of a city faintly etched on the horizon. A seemingly flat, one-dimensional sketch of tall, narrow buildings, square-shaped buildings, domes, and towers that seemed to hang in the air, then vanish. Moments later they rattled into the station.

"Hoboken," the conductor cried as he walked down the center of the train collecting tickets, "Hoboken."

Other trains were pulling in and sleepy-eyed passengers shuffled along the platform. Grace followed them into the waiting rooms, then out through the revolving door to the dock where the ferry boat was moored. She paid her nickel and walked up the ramp.

The boat was a wide, shallow vessel, with benches all around the deck and a roomy cabin outfitted in dark, polished wood. She pushed open the frosted glass door and was greeted by a delicious smell of fresh brewed coffee. She realized how hungry she was and joined a small group at the counter where she ordered a coffee and pastry.

Although it was still very early there were several well-dressed businessmen among the passengers, and a few women. She was pleased to note that she fitted right in with her gray suit and short jacket. She felt a stirring of excitement. This was her style.

She finished her welcome breakfast and went back on deck, bracing herself against the cold wind that whipped across the water. The ferry chugged across the Hudson at a steady pace, and Grace leaned against the rail drinking it all in. Rising up out of the choppy water was the Statue of Liberty, a huge gray-green figure silhouetted against the sky. Behind her was Ellis Island, probably already crowded with masses of tired, bewildered people. But Grace was not looking backward—ahead, drawing closer and closer, was the skyline of New York. New York, alive with all the excitement of a thriving city: the buying, selling, banking; the shopping, concerts and theaters; and people, hundreds of people, all hurrying, bustling, jostling. She felt her heart beat faster as the ferry maneuvered its way into the slip, and the heavy ropes were thrown ashore and pulled tight around the stanchions. Passengers crowded on deck, and before the wide gangplank had even touched the ground they surged forward, Grace among them, to spill out onto the quay at Chambers Street.

When she emerged into the street her fellow passengers fanned out in all directions, but she stood for a moment bewildered by the noise and traffic. Carts, cabs, and trolley cars jockeyed for space as they rattled past her. Overhead the sky was blotted out by the massive road of steel that carried the elevated trains. As one came hurtling through Grace felt she had never before been engulfed in such a thunderous noise. She hesitated at the edge of the pavement, watching in amazement as people casually crossed over, dodging in and out of the traffic which seemed never to stop. Finally she took a deep breath, clasped her valise firmly in her hand, and following close on the heels of a fellow pedestrian, dashed across to safety.

Now the city stretched out before her, waking up and

coming alive. She walked briskly along, past a string of little stores, above which were the crowded sewing shops where girls and women, bent over sewing machines, treadled incessantly. Now and then, huddled in a doorway, a tramp lay curled up against the cold, a cheap bottle of wine hidden under his threadbare coat, part of the flotsam and jetsam washed up by all great cities.

She continued uptown, catching a glimpse of teeming tenements—wash strung from window to window, narrow streets choked with pushcarts and swarming children. Even now, with windows and doors closed against the cold air, she could sense the reek of garlic and unwashed humanity. She quickened her pace.

Her valise was growing heavy and she was tiring. She had no idea where she was heading and decided it was time to ask directions. She stopped at a busy corner and watched the faces of those hurrying by until she saw one that seemed friendly.

"Excuse me, ma'am, is there a tram—trolley—that I could take from here?" The woman looked at her blankly.

"Where d'ja wanna go?" she asked.

"Oh," said Grace, then on the spur of the moment she exclaimed, "Pennsylvania Station."

"That's easy," said the woman. "Trolley stops on this corner. It'll be marked Penn Station, don't go no further."

The first thing that struck Grace as she entered the station was the fact that she couldn't see any trains. She walked around the huge waiting area with its lofty ceiling and enormous clock. There were listings of trains, rows of ticket windows, newspaper booths, shoe shine boys, doughnut stands, and masses of people hurrying in one direction or another, but no train tracks and no trains. She found a fairly quiet corner and put down her valise. It was all so confusing; she hadn't realized New York was so big or so crowded.

"Excuse me, miss, do you know what time the Long

Island train gets in?'' A middle-aged woman, wearing a shabby but respectable suit and a small hat with a veil over her face, was at Grace's side. Grace shook her head.

"No, I'm afraid not.''

"When I saw you standing here I thought maybe you were meeting someone.''

"No,'' said Grace.

"You're catching a train then?''

"No, I just got here. I'd like to get a cup of coffee and maybe check my valise.''

"There's lockers over by the West Gate, and there's a coffee shop on the lower level,'' said the woman. "You look confused. Here I'll show you, follow me.'' The woman picked up Grace's valise and began to walk swiftly across the crowded concourse with Grace close behind her. What happened next was always a blur in her mind. As they pushed through the crowd, someone bumped heavily into her almost knocking her off her feet. She felt a tug at her arm, and before she could regain her balance her purse was gone and whoever had it had melted into the crowd. She looked around wildly but could see no sign of her assailant. She broke into a stumbling run, dodging around the stream of people who were hurrying towards the exits, trying to catch up with the woman who had her valise, but as she worked her way through the crowd a sense of desperation began to overwhelm her. The woman, too, had disappeared, completely swallowed up by the surging mass of people.

She felt her knees growing weak and she made her way, more slowly now, to where rows of lockers, their brass doors gleaming in the yellow light, lined the walls. She leaned against them and scanned the cavernous room searching in vain for her erstwhile good Samaritan. For a moment she thought she was going to faint. The room seemed to grow dim, and her heart began to pound as she made her way, shakily, to a bench and sat down, and the awful realization swept over her that she'd been robbed of everything she owned.

She stared with unseeing eyes at the crowds of people hurrying by oblivious to her and her plight. After a while she noticed two policemen walking slowly across the waiting room, swinging their nightsticks. *I should go to them,* she thought, *and report what happened.* But then a feeling of shame swept over her. How could she admit she'd been so foolish, so trusting? *I must look like a greenhorn,* she thought bitterly.

She began to desperately search her pockets in the vain hope that she'd find a few dollars, but all she discovered was a quarter and two nickels, barely enough to get back to Paterson. She fingered the coins, then sat up straight. No, no, she could never go back. She could hear Aunt Flora now telling her she was lazy, stupid, and ungrateful. She'd rather starve, beg in the streets, than go back. She'd find something. Somewhere.

She stood up and walked out of the station, back to the busy streets now thronged with people. Her mind was still in a daze and she wandered aimlessly, unable to concentrate on anything. Her mood ranged from anger to shame. Every once in a while she thrust her hand into her pocket and fingered the coins; they would just about buy her dinner, but she wasn't hungry. She was too upset to eat. And so she walked back and forth across Manhattan, street by street, gradually working her way uptown. When she came to Fifth Avenue and 50th Street, she turned onto Fifth Avenue, gazing at the huge blocks of granite and marble that housed New York's richest rich—the Astors, the Vanderbilts, the Goulds—each mansion more splendid than the last, and each served by elegant carriages and an occasional motor car. Here was the New York of her dreams, but as unreachable as the moon.

She walked steadily until she came to Central Park, where she sat down on a bench and watched the pigeons strutting back and forth. The grass had faded to a dull

brown and trees were leafless. There was a damp chill to
the air and she shivered. An old man came shuffling along,
and when he saw Grace he stopped.

"Got a nickel for a poor old man, miss?" She stared
at him blankly. "Nice young lady like you could give a
nickel to a poor old man down on his luck." He leaned
towards her and she jumped up and hurried out of the
park. She found herself walking along narrow streets,
whipped by a cold wind blowing in from the river. She
knew she had to eat something soon; it had been hours
since her last meal on the ferry this morning. Could it
have only been this morning? It was as if the ferry boat
ride had happened in another lifetime, and since then she'd
been walking the gray streets of the city.

The work day was almost over—people were pouring
out of buildings and hurrying towards home, or meeting
each other in restaurants; smiling, laughing, taking off their
coats and settling themselves at small tables lit by flickering candles. Grace leaned against the window of one
such restaurant and read the menu posted there: fresh
back-bay oysters, Long Island duckling, stuffed capon. It
was an elegant setting, with flowers on the table and crys-
tal chandeliers in the lobby. She watched with envy as
women, swathed in silks and furs, all with escorts, were
welcomed by the maître d'hotel.

She turned away and found a small storefront kitchen
that promised a bowl of soup for a dime. She slipped
inside and sat down at a corner table that was covered with
a yellow oilcloth. She ordered a bowl of vegetable soup
from a weary looking waitress. It came accompanied by a
plate of crackers and she ate hungrily, dipping the crackers
into the soup to try to make it last longer. Hunger made
it delicious and she lingered over it as long as she could,
but finally had to leave, paying her dime and feeling guilty
about not leaving a tip.

Back in the streets she automatically followed the crowd
and found her way to Broadway, that brilliant glorification

of commerce that slashes across the heart of the city like
a diamond-studded sash. Here was a happy, jostling crowd,
mostly theater-bound. She allowed herself to be carried
along with it, pausing under the marquees to study the
garish posters.

"Seats available for this performance," announced a
man in a striped coat. "Seats available."

"How much?" asked Grace on a sudden impulse.

"Fifty cents stall, twenty-five cents loge, and ten cents
for the balcony."

"I'll take a ten-cent ticket," she said, parting with two
more precious nickels. A feeling of recklessness had overcome her. Maybe this would be her last night of freedom—she might as well enjoy it. Besides, it was warm
inside.

She was quickly hustled through the red plush lobby and
began the long, steep climb, the stairs growing narrower
and steeper the higher she went. She emerged close to the
roof and looked down the dizzying slope to the floor below, where she could see a miniscule stage. She quickly
found a seat and clung to it while more practiced patrons
strolled up and down the steep steps with the nonchalance
of hardy mountaineers.

The show was something called vaudeville, the acts
varying from sweetly sentimental to bawdy, but she saw it
all through a blue haze of tobacco smoke that hung like
wreaths from the ceiling. The music floated upwards and
disembodied voices hung in the air adding to the unreality.
There were patterns of color made by tiny dancers, who
appeared to be in a state of undress that would have caused
Aunt Flora to faint, but actually it was a dream and soon
she would awake to find herself in bed. Then she slipped
her hand into her pocket and felt the three little coins,
cold, hard and solid, and a chill swept over her. It was
not a dream.

The final curtain came down, the applause died away,
and there was a sudden stampede for the stairway. Grace

found herself pushed towards the exit, and then pulled away. A tall, smartly dressed man was holding her arm.

"You don't want to go rushing down with that crowd, young lady. Good way to break a leg." He had a thick mustache and heavy lidded eyes. He smelled of whiskey.

"Enjoy the show?" he asked.

"Yes, thank you," said Grace, edging away.

"How about joining me for an after-theater drink?"

"I don't drink," she said quickly.

"A cup of coffee, then. I know a nice little cafe nearby." He slid his arm around her waist and gave her a squeeze. Alarmed she pulled away.

"I have a train to catch," she gasped, thrusting herself into the middle of the crowd hurtling down the staircase. Once outside she continued the pretense and set off for Penn Station.

A welcome blast of warm air greeted her in the huge waiting room. She found the ladies' room and freshened up, then joined the milling crowd of theater goers who were awaiting trains for the suburbs. She settled down on a bench where she retrieved a secondhand newspaper and pretended to read, while snatches of conversation drifted around her.

"Of course Mother wants me to go to her dressmaker, but she'll make me look like a dowdy old matron. I want to get my gown from Saks."

"I know, my mother's the same way, but I wangled an allowance out of Daddy, so at least I can buy some decent shoes and hats."

"Come along girls." An elderly lady waving tickets bustled around shepherding her two elegantly dressed charges towards their train. Grace couldn't suppress a pang of envy as she listened to talk of golf games and bridge parties, dinner engagements and teas, until finally weariness overcame everything and she leaned against the arm rest and fell asleep.

"Wake up, miss, wake up. Last train leaving for

Westchester.'' Grace woke with a start to find a uniformed stationmaster standing over her. She looked around in confusion until she remembered she was at the railway station. It was almost empty now, and sweepers, all negroes, were slowly pushing their wide brooms across the floor. ''If you hurry you can still make it, platform 3.''

''I'm not catching a train, I'm—I'm meeting someone from Long Island.''

''Last train came in from Long Island an hour ago. No more now till morning.''

''Oh, dear, I must have missed her.'' Grace was surprised at how quickly the lies came.

''Would you like me to call you a cab, miss?'' He was being very kind, but then she didn't look like a vagrant.

''No, thank you. I have a carriage waiting.'' She folded the newspaper and walked briskly back out into the cold, damp night.

As her footsteps took her further away from the station, a feeling of panic overtook her. Three young men came stumbling towards her, obviously drunk—they were hanging onto each other and singing. When they spied Grace they called out to her. She turned and fled, running desperately down the dark narrow streets that led she knew not where. At last, out of breath, she stopped and leaned against a lamppost. The thin, cold-blue gaslight showed a row of dark and empty stores.

What was she to do? There were still several hours until morning. She couldn't walk the streets without either being accosted or arrested; she had to find someplace to hide. A dark doorway beckoned. Checking to make sure it was empty she crept in, sank down in the corner and spread the newspaper around her. Then she put her head down on her knees, and once more overcome by sheer exhaustion, she slept.

The first gray streaks of dawn were lightening the sky when Grace awoke from her first night in the city, stiff, sore, cold, and miserable. *Thank heavens Aunt Flora can't see me now,* she thought. *Or Ian. Oh, God, Ian.* What would he think of her huddled in a doorway like an old tramp? *I must be crazy,* she thought. *Why am I here all alone when I could be warm and safe with Ian?* All she had to do was go back to the ferry. After that she could find her way back to Paterson. Paterson, and Aunt Flora's thin, pinched lips saying "I told you so, Miss know-it-all." *I can't go back,* she thought, *no matter what becomes of me I can't go back.* But what was going to become of her?

She heard a shuffling noise and shrank back into the recess of the doorway. An old woman came into view, wearing a man's jacket, tattered and threadbare, which flapped open to reveal a filthy cotton dress. The woman squatted down and began sifting through the dirt in the gutter. She spat on something and began rubbing it on the corner of her jacket, then pocketing her find and groaning slightly, she rose from her crouched position and shuffled away.

Horrified, Grace got quickly to her feet and abandoned the doorway. She hurried back towards the by now familiar, almost friendly, Pennsylvania Station. There, in the steamy warmth of the ladies room, she washed up as best she could. If only she had a comb, without one she didn't dare let down her hair, just secured the loose pins with a quick twist and refastened her hat. There was a new attendant, wearing a fresh white apron, who offered to help brush down her skirt, but Grace shook her head.

Her footsteps rang out as she crossed the almost empty concourse. Back in the streets the city was waking up, carts rumbled by and a few carriages and trolleys were on the move. She walked purposefully, as if she knew exactly where she was headed. She had a purpose. A reason for being here. She was going to find a job.

She was ravenously hungry. A small lunch room caught her eye with a sign in the window which read, "Breakfast being served."

A bell jangled as Grace pushed open the door. The heavenly aroma of bacon and freshly perking coffee greeted her, overwhelming her good intentions of just ordering something to drink. She swayed slightly as she approached the counter. A pretty girl and slightly balding man were engrossed in conversation.

"What can I order for fifteen cents?" she gasped. They turned to stare at her, and the next thing she knew they were both on the other side of the counter, gently pushing her into a chair, and offering her a glass of water.

"Here, honey, you drink this," said the girl. "Mike, get this young lady some food. When was the last time you had a meal, Sugar?"

"I had some soup yesterday," she said. "I've only got fifteen cents, someone stole my purse." To her horror she felt tears trickling down her cheeks.

"Don't try to explain now," said the girl. "When you've had something to eat we'll talk."

"That's right," said Mike, cracking two eggs onto the sizzling griddle, "we can't have youse fainting from hunger, wouldn't look good to our customers." In a few minutes he set a tray in front of her—bacon, eggs, toast, coffee, and fresh orange juice.

"Maisie, lets you and me jern this here young lady wit' a cuppa coffee, ain't no one comin' in this oily." Maisie filled two big white cups and they both sat down with Grace, who was trying not to swallow everything whole. Finally she wiped up the last trace of egg with her toast and sat back to study her benefactors.

Mike was obviously the cook, and as she learned later, the owner. His squashed-in nose and crooked teeth gave him a rough look, but his manner was as gentle as his appearance was tough. Maisie, on the other hand, was as pleasant as she looked, with sparkling brown eyes, a pert turned-up nose, and thick brown hair that escaped in bouncy curls from under her cap. Both wore long white aprons.

"I don't know how to thank you," said Grace, tears springing to her eyes again. "If there's anything I can do—wash dishes—anything . . ."

"Can you wait on table?" said Maisie, laughing. "We're short-handed."

"Yes, yes, I can wait on table," said Grace fervently.

"Oh, come on, I was only kidding—a lady like you!"

"You ain't cut out to be no waitress," said Mike. "Youse speaks too nice."

"No, I mean it," said Grace. "I need a job. I'll do anything. I'm good with figures, too." Mike and Maisie exchanged glances.

"We need someone to mind the till," said Maisie. "And she could help with the tables when we're busy." Mike grinned.

"Why not? Two beautiful goils should bring in twice as much business." The jangling bell interrupted their discussion and Grace went behind the counter to begin her job as waitress/cashier at Mike's Luncheonette, on the corner of Broadway and 48th Street.

# CHAPTER

## ❧ 8 ❧

IT started like any other morning. Maggie and Aunt Flora were eating their porridge, Ian was drinking a cup of tea, when Jeannie came bursting into the kitchen, eyes wild, pigtails flying.

"She's gone, Grace's gone," she cried. "Her room's empty. She left a note." Jeannie read it aloud. When she reached the end, she paused, then said in a choked whisper, " 'P.S. Say goodbye to Ian for me.' "

Maggie watched the color drain from Ian's face and the skin tighten over his bones until he looked like a death mask. He didn't say a word, but stood up, reached for his coat, and walked out of the house. Her heart was filled with pity, but even as the door closed behind him a small, traitorous voice whispered in her ear: *She's left him. Grace has left him.*

"Well, of all the wicked, ungrateful girls," Aunt Flora was a torrent of fury, her burr growing thicker as her anger increased. "Tae think that my ain sister could have borne such a hussy. But what can ye expect from a Cameron? I told her she nay should ha'e married that wastrel."

"But what will Grace do? How will she live?" sobbed Jeannie.

"Och, she'll find some wickedness nae doot. She's nae

gude and I'm glad she's awa' from here. Good riddance tae bad rubbish.''

"But Grace was always kind tae us," said Jeannie.

"Aye, that's true, Aunt Flora." Maggie couldn't think of Grace as wicked.

"Kind! Ye think it's kind to fill young girls' heads full of sinful ideas. Leavin' ye her books is she? Well, we'll see aboot that. That's where she got those high and mighty ideas from in the first place. Not content wi' the Gude Book, oh, no. Poetry and novels, well they'll nay corrupt ye. Now get tae work, the two of ye.''

"Please dinna get rid of her books," wailed Jeannie. "She gave them tae me.''

"And I'm your guardian. D'ye think I'll stand by an' let ye swallow poison? 'Tis my Christian duty tae protect ye from such filth.''

"How do ye know it's filth if ye've never read any of it?''

Aunt Flora's face turned bright red. "And I never will," she exclaimed. "Don't ye argue wi' me, miss. Get tae work, both of ye.''

Jeannie made a quick dash upstairs, leaving Aunt Flora muttering to herself by the stove. She came down a minute later wearing her wool cape around her shoulders. Once outside she ran towards the back yard.

"Got to check the chickens," she called out to Maggie, who waited patiently by the gate. When she reappeared she set off so quickly that Maggie had to run to catch up with her.

"What are ye up to? Ye collected the eggs this morning, ye know ye did.''

"It's Aunt Flora," said Jeannie. "She'll get rid of the books. She hates book learning. That's one reason she hates Grace.''

"She doesna *hate* Grace.''

"Yes she does, because Grace is smarter than she is, and that's because of the books. She'll be rid of them before we get home, but I rescued a few and they're hid in the chicken coop. Ye won't tell on me, will ye, Maggie?''

"Ye know I never tell on ye," said Maggie, although she couldn't understand such a fuss over a few books. "Do ye think she'll get rid of the music box too?"

"No, it plays 'The Blue Bells o' Scotland' so that'll be allowed to stay." Jeannie's voice was bitter. Maggie glanced at her sister in surprise. Her thin face was pale and pinched with the cold, and she couldn't read the expression on it.

They walked in silence for a few blocks, each trying to grasp the full realization of Grace's flight.

"Poor Ian," said Maggie. "I can understand her wanting tae leave the mill, and even Aunt Flora, but how could she be sae cruel to Ian?"

"It may seem cruel now, but in a way she's really being kind."

"Kind!" Maggie stopped to stare at her.

"Aye. Grace would never have married Ian. He's not what she wants."

"Not what she wants?!" Maggie was shocked. How could any girl not want Ian? Her own cheeks flamed at the thought of him, and again, a wild, traitorous gleam of hope entered her heart, but she squashed it in panic. "What does Grace want, then?"

"Life, excitement, riches. She wasna' meant to live in a mill town and be a good little housewife. Can ye picture Grace down on her knees scrubbing the floor?"

Maggie was astonished. When had Jeannie grown so worldly? She didn't look any different—her two thick braids were pushed back behind her ears and her black felt hat pulled firmly down on her head. Her step was quick and light in spite of the heavy boots she had to wear. Her cotton skirt, worn over a host of heavy petticoats, reached almost to her ankles. She looked the same as she always did, and yet Maggie sensed that somehow she had grown.

It was almost as if Jeannie were the older and she, Maggie, the younger of the two. What a strange morning it had been—everything had changed in one brief moment. Everything.

Ian got through the day somehow. He was grateful for the clatter of the looms. He watched the shuttle flying back and forth with the thrust and speed of a bullet as the elaborate frame rose and fell displaying the warp and weft of the broadsilk, where one thread breaking or knotting could ruin the smooth surface of the fabric, or one errant spool of foreign silk could change the entire pattern of the cloth.

All day he watched the looms, listened to their hypnotic rhythm, willed himself not to think. For the most part he blocked out all thoughts and feelings, but a shifting shaft of sunlight illuminating a delicate red-gold thread caused him to flinch as from a knife wound. When the day ended he spoke to no one, and something in his face and manner showed clearly he wanted to be left alone. He walked deliberately into the Nags Head and ordered a whiskey, then another and another, and continued until he was totally and joylessly drunk.

Aunt Flora stood in the corner of the backyard, out of the wind. Her old black coat pulled around her, a long stick in her hand, she poked at the small bonfire that burned brightly. She had cleaned out Grace's bedroom, stripping it bare. Everything she owned—a few picture postcards, a couple of pretty boxes she used to keep her handkerchiefs in, and her books—all fed the flames. She watched with deep satisfaction as the pages charred, curled, and then were finally consumed. She saw names like Scott, Thackeray, Bronte, Dickens, each reduced to a handful of ashes. She tossed in a small volume marked "Selected Poems of Christina Rossetti," and watched it explode into flames with the double satisfaction of having eliminated both a poet and foreigner.

"There, Miss Grace Cameron, with your high and mighty ideas, ye'll not infect young Jeannie with your trash. As for Ian, he's a fool if he loses any sleep over the likes of you."

When the girls got home that night there was a sign in the front room window: Room for Rent. *She hasn't wasted any time,* thought Jeannie as she dashed around to the chicken coop past the smoldering remains of the bonfire. *I knew it. I knew she would destroy everything.* In the darkness of the coop she reached up between two squawking, flapping chickens and felt the hard spines of her rescued books—at least they were safe.

Maggie slowly climbed the stairs. Grace's door was open. The bed was neatly made, the coverlet newly washed and ironed, as were the curtains. The bureau was bare. It was as if Grace had never existed. She went into her own room, the one she shared with Jeannie, and there on the dressing table was the music box. She picked it up. It was a pretty little box, with a filigreed clasp and a picture of a heather-clad hillside on the top. She opened it slowly and listened to the faint, tinkling melody. It wasn't the "Blue Bells of Scotland," but "Comin' through the Rye." Maggie whispered the words:

"Every lassie, hae her laddy
Nae'ne they say hae I
But all the lads they smile on me
When comin' through the rye."

# CHAPTER
## ❧ 9 ❧

THE work at the luncheonette was hard, but it was not like the mindless, backbreaking work at the mill. Grace enjoyed meeting the customers, most of whom were businessmen who commuted in from the suburbs. They were well dressed and polite, and even when they engaged in bantering conversations with Maisie they seldom got fresh. And if they did, Mike was at her side in a moment. They never bantered with Grace. There was something about her that checked even the most exuberant. Also, unless they were extremely rushed, Grace seldom waited on table but instead remained behind the counter. In no time at all she found herself in full charge of the cash register, totalling the receipts at night and balancing Mike's simple books for him.

"Youse is too smart to be woikin' here," he told her. "Youse should be in some big fancy office."

"One day, Mike," she said with a sigh. "One day."

It was Maisie's boyfriend, Joseph Schmidt, who showed her the way.

Grace had moved in with Maisie. They shared a little one-room walk-up off Third Avenue. Maisie had taken Grace under her wing ever since that first day when she'd stumbled into Mike's place, cold, hungry and desperate.

She realized Grace had no place to go and had taken her home for the night.

"I have two pull-down beds, so I can put you up," she said. After her previous night of sleeping in a doorway, a pull-down bed sounded like heaven to Grace, and she accepted the offer gratefully. Maisie's room was on the third floor of a boarding house run by a middle-aged widow. It was a fair sized room, with a sink and gas ring, which served as a kitchen, and a window that looked out onto an alleyway, the windowsill sometimes serving as an ice-box. Mrs. Murphy ran a decent house. It even had central heating, although as Maisie explained, the steam seldom reached the third floor, in spite of vigorous banging on the pipes by shivering tenants.

There was a bathroom down the hall which was shared by two other tenants. It did have hot water and Grace welcomed the chance to really wash. Later when both girls were in their nightclothes, Grace's loaned to her by Maisie, they sat on their respective beds drinking hot cocoa and sharing confidences. Grace did not say much about her life in Paterson, merely that she had come to New York looking for work. Maisie told her that she was the oldest of eight children, and her family lived in Brooklyn.

"But the place was so crowded I think they were glad when I moved out. I try to send them something every now and then, but I'm saving up to get married. What about you, Grace, do you have a boyfriend?"

Grace winced. She had tried not to even think of Ian, it caused such an ache in her heart. "No one special," she said not looking up, and Maisie, sensing that she had touched a nerve, changed the subject.

"Do you think you'll stay at the luncheonette? Mike's a good guy, you could do a lot worse. If you like you can move in with me and we'll share expenses. I know Mrs. Murphy won't mind."

"I won't be able to pay you anything until I've earned some wages," said Grace.

"We'll settle up at the end of the month, then," said Maisie. And as Grace lay down in the narrow bed, she thought, *I'm in New York, I have a job and a place to live. I won't ever have to go back to Aunt Flora.*

The days slipped by quickly. Grace soon became used to the noise and bustle of New York, and became adept at dodging in and out of traffic, jumping on and off of streetcars. She managed to squeeze a little money from her wages to buy herself a few clothes each week. She chose carefully, but at the same time, she fingered the fine linens and silks and promised herself that one day she would be able to buy such fine clothes.

"If you want to wear satins and silks you're going to have to get a better job than slinging hash at Mike's place," Maisie told her. "Do you want to come with me and my Joe? We're going to sign up for night school. My Joe says education is the way to get on in this country. He's planning to become real rich one of these days." Maisie always referred to her boyfriend as "my Joe." She had staked out her claim. Joe was her territory, and that was fine with Grace. A boyfriend was the last thing she was interested in. But getting rich, that was something that did interest her.

She had liked Joe Schmidt from the moment she met him. He was a tall, thin young man, wearing the usual tell-tale black woollen suit that marked him as an immigrant just as surely as his heavy German accent. But Grace quickly recognized a kindred spirit. Joe was fiercely ambitious, and she knew he would soon be shedding both the suit and the accent.

"You can become anything you wish here in this country," he told her. "It iss true. If you study hard, nothing can stop you."

*Nothing can stop you,* thought Grace. Those were the words she'd been longing to hear.

So she and Maisie began going to night school, banging away on ancient typewriters, poring over the baffling signs and symbols of shorthand, and studying the advanced forms of bookkeeping at which Grace excelled.

"You would make a good accountant," said Joe one evening as they were walking home.

"A woman accountant—are you crazy?"

"Do you see some of the subjects the Jewish girls study?"

Grace nodded. A large number of the students were Jewish, and Grace was a little in awe of them. Dressed in drab clothes, the young men often wearing those funny looking skull caps on their heads, nevertheless they were fervent scholars, some of them so brilliant that Grace felt ignorant beside them. It seemed to her they were never seen without their heads buried in a book. *They are encouraged to learn*, she thought. *Their parents believe in education.* Not like Aunt Flora, who feared knowledge as if it were the teachings of the devil.

"Do you think I really could study accounting?" she asked.

"I do not see reason not to," Joe said.

Not long after that conversation, Grace enrolled in a class and began learning the intricacies of stocks and bonds. She loved it. She only wished she really had money to invest. She wouldn't be as bold and reckless as some of the men in the class, but she wouldn't be afraid, either. She would prefer to invest in something tangible. Something you could see and feel. Something like silk.

She'd been attending a series of lectures on various investment opportunities, and tonight the subject was the profit potential of the silk mill. She knew from that fateful night spent working on the books at Potter's mill that there was money to be made in silk, even from a poorly run mill like Potter's.

There were two speakers on the platform. The older man, a Mr. Wylie, was an investment broker, and the other was introduced as Mr. DeWitt-Kenton, whose family owned several silk mills in Paterson and Pennsylvania.

Grace sat up. Which mills? What kind of silk did they produce? Broadsilk? Jacquard? Silk ribbons? All of them were immensely profitable. He must be extremely wealthy, and so young. Inevitably she thought of Ian, working night and day, struggling to save enough money for a small apartment. It was a heart-wrenching thought and she pushed it away.

After the lecture Grace found herself being introduced to the younger man. They shook hands.

"Tell me, Miss Cameron, are you thinking of making an investment? I know a lot of fashionable young women are dabbling in the stock market these days. It's the latest thing to do."

"I'm not quite ready to invest yet," said Grace with a laugh. "I want to know more about it."

"Then allow me to be your adviser. Austin DeWitt-Kenton at your service ma'am. Say, it's rather noisy in here. Perhaps you would join me for a cup of coffee somewhere quiet, and we can discuss your portfolio."

Grace was amused, but she did join him. He took her to a small but elegant restaurant nearby. Once there he insisted she call him Austin. "After all, I'm merely offering advice as a friend, it is not a business arrangement." He ordered coffee and pastries, and then endeavored to learn more about Grace. She fielded most of his questions, but did say that she was simply a working girl, not a socialite. She didn't mention Mike's Luncheonette—somehow she knew that Austin would not appreciate being seen with a waitress, or even a part-time cashier. Instead she gave the vague impression that she had experience in the silk trade. Which was true, she thought wryly, but she certainly wasn't going to tell him that her experience took place in the dreadful basement of Potter's mill.

"And you, Mr. . . . Austin, are also in the silk business?"

"Well, I'm supposed to be learning it. The heir apparent, don't you know. Just finishing up at Princeton, and would really like to give the old brain a rest, but Mother thinks it's time I joined the family firm. We own three silk mills in Paterson, and two in Pennsylvania. Actually my mother owns them. My father died several years ago, but they were Mother's anyway—she inherited them from her father.'' This was the most he had ever said about his family, but now he continued. ''The best silk comes from Paterson, but the Pennsylvania mills are cheaper to run. Now if I had my way, I'd like to see us get into the buying and selling rather than the manufacturing. Not that there's not good money in the mills, but you have to deal with those wretched workers. And now with all these foreigners pouring in, bringing their anarchist ideas, asking for higher wages, I can see trouble ahead. They're lazy louts, too, next thing they'll be demanding shorter hours. You wouldn't believe the gall of these people.''

Grace thought of the long days of misery spent working at the swifts, and of the soakers bent over their greasy vats hour after hour—all for a few meager dollars a week. But she didn't say anything. This was the other side of the picture—she must keep still and learn.

She started meeting Austin occasionally after class. They usually just went out for a cup of coffee.

''I can't get over meeting someone like you here,'' he said. ''You've no idea how pleased I was to see you in the audience during the lecture. You were an oasis of light in that sea of black-eyed, black-clad foreigners. I don't know what this country is coming to with all the riff-raff they're letting in these days.''

*Why, he's just as narrow-minded as Aunt Flora,* thought Grace, *for all his education and money.* But Austin was also fun to be with. He plied her with compliments which both pleased and embarrassed her. But she got the feeling that they were both tip-toeing around each other. She never let him take her home, never introduced him to Maisie, and tried at all costs to avoid the subject of her job. He, on the other hand, did not include her in his circle of friends, and made no mention of letting her meet his family.

"Maisie, I've simply got to get a better job," Grace said one day. "If Austin discovers I'm working here for Mike I think I'll die."

"I agree you're ready for a different job," said Maisie, "but not because you're ashamed of Mike. You'll go a long way before you meet a better person, even if he does look like a beat up thug." Grace was immediately contrite.

"Oh, Maisie, I'm not ashamed of Mike. I can never be grateful enough for all he's done for me. It's just that I don't think Austin would understand."

"Then maybe you should get rid of Austin," said Maisie tartly. It was the first time they had had words, and Grace was upset. She loved Maisie like a sister. But then why hadn't she introduced her to Austin? Because Maisie was as honest as an Irish saint—she would never pretend to be anything other than herself. *I'm turning into a snob*, thought Grace, with a shock. And yet she knew if it came to a choice she did not want to get rid of Austin.

Grace never saw him on weekends, as he usually spent Saturdays and Sundays at his home in Westchester, or else out in the Hamptons, and she was never included in these excursions. She was surprised, therefore, when he suggested she meet him on a Sunday morning in the park. She wondered if this was going to mean a change in their relationship. She didn't say anything to Maisie, but on Sunday morning she rose early and began to dress with care.

"Where are you going?" asked Maisie, sleepily.

"I'm meeting Austin," she said.

"On Sunday!" Maisie's eyes flew open. "What's the occasion? Is he going to take you home to meet the family?"

"No, nothing like that," said Grace quickly. "Just that it's a nice day for a walk in the park."

"Hmph," said Maisie. "If you ask me you're wasting your time with Mr. DeWitt-Kenton." Maisie's opinion of Austin had obviously not changed, but Grace pretended not to notice. She had enough trouble quieting her own misgivings.

The weather was spring-like, and once she got past the huddled masses of tenements and onto the avenue, there were actually trees coming into leaf. Her spirits lifted. It was good to be out in the fresh air. She felt a little guilty about Maisie, whom she had left cleaning the apartment.

She spotted Austin coming towards her on the path, but to her surprise he was not alone. There were two girls with him, and she noticed with dismay that they were all carrying tennis racquets.

"Hi there," he called out. "Perfect day for a game!" He introduced the two girls casually as Helen and Susie. They were neighbors in Austin's town apartment. "I was hoping you'd bring your racquet when you saw what a beautiful day it was. We could play doubles, although I warn you, Susie has a wicked backhand."

"Sorry," said Grace, "I never gave it a thought."

"Say, maybe we could borrow a racquet for you," said Susie.

Grace experienced a moment of panic. She had never played tennis in her life. "I'm afraid it wouldn't do any good. I'm still getting over a sprained wrist," she lied.

"Too bad. We'll have to make it another time," said Austin.

"Heaven knows when that will be. You don't spend many weekends in the city," said Susie. They nodded to Grace and took their places on the court. She and Austin watched for a while, Austin making comments every now and then such as, "Good serve!" and "Oh, oh, fault, double fault." Grace said nothing, so as not to betray her ignorance, but she realized that if she ever expected to move in these circles she would have to learn to play this game.

After a while they tired of watching and began to stroll down the tree-lined paths.

"How come you stayed in the city on a beautiful weekend like this?" she asked.

"Mother and I went to the annual silk merchants dinner last night. Have to attend these affairs, you know. After all, these are the chaps who buy our silk." He looked at his watch. "I have to pick Mother up at noon, we're due at the Plaza for lunch. However, we do have time to stop for a hot chocolate, and there's a nice little cafe along here."

Grace felt herself flush with annoyance. She was merely a fill-in until he had to meet his mother. Just someone at his beck and call. Well, she'd show him that she wasn't.

"I'm sorry, Austin, but I'm afraid I, too, am meeting someone for lunch, so I really haven't time for hot chocolate." She noted with satisfaction the look of surprise that crossed his face. "In fact, I really have to run. I just made a detour through the park to say hello and goodbye. Perhaps we'll see each other sometime. I'm signing up for some new courses, so I don't know when I'll be free."

"But Grace, you can't abandon me like this."

*Oh, yes I can,* she thought.

"I particularly wanted to talk to you." He sounded cross. "I was planning to ask you out to dinner next week, and then, well, I thought perhaps you could meet my mother."

"Really, well I don't know if I can fit you in, Austin. My calendar is very full right now." And she turned quickly and walked away, glancing back when she reached the corner to see him standing staring at her, his mouth open in wordless protest. *Maisie would be proud of me,* she thought, but she knew she wouldn't tell Maisie. She wasn't very proud of herself at the moment. If she saw Austin again it would be on her own terms. She wasn't going to be a casual fill-in, not for anyone.

# CHAPTER

## ❧ 10 ❧

MAISIE'S announcement that she and Joe were getting married galvanized Grace into action. She knew she couldn't stay working at the luncheonette without Maisie, no matter how much she liked Mike. She had to find another job. She began scanning the papers and spotted an advertisement by Harwood Associates, a silk importing firm. If they were connected with silk, Austin could probably tell her something about them. She had started seeing him again, but not on a regular basis. It amused her to note that the less interested she appeared, the more enthusiastic he became. She wouldn't be surprised if he actually overcame his awe of his mother and introduced her one of these days. Grace was curious to meet this matriarch who wielded so much power.

Austin was impressed when she mentioned Harwood Associates. She let it appear that she was thinking of investing in them, and in a way she was.

"They import raw silk from France and Italy," he told her. "That's where the best silk comes from, something to do with better fed silkworms and larger cocoons. Whatever the reason, when you buy your silk from Harwood's you know you're getting quality. I'd like to know how you found out he was thinking of selling stock. I'd heard a rumor, heard he was expanding and getting into the Japanese market, but didn't think he'd ever go public. Harwood's pretty much a self-made man, the sort that keeps a tight hold on the reins. Boy, do I know some people who would like to get their hands on his business.''

"Then you think it would be a good investment?'' murmured Grace.

"If you can get hold of some of Harwood's stock, then by all means get it. And let me know.''

*I don't know about stock,* thought Grace, as she paced the pavement in front of a granite edifice that rose several stories, *but I hope I get this job.* Harwood was looking for a switchboard operator; it didn't exactly sound like the road to riches, but she had to start somewhere. Gathering her courage, she swept through the revolving door into the cavernous lobby. It reminded her of a museum. Brown marble walls rose almost two stories to a vaulted ceiling. In the center of the floor, also marble, was a star-shaped black inlay, and in the center of the star was a desk. She walked over, her heels clicking loudly, and asked the man seated there how to find Harwood Associates.

"Third floor, miss. Take the elevator to your left.''

The operator clanged the gates and the elevator rose slowly. She felt a tremor in the pit of her stomach. What would she say when they asked what experience she'd had? Six months working at Mike's Luncheonette. The elevator settled with a slight bounce and she stepped out into a smaller version of the downstairs lobby. Facing her was a frosted glass door with the name Harwood Associates printed in gold lettering. She opened it hesitantly. She had a blurred impression of a large room where several men in white shirtsleeves were bent over desks. In front of them, a young woman sat behind a counter. Grace approached her.

"I'm here about the job that was advertised in the paper,'' she said breathlessly.

"Yeah, you got an appointment?''

"I didn't know you needed an appointment.''

"Well, maybe you don't. Follow me." She led Grace through a labyrinth of corridors until they came to a narrow room where a row of girls sat in front of an enormous switchboard. A middle-aged woman, whose gray hair was piled in a series of coils to an extraordinary height, stepped forward and was introduced as Miss Finch. Miss Finch looked her over carefully.

"Do you have any experience working a switchboard, Miss . . . ?"

"Cameron," said Grace. "No, but I've been—"

"Where are you from, Miss Cameron?"

"Scotland, originally."

"You don't sound like a Scot, thank heavens. Half the girls that come here have an accent of some sort. You've no idea how difficult it is to find someone who speaks properly. The Irish are the worst." She rolled her eyes in horror at the thought of a gentle Irish brogue and handed Grace a slip of paper. "Read this, please."

"Good morning, Harwood Associates, Importers of Fine Silks. May I help you?" Grace read.

"Hmm, not bad," said Miss Finch. "Where are you working now?"

"I'm a . . . cashier. I've been taking business courses at night school. I can take shorthand and type and—"

"We've no need for a shorthand typist, but we do need a telephone operator. Leave your name and address and we'll be in touch with you." Grace sat down at a small table and wrote her name and address on the form Miss Finch had given her. There were already several other forms in a tray, and she put hers on top. Miss Finch had disappeared and all the girls were busy, so she attempted to find her way back to the elevator. It was hopeless. Every corridor seemed to be a dead end. She was turning back when a door opened giving her a glimpse of rich oak panelling and thick oriental carpets. An extremely well-dressed man stepped out. He looked at her in surprise.

"I seem to be lost," said Grace, apologetically. "I'm

trying to find my way back to the elevator.'' His face relaxed into a smile.

''Yes, it is confusing. You have to go through this door.'' He opened another door and Grace found herself back in the room where the young men in shirtsleeves were still bent over their desks. As she thanked her rescuer, she was aware of the curious looks she was getting from the occupants of the crowded office. *I must have stumbled into the boss' domain,* she thought. *Perhaps this is Mr. Harwood himself.* If so he seemed like a nice man. Suddenly she wanted this job, wanted to work in these marbled halls where there were panelled offices and plush carpets, even if she only caught a glimpse of them once in a while.

To Grace's surprise and delight, she received a letter a few days later. The job was hers.

Mike was philosophical about it. ''So I'm going to be losing both you goils at the same time. It won't be the same without youse.''

''Me and my Joe'll be in to see you, Mike. I could even help out a bit if you get stuck. But I'm going to be living across the river, you know.'' Maisie and Joe had found a tiny two-room apartment in Brooklyn. ''And here I thought I'd escaped Brooklyn forever,'' said Maisie with a laugh. ''But I don't mind, as long as Joe is with me.''

Maisie's future was secure. Joe would finish night school, get a good job, they would move to a bigger apartment, have a baby . . . Grace bit her lip. *Why can't I be like that?* she thought. *I could be married to Ian by now.* Her whole being still longed for Ian, but the thought of Paterson always came down on her like a damp depressing fog. *Why can't Ian see what a dreadful place it is? Why can't he want to move up, like Joe?* she thought angrily. She often found herself getting angry with Ian these days, especially when she was with Austin. Austin had access to everything she'd ever wanted, but he wasn't Ian.

''I want you both to come to the wedding,'' said Maisie. ''Think you can manage it, Mike? Saturday morning.

We're getting married at City Hall, then breakfast at Schrafft's. Our treat.''

"Nothin' doin'," said Mike. "It's my treat or I ain't goin'."

"Oh, Mike, I'm going to miss you," said Maisie, giving him a hug.

"Nothin' lasts forever," said Mike. "Wot with youse getting married, and Grace here startin' her new job. Seems like 1911's a good year for goils. Not so good for old guys like me—but what can youse do?" He gave a mournful shrug and began polishing the counter.

"And I'll be in to see you, Grace," said Maisie. "Now that you've got a posh job uptown, you can meet me on your lunch hour. We can go somewhere fancy and splurge."

Grace didn't think she'd be doing too much splurging. Her salary was probably going to be less than she made at Mike's, and her expenses would be higher now that she didn't have Maisie to share them with her. She was going to stay on at Mrs. Murphy's by herself, at least for a while. But none of that mattered in her anticipation of finally working at an interesting job in elegant surroundings. She felt that, at last, she was on her way to that golden future, the promise of which, temptingly portrayed in advertisements and steamship ads, helped entice an endless stream of immigrants to the bountiful, but sometimes cruel and heartless shores of America.

Grace started her new job at Harwood Associates the Monday after Maisie's wedding. They had toasted the bride and groom with coffee and tea, indulged in a breakfast of ham and eggs, and flung a handful of rice at the ferry as Joe and Maisie drifted across the river to Brooklyn. Maisie had looked as pretty as a picture in her blue cotton dress and new straw hat decorated with white cabbage roses. Joe was in his usual black wool suit, all steamed and pressed for the occasion. They were going to join Maisie's

family, to be feted with a large home-cooked dinner and
a small array of gifts, before settling in their own little flat
for a one-day honeymoon.

Grace sighed as she looked around her empty apartment. She had dressed with care in her lavender chambray,
made fresh with new white collar and cuffs, but there was
no one to tell her how nice she looked. She left early, not
sure how long it would take her to get there on the trolley,
and arrived even before Miss Finch. Once that lady appeared, however, she quickly put Grace to work, explaining how to plug in and out of the board, and how to speak
into the mouthpiece. By lunchtime Grace was an old hand.

She soon settled into the life of a switchboard operator.
It wasn't difficult, but in spite of the fact that there were
at least ten girls working the board, it was lonely. She
missed the casual comings and goings of Mike's place.
Compared to the luncheonette, working the switchboard
was like being back in school. They were not allowed to
leave the board without permission, but spent the entire
day perched on their stools, elbow to elbow, while Miss
Finch marched up and down making sure there were no
slackers. Nor was there any opportunity to meet the other
employees; she never as much as glimpsed the young men
in shirtsleeves, and there were few chances to talk to the
other switchboard operators. The only break was at lunchtime when they ate their sandwiches in a tiny room off the
storage area. Better than Potter's she thought, but not
much.

The work was mostly routine, except once in a while
when a flurry of buying and selling set the board flashing
like Broadway and Forty-Second Street. Grace enjoyed
these moments, although she heard the other operators
grumble at the pace. The girls were all pleasant, but Grace
found she didn't share their goals and interests, and they
thought she was cold and standoffish. They also couldn't
understand her concern for the company. Most of them
were just marking time until they got married.

*What's wrong with me?* thought Grace. *Why am I so different?* She was different. While the other girls had no real interest in Harwood Associates, didn't care that Mr. Harwood travelled to France and Italy buying raw silk—silk that would then be made into shimmering bolts of cloth—Grace found it fascinating. But she was the only one who did.

It was this loneliness that led her to spend more time with Austin. She had saved her money and purchased a tennis racquet, much to Maisie's horror—"All that money for something to hit a silly ball with," had been her comment. But Grace knew it was more than just hitting a ball—it was a way of life. She had read up on the rules, and practiced serving in the late evening hours when most of the players had left the park. She told Austin that she was thinking of taking lessons to improve her game. He immediately volunteered to coach her, and made a date for next Sunday morning.

"In fact, why don't you plan on coming back to the apartment with me for lunch? Mother would like to meet you."

"I'd love to meet your mother," said Grace, concealing her astonishment and fighting down a rising sense of panic. She had a feeling that Mrs. DeWitt-Kenton would not be content with vague explanations, but would want to know full details of her background and what she was doing in New York. *What will she say if I tell her I'm a "woiking goil?"* thought Grace, suppressing a nervous giggle.

The weather on Sunday turned out to be crisp and clear, and Grace rose early. It took her some time to reach Central Park, and Austin was already there waiting for her. She was pleased to discover that they had the courts to themselves, with no one standing around to watch and criticize.

"Just concentrate on returning the ball," said Austin. "Don't worry about the rules of the game." She found it was fun to hit the ball back and forth, and quickly became quite good at it, hearing with pleasure the plangent "thwack" as the ball met the racquet.

"Oh, I say, jolly good," exclaimed Austin. "I think you're ready to start controlling your forehand. Here, let me show you."

He jumped easily over the net and began to demonstrate the correct arm swing. "Hold your racquet like this." He stood behind her and placed one arm around her waist, grasped her wrist with the other, and began to swing the racquet back and forth.

Grace instinctively stiffened. "Relax, let your arm swing all the way back," he said. She pulled away.

"I think I have the idea now, Austin, thank you. You can go back to your own side of the court."

He gave her a sly wink. "It's more fun on this side."

"We can't play tennis if we're both on the same side of the net."

"I think we've had enough tennis for today. We'll continue this lesson another time. How about sitting over there in the shade for a while? I need to cool off before we go for lunch." He led her to a bench under a tree, and Grace began to feel a little uneasy. She had never consciously flirted with Austin, and this was not the day to start.

"How come you stayed in town today?" she asked. "Another dinner party?"

"Actually Mother's suffering from a touch of sciatica. She's confined to her bed. But she wants to meet you anyway. I—er—I've been telling her about you."

"What did you tell her?"

"About your interest in investing in silk, that sort of thing." Austin looked uncomfortable.

"I'm only studying the market."

"Yes, I explained that. Come on, I think it's time to go."

The DeWitt-Kentons' apartment was larger than most houses Grace had been in. A doorman resplendent in his gold-braided uniform guarded the entrance, but the apartment itself was presided over by a butler·and a house-keeper. It was the butler who greeted them, relieved them of their tennis racquets, and ushered them across the spacious entrance hall to a small luxurious sitting room.

"Cooper will be with you in a minute, sir," he said as he silently backed away. Cooper, apparently, was Mrs. Cooper the housekeeper, a middle-aged, severely dressed woman who quickly appeared in the doorway.

"Good morning, Mr. Austin. Is this the young lady who will be staying for lunch?"

"Yes, Cooper, this is Miss Cameron."

Cooper gave her a shrewd assessing glance, and Grace saw that she was not impressed.

"We'd like to see Mother first," said Austin. "Is she receiving?"

"Wait here and I will check."

"Austin, I feel very untidy. What will your mother think?"

"She'll think you've been playing tennis. Don't worry about it."

Grace glanced around the room. In spite of the luxury there was something oppressive in the dark red draperies, the intricately carved chairs, and the heavy-footed table on which stood a bowl of overblown roses. The walls were lined with curio cabinets filled with ivory and jade, and a massive carved firescreen shielded the empty fireplace. But for all its furnishings, the room struck her as being cold.

"Mrs. DeWitt-Kenton will see you now." Grace jumped, she had not heard Cooper return. *Do they always creep around so silently?* she wondered. It was a silent house. There would never be anyone yelling up the stairs, or banging on the pipes in these apartments, she thought.

Mrs. DeWitt-Kenton was not in bed, but rather reclining on a chaise lounge in her sitting room. She was not alone. A thin, solemn-faced man was seated on a chair next to her. He rose as they entered and Austin exclaimed.

"Hello, Uncle Thomas! Didn't know you were here.

Mother, this is Miss Grace Cameron. Grace, this is my mother and my Uncle Thomas.''

Grace extended her hand and received an limp handshake from both of them. She guessed they were brother and sister, as Mrs. DeWitt-Kenton was equally thin and solemn-faced.

"Do sit down, Miss Cameron. I am so pleased to finally meet you. Austin has been telling me all about you.'' Mrs. DeWitt-Kenton's appraisal of Grace didn't look any more promising than that of her housekeeper, but Grace was determined not to let it bother her. Instead she straightened her back and held her head a little higher.

"I am delighted to meet you, Mrs. DeWitt-Kenton.'' She sat down on a straight-backed chair and folded her arms in her lap. *Now for the third degree*, she thought, but it was Uncle Thomas who spoke instead.

"I hear you're dabbling in the market, Miss Cameron. Seems a lot of you gals are taking flyers with stocks these days. Old Fitzwilliam's daughter made a packet for herself on Coca-Cola, of all things.''

"Well, I'm really only studying the market at the moment,'' she said. "Austin is advising me.''

"Austin would be better occupied studying the silk market,'' said his mother severely. "But I understand it is silk that interests you.''

"Harwood's, to be exact,'' said Uncle Thomas. "Austin tells me you're thinking of investing in Harwood's. Sound company. Good buy.'' He paused and glanced nervously towards Austin. "Any ideas just when the stock is coming on the market? Austin seems to think you've got an inside track.'' He gave an embarrassed laugh. "Just curious, you know. Not really interested myself.''

*So that's it*, thought Grace. *They think I know something about Harwood's stock. What would they say if I were to tell them that I'm merely a switchboard operator for the firm? I would probably be thrown out.* But now she was curious. What did they want with Harwood's? Something not quite aboveboard obviously. She looked at Austin, whose face was flushed and who was fiddling with his tie.

"Actually, I'm waiting to hear myself. It's all rather indefinite at the moment." Both Austin and his uncle seemed to breathe a sigh of relief, but Mrs. DeWitt-Kenton's pursed lips spoke of annoyance.

"Well, good luck on your investments, whenever they come about," said Uncle Thomas. "And now, my dear sister, I really must be going."

"Aren't you going to stay for lunch?"

"No, Estelle is expecting me." He gave a quick peck on the cheek to Mrs. DeWitt-Kenton, another limp hand-shake to Grace, tapped Austin on the shoulder, and left. Fortunately, for Grace anyway, Cooper returned at that moment to announce that lunch was served.

"Go along then, Austin, I'm having my lunch here. Cooper you can bring me a tray. It was very nice meeting you, Miss Cameron. Austin must bring you again some-time." As Grace followed Austin towards the dining room, it occurred to her that not once had she seen Mrs. DeWitt-Kenton smile.

# CHAPTER
## ❧ 11 ❧

It was strange, thought Grace. She had invented her story about buying stock in Harwood's in order to avoid telling Austin the real reason for her interest in the company. But now it seemed that Mr. Harwood was considering getting into the Japanese market and forming an auxiliary company which would handle finished goods. Consequently, he was looking for investors. It was all highly confidential, however, and they had been warned by Miss Finch to make no mention of it to anyone whatsoever. Although she had not consciously done so, Grace found herself plagued by vague feelings of guilt.

Over the next couple of weeks she put through several calls to Harwood's attorney and broker, and it finally looked as if a deal were set. There were two prospective investors—one who already had connections in Japan, and the other a buyer of finished goods.

On looking back on it, Grace decided it was fate that drew her to the coffee shop at that particular time, on that particular day, although she had no premonition of it at the time. In reality she was doing her best to hide her disappointment. She and Maisie had planned to meet for lunch, but at the last minute Maisie called to say she couldn't make it. Grace felt bereft. She missed Maisie terribly and had been looking forward to this outing all week. She couldn't face another day eating in the stuffy little storage room where the operators usually spent their lunch break, so she decided to go somewhere by herself. There was a coffee shop on the main floor. It was expensive, but she didn't care. She needed something to cheer her up.

She slid into a booth, ordered a sandwich and a cup of tea, and sat back. It was still early and the place wasn't crowded. Two men entered and took the booth in front of hers. She recognized them with a start. She had seen them speaking to Miss Finch, asking her to relay any calls they might have, but she had never before seen them together. They were the two potential buyers of Harwood's stock, and Grace knew enough from handling the calls that they were totally separate deals. Why were these men lunching together, she wondered?

*Well, it's no concern of mine,* she thought, as the waiter brought her order. She sat back to enjoy her lunch, when one of the men began signalling to someone across the room. She looked up to see a tall, thin man entering the coffee shop. To her astonishment she recognized him, also. It was Austin's Uncle Thomas. She shrank back in her seat and buried herself in the large menu. She definitely didn't want to meet Uncle Thomas, but she needn't have worried—he walked right by her without a glance and joined the other two men in the booth.

At first she paid no attention to their conversation. She ate her sandwich and sipped her tea, but gradually the impact of what they were saying, which she could hear quite clearly, began to disturb her.

"You're sure my name has never been mentioned," said Uncle Thomas.

"Never, he has no idea."

"And once you've got the stock, there's no way he can halt the transaction."

"It will be tied up solid."

She heard a laugh.

"It will certainly boost our profits. Japanese silk sold at European prices, and who's to know."

"He'll have to buy, you know, it's in the deal."

Grace hastily finished her tea and paid her bill. She hurried from the coffee shop back upstairs to the switchboard.

"Is Mr. Harwood in his office?" she asked Mary, the girl who sat next to her.

"Far as I know," she replied. "Ask Miss Finch when she gets back from lunch." Grace watched the clock apprehensively. She had to get a message to Mr. Harwood before she lost her nerve. Taking a note pad she quickly wrote a few lines.

"Mary, I've got to give this note to Mr. Harwood. I can't wait for Miss Finch, I'm going to take it to him myself." She didn't wait for Mary's protests that they weren't allowed to leave the board, but hurried through to the inner sanctum. She was immediately stopped by a gray-haired secretary.

"I have a message for Mr. Harwood," said Grace breathlessly. "It's very urgent."

"You may give it to me. I'll see that he gets it." Grace hesitated, but at that moment Mr. Harwood stepped out of his office. She immediately confronted him.

"I have an urgent message for you, sir." She handed him the slip of paper and watched nervously while he read it. His expression didn't change, but when he'd finished he looked directly at her.

"Are you quite sure about this?"

"Yes, sir," she replied.

"Then thank you very much, Miss . . . ?"

"Cameron."

"Miss Cameron. I will look into it." He folded the paper and put it in his inside pocket, then nodded to his secretary.

"When Mr. Everett arrives show him in, please." He returned to his office, closing the door behind him.

Grace went back to her seat at the board, but not before she caught a glimpse of one of the men from the coffee shop heading towards Mr. Harwood's office. She started to shake. What if she was wrong? What if it was all a mistake? The other girls eyed her curiously, but there was no time for questions; the board buzzed constantly and she was grateful for it. The day was almost over when Miss Finch called her to the desk with a puzzled expression on her face.

"Grace, Mr. Harwood wants to see you right away. Have you any idea why?"

"I had to give him an urgent message while you were at lunch," explained Grace.

"You know you girls aren't supposed to leave the board without my permission," she said. Then she added kindly, "But you're a good worker, and I'll be glad to say so if you need me to."

Grace was touched, and she thanked her but added that she didn't think there would be a problem. Then, looking more confident that she was feeling, she entered the domain of Mr. Robert Harwood. This time the secretary ushered her directly into his richly furnished office and then left, closing the door behind her. Grace stood quite still. Mr. Harwood was seated behind an enormous oak desk. He was a man of medium height and build, with dark, crisply curling hair lightly touched with gray. He had a high color that contrasted with his light blue eyes, eyes that seemed to look through her, and even though he sat perfectly motionless there was an energy radiating from him that charged the atmosphere.

"Sit down, Miss Cameron." Grace quickly perched on the edge of the nearest chair. He continued to stare at her.

"How did you know?" he said at last.

"I overhead them talking in the coffee shop." Realizing that switchboard operators didn't usually eat there, she added hastily, "I was supposed to be meeting a friend, but she couldn't come."

"I mean, how did you realize they were conspiring against me?" He took the note out of his pocket and read it aloud:

"Mr. Harwood,
I have reason to believe that the two men interested in buying your stock are conspiring to defraud your company."

He repocketed the note. "You were right, you know. They were in collusion with some unscrupulous mill owners to sell inferior goods at inflated prices."

Grace gave a small sigh of relief, she hadn't imagined it all. "I overheard them saying that once they gained control of the subsidiary, they could sell you Japanese silk at European prices."

"It was very astute of you to put two and two together and realize the implications. I don't think many of the young ladies working the switchboard would have recognized what was going on."

"I've been taking business courses at night. We've been studying the silk industry."

He looked at her curiously. "Isn't that rather dull for such a beaut—for such a young woman?"

"Oh, no," she exclaimed. "It's not dull at all. I enjoy it." He continued to stare at her with his light blue eyes and she felt as if an electric current were coursing between them, but when he spoke it was in a distant tone.

"Well, thank you again, Miss Cameron. What is your first name, by the way?" She told him and he wrote something down on a notepad. "You'll be getting a small bonus in your next paycheck," he said. Then he smiled. "And keep up the night school." It was a dismissal, but as Grace emerged, slightly dazed by what had taken place, she had the distinct feeling that her life had somehow changed direction.

* * *

However, except for a doubling of her paycheck for one week, nothing further happened. She knew the stock sale was off, and life at Harwood's continued much as before. She continued to see Austin. He made no mention of Harwood's stock, and neither did she. She was not, however, invited back to the apartment, nor was she included in his trips to Westchester or the Hamptons. But she was invited to a charity bridge game, sponsored by Mrs. DeWitt-Kenton, to raise funds for the Council for the Training of Indigent Females.

"Mother's on the Board, you know. She says someone has to see that the money isn't wasted and that the girls get a proper training."

"What are they trained for?"

"Domestic service, of course. What else could they do? Most of them aren't capable of being much more than scullery maids, but once in a while Mother says one of the brighter girls gets a chance of becoming a parlor maid. Of course, if they have babies, and you'd be astonished how many of them do, the Council arranges for adoption."

*Now I know what they mean when they say "cold as charity,"* thought Grace, but she kept her views to herself. No doubt both Austin and his mother thought they were doing their Christian duty, but it all sounded so businesslike.

Grace was somewhat taken aback to discover that she had to pay to get in to the bridge game. A token amount, said Austin, but it was a lot of money to her and would mean pretty lean lunches for the rest of the week. *Oh, well I suppose it's for a good cause,* she thought. She had only recently taught herself to play bridge, but she had frequently made up a table of whist with Lady McLeod and the games were similar. With her mathematically oriented mind she was a natural.

The bridge party was held in a somewhat shabby brownstone which was the headquarters for the Council and several other charitable organizations. It was quite crowded, and although most of the players were older than Grace, they were all obviously extremely fashionable. She caught a glimpse of Mrs. DeWitt-Kenton in an exquisitely tailored grey linen suit, ramrod straight, obviously recovered from her bout with sciatica, proceeding around the room acknowledging friends and acquaintances like royalty.

Once the game began a quiet hum filled the room. She was paired with Austin, who was a mediocre player. In fact most of the players were of average skill and Grace began to feel more confident. They progressed from table to table until they were playing opposite Mrs. DeWitt-Kenton and Uncle Thomas.

"You play very well, Miss Cameron," said Uncle Thomas admiringly. "Have you been a bridge player long?"

"Not really," she said, "but I used to play whist with Lady McLeod." She noticed a gleam of interest in Mrs. DeWitt-Kenton's eyes at the mention of Lady McLeod and an exchange of looks between her and her brother. It still amazed her how, in this democratic society, the mere mention of a title made everyone sit up and take notice.

Austin dealt and Grace noticed a smug expression flit briefly across his mother's face as she studied her hand. Grace's hand was poor, but she did have a few low hearts, which were trumps. Mrs. DeWitt-Kenton led with hearts and began taking tricks with no opposition, then she switched to clubs, but Austin had the Queen and King. *She's got the ace,* thought Grace, *but I still have the two of hearts*. She dropped it neatly on Mrs. DeWitt-Kenton's ace of clubs, and took the game.

Afterwards, when Grace and Austin were awarded their second-place prize, Austin took her aside.

"That wasn't very nice of you, Grace, trumping Mother's ace like that."

"But Austin, that's how you play the game. It was perfectly fair and square."

"I know, but after all, Mother invited you."

She stared at him incredulously.

"She likes to win, you know," he said.

"I like to win too, Austin. You'd better remember that." She collected her prize, a set of fine embroidered handkerchiefs, exchanged a chilly goodnight with Mrs. DeWitt-Kenton, and ignoring Austin's offers to accompany her, left on her own.

*Why do I bother with him?* she asked herself on her way home. *He's spineless and weak.* But she was lonely. Lonelier than she'd ever before been in her life. *I just don't fit in anywhere,* she thought. *I'm not part of the DeWitt-Kentons' world, and I have nothing in common with the girls on the switchboard. There must be someone out there who feels as I do. Oh, Ian,* her heart cried out. *Oh, Ian.*

# CHAPTER
## ❧ 12 ❧

"HERE'S a postcard from Grace," exclaimed Jeannie. "She says she has a fine new job."

"Hmp, what kind o' job?" asked Aunt Flora.

"She says she's working for a big silk importing company."

"What does that mean?" asked Maggie, with a sideways glance at Ian who was sitting at the table quietly drinking his tea.

"It's a company that buys raw silk, and then sells it to the mills," explained Jeannie. "She says she works the switchboard."

"Ye mean she talks on the telephone." Maggie was impressed.

"She thinks she's tae good to work on the looms, but she'll spend her day speakin' into one o' those newfangled Godless machines. Devices of the devil, if ye ask me."

"Oh, Aunt Flora. There's nothing wrong with the telephone. 'Tis a wonderful invention," said Jeannie.

"If God had wanted us tae talk tae people miles away he would ha'e given us louder voices," said Aunt Flora with a sniff. "No good will come o' it, believe me. What do ye think, Ian?"

"It's no concern of mine," said Ian, jumping up. "I have to go to the shop." He almost ran out of the kitchen, letting the door slam behind him. Maggie stared after him. *He's still in love with her,* she thought miserably. *Even though he never mentions her, he's still in love with her.*

"Well I say good for Grace," said Jeannie. "I'm glad she's found a job she likes. And just think, Maggie, if Grace hadn't quit Potter's and gone to New York, we'd never have met Moira."

Moira was a cheerful Irish lass who had taken Grace's place in Potter's basement. She lived by herself in a tiny room on Straight Street and the three girls had become good friends. They'd started spending their Saturday afternoons together, usually window-shopping in Paterson. Moira was not particularly welcome at Aunt Flora's.

"I dinna know why ye girls keep getting yourself mixed up with these Catholics," she complained. "But at least she speaks English, if ye can call it that, not like those dreadful Eyetalians."

Jeannie had become quite friendly with the Simonetti girls. She had offered to help them learn English, and they had invited her home to meet Mama and get her approval. Unlike Aunt Flora, Mama Simonetti had immediately clasped Jeannie to her ample bosom, and declared that she was welcome any time. She still remembered the sudden rush of tears that had come to her eyes at that loving gesture. It was the first time anyone had hugged her since her mother died, and Jeannie found herself drawn back again and again to the warmth of the Simonetti household where she was accepted like a daughter.

"I may leave you and Moira and go over to see Mama Simonetti for a while," she said as she and Maggie walked toward Straight Street. "Anthony has promised to lend me some of his books. Ye won't tell Aunt Flora will ye?"

"Now ye know I won't," said Maggie, "but I dinna ken what ye want those old school books for." She never could understand Jeannie's hunger for school and learning, or why she was so envious of Anthony Simonetti, who

was going to high school. She'd persuaded Anthony to
share his lessons with her and spent hours poring over
notebooks and textbooks.

"It was book learning that helped Grace get out of the
mill and into a fine job in New York," said Jeannie.

"Och, Jeannie, you're nae thinking of runnin' off to that
wicked city, are ye?" Maggie looked at her sister in alarm.
New York was a modern Sodom and Gomorrah according
to Aunt Flora.

Jeannie laughed, "No, I'm afraid I'm stuck at Potter's
for a while. Thank God for Moira, I don't think I could
stand it otherwise. And here she is." Moira came running
down the steps of her rooming house to meet them. She
was a pretty little thing, with a smattering of freckles
across her nose, a mass of dark auburn hair, and a brogue
as thick as a peat bog.

"What took ye so long? 'Tis watchin' and waitin' I've
been half the day."

"We got a postcard from Grace, and that set Aunt Flora
off," said Jeannie.

"Is she the cousin who ran off to New York?"

"And abandoned Ian," said Maggie. It slipped out. She
usually never mentioned Ian, just the sound of his name
caused her to blush.

" 'Tis mad she must be," said Moira. "But sure'n he's
forgotten her by now. 'Tis ye he likes, Maggie, I've seen
him looking at ye."

"At Maggie!" exclaimed Jeannie, usually so observant
but now completely surprised by her sister's blushes.
"Well, that's an interesting thought."

It was a thought that Maggie did not dare indulge in,
and she quickened her pace, hurrying the girls to the five-
and-ten where they soon became lost in a bewildering se-
lection of buttons and ribbons and fancy bottles of cheap
cologne.

After they had spent their few pennies, and Jeannie had
departed for the Simonettis with a promise to meet Maggie

in an hour, Moira announced that she had to go to confession. Maggie was appalled.

"Ye mean in a church." She didn't say *Catholic* church, but she was thinking it. A den of iniquity, that was what Aunt Flora called the Catholic Church; and although Maggie wasn't quite sure what iniquity was, it sounded bad. And confession! She couldn't imagine it.

"What do ye do in confession?" she asked, half afraid to hear the answer.

"Well Father sits in a little box with a curtain in front of him, so he can't see who ye are. Then ye go in and kneel down and tell him all your sins. He gives ye absolution—that means he forgives ye—and ye have tae do penance. Usually it's three Our Fathers and three Hail Marys. If ye have a lot to tell it may be five, and if ye're a real sinner ye'll get ten of each and a Hail Holy Queen too."

"How awful," said Maggie. "Suppose he tells everyone what ye've done?"

"A priest can never tell anything he hears in confession on pain of mortal sin. Even if I went in and told him I'd strangled someone wi' my bare hands, 'tis nought he could say. Not even to the cops if they came askin' him."

"Well I'm sure ye've nae strangled anyone," said Maggie with a nervous laugh.

"Nay, but sometimes I'd like to strangle Mrs. Anderson, and that's a sinful thought. Or is it just a temptation? Jesus himself was tempted, so that's allowed."

"Ye mean ye have tae confess your sinful thoughts?"

Moira nodded. Maggie found herself blushing again. She was glad she wasn't a Catholic. It seemed like a terrible religion to her.

She waited outside while Moira went in, walking up and down nervously in front of a white statue of a woman with a baby in her arms. She was relieved to see her friend emerge none the worse for wear. In fact, she seemed positively light-hearted. Aunt Flora was right, they were strange people these Catholics.

* * *

Ian was working on a broken loom in McPherson's shop. Normally he enjoyed the work, but today he couldn't concentrate. As long as no one spoke about Grace he was all right. He could keep her out of his mind and convince himself he had forgotten all about her. But just the mention of her name reawoke that long-buried ache that dragged at him, pulling him down. If she had only stayed with him. If she were only waiting for him now, in a little flat all their own, how eagerly he would do this extra work, whistling cheerfully as he wielded his wrenches, taking pride in the renovation, listening for the smooth, steady click of the newly mended loom. What a spring there would be in his step as he hurried home. *Home.* He sighed at the word and tried to squash the vision that haunted his dreams. Grace returning, Grace admitting she'd made a mistake, Grace running into his outstretched arms and nestling there like a gentle bird. But he knew in his heart that she was no little nesting bird. Grace wanted to fly, to soar, to reach the cold mountain peaks of worldly success, while he remained, his feet firmly on the ground, mending his looms.

It was both to keep his mind off Grace and to make some extra money that he decided to hire on at Lambert Castle for Mrs. and Mrs. Lambert's annual ball. He told Maggie and Jeannie about it as they walked home from the mills.

"I don't know if you girls would be interested, but Mr. Lambert's looking for some extra help at the castle on Saturday night."

"What kind o' help?"

"People to work in the kitchen, set and clear the tables, help the ladies with their wraps, that sort of thing."

" 'Twould be a lovely chance tae see inside the castle," said Maggie, "and tae see all the ladies in their fine dresses."

"How much will he pay us?" asked Jeannie, ever practical. "I hear he's a regular old skinflint."

"That depends on the job, but you could probably make an extra dollar or two for the night."

"Are you going?" asked Maggie.

"I've been thinking about it. I'd like to buy a lathe and this would help."

"Then we'll go, too. Won't we, Jeannie?"

" 'Twould be nice tae have some money in my pocket for a change," said Jeannie, who always dutifully handed her pay envelope to Aunt Flora in return for carfare and tea money. "Aye, I'll go."

"Will there be a lot of people there?" asked Maggie.

"Probably over a hundred. Mr. Lambert throws a big party once a year for all the mill owners and silk merchants. He hires a train to bring them to Paterson, and then coaches to bring them from the station to the castle. It's the biggest event of the year. You can see the lights shining from the castle as far away as Passaic."

Maggie's eyes were round with wonder and she looked at Ian warmly. *Isn't it kind of him,* she thought, *tae give us a chance to be part of such a grand affair*.

"I hear Mr. Lambert sometimes has fireworks at his parties. D'ye think we'll get a chance tae see them?" Maggie asked.

"Maybe," said Ian, "we'll find out on Saturday night."

Grace was surprised when Austin invited her to go to a dance with him on Saturday night. She almost asked if his mother's sciatica was acting up again, but he forestalled her.

"Mother and Uncle Thomas will be there, too. We received four invitations. Actually it's more like a royal summons when you receive an invitation from Mr. and Mrs. Catholina Lambert."

"Lambert! You mean the dance is to be held at Lambert Castle?" exclaimed Grace.

"Then you do know the Lamberts," he said.

"I know of them," she said cautiously. "I'm sure anyone who knows anything about the silk industry has heard of Catholina Lambert."

"I told Mother you'd probably know him. He's a good man to know, old Lina, regular robber baron, but he knows how to make money. He's got an art collection that outdoes any museum. Perhaps you've seen it? Have you ever been to the castle?"

"I've never been inside, but I know where it is—it's in Paterson." The mere mention of Paterson brought back a flood of memories. She felt a shiver pass through her at the thought of the dark dreary basement of Potter's mill, the sickening smell of the wet skeins of silk, the long backbreaking hours spent at the swifts.

"You don't look very thrilled," said Austin, "but I promise you that you'll have a good time. Lambert really puts on a spiffy show."

Grace already knew that. She remembered the little old gardener telling her about the fountains, the lights, and the fireworks when she visited the grounds on that dreary November day, following her final confrontation with Mrs. Anderson. Her last day in Paterson. And now she'd be returning. Returning as a guest of the most powerful man in the city. It was a satisfying thought.

# CHAPTER

## ❧ 13 ❧

GRACE'S dress was simple but elegant. Maisie had introduced her to a little shop on Third Avenue where prices were lower. So much lower, in fact, that she had been able to purchase a silk-lined wrap. Fortunately it was summer, so no one would be wearing velvets and furs.

When she'd told Maisie about her forthcoming outing, her friend had insisted on coming over on Saturday evening to help her get ready.

"Oh, my, Grace, anyone would think you belonged to New York's Four Hundred," said Maisie admiringly.

Grace looked at herself critically. Her mirror was small so she couldn't see her feet, which were shod in a pair of white kidskin boots, but if she stood back and twisted this way and that she could see most of her dress. It was cream-colored moire silk with a square neck, fitted bodice, smooth over her waist and hips, but with a slight ruffle in the back. The sleeves were fashionably puffed. Her hair was piled high with a few curls trained alongside her cheeks, which were innocent of rouge but pink with the healthy flush of youth.

Maisie sighed. "You'll be the prettiest girl at the castle. Imagine going to a ball at a real castle, just like Cinderella. Although I still don't think Austin's much of a prince."

"I'm not interested in princes, and I'm definitely not planning on losing a slipper," said Grace. She surveyed her neatly buttoned boots with pride.

Maisie saw her safely into the cab, and waved her away with repeated urgings to have a good time. And so Grace set off on her first trip to Paterson since that fateful morning when she had run away from Aunt Flora's. She couldn't help reflecting with satisfaction on the difference in her situation. She had definitely put Potter's Mill behind her. And even though she knew she was only on the outer fringes of this rich and elegant crowd, who swarmed over the ferry boat and later filled the private train, she found them casually accepting of her. Happily she and Austin had become separated from Mrs. DeWitt-Kenton and Uncle Thomas, who were in a different carriage, and Austin, once out from under his mother's eagle eye, became quite the man-about-town. He assumed a proprietary air and introduced her to numerous acquaintances on the train.

"If this is your first visit to Lambert Castle, Miss Cameron, you're in for a treat."

"Why?" exclaimed a cigar smoking man. "It's nothing but a great heaping pile of stones. On top of a mountain, of all places."

"But it does give Lina a great view of Paterson. He can count his workers as they go into the mill."

"And fire anyone who shows up late." There was a burst of laughter. Everyone seemed in a happy, carefree mood and Grace listened eagerly to the gossip that swirled around her.

"It really is overdecorated," complained a tall lady wearing a headdress of ostrich feathers. "All those pictures! Why, there's not an inch of wall space."

"My dear, they're not just pictures, they're art. A priceless collection, and Lina's pride and joy."

"And the gardens are magnificent."

"Come on, Josh, you just like the naked statues." There

was another burst of laughter as the train pulled into the station.

A row of carriages was lined up to meet the train, and Grace and Austin were soon whisked through the once familiar streets and up the long driveway to the gatehouse of the castle. Grace had never seen such a crush of people. Their host and hostess greeted them on the terrace. Mr. Lambert was a short, rotund man, who exuded a force of energy that entirely made up for his lack of stature. His wife, Harriet, stood by his side wearing the most exquisitely embroidered faille silk dress that Grace had ever seen. She knew this was Lambert's second wife, the younger sister of the beautiful Belle, who had died some ten years earlier, and for whom the castle had been named.

While Grace was meeting her host, Maggie and Jeannie were lined up in the kitchen with the rest of the temporary help. Poor Moira, who had come along at the last minute, had been relegated to the sculleries to wash dishes.

"Sure an' I only came so I could see all the foine silk dresses," she lamented.

"Don't worry," said Jeannie, "I'll sneak you out sometime during the evening. Whew, what a mob."

The kitchen was, if possible, even more crowded than the rest of the house, and several degrees hotter. Both Jeannie and Maggie had been outfitted with white caps and starched white aprons over black cotton dresses, and were receiving their instructions.

"Now carry your tray in front of you. Stand quite still while the guests help themselves. Don't worry about dirty plates and glasses as the menservants will take care of them. Speak only if you are spoken to, and do not engage in conversation either with the guests or with each other." They were further warned to watch where they were going and not to bump into the ladies and gentlemen.

Mindful of these warnings they set off, each carefully balancing a tray of drinks. Their faces were flushed from the heat of the kitchen, Maggie's brown curls clung to her forehead, while Jeannie had wrapped her braids around her head in an effort to look older. Both stared wide-eyed at the beautiful gowns worn by the ladies, and were dazzled by the array of jewels which ranged from garnets and emeralds, to rubies and pearls.

"Och, did ye ever see the like?" whispered Maggie. " 'Tis like being at the royal palace." Indeed, Maggie found it hard not to curtsey so overwhelmed was she by the richness of her surroundings. She hung back, but Jeannie, who was not so easily intimidated, advanced towards the crowd. A large matron wearing a rose-colored watered silk tapped her on the arm with a fan and nodded towards the glasses.

"Is it sec or brut?" she asked.

" 'Tis champagne, ma'am," said Jeannie.

"Of course it's champagne you silly girl."

"Oh, come, Matilda, what should this child know of wine?" exclaimed a red-faced man with gingery whiskers. "Whatever it is, Catholina Lambert serves only the finest." He took two glasses from her tray and winked kindly at Jeannie. The heavy set lady took a glass and waddled away. Jeannie watched her go, resisting the temptation to stick out her tongue. Maggie was still standing by the kitchen door, her knees shaking.

"Jeannie, I'm scared. Suppose I drop something."

"Dinna worry, what can they do tae ye anyway? Throw ye in a dungeon?"

"Where's Ian?" she asked, looking around anxiously.

"He's out wi' the carriages, but he'll be here later to collect the glasses." Maggie's spirits lifted at the thought of Ian. Perhaps they could go around together—she wouldn't be so nervous with Ian at her side.

"We'd better get goin'," said Jeannie. "Yon slave driver is givin' us the evil eye." She nodded towards the black-clad majordomo who appeared to be heading towards them. Alarmed, the two girls quickly separated and began moving through the crowd.

After Grace and Austin had left the receiving line, she suggested that they go and look at the gardens. She had seen Mrs. DeWitt-Kenton and Uncle Thomas disappear into the house, and the longer she could avoid them the better. Austin apparently felt the same way.

"Capital idea," he said. "A stroll in the gardens is just the ticket. After all, it's not every night that I have such a beautiful woman on my arm. I'm the envy of every man here." His look was all-encompassing, and there was a light in his eye that she had not seen before. He almost seemed to be asserting himself, she thought. He guarded her possessively, and she noticed several people glance at them admiringly as they made their way along the well-lit paths. It was as if they were actually being seen as a couple. Grace wondered how Mrs. DeWitt-Kenton would react to that idea. She wondered how *she* would react to that idea, if she ever decided to take it seriously. But tonight she wasn't going to take anything seriously, just enjoy herself.

She looked around her. The bare, dreary gardens she had walked through that fateful November day had been transformed. Now the fountains were playing, their delicate spray reflecting the lights of hundreds of tiny electric lights strung from tree to tree, while among the banks of greenery and flowers the statues gleamed white. The paths were no longer deserted but thronged with people, the women beautiful in silk gowns of every hue, the men elegant in their swallow-tail coats and stiff white shirt fronts. Even out here in the open, the hum of conversation and tinkle of glasses filled the air.

As they promenaded around the gardens she noticed Mr. Lambert making his way through the crowd, pausing every now and then to speak to one or two of the men. When he reached them he stopped.

"Ah! Kenton. Your mother is looking for you. She's in the library, having a little tête-à-tête with Henry Doherty and the others. I'll probably be joining them in a little while." Austin looked apologetically at Grace. "Ha! you're worried about leaving this beautiful young lady without an escort, and so you should be young man, so you should be. But no need to worry. If you'll introduce me, I'll be her escort."

Austin's eyes opened wide in surprise, but he dutifully introduced Grace, and then was quickly waved away by his host.

"I must warn you, Miss Cameron, that whenever I have first-time visitors to Belle Vista I insist on showing them my art collection."

"I'd love to see your collection, Mr. Lambert," replied Grace with a smile. "I've heard so much about it."

"Splendid. Come with me."

Grace realized she was being singularly honored, and once more she found herself silently blessing Lady McLeod for enabling her to recognize the names of the painters on display in the gallery. Lambert's collection included a Rembrandt and an El Greco, in addition to the works of Sir Joshua Reynolds, Gainsborough, Hogarth, and the great landscape artist, Constable. She also noted some modern French artists such as Renoir and Monet. A remarkable achievement for a man who had started out working in a cotton thread mill in England when he was ten years old. She looked at her host with renewed admiration.

They were still examining the numerous paintings that covered the walls when a manservant appeared at their side.

"I beg your pardon, sir, but Mrs. Lambert sent me to tell you they are awaiting you in the library."

"Duty calls, Miss Cameron, but feel free to browse as long as you wish, and I promise I'll send young Kenton back to you as soon as possible."

Grace lingered for a while in the upper gallery, then decided to go downstairs to the ballroom. The music drifting up from below set her feet tapping. She would watch the dancers until Austin could escape from his mother's clutches. She wondered if he could waltz.

Ian had finally finished seeing to the carriages and had reluctantly joined the kitchen help. A towel over his arm and a large tray in his hands, he joined Maggie and Jeannie on the fringes of the ballroom.

"How are you girls doing?" he asked.

"It's nay so bad, once ye get used tae it," said Maggie. "And the dresses are beautiful."

Jeannie wrinkled her nose. "See that fat lady over there? She's had about six glasses of champagne already. They're going tae have tae carry her out o' here. If this is high society, I'll take Big Nellie any day."

The black-clad majordomo bore down on them. "No talking, no talking. Circulate."

"Circulate, circulate," muttered Jeannie. "I'm going tae rescue poor Moira for a minute."

"Ian, if ye stay alongside me, then the ladies and gentlemen will have somewhere tae put their empty glasses," said Maggie.

"Good idea. We'll stick together. This doesn't look like the friendliest crowd. I've never seen so many—"

He broke off with a muffled choking sound. Maggie looked at his awe-struck face and then followed his gaze. He was staring towards the stairs with an intensity that frightened her.

The stairs were a major feature of the castle. They had been specially designed with a life-sized frame on the lower landing so that Lambert's lovely wife, or any beautiful woman descending them, would be caught as in a picture. And in that picture, looking breathtakingly beautiful, stood Grace. Her red-gold hair shimmered in the soft light, and her simple creamy silk dress clung to her willowy figure. She had no need of jewels. "Oh no," breathed Maggie. "Please God, no."

As Grace descended the stairs she paused to look around the laughing, jostling crowd to see if Austin had escaped from the library. Then she gasped and the room seemed to swim before her. She clutched the bannister for support. For a moment the tableau before her froze. She glimpsed Austin emerging from the library, she saw a stricken Maggie, noted two young girls, one of them Jeannie, peeping out from the kitchen door, and in the center of it all was Ian. Their eyes met and held, and she watched mesmerized as he abandoned his towel and his tray and moved slowly towards her. When he reached the foot of the stairs he simply took her hand and led her, wordlessly, to the ballroom where the orchestra was playing a waltz. Then, his arm around her waist, he guided her onto the dance floor where they drew together instinctively.

Grace had never before danced with Ian, but they both moved with such a natural ease and rhythm that they seemed to become one with the music. There was something sensual and disturbing in the way they dipped and swayed and the other dancers gradually withdrew to allow them the floor. They had eyes only for each other as they whirled around and around oblivious to the shocked but admiring glances of the bystanders. Oblivious to the open-mouthed stare of Austin, the pursed-mouthed condemnation of his mother, the astonished gasps that came from Jeannie and Moira who were peeking out from the kitchen, and quite oblivious to the silent tears that rolled down Maggie's cheeks.

When the music stopped they stepped back onto the sidelines where they were immediately confronted by a furious majordomo.

"My deepest apologies, ma'am." He glared at Ian. "I don't know what could have possessed this . . . this . . . bus boy."

Ian returned his gaze contemptuously, and without saying a word, turned on his heel and strode out of the ballroom, out of the castle, and into the night. The irate manservant continued to mumble apologies to Grace, who appeared in a daze. In a few moments Austin reached her side. He waved the man away, and took Grace's elbow, steering her away from the dance floor.

"I say, are you all right?" He looked bewildered. "Didn't you realize he was one of the hired help? No, I suppose you didn't, he'd taken off his apron, but my God, Grace, he was certainly no gentleman, embarrassing you like that. He ought to be horsewhipped."

"Austin, I'd like to leave now," said Grace. "Will you please take me home?"

"Now? But the party's not over yet. My dear, you don't have to leave just because of some millhand. I'm sure no one's going to actually blame you for what happened. Besides, I don't think Mother is ready to go yet."

"Oh, forget about your mother for once. For heaven's sakes, Austin, can't you do anything on your own?"

"I say, you *are* upset. Come on, let's walk outside for a bit." He took her arm and they went onto the terrace.

To say she was upset was putting it mildly. Grace was in a turmoil. The sight of Ian had awakened all the latent fires she thought she had smothered. The feel of his arms around her had aroused her in a way Austin's never did. She wanted more. She wanted to feel Ian's cheek against hers, his lips against hers. Oh, God, she thought, she wanted Ian with every fiber of her being.

The evening ended with a fireworks display. The three girls watched it from behind the house along with the other servants. They had been paid for their night's work, although Jeannie had been severely rebuked for talking too much, and Maggie for running into the kitchen to cry, and as for Ian, well, he wasn't going to get paid at all.

"He'll never work here again," said the majordomo.

"Ye dinna have to worry on that account," said Jeannie, pocketing her two dollars. "It'll be a long time afore any of us come looking tae work for Mr. Catholina Lambert."

But the fireworks were thrilling. The watchers cowered in terror at the thunderous booms of the rockets and gasped with astonishment as the sky was filled with red, blue, gold, and silver exploding stars.

"Grace should have stayed tae see this," said Jeannie. "Ian, too." At the mention of Grace and Ian, Maggie's depression returned, and she turned aside to brush away the tears that seemed to spring unbidden to her eyes. Moira put her arm around her friend.

"Don't worry, Maggie. 'Twas just a lark, Ian dancing with your cousin like that. And isn't she safely back in New York by now wi' no harm done."

But Maggie had seen the hunger in Ian's eyes when he looked at Grace—Grace, who was more beautiful than ever—and felt much harm had been done.

# CHAPTER
## ❦ 14 ❦

GRACE paced the floor in her tiny apartment trying to sort out her feelings, but all she could think of was Ian. He was still the most desirable man she'd ever met. There was a strength, a power, an integrity to Ian that made Austin appear to be a jellyfish by comparison. But it was just that strength and integrity that kept them apart. If only . . . She shook her head. It was hopeless.

Austin had finally braved his mother's wrath and taken Grace home from the ill-fated ball. She had not seen or heard from him until, just when she figured he was probably out of her life forever, she received a graven invitation to have tea on Saturday afternoon with Mrs. DeWitt-Kenton. *Where,* she wondered, *did she obtain my address?* Grace had always kept her tiny apartment a secret, and had let Austin assume that she lived somewhere on the upper West Side. Even when they returned from Lambert castle she had insisted he put her in a carriage when they left the ferryboat. She thought he had the vague idea that she lived with Lady McLeod, although she had never said so. However the invitation bore her name and was sent directly to the house on Third Avenue. She was almost tempted to send her regrets, but decided that would be cowardly. She had started this charade and now she must finish it.

She dressed in her most expensive suit, adjusted her simple straw hat, and drew on her new kid gloves. She looked every inch a young lady of quality. *And I am,* she thought. *All I lack is money.*

Mrs. DeWitt-Kenton received her in the rather chilly parlor Grace had seen on her first visit. Austin was nowhere in sight, but Uncle Thomas was there, dour-faced as ever. They both greeted Grace coldly and she was invited to sit. So all three sat, straight-backed and rigid on the edge of their chairs while the housekeeper brought in the tea tray. Mrs. DeWitt-Kenton poured, then handed out the delicate white china cups. Grace put hers down untouched and waited. After an interminable silence Mrs. DeWitt-Kenton spoke.

"Miss Cameron, do you have an explanation for your extraordinary behaviour the other night? You greatly embarrassed my son by dancing with a waiter."

"He's not a waiter," exclaimed Grace.

"Ah, so you do know him! He is not, as my naive son believed, a total stranger. He is some sort of an acquaintance of yours. Someone from your unsavory past, no doubt."

"There is nothing unsavory about my past, Mrs. DeWitt-Kenton."

"But what about the present?" This from Uncle Thomas. "I have been checking up on you, Miss Cameron. First of all, as you can see, we discovered where you live."

"In a dreary little cold water flat!"

"It has central heating," said Grace defensively. Mrs. Murphy would be insulted at her description.

"And what is more, you have a job. You work for your living. Your pretense about studying the market in order to improve your investments, was just that—pretense." Uncle Thomas looked down his long, aquiline nose. "But let us discuss this job of yours, Miss Cameron. You work for Robert Harwood, do you not? What are you, a spy?"

"I'm a telephone operator," said Grace. Mrs. DeWitt-Kenton laughed. It was a high-pitched, mirthless sound.

"And telephone operators have inside information on investment opportunities within the firm, I suppose." She leaned forward. "Just why did you bring this to my son's attention? What were your motives? What is Harwood doing? Testing the waters?"

"I have no idea what Mr. Harwood's intentions are," said Grace. "When I discussed buying stock in the firm, it was purely hypothetical." *In other words,* thought Grace, *I made it all up, but I can't possibly explain that to these two, whose motives are far more devious than mine.*

"Well, Miss Cameron, I think it should be obvious, even to you, that your behaviour has been utterly shameful. You may be sure that I will see that you are no longer accepted in any polite society, and my son will no longer be seeing you."

"I would think that decision was up to Austin," said Grace, getting to her feet. "But rest assured, I have no interest in any society that *you* might consider polite. I have higher standards than that."

"Such insolence!" exclaimed Mrs. DeWitt-Kenton, flushing a bright red. "I deal with girls of your caliber every day, young woman, and I predict you will come to a bad end." She yanked on the bell pull. "Cooper will show you out."

"I can find my own way out," said Grace, brushing past an appalled Uncle Thomas and almost colliding with the silent-footed housekeeper.

Once out in the streets Grace's anger swept her along, oblivious to the activities around her—the nursemaids pushing carriages, children playing, old people sitting on park benches in the shade of dusty city trees—she saw none of them. Instead, the condescending features of Austin's mother swam before her eyes. It wasn't until she'd left the upper part of town and was pushing her way through the East Side, through crowded streets lined with pushcarts piled with fruit, vegetables, and cheap clothing, did the bleakness of her situation begin to register. As she hurried past the teeming tenements, with children swarming up and down the stoops, and babies taking care of babies while their mothers sat upstairs hunched over sewing machines in hot, crowded rooms, she began to shiver. Was there no way to escape from the stigma of poverty? She was attractive, intelligent, well read, but because her father didn't own a couple of mills, or wasn't a bank president, women like Mrs. DeWitt-Kenton looked down on her. Despised her. Doors were slammed in her face. *Face it, Grace,* she told herself bitterly, *you're no closer to reaching your goals than you were the day you stepped off the boat at Ellis Island.*

It was a very dejected young woman who let herself in and began the long, slow climb up to her tiny, solitary apartment. She didn't even notice Mrs. Murphy who appeared at the foot of the stairs, bursting with excitement.

"Grace," she called after her, "sure'n ye've got a visitor. A nice young man. I've put him in the parlor."

*I don't believe it,* thought Grace, *Austin is actually defying his mother and coming to see me.* She wondered what he was going to say. She thanked Mrs. Murphy and hurried down the hall. She pulled open the door and stepped inside. A young man quickly rose from an arm chair and stood facing her.

"Hello, Grace," he said softly.

"Ian!" she exclaimed. "Oh, my God, it's Ian." And she flung herself into his arms. "Let me look at you. I can't believe you're really here. How did you find me?"

"Jeannie gave me your address. Ever since I saw you at the castle the other night I . . . Grace, I've missed you. You don't know how much."

"I missed you, too, but now you're here. You're really here."

They hugged each other again, exclaiming over and over

how wonderful the other looked, how they had missed
each other, and how lonely each one had been.

"Come on, we don't want to stay in this stuffy little
parlor all day," said Grace. "Let's go and explore the
city."

They thanked Mrs. Murphy and set off, arm-in-arm, to
walk the length and breadth of the city. But surely these
were not the same bleak and dirty streets she had traveled
just a short while ago. This was the New York she had
dreamed about. A shining city, a city of charm and elegance, a city of joy—and all because of Ian. Arms entwined, faces radiant, they admired the huge mansions on
Fifth Avenue, laughed at the antics of the hucksters on
Broadway, craned their necks in wonder at the tall, slender
Metropolitan Life Building that seemed to reach up to the
sky, and even rejoiced in the overflowing tenements of the
poor that somehow, magically, were no longer pockets of
despair but bursting with life and hope.

Later on they had dinner in a small restaurant with tiny
tables set with checkered tablecloths and flickering candles. Ian ordered a bottle of dark red wine and the food
was delicious, although Grace had no memory of what she
ate. All she remembered was Ian's face—the strong bone
structure of his cheek and jaw, accentuated by the shadows
from the candlelight, and his clear, gray-green eyes, that
looked at her with a desire and longing that sent tremors
of delight throughout her.

What followed was so right, so wonderful and so in-
evitable that Grace could never think of it as sin. They
walked home hand-in-hand, let themselves in, and crept
quietly up the three flights of stairs to Grace's room. Once
inside they flew into each others arms, their kisses growing deeper and hungrier by the minute. At last, breathless,
Ian paused, and slowly and deliberately took the pins out
of her hair. It tumbled down around her shoulders, a shining mass of burnished gold, and he buried his face in it.
Then, picking her up gently, he carried her over to the

small bed, where, with a long, shuddering moan of joy, he possessed her at last.

The next morning Grace set the table for breakfast, humming softly to herself, while Ian slept. When he awoke, sleepy-eyed and tousle-haired, he was confused for a moment, wondering where he was, then remembering with a rush of joy.

"You'd better get up sleepy head," said Grace. "I think you should leave while Mrs. Murphy's at church. I don't think she'd approve of your being here." Then feeling strangely shy, Grace turned her back to allow Ian a chance to dress. He quickly pulled on his clothes, then came up behind her and put his arms around her.

"Not sorry, are you Grace?" he asked.

"Oh, no, Ian, no." She turned to kiss him.

He looked around and sighed. "You don't know how often I've dreamed of this moment. The two of us in our own little apartment. You fixing breakfast."

"And I'd better hurry up and fix it because you have to leave."

"I know. But soon I'll be able to stay. Once we're married you're never going to get rid of me." They clung to each other for a moment, then Grace went back to her kettle simmering on the gas ring.

"We'll have to look for a bigger apartment. And you'll need a job—"

"I have a job," he said.

"But that's in Paterson," she exclaimed. "I thought—"

"You thought I wanted to move to New York. Grace, what would I do in New York?"

"You could go to school—night school. That's what I've been doing."

He laughed. "Do they teach loom fixing? Even if they did, which I doubt, they couldn't be any better at it than old McPherson. Grace, I'm going to be a loom fixer any day now. And eventually I'm going to open my own shop.

And if we can't get an apartment right away, we could probably stay at Aunt Flora's for a while, fix up the attic . . .''
Ian's face glowed, but for Grace a cloud seemed to drift
across the sun and for a brief moment the shine went from
the morning.

She managed to scramble two eggs on the little burner
and make a pot of tea. When she carried it over to the
table, and saw Ian sitting there looking as handsome as
ever, she felt a thrill run through her. The sun had come
out again, and this time she was not going to let any shadows get in its way. She still had trouble realizing he was
actually here, and she wanted him to stay more than anything else in the world. Austin and his mother and Uncle
Thomas were all forgotten. They were unimportant. Ian
was important. But they needed time together—time to
talk, to plan, to dream.

She reached over and took his hand. "Oh, Ian, I love
you.''

# CHAPTER
## ❧ 15 ❧

FOR the next few days Grace simply floated. She was present and yet she was absent. She did her work as quietly and efficiently as always, but between times her eyes took on a far-away, dreamy look that caused the girls at the switchboard to nod to each other knowingly.

"The Ice Queen's in love," one of them whispered. "Wonder who the poor guy is."

Grace's day dreams, unlike Ian's, did not extend to the future. That was hazy and unclear. Instead she relived the wonderful day and even more wonderful night they'd spent together. She knew he was probably already rebuking himself, and would now feel a quick marriage was imperative, but she was content to drift, basking in the warm glow of desire, reliving an experience that must surely be unique in all the world.

In her euphoric state she remained both calm and detached when a flustered Miss Finch told her she had been summoned to Mr. Harwood's office. *I'm probably going to be fired,* she told herself. Undoubtedly Mrs. DeWitt-Kenton had informed Mr. Harwood that she'd been giving away trade secrets. She wondered idly if she should defend herself or simply pack up and leave. Ian would be delighted if she left, but the thought of returning to Paterson was as chilling as a cold errant breeze on a summer afternoon.

Still feeling remote from her surroundings, she drifted into the elegant office and sank into one of the immense leather chairs. Mr. Harwood took his seat behind his massive desk and once more she became aware of the magnetism of the man. He surveyed her with his pale but brilliant eyes, and she quickly emerged from her semi-dazed state to a sharp awareness of her situation. She sat up a little straighter. But his first question took her completely by surprise.

"Are you still attending night school, Miss Cameron?" he asked.

"Why, yes," she replied, puzzled.

"Can you type? Take dictation?"

"I've taken classes, but I've never actually worked as a stenographer," she answered.

"Do you like working for Harwood Enterprises?"

"Yes, sir, I do." She looked at him curiously. What was he leading up to? Was she going to get a lecture on company loyalty? Surely he would have relegated that task to Miss Finch. He continued to eye her speculatively.

"You seem to have a good grasp of the silk industry, Miss Cameron, and what's more important, I believe you care about it." He leaned forward. "How would you like to work for me?" He smiled at her obvious confusion. "I mean here, in this office, as my private secretary." She stared at him in astonishment. "Miss Avery is retiring. She is willing, however, to stay for a couple of weeks to show you the ropes. Once you take over, of course, you will receive a substantial raise. Do you think you can handle the job?"

Handle it, she'd revel in it! "Oh, yes, Mr. Harwood, yes." Her face was eager. "I'd love the job, and thank you so much for offering it to me."

"I told you I wouldn't forget you, Miss Cameron. Ever

since that day you warned me about the stock deal, I've had you in mind. And now let's get started.''

He summoned Miss Avery into the room and told her to take Miss Cameron under her wing. The older woman's smile was friendly, and she suggested they start working together right away.

"Go down to the switchboard and fetch your things. I've already explained to Miss Finch that you're leaving. From now on you'll come directly to the front office. The hours are eight-thirty to six, but you may have to work later.''

"Oh, I won't mind," said Grace.

"I'm glad to hear that. This isn't a job for a clock watcher. But Mr. Harwood's a wonderful boss. You're lucky to be working for him.''

"I know," breathed Grace, "I know." It was a dream come true. *It's almost too much,* she thought. *First Ian, and now this. What more could I possibly ask for?*

When Grace emerged that evening, she was so keyed up she simply had to talk to someone. If only Maisie were nearby, she thought, but Brooklyn was too far. However, Mike's Luncheonette was within walking distance. She'd go and see Mike and tell him her good news.

Her head was still spinning from the reams of information Miss Avery had been piling on her, but she had rejoiced in it. No more would she be performing a dull, boring job. Now every day would be a challenge. Every day she'd be learning something new.

"I want to learn everything," she had said. And Miss Avery and Mr. Harwood had looked at each other and smiled knowingly.

She had spent the afternoon typing short letters and being introduced to the intricate filing system. She was made privy to Mr. Harwood's private appointment book and warned to remind him of all upcoming meetings and luncheons. She was given a list of frequent callers who could be put through directly, although she was already familiar with those names. Before she even realized it, Miss Avery was putting on her hat and locking up the office.

"I'll see you in the morning, Grace. I feel much better about leaving now," she said. "I think you are going to make a splendid secretary."

Those words of praise ringing in her ears, she made her way to Mike's place. Mike had an older woman waiting on table, and he was behind the counter. He greeted Grace with pleasure.

"Now here's a sight for sore eyes. Look at you, if you ain't the fine lady."

"Oh, Mike, I've just got a wonderful new job. I'm going to be Mr. Harwood's private secretary. I'll have my own office, get a raise, and everything."

"I always knew youse belonged in a fancy office. Wouldn't surprise me if youse didn't own the company one of these days. Congratulations, Grace." Mike was genuinely pleased.

"Will you be seeing Maisie? Tell her I want to meet her so we can go and celebrate."

"Sure thing. She comes in on Fridays sometimes. I'll tell her."

Grace had a cup of coffee and a sandwich, although she was too excited to care about eating. She took the trolley back to her room, all the time marvelling at her good fortune. *I'll have to write to Ian,* she thought. *This time when he comes to town I'll treat him. I'll buy a bottle of champagne and cook a chicken. Perhaps Mrs. Murphy will let me use her oven.* Her head was so full of wonderful plans she didn't know what to think about first. It was like a cascade of golden pennies running through her fingers— she tried to catch as many as possible and hold on to them, but she couldn't hold them all.

* * *

Grace's note to Ian had been brief in the extreme: "I've got some wonderful news. When you come in we'll celebrate. Love, Grace."

He tried to imagine what the wonderful news was, but he had a nagging feeling that it wasn't going to be wonderful for him. Grace was as still as difficult to pin down as a butterfly. He'd seen her expression change whenever he mentioned settling down, and he couldn't understand it. He thought that all girls longed to be married, to have a home of their own, to have children. Why was Grace so different?

When he saw her, glowing with excitement, he knew it wasn't for him. Not that she wasn't overjoyed to see him. She hugged him close and he felt that familiar stirring inside of him, but her thoughts were elsewhere.

"Look at me, Ian, you might think I'm the same old Grace, but I'm not. You're looking at Miss Grace Cameron, private secretary to Mr. Robert Harwood, President of Harwood Enterprises. Can you believe it? I'm still pinching myself to make sure I'm not dreaming."

But Ian knew this was no dream, and he felt a sudden upsurge of hatred for Mr. Robert Harwood. Damn it, why did he choose Grace? And why now, now of all times, when he was so close to coaxing her to come back to him? A feeling of black despair came over him.

The special dinner was not a great success. Grace was not an experienced cook. The chicken was tough, the potatoes hard in the middle, and even the champagne didn't seem to have much fizz.

"To us," said Grace, raising her glass.

"To us?" said Ian. "Or to Mr. Robert Harwood?"

"Oh, Ian, you don't have to be jealous. He's only the man I work for."

But with a slight feeling of guilt, she did recall the electrifying current that seemed to run between them. *That's because we share the same enthusiasms,* she thought, and again a guilty twinge ran through her. What she shared with Ian was far more than enthusiasm for a job. But Ian was picking dejectedly at his dinner, and their special day seemed to be turning to ashes.

Ian couldn't think of anything to say. He had planned to tell her about the difficult repair job he'd done on a jaquard loom, and how much he'd earned. He'd been going to describe the apartments he'd looked at, figuring to see if they could afford the rent. He'd pictured her laughing when he told her about gazing into shop windows, picking out furniture. But he didn't think any of that would interest her. Not now. She'd moved into another world. A world in which he could have no part.

"I can't stay, Grace. I promised McPherson I'd give him a hand tomorrow, even though it is Sunday." He'd made that promise for two reasons. One was, he didn't trust himself. He wanted Grace more than anything else in the world, but he vowed he wouldn't touch her again until they were married. And the second reason was that the more money he could earn the sooner the marriage could take place. At least that's what he'd thought, until Grace met him, bubbling with excitement over her new job. Once more it seemed as if all his hopes and dreams were crashing down around him.

She walked with him to the ferry.

"Next Saturday, Grace, the Scottish Club is having a ball game and picnic. I don't usually play, but this time I've been roped in. Do you think you could come out and cheer me on? I know the girls would love to see you." He looked at her anxiously, as if knowing that her answer would determine their future.

Grace avoided his eyes, and sighed.

"I'm sorry, Ian, but I can't. I promised Mr. Harwood I'd work next Saturday. There's so much I have to learn."

"I see," he said bitterly. "And we can't disappoint Mr. Harwood, can we?"

"Oh, Ian, don't you understand? It's a new job. I can't possibly refuse to work. I'd love to go and watch you play, believe me."

"But it's not that important, is it?" *Why am I quarrelling with Grace*, he thought miserably. *I should take her in my arms and kiss her until she's breathless, then she'd come with me.* But would she? She was the most beautiful, wonderful, bewildering, confusing girl he'd ever met. She could fill him with joy and lacerate him with pain. Life with Grace would be a roller coaster of highs and lows, and life without her would be empty and dull. But somehow he knew that the choice would not be his, either way.

They said goodbye, promising to write but without making a definite date to see each other again. Her hand lingered in his until it was time for him to board the ferry. He stood on the deck and waved as the boat pulled out into the harbor. The distance between them grew wider and wider, until they both became little specks standing on distant shores.

# CHAPTER
## ❧ 16 ❧

GRACE didn't see or hear from Ian over the next few weeks, but she wasn't too concerned. With the long hours he spent at the mill, plus the nights and weekends working for McPherson, it was not easy for him to get to New York, and she knew he wasn't much for writing letters. She did write to him telling him all about her job, although she wondered if he was interested. She did experience a slight twinge of conscience for not going to Paterson when he asked her to, but felt sure he would understand. After all, he was in love with her. He had always been in love with her, and that love set them apart from other men and women. She still felt shivers of delight at the memory of their night together. She knew that night had changed them forever, for now they were no longer two separate people—they were one. Even though he was in Paterson and she in New York, they were joined as if by a silken thread—slender and delicate, and yet strong and pliant. A gentle pull upon the thread and he would come to her; he would realize that life in Paterson was a treadmill that led nowhere, but here in New York there were no limits to the heights they could reach together. And so with this comforting thought to reassure her, she plunged into the world of business and finance that had always held such fascination for her.

Perhaps it was Grace's nature to accept the extraordinary as commonplace: Ian's unwavering devotion in the face of her desertion, and now Mr. Harwood's generosity by including her in all aspects of his business. She sat in on meetings with accountants and legal advisors, and afterwards he would discuss the issues with her. "How did I ever get along before you came, Miss Cameron?" he'd say over and over, and she'd wonder how she ever endured working in the boring jobs she'd had before. Now she looked forward to each day, anxious to sit across from this dynamic man and feel the energy that emanated from him as he went over the various deals he was engaged in. There was an intimacy between them that allowed them to anticipate each other's thoughts.

"Close the door, Miss Cameron, and pull your chair over here—I want you to look over these patterns. Now which one do you like best?" She showed him. "Ah, I thought you'd like that one," he said. "It's sophisticated yet subtle." He looked at her admiringly.

He took time to explain to her the intricate chain of events that led to the creation of silk, from the spinning of the cocoons to the reeling of the thread. She learned the difference between organzine and tram, between European and Oriental silk. She learned to recognize the personal trademarks of the Japanese manufacturers, some of them as beautiful as works of art.

"The Japanese are smart traders," he told her. "They knew the problems we'd been having with silk from China, which was often weighted with acetate of lead. Silk is judged by weight, you see. The Chinese never identify their manufacturers, so the buyer has no redress. So naturally we prefer to do business with the Japanese. And that leads me to Mr. Kawasaki."

Grace knew that he had been negotiating a deal with Mr. Kawasaki, a wealthy Japanese silk merchant who was visiting the United States.

"He's something of a recluse, you know. He's rented

an oceanfront mansion just outside of Atlantic City over
in New Jersey, and refuses to come to the city. I need to
get his signature on a contract, but I'm committed to speak
at the annual gathering of silk buyers." He eyed her speculatively. "Miss Cameron, how would you like to spend
a couple of days at the Jersey shore?"

"Me?" she exclaimed.

He laughed. "All expenses paid, of course. I'd like to
have this contract hand delivered. The actual business
dealings with Mr. Kawasaki will have to be handled by
Gorman and Gorman, our solicitors. I'm afraid an elderly
Japanese gentleman would not do business with a woman,
no matter how competent she is. Luckily Gorman senior
spends his summers in Atlantic City, so he's available."

And that's how Grace found herself booked into the
Blescoe Inn on the Boardwalk in Atlantic City. It was a
highly respectable family hotel where dowagers brought
their daughters and eventually their granddaughters. The
people who stayed there were already friends and neighbors. They shared the same clubs and schools, played
bridge and tennis with each other at home, and played
bridge and tennis with each other while away. They had
little use for strangers.

*Well,* thought Grace, *I'm not here for bridge or tennis.
I'm here to work.* Her job consisted mainly of sitting quietly on the sidelines while Mr. Gorman senior explained
the terms of the contract to Mr. Kawasaki. He was, as Mr.
Harwood had described him, an elderly Japanese gentleman, precise and exacting, albeit with exquisite manners.
After much deliberation, and numerous delicate little cups
of tea, the contract was signed, a copy secured in Gorman
and Gorman's safe, and Grace returned to the hotel bearing the original. Mr. Gorman insisted on having her driven
there in his silver-gray Daimler, which caused several
raised eyebrows among the dowagers gently rocking on
the veranda, as well as sighs of envy from the bus boys
and stewards.

She was elated with the success of the mission, and in a moment of recklessness, decided to go unescorted into the dining room where a tea dance was in progress. She allowed the maître d' to seat her in a quiet secluded corner sheltered by potted palms, and watched, with a slight pang of envy, as young men in flannels and striped blazers and young women in flowered silks whirled by on the dance floor.

"So you're the mystery woman everyone's been talking about!"

Grace looked up in surprise to see Austin standing over her. She gave a slight groan. She should have known this was the kind of place frequented by the DeWitt-Kentons. She glanced around.

"Mother hasn't arrived yet," said Austin quickly. "I'm the advance guard. May I sit down?"

"If you wish," she said, "but I'm not staying. I have work to do." She made a motion to leave, but he reached across the table and grasped her hand.

"Grace, don't run away from me. You know how I feel. I can't help it if Mother got the wrong idea about you."

"But she didn't get the wrong idea, Austin. She was absolutely right about me. I'm not your type of girl. I don't spend my days going to luncheons and teas, shopping at Saks, or touring Europe. I work for my living. And, although you may find this hard to believe, I like what I do."

"Well, bully for you," said Austin. "I like a girl with spunk."

*That's because you don't have any,* thought Grace. But then he surprised her.

"Have dinner with me tonight. I know a great little restaurant overlooking the ocean. We could eat lobster and listen to the breakers. Later we can watch the moon rise."

It was tempting. Grace had been having dinner alone in her room, and it would be pleasant to have someone to talk to, although she had grave reservations about watch-

ing the moon with Austin at her side. If only it were
Ian. . . .

"No, Austin," she said. "Thank you for the invitation,
but I have a report to write and packing to do. And you
have to prepare for your mother."

"Oh, bother Mother. She's not coming down until tomorrow. Tonight I'm a free man."

"There are lots of pretty girls here. I'm sure you can
find someone to accompany you to dinner. Now, I must
be getting up to my room." He released her hand and she
stood up.

"I'm not going to take no for an answer, Grace. You
haven't heard the last of me."

*Oh, yes I have,* she thought, as she returned to the lobby.
She was just running up the stairs when the desk clerk
called out to her.

"Excuse me, Miss Cameron. This package came for
you." He handed her a large box wrapped in white em-
bossed paper and tied with a white and silver bow.

"For me," exclaimed Grace. "Are you sure it's for
me?"

He gave her the acompanying envelope addressed to
Miss Grace Cameron, Blescoe Hotel. Puzzled, she hurried
to her room where she quickly ripped open the envelope.
Inside was a card which said: "My sincere compliments.
C. Kawasaki." With trembling fingers she opened the
package. Among folds of tissue paper lay an exquisite kimono. She lifted it out. It was made of creamy silk, delicate as spun angel hair. She turned it around and gasped
in astonishment. The entire back panel was embroidered
with a carpet of delicate flowers, in the midst of which lay
a curved and stylized dragon, each scale glowing like a
precious jewel.

"Oh, it's so beautiful," she murmured. "Almost too
lovely to wear."

She laid it on the bed while she ran a bath, sprinkling
a scattering of pink bath salts into the water. A faint scent

of roses filled the air as she slid down into the tub. Then, after rubbing herself dry with a big bath towel, and feeling sinfully luxurious, she slipped into the kimono. It was as light as a feather, cool and soft against her skin. She found the wide sash, or obi as she knew it was called, and wrapped it around her slim waist. Then she pirouetted around the room, lifting her arms so that the long square-shaped sleeves spread out like wings. *What a pity Ian isn't here to admire it,* she thought with a pang.

She unpinned her hair and let it tumble around her shoulders. Then she lay down on the bed. The maid had lowered the shades and a soft yellow light filtered into the room. Outside she could hear the shouts and laughter of children drifting up from the beach. A faint breeze stirred the shades slightly, but it was a hot breeze. A pleasant drowsiness engulfed her as the outside noises grew fainter and farther away.

A sharp tap on the door roused her.

"Room service," came a muffled voice.

"I didn't order room service," murmured Grace. She rose from the bed and tightened the sash around her. Then she opened the door.

"Austin! What are you doing here?"

"Champagne for the lady," said Austin, pushing his way into the room. He had a bottle in one hand and two glasses in the other. Then he looked at Grace and caught his breath. "God, you're beautiful," he exclaimed. He kicked the door shut and set the champagne down on a small table. Then he advanced towards Grace. She backed quickly away.

"Austin, are you mad? Take your champagne and go. You've no business coming here at all."

"But I am here. We're both here. Grace, we can't waste this precious opportunity." He pulled her towards him, and ignoring her protests gave her a long hard kiss while his hand began exploring the inside of her kimono. She responded with a stinging slap across his face.

"Get out! Do you hear me? Out." She tore herself away from him and wrenched open the door. "Are you going to leave, or do I have to call the manager?"

"Oh, come on, Grace. Don't be such a prude." She gave him a push that sent him stumbling into the hallway.

"I never want to see you again, Austin. Do you understand?"

"But Grace . . ." Austin looked around him desperately, "I thought you liked . . ." Suddenly his voice trailed off and his face turned an assortment of colors. "Oh, my God," he murmured.

Grace followed his glance and saw the reason for his alarm, for advancing down the corridor, immaculately attired in a pale gray traveling suit with a white straw hat and gray gloves, was Mrs. DeWitt-Kenton. She skimmed towards them like an elegant yacht before a stiff breeze.

"M-Mother. I d-didn't expect you until tomorrow."

"Obviously not." She gave Grace a look that would have withered a garden of roses. "When did you plan this sordid little assignation?"

"It was an accident. I mean, I didn't know Grace was going to be here."

"There was no assignation," said Grace coldly. "Your son forced his way into my room under the pretext of room service. Here's your champagne, Austin." She thrust the bottle into his hands and slammed the door, leaving the two DeWitt-Kentons standing open-mouthed in the hallway.

Nevertheless Grace was severely shaken. She knew she could not remain under the same roof with Austin and his mother. She would leave now. She took off the kimono, fingering its soft silkiness and wondering if she would ever be able to wear it again without feeling a sense of shame and embarrassment. The colors of the dragon glowed in the dim light that filtered through the blinds and seemed to mock her with their beauty. *What a fool I've been,* she thought, *in not seeing what selfish and shallow people the*

*DeWitt-Kentons are. I let myself be blinded by their money and position.*

It took no time at all to pack her one small suitcase, making sure she had the precious contract safely stowed away. She didn't bother calling for the steward but carried it down herself and approached the desk to check out.

"We're sorry you're leaving us so soon, Miss Cameron, especially now that the weather is so beautiful."

"I've business to attend to in New York," she replied. "I'm afraid I've already lingered here too long."

The desk clerk arranged for a carriage to take her to the station. "If you'd like to wait on the veranda, I'll let you know when the carriage is here."

She thanked him and took a seat on one of the white wicker chairs. Except for a few elderly ladies, it was almost deserted. She sat looking out beyond the flower boxes filled with pink and white petunias to where the blue-green ocean curled against the sand. She could hear the softly breaking waves, punctuated by the far-off cry of the gulls, who wheeled and soared, their wings flashing in the brilliant sunshine. *Next time I come to a place like this,* she thought, *I'm coming with Ian.*

A carriage pulled up and a woman got out, accompanied by her two daughters, fashionably dressed young ladies, who were quickly surrounded by porters and stewards as bags, trunks, tennis racquets, squash racquets, hat and shoe boxes piled up around them. Grace picked up her solitary suitcase and approached the now empty carriage.

"To the train station," she said to the driver. "And hurry."

# CHAPTER
## ❧ 17 ❧

GRACE was right about Ian being busy. Mc-Pherson had acquired a collection of broken looms from a derelict mill, and they crowded the small shop.

"They'll take some time tae fix, laddie," McPherson said, "but we should sell them at a fair profit. If we do I'll gi'e ye a bonus."

Ian was glad of the work and the money, but sorry that it meant not seeing Grace. He needed to see Grace. He was still unhappy over his last visit, still felt great surges of jealousy towards this Mr. Robert Harwood, who was now monopolizing Grace's time. Even though he tried to tell himself it was no different from the time he spent working with McPherson, he knew it *was* different. He knew it was dangerous. Grace was being given a look at the world of money and power, a world she seemed to aspire to, but one that held no interest for him. Already they were being pulled apart again.

He picked up one of the heavy shuttles, balancing it in his hands, enjoying the feel of the smooth, polished wood. His fingers explored the sharply pointed metal ends that gave it the appearance of a bullet. He knew if a shuttle broke loose it could kill a man instantly, and he carefully tightened one of the deepset screws. When installed, this shuttle would fly back and forth with the speed of an actual bullet, and from the rise and fall of the intricate machinery, a shining silken cloth would emerge. Surely this was work to be proud of—far more satisfying than sitting on a stool adding up columns of figures. Ian shook his head. He would never understand the admiration of penpushers over craftsmen.

He began to examine the looms around him, studying each one carefully. There was a reason for his interest. McPherson had made him an offer that required much thought.

"Why dinna ye buy a couple o' looms yourself, laddie? I'll wager ye could get work for 'em. The big fellas often farm out small jobs to independent shops. 'Twould be a start for ye, and who knows where it might lead?"

Ian realized this was the opportunity he'd been waiting for—the chance to start up his own business. McPherson would let him pay it off in weekly installments, and the jobs would probably cover the payments. Once the looms were paid for, it would be all profit, and if there were any problems he would be able to fix them. He knew there were several small independent weavers, often husband and wife teams, in and around Paterson, some of them quite successful. He could be successful, he knew it, but he'd need Grace's cooperation. Would she be willing to work alongside of him in a small shop? It wasn't Grace's style, but perhaps if she saw what the possibilities were she would agree. After all, everyone had to start somewhere, and as Old Mac said, who knows where it might lead. There was really no reason to hesitate, and yet . . . He decided to sacrifice a Saturday afternoon to go into New York again.

"I'll make up the time, Mac, I promise," he said.

"Aye, I know ye will, but the sooner we start gettin' these looms fixed, the sooner we'll ha'e some money in our pockets. Right now mine are empty."

Mac knew that Ian was going to New York to see Grace. He knew all about Grace, having heard the tale from Aunt

Flora. Although he recognized Flora's prejudices, he knew
in his heart that Grace was not good for Ian. She was not
the kind of woman who would stick by his side and help
him work towards his goals. As far as Mac was concerned,
Grace was selfish and vain, and he feared for Ian. But
there was naught he could say. *Young men have tae learn
for themselves,* he thought, and a wave of pity swept over
him.

Ian took the morning train. He knew the way by now,
and hurried straight to Grace's apartment. He hadn't both-
ered to let her know he was coming. He didn't want her
to feel that she had to buy more champagne, which he
hadn't particularly enjoyed; he just wanted to sit down and
talk to her. He rang the bell and waited for Mrs. Murphy
to let him in. He heard her grumbling to herself as she
unlocked the door, but her smile was welcoming when she
saw who it was.

"Why 'tis the young man from New Jersey. Mr. Campbell is it not? From Paterson? Sure'n a shame it is ye've
come all this way for nothing, Mr. Campbell. But look at
me keeping ye standin' on the doorstep. Come inside."
Ian felt a great sense of foreboding as he followed her into
the small parlor. What did she mean, "come all this way
for nothing?"

"Grace isn't here, you see. She's off on an important
business trip." She motioned him to sit on one of the stiff,
overstuffed chairs. "Ye know she has a fine new job. Private secretary, she is. And doesn't her boss treat her as if
she were a society lady. Came for her in his own carriage—such a handsome gentleman—carried her bag for
her, and settled her into one o' the foine plush seats. She
looked so pretty and smart ye'd have t'ought she lived in
one of those big Fifth Avenue mansions, instead of Mrs.
Murphy's boarding house." Her landlady was obviously
bursting with pride at Grace's rise in the working world.
" 'Tis a shame, though, here you've come all the way to
New York, and the two of them off to New Jersey."

Ian felt as if he had received a blow to his stomach. Grace and Mr. Harwood going away together! He couldn't believe it. He wouldn't believe it.

"New Jersey! Are you sure?"

"Atlantic City, she told me, staying at some grand hotel. Are ye anywhere near the seashore, Mr. Campbell?" Ian shook his head. "Ah, 'tis too bad, then, ye might have seen them there."

"How long have they been gone?"

"Two days, and she didn't say when she'd be back." She looked around. "Perhaps 'tis a note ye'd like to write. I'll pin it to her door for ye."

"No, thank you." Ian got slowly to his feet. "I just stopped in on the off chance she'd be here. There's no need to even tell her I came. It was nothing important."

He left Mrs. Murphy protesting that she'd be glad to give Grace a message, and walked heedlessly through the crowded streets back to the ferry. Finally back on the train to Paterson, he stared out at the waving grasses of the Jersey meadows, where flocks of birds rose like clouds at the passing of the train, but he didn't see them. He had to struggle not to grind his teeth and groan aloud with the pain of it. Grace off to some grand hotel with this Mr. Harwood. How could she? How could she after the night they had spent together? To him, that had meant a betrothal—a promise as binding and holy as any given in church. But not, apparently, to Grace.

Ian decided to buy the looms, and spent all of his free time at McPherson's. He worked late into the night, on Saturdays, and even Sundays in spite of Aunt Flora's disapproval. He never spoke of Grace. He did receive some letters from her, but threw them away unopened. He felt as if there was a raw open wound where his heart was, and any reminder of Grace was like rubbing salt in that wound. Just when he thought she might become his forever, she had moved out of his reach. He could not compete with the likes of Mr. Harwood, with his money, prestige and, according to Mrs. Murphy, good looks besides. This man, whom he would hate for the rest of his life, could give Grace everything she'd ever dreamed about. Fine carriages, beautiful clothes, trips to fancy hotels by the shore. What could he give her? Endless days in a small, dank repair shop?

Even though Ian's mind was numb with despair, his hands—his strong, skillful hands—worked endlessly, planing, sanding, tightening, oiling, and soon his two looms were working smoothly. Now all he needed was a contract.

It was McPherson who found him his first job.

"It's an odd lot, laddie. They dinna want to set up two looms for such a small job, so I told them ye were available. Ye'll have to work steady on it—they want the goods by the end o' next week." For the first time since his disastrous trip to New York, Ian felt a slight surge of satisfaction. But how was he going to do the job? He couldn't abandon the other work he was doing for McPherson. And suddenly it came to him. Maggie! Maggie would help him out.

That night he presented himself at the dinner table, amid cries of, "Welcome back stranger." Jeannie quickly set a place for him, and Aunt Flora threw a few more potatoes into the pot. Maggie looked at him shyly. She knew he had gone to see Grace after that dreadful evening at Lambert's castle and had returned home bursting with happiness, while she quietly cried herself to sleep night after night. But something had changed, something had happened between Grace and Ian. She wouldn't dare ask, but Jeannie told her that Grace had written to her about an exciting new job. Surely she couldn't want a job instead of Ian. Maggie shook her head; she would never understand Grace. But whatever the reason, for the last few weeks Ian had been in a deep depression. And the deeper his depression, the lighter Maggie's heart became, because that meant he was no longer seeing her. Perhaps it was truly all over between them.

"I hear ye've been doin' some fine work for McPherson," she said. "I heard the looms you've been fixin' are better than new."

"Thanks, Maggie. But you know I haven't only been working for McPherson. I bought two of those looms myself." All three looked at him in astonishment.

"Och, Ian, ye didna'," cried Jeannie. "That's wonderful. Next thing ye know ye'll have your own mill."

"Not so fast," said Ian. "Two looms is a far cry from a mill. But it's a start, and I've got my first contract. I'm running a couple of bolts of broadsilk for Lambert. It's an odd looking purple color, and he doesn't want the bother of setting up a run for it. I'm going to need some help, though. Maggie, do you think you could find time to do some weaving for me?"

"Me?" Maggie's face was radiant. "Och, Ian, I'd be glad tae do anything tae help ye. But ye know I've not done a lot o' weavin'. I have taken over the looms when one o' the men were out sick, but I'm nae expert."

"You're a fine weaver, Maggie. I know, I've heard from some of the men you've covered for. They say you're as good as a full-fledged operator any day."

Maggie blushed with pleasure. The thought of working alongside of Ian filled her with joy. She couldn't wait to get started. "When do you want me to begin?"

"After work tomorrow if possible."

"Ye canna keep Maggie working those late hours ye've been keeping lately," said Aunt Flora. "Young girls need their rest."

"I promise I won't keep her out too late," said Ian. He smiled at Maggie, and she felt herself dissolving inside. "Just remind me of the time once in a while, Maggie—I tend to lose track of it."

Maggie knew she would never have the heart to remind

him—any time spent with Ian was precious to her, she wasn't going to do anything to cut it short.

All the next day she waited impatiently for the final whistle to blow at the mill. Even though she'd put in twelve hard hours tending the winding machines, she was ready to work several more hours on Ian's looms. He was waiting for her when she emerged from Potter's side door, they waved to Jeannie and Moira who were chatting on the sidewalk, and set off for McPherson's shop. It wasn't much more than a shed, with rough board walls, a concrete floor, and a few grime-stained windows. A couple of solitary light bulbs hung suspended from primitive wires running across the ceiling, and a small pot-bellied stove stood in the corner.

"It can get cold in here in the winter," said Ian. "The wind whistles through the cracks."

*It could do with a good sweeping,* thought Maggie. *On Saturday I'll come over with a bucket and broom and clean the place up a little.* But if the shed was dirty, the looms were polished and shining, and they spent the next few hours setting up the warping frame.

While they were working, McPherson arrived with a plateful of cold mutton pies. He was a small, wiry man, with short sandy hair that seemed to stick up in all directions. He watched with approval as Maggie deftly handled the delicate threads. She knew what she was doing.

"Can ye take a break and ha'e something tae eat?" he said.

"Sure," said Ian, wiping his hands on his trousers. "We've got the worst of it done."

"It wasn't so hard," said Maggie. "But I'm ready for dinner."

"Not much of a dinner," said Ian apologetically, "and we don't even have a table."

"It's just fine," said Maggie, smiling cheerfully as the three of them sat on wooden crates eating their pies.

"There's a place out back," muttered McPherson,

pointing to a small shed barely visible from the window. "Better take a candle with you." Maggie mumbled an acknowledgement and hoped she'd never have to go there.

"I'm going to be grindin' down a few small pieces, laddie. I'll be finished afore ye are, so be sure ye lock up."

"We can't stay late tonight, or Aunt Flora'll have my hide. Anyway, Maggie must be tired." Ian smiled at her. "You're doing a great job, but I don't want to wear you out." Maggie, whose back had been aching for the last two hours, suddenly found she wasn't tired at all. But Ian insisted they get home before ten. "Tomorrow's another day," he said as he took her arm. Maggie's step was light as she thought of tomorrow and the next day and the next day. All spent with Ian. What more could she ask?

On Saturday when Ian came down to breakfast, Aunt Flora informed him that Maggie had beaten him to it and was already over in the shop. He found her there, up to her elbows in soapsuds. The floor was clean, the windows sparkling. A small crate had been covered with a cloth to make a table, and a couple of boxes set up as chairs.

"Gosh, Maggie, it looks great. Wait till old Mac gets here—he'll think he's in the wrong shop. I guess we needed a woman's touch. Thanks."

He put his arm around her shoulders and gave her a brief hug. Maggie felt her heart leap for joy, the color rushed into her cheeks and she could hardly speak.

" 'Twas nothin' Ian," she murmured. "And now we'd better be gettin' to work."

Once the looms were running it was impossible to talk, but Maggie didn't mind. She was in charge of the weaving, while Ian and McPherson concentrated on the repair work. The day was warm, so the door stood open and the sun shone in. Light also streamed in through the now clean windows, brightening everything. She could see Ian at his workbench, his shoulders broad under his heavy blue shirt, his hair falling casually over his forehead. Old Mac bobbed up and down, running his grease-stained hands through his spiky hair and grinning cheerfully. The purple cloth flowed like a jeweled carpet from the looms that clickety-clacked their steady familiar rhythm. Ian looked up from his bench and smiled at her, and Maggie knew she had never been so happy in her whole life.

# CHAPTER
## ❧ 18 ❧

GRACE was worried. She hadn't heard a word from Ian. She'd written and told him about her trip to Atlantic City, not mentioning Austin, of course, and she'd written again asking him to come over on a Sunday. She knew he usually worked all day on Saturday, but still she received no reply. What could be wrong?

New York was in the grip of a heatwave, and as day after endless day went by Grace began to look a little peaked. The office was stifling in spite of the fan set on the windowsill, and she found herself making several trips to the ladies' room to wash her face and splash on some cooling cologne.

"You need a vacation, Miss Cameron—a few days by the sea, perhaps," Mr. Harwood suggested. But a vacation by the sea was the last thing she wanted; even now, the memory of Austin caused her to blush hotly. She picked up a paper and fanned herself.

"It's the heat," she said. "But it's bound to break soon, and we're too busy to think about vacations."

He shook his head. "You're incredible. One in a million. What did I ever do to deserve such devotion?" He smiled at her warmly. "But I certainly do appreciate it. And you're right, business has never been better, especially now that we have secured the Kawasaki account.

Both he and Mr. Gorman were impressed with your professionalism, by the way.''

''But I hardly said a word,'' she said.

He laughed. ''Perhaps that's what impressed them.''

His eyes, however, told her that it was more than her silence that pleased them. He always treated her with the utmost formality, but she often glanced up to see him looking at her with an intensity that was pleasantly disturbing, and occasionally, when their eyes met, she could feel an almost tangible current coursing between them. He was a man who exuded power and excitement without moving from his chair. She admired that.

''Well, if it's work you want, we certainly have plenty of it,'' he said. ''Do you think you could type up these specs before you leave tonight?''

She was glad of the opportunity. Glad to have work that occupied her mind so that she didn't have to think about . . . about anything.

She stayed late, but it was still suffocating when she emerged onto the street. She was more tired than she wanted to admit and was relieved that it was Friday, even though a lonely weekend awaited her. Most people had left the city. Who could blame them? she thought as she clung to the strap of the rattling, swaying trolley car that eventually disgorged her back onto the hot pavement. Waves of sultry, putrid air beat back at her from the walls and sidewalks until at last she climbed the stairs into the dim, comparative coolness of her room.

She leaned back against the door and closed her eyes, waiting for the slight dizziness to pass. Then she removed her hat and gloves and hurried down the hall to the bathroom which she shared with the other girls on the floor. It was not just to splash on cologne that Grace had been making her frequent trips to the ladies' room. She was late. Later than she'd ever been before. At first she'd thought nothing of it, but the other morning, as she poured herself a cup of coffee, she had been engulfed by a wave of nausea. She still couldn't believe it. One brief moment of passion. One night spent in Ian's arms. Surely that couldn't result in a baby. But from the evidence, or rather lack of evidence, it appeared it could. She looked at herself in the tiny, cracked mirror. She looked the same, a little pale perhaps, but the same.

"Oh, Ian," she murmured. "Please come soon. I need you."

As she was on her way back to her room, Mrs. Murphy called up the stairs. "Grace, sure'n I have a letter for ye." Relief flooded her, and she ran down the stairs to clutch the small envelope from the landlady's hands, then stared at it in disappointment. It was from Jeannie.

"I completely forgot to tell ye, although he did say it wasn't important . . ."

Mrs. Murphy was rambling on about something but Grace wasn't paying any attention, she was still staring at the small, rather grubby envelope from her cousin. Why, oh why wasn't it from Ian? But gradually the force of Mrs. Murphy's words began to penetrate.

"What did you say, Mrs. Murphy?"

"I've been trying to tell ye. That nice young man from New Jersey came to see ye, and wasn't it the same time ye were off to Atlantic City with that handsome boss of yours . . ." Grace stared at her in horror.

"But Mrs. Murphy, I didn't go away with Mr. Harwood. He just took me to the station. I was alone in Atlantic City."

"Well, an' how was I to know that when you drove away together? I thought ye had to attend some important meetin' . . ." She looked at Grace's pale, unhappy face, and was immediately contrite. "Oh, Grace, now I never thought for a minute that ye were doin' anything improper. I hope that young man didn't—"

"No, I'm sure he didn't. Don't worry about it, Mrs. Murphy."

Grace went slowly back upstairs. Now she knew why

she hadn't heard from Ian. Why he hadn't answered her letters. He was hurt. It seemed that she was always hurting Ian. But surely he couldn't believe she would start an affair with her boss after what had happened between them. She was Ian's, and Ian was hers. And now she was carrying his baby. She felt a tremor of wonder at the thought. Ian's baby. Once he knew that, he would come to her with open arms. She would write to him immediately, but first she would see what Jeannie had to say.

She sat down, opened the envelope, and studied the carefully penciled words. Jeannie wrote well, and Grace always enjoyed her letters. She began to read:

"Dear Grace,
Wait until you hear my news. I think it's grand. 'Tis about Ian. He's bought himself two looms, and he's starting his own business. But that's not all. He's walking out with Maggie. Of course, 'tis nothing official yet. They're not engaged or anything, but Maggie's helping him at the shop, and they spend all their time together. Dinna ye think they'll make the perfect pair? Of course, Maggie's been in love wi' Ian since the first day we got here . . ."

Grace put the letter down. She couldn't read any more. Maggie and Ian. Yes, they were the perfect pair. Little Maggie, who'd been in love with him forever. She'd never run off and leave him. She'd be loyal and true no matter what happened. She'd put Ian's needs above her own in a way she, Grace, had never been able to. She stood up and paced the floor. She could picture Maggie working in the shop, her happy rosy face beaming up at Ian; picture her cheerfully scrubbing, cleaning, and cooking for Ian. *I can't come between them now,* she thought.

Her mind was in a turmoil. *I'm being punished,* she thought wildly. *God is punishing me.* She needed Ian, needed him desperately in a way she'd never needed him before. She wanted him by her side. She wanted to see the look of wonder on his face when he learned about the baby. His baby. *But I can't tell him now,* she thought, tears running down her cheeks. *He must never know. No one must ever know.*

The days slid by one after another and Grace managed to perform all her necessary tasks. She rose, dressed, breakfasted, and went to work. There she concentrated on her secretarial duties. Never had the files been so up-to-date, the invoices paid so promptly, letters typed so rapidly. Outwardly she was the perfect secretary—cool, composed, efficient—but inside she was dead.

She moved in a small vacuum of detachment. She gave no thought to the past, made no plans for the future, but was gripped by a spiritual and emotional lethargy. Just as the heavy hand of summer held the earth in bondage, oppressing the land, silencing even the birds, so the heaviness of her heart dragged at her spirit. She no longer cared. Nothing mattered.

As if unaware of her condition, she frowned in puzzlement when her skirt failed to button, nodded in vacant agreement when Mr. Harwood scheduled meetings for October and November, and stared blankly at Mrs. Murphy when she suggested she get a new roommate. Worry had been replaced by paralysis which continued until the afternoon when, sitting across from Mr. Harwood, notebook in hand, she felt a tiny but definite kick in her ribs. She sat bolt upright, her eyes wide. Mr. Harwood looked at her curiously.

"Is something wrong, Miss Cameron?" he asked.

"No, it's just—Would you excuse me for a moment, please?" She left his office and went directly to the ladies' room. There she stood, clutching the sink and looking, as if for the first time, at the pale face and dark circled eyes reflected in the mirror. And then she felt it again. That small determined kick. Proof that a real, live, little human being was growing inside of her! The wonder of it washed over her, causing her legs to tremble, as she was alternately filled with elation and despair. Now it was real. Now it was no longer possible to deny it. She was having a baby.

Unable to settle down to work, Grace wrote a note for Mr. Harwood explaining that she was not feeling well and left the office. She walked the streets of New York, stopping to stare in a store window at a display of baby clothes, bassinets, cribs, and baby carriages. She tried to imagine having a crib delivered to her room at Mrs. Murphy's. Her landlady would be shocked. A wave of hysteria swept over her. What was she going to do once the baby was born? Bring it to the office? Keep it in a cradle beside her desk? Hide it in the filing cabinet? She fought down the urge to burst into a wild and reckless laughter that hovered on the brink of tears. The days of denial were over. Soon there would be no way to conceal the fact that Miss Grace Cameron, an unmarried woman, was in the family way.

She walked on, her feet finally leading her to the river. Leaning on the rail she looked down into the dark, swirling depths. Was this the answer? Was dying the only way out? She remembered the long, sad poem that was one of Lady McLeod's favorites. She had never really grasped its meaning, but now she did.

Take her up tenderly
Lift her with care
Fashioned so slenderly
Young and so fair.

*No*, thought Grace, *no,no, no*. She turned away from the dark seductive waters of the river, away from the soft lapping sounds that whispered of sleep and safekeeping. She wouldn't die. She couldn't kill the small life stirring within her. She didn't know what she was going to do, but she would not give in.

That night as she sat in her room, Grace tried to assess

her future. She realized that she had no one to turn to. Whatever happened to her, she would have to face it alone. She had managed to save a few dollars, but how long would they last once she stopped working? She knew she couldn't continue to work at Harwood Enterprises in her condition, neither could she stay at Mrs. Murphy's; not only because she would no longer be able to afford to pay the rent, but Mrs. Murphy prided herself on keeping a respectable house—an unmarried mother would be a disgrace. She would have to look for a cheap room somewhere and find some work she could do at home. Sewing perhaps. Grace sighed. She had learned to sew from necessity, but she hated it.

The next day she called Miss Finch at the switchboard and asked her to tell Mr. Harwood she would not be in for a few days. She didn't want to speak to him personally; she had a feeling that he would soon see through her excuses and get right to the heart of her secret. She couldn't face that. Neither could she face the knowing looks of the girls at the office, the gossip and speculation, the snide remarks. She knew that she had left Harwood Enterprises forever, and the thought added to her feeling of despair.

Grace found a small room for rent just off Mulberry Street. She bought herself a cheap gold-colored ring and gave her name as Mrs. Cameron, explaining that her husband was away at sea. He hoped to be home before the baby was born. The janitor, who spoke little English, nodded and grinned. Grace looked around. She shuddered at the noise, the heat, the dirt, and the smell. It was that same awful smell that she had endured on the journey over—a mixture of wet wool, garlic, and unwashed humanity. She fanned herself with her hankie. The janitor grinned again and gestured to the grimy window that let out onto an iron fire-escape. Grace looked out and saw old mattresses and bedding on the platforms, and even on some of the steps, where whole families slept to escape the unbearable heat. Down below the street was swarming with people. She hated it already, but it was all she could afford.

She returned to Mrs. Murphy's and gathered up her few things. She had decided to tell her landlady that she had to leave New York for a while and thought it best to vacate the apartment.

"Sure'n I'll be glad to hold it for you, Grace. How long do ye expect to be gone?"

"I'm really not sure, Mrs. Murphy. I'll look you up when I get back, but I think you'd better find a new tenant."

"An' what of your fine new job, indeed, you're not givin' that up are ye?"

"No, no. This is really a business trip. I—I'll be buying silk."

"Fancy that now. My, Grace, ye really are gettin' up in the world," said Mrs. Murphy. "Next thing you'll be livin' on Fifth Avenue with all those society ladies."

*Oh, how I wish,* thought Grace, and she hoped Mrs. Murphy would never find out that she was moving to Mulberry Street. *I'm not going up in the world,* she thought bitterly, *I'm going down, down, down.* She bade her a quick goodbye and hurried away.

A week or so later Mrs. Murphy received an unexpected visitor. It was Mr. Harwood. He was looking for Grace.

"But she's off on a business trip." Mrs. Murphy eyed him suspiciously. "Sure'n you're her boss, ye must know where she is."

"I'm afraid I don't, Mrs. Murphy. She left without saying a word."

"An why would she be doin' that now? She told me she was to be buyin' silk. What kind of a firm is it that sends a young girl off to buy silk, and then says they don't know where she is. Did she go off to foreign parts? Is she in some kind of trouble?"

"We didn't send her to any foreign parts. Did she leave with anyone, Mrs. Murphy—a young man, perhaps?"

Mrs. Murphy was indignant.

"And what are you suggestin', sir? Grace was a good Christian girl. She'd not be goin' off with some young man."

"I'm sorry, I'm just trying to think where she might have gone. I do need to get in touch with her. Did she leave a forwarding address?"

"She did not. All she said was that she'd be gone for a while, but that she'd look me up when she got back."

"If you learn where she went or if you hear from her, a postcard even, would you please call me immediately? It's most important. Here's my card."

"Well, I suppose it can do no harm, although ye'll probably be gettin' a letter before I do."

"Perhaps. But, please, even if it's several months before you hear from her, call me just the same, right away. And please take this to cover the cost of the phone call." He handed her a twenty dollar bill, and she gasped in astonishment.

"Thank ye, sir. I'll be sure to call ye if I hear anything at all."

The next few months were sheer misery for Grace. She did get some sewing jobs from the several small shirt factories in the neighborhood, mostly making buttonholes and sewing on buttons. She made very little money and had to work long hours. Gradually the stifling heat gave way to a raw damp cold. Her room was never warm, and as the days grew shorter, she sat, wrapped in layers of sweaters, huddled over a small table working by the light of a single low wattage bulb, late into the night.

She did try to eat a proper meal at least once a day, and dutifully drank a glass of milk. The baby grew inside of her and kicked vigorously, so that she was constantly aware of her condition, which was now obvious to everyone. The other women in the tenement pointed to her stomach and smiled. "Bambino—big bambino," they told her. In their broken English they directed her to a clinic where she could have her baby for free.

She hated the clinic. The women had to line up in the hall outside the dispensary, sometimes for hours, before they went in for a cursory examination by an elderly doctor who spoke only German. He counted the months on his fingers and wrote something down in a ledger.

"February," said the nurse. "You'll probably deliver in February. Come to the outpatient clinic when you start getting pains regularly. Show them this card and they'll try to find you a bed in the ward."

# CHAPTER
## ❧ 19 ❧

Ian didn't know what he would have done without Maggie. He insisted on paying her for the weaving, but she was reluctant to take it.

"Nay, nay, that's too much, Ian. I dinna want any money. I'm happy tae be able tae help ye."

"I know you are, Maggie, but if you don't let me pay you, I won't feel I can ask you again. And you've done such a good job . . ." He looked at her hopefully.

"Ye know I'll help ye any time ye ask, Ian."

"But I won't ask if you don't let me pay you. Besides, Mac will throw me out if he thinks I'm letting you work for free."

She finally gave in and pocketed the few extra dollars. She didn't feel right about spending them, so she decided to start a savings account. The idea of going into a bank by herself terrified her, so Jeannie came with her and showed her how to fill out the form and where to sign her name. Jeannie didn't seem at all intimidated by the great marble pillars and polished floors of the bank, and was quite unimpressed by the haughty young woman who took Maggie's money, explained something about interest, and handed her a little black book showing the amount of twelve dollars and seventy-five cents. Maggie pocketed the little black book with pride. *Now*, she thought, *if Ian needs some money for a project I'll be able to lend it to him.* Somehow that made it all right to let him pay her.

She continued to accompany him to the shop, even when there wasn't any weaving to be done. She kept the place clean, and as the nights grew chill she stoked up the little pot-bellied stove and kept a pot of soup simmering on it, or boiled water for tea.

"Aye, lass, ye've brightened this place up for us, nae doot aboot that," said McPherson with a sigh of satisfaction. " 'Tis a fine young woman ye have here, laddie—better not let her get away." He winked broadly at Maggie, who blushed prettily.

Ian said nothing, but sipped his tea and looked around him. Maggie was certainly a wonderful help to him. She was the kind of girl who didn't mind scrimping and saving, and who'd enjoy working alongside her man to help him reach his goals. She would be content to share the hard times along with the good times, whereas Grace . . . He closed his eyes and gritted his teeth. He would not think of Grace.

"Time to get back to work," he said, standing up.

At Christmas Ian invited Maggie to the holiday dance held every year by the Scottish Club. It was a festive occasion. Several of the men wore dress kilts and the ladies wore tartan sashes over their gowns. Maggie felt very stylish in her dress of rose pink sateen with a wine velveteen jacket, Aunt Flora's cameo broach at her neck, and tucked in her sleeve, a beautiful embroidered hankie that had been a present from Grace. With her shy glances, pink cheeks, and bouncy curls, she quite captivated the crowd and Ian found himself receiving several bantering compliments as they spun around the dance floor. Ian had a smooth natural rhythm, and Maggie a bubbly enthusiasm, which made them an endearing couple.

Whenever Maggie looked back on that evening it seemed to her that everything about it was perfect. The men drank their good Scotch whiskey, and she had a shandy with the other ladies as they all sat down to watch the Paterson Thistle Dancers put on a demonstration of jigs and reels. When the dancers finished their performance the crowd was so enthusiastic that several of the guests got up to perform their own sets. Skirts were raised, heels kicked up, fingers snapped, arms linked as the pipes skirled and the old tunes echoed all the way from the Culins to the lowlands, bringing, for a brief moment, the tang o' the heather into a small, stuffy hall in the heart of Paterson.

It was afterwards, when the dancers were mopping their brows and fanning themselves, that Ian and Maggie stepped outside for a breath of fresh air, and Ian kissed her. To Maggie it was as if all the stars in the frosty sky exploded into light. She could feel her heart pounding in her chest, and she clung to him, returning his kisses with a passion that astonished both of them.

And Ian, with Maggie's firm young body pressed close to his, inhaling the sweet scent of her hair and skin, the warmth of her kisses on his lips, found himself caught up in the moment. After the loneliness and rejection of the past months it was a heady experience and he found himself murmuring, "I love you, Maggie. Marry me, marry me." And Maggie didn't hesitate for a second.

"Yes," she said, "oh, Ian, yes, yes, yes."

And so they became officially engaged. Maggie was ecstatic, Ian seemed well pleased, Aunt Flora was gratified, and Jeannie declared it was a match made in heaven. The wedding was set for June.

For Grace, Christmas was just another day. A day of trying to keep warm by drinking endless cups of weak tea. She wondered what Maggie and Jeannie and Aunt Flora were doing. Particularly she wondered what Maggie and Ian were doing. Were they quietly holding hands in church? Would Ian kiss Maggie under the mistletoe? She couldn't bear to think of Ian kissing anyone else, not even Maggie.

*But it's your own fault,* she told herself. *You were greedy. You tried to have it all and you've ended up with nothing.* But that wasn't true, and a firm pressure under her ribs reminded her that far from ending up with nothing she was responsible for a new life. A child.

Her own life seemed so unreal that she had trouble visualizing actually having the baby, holding it in her arms, feeding it, changing it, rocking it to sleep. It wasn't until some of the women in the other apartments offered her a few well-washed and mended baby clothes did she realize she would need a layette. In between her buttons and button-holes she started to sew scraps of linen. Holding up the tiny dresses and nightgowns she kept telling herself that soon she would no longer be alone; there would be two of them in this ugly little room. Herself and the baby. Ian's baby. She put her head down on the table and began to weep.

She had sent a short note to Aunt Flora wishing her and the girls a Merry Christmas, and sent them each an embroidered handkerchief from the set she had won playing bridge with Mrs. DeWitt-Kenton. She had told them she was very busy with her job and had not put a return address on the letter. She did the same with Maisie. She wondered if she would ever see any of them again.

It was a relief actually when the holidays were over and life returned to normal. This was a slack time for the garment workers, and Grace had not been able to get much work. She had finished the layette, scraping up her last few dollars to buy a woollen shawl to wrap the baby in when she brought it home. She never tried to speculate on whether it would be a boy or girl, but the women pointed to her prominent belly, grinned, and said, "Boy."

Grace, like many young women, knew little about the physical aspects of giving birth, but she knew enough to recognize the brief, intense pain that came to her one cold, sleety morning in February. She quickly dressed, blowing on her fingers to warm them before she could button her boots. She made herself a cup of tea and waited. The pain came again. She packed a few personal things in a bag, made up her small bed, looked at the little pile of baby clothes, and then, realizing she would need something to dress the baby in, she picked out the smallest of the wrappers, a tiny sweater and bonnet, and the precious wool shawl. She was ready.

She walked to the clinic, head bent against the icy rain, until she arrived at the outpatient door. A gust of warm, stuffy air greeted her and she welcomed the warmth. The clinic was already crowded with people, some wracked by coughing, others flushed with fever, some, white-faced and hollow-eyed simply sat and stared into space. The place smelled of sickness and despair.

She took her card to the desk where a harried clerk checked it.

"How far apart?" she said. Grace looked at her puzzled. "How often are you getting the pains?"

"I'm getting one now," said Grace, gripping her bag and leaning on the counter.

"Better have the doctor take a look at you while I see if I can get you a bed. He's over there." She nodded to where there was a long line of women in various stages of pregnancy. Grace groaned but took her place at the end of the row. The line moved slowly, and Grace could see it might be several hours before she saw the doctor. The pains were not coming too often, but when they did come they were severe, causing her to double over and catch her breath. When the other women realized she was actually in labor, they moved her up to the front of the line, murmuring sympathetically and shaking their heads over the inhuman system.

The doctor gave her a quick examination and ordered a bed for her in the charity ward. Grace flushed with embarrassment that she should be having her baby in the charity ward, but to the people at the hospital she was just another poor immigrant mother, and they thought nothing of it. She was led to a long, narrow room lined with rows of iron beds placed side by side with barely room to move between them. She was shown a bed at the far end of the room and was told to get undressed and put on the stiff, white garment known as a hospital gown.

"I'll see if I can find you a screen," said the nurse, and returned a moment later with a small screen, behind which Grace struggled out of her damp clothes and into the gown. It was harsh and scratchy, but it was clean. She folded her own clothes and slid them under the bed. Then she climbed into the high, narrow bed, and was horrified to discover that she had to lie on a rubber sheet, propped up by a pillow that felt as if it were filled with rocks.

The nurse came again, and this time she had a notepad with her and began asking Grace for her history.

"Is this your first pregnancy?"

"Yes."

"Do you suffer from tuberculosis or any other debilitating disease?"

"No."

"Religion?"

"Presbyterian, I guess," said Grace.

"Husband's full name?" Grace stared at her blankly. She had never given a thought to a first name for her imaginary husband. The nurse shrugged and continued questioning her, until a gut-wrenching pain hit Grace and the nurse quickly put away her notebook and placed her hands on Grace's stomach.

"Baby's starting to descend," she said. "I'll be back." Grace leaned back and sighed.

"Hurts, don't it?" The remark came from the next bed where a young girl, who didn't look much more than seventeen, was sitting up and watching her.

"Yes, it does," said Grace.

"Don't get no better either," said her fellow sufferer. "I'm 'aving my third, so I know." Grace looked at the girl in amazement—she seemed so young. "I 'eard them

askin' you all them questions. Nosy bunch aren't they?
Wot's it to them if you're married or not. But the nurses
ain't nothing to them society ladies wot comes in 'ere with
their noses in the air. Do gooders they're supposed to be.
Don't do much good as far as I sees it.''

Grace was swept by a terrible premonition.

"Who are these society ladies?" she asked.

"Calls themselves a Society for some sort o' females."

"Council for the Training of Indigent Females?" said
Grace.

"That's it, although if you ask me, all they're really
interested in is gettin' cheap help. They come in 'ere and
starts asking you all sorts of questions. Then they tries to
take your baby away and get you to go to work in their big
fancy houses. That Mrs. Ken something, she's the worst.''

"Mrs. DeWitt-Kenton," said Grace faintly.

"That's the one. I see you've been up against them before."

*Yes,* thought Grace, *I've been up against them before.*
And suddenly she knew she couldn't stay in this bed, in
this hospital. No matter what happened to her, she could
not face Mrs. DeWitt-Kenton.

"I—I don't feel well," she said. "Where's the bathroom?"

"You ain't supposed to go to the bathroom. They'll
bring you a spit basin, or a bedpan if you 'ave to go."

"No, I must get to the bathroom," said Grace. She slid
out of bed and retrieved her bundle of clothes.

"The bathroom's through that door and down the hall.
But you'll get into awful trouble they finds you there."

"Don't worry about me," said Grace. "I won't get into
trouble."

She looked up and down the ward. The head nurse sat
at the desk, but she was intent on her paperwork. The
other nurse was attending a patient behind a screen, so
Grace quickly slipped out of the door and down the hallway until she found the bathroom. There she dressed,

shuddering as she put on her cold, damp clothes. She abandoned the hospital robe in the bathroom, found the nearest exit, and escaped into a narrow alleyway lined with trash cans, that eventually led back into the street. A stinging, icy rain was falling, and she ducked into a doorway, clutching her bag as pain gripped her once more.

Where to go? She couldn't face the thought of returning to her empty room. She needed help. Someone, anyone, who knew about birthing babies. She had to think, to collect her wits, or she'd wind up having the baby here on a street corner. She pulled herself upright and made her way to the curb just in time to board the cross-town trolley. There was really only one place she could go, one place where she knew she would be taken in. Mrs. Murphy's.

By the time she got to the door of her old boarding house she was soaked to the skin and shivering violently. She rang the bell and waited as she heard Mrs. Murphy shuffling along the hall. The door opened and Grace all but fell inside.

"Help me," she said, and clutched her stomach.

"Glory be to God and all the saints," exclaimed Mrs. Murphy. " 'Tis Grace. Sure'n an' come inside, 'tis soaking wet yet are, and chilled to the bone."

"Mrs. Murphy. I need a doctor, or someone."

The landlady now looked at Grace, and her eyes widened in amazement as she took in her condition. "Jesus, Mary, and Joseph, don't be tellin' me now that your time has come." Grace nodded wordlessly. "Set down, set down an' I'll try to get a hold of Mrs. Flynn, 'tis she who delivers all the babies in the neighborhood. Ah, Grace, 'tis hard times ye've fallen on. Mother of God, who'd have thought this . . ."

She left Grace in her small sitting room huddled by the radiator, and went down the hallway to the telephone. There she called the corner stationery store and left word for Mrs. Flynn to come to the house.

"She's off on a case," she explained to Grace on her

return. ''Don't know when she'll get back, but she always stops in the store before she goes home, and they'll send her over here.''

Grace didn't say anything, just moved even closer to the radiator. She was shivering violently.

*Dear God, now what am I going to do?* thought Mrs. Murphy. Grace acted like she was going to have the baby any minute, and besides, she looked really ill. Maybe pneumonia. She should have a doctor, but who would pay for it? Then she remembered the twenty dollar bill and Mr. Harwood's request. *No matter when you hear from her let me know.* Did he expect something like this? Was he responsible? Mrs. Murphy fumbled in her pocket and found his card.

It took her some time to get past the switchboard, but she finally got through to a secretary.

''If you leave the message with me, ma'am, I'll see that he gets it.''

'' 'Tis Mr. Harwood himself I must speak to. 'Tis personal and very urgent.'' After some muffled conversation back and forth he came on the line.

''Harwood here.''

''Oh, sir, 'tis Grace. Miss Cameron. Ye said to call you whenever I heard from her. Well she's here. An' she's sick, she's . . . sir, she needs a doctor, now, right away.''

''Mrs. Murphy I'm on my way, and I'll bring a doctor with me. And thank you.''

She returned to where Grace sat shivering.

''Mrs. Flynn will be here as soon as she can. In the meantime ye'd better get out o' those wet clothes, you'll catch your death o' cold.''

She showed Grace into the bedroom and helped her get undressed and into bed. She didn't mention Mr. Harwood—she had a feeling that Grace would not be pleased that she had called him—but if he was the one who made the poor girl pregnant, then it was his duty to take care of her. Besides, it seemed as if he wanted to.

By now Grace was only too glad to get into bed. The pains were coming closer together and getting stronger. She moaned aloud and gripped the bedclothes. God, she never knew having a baby was so painful. She was dimly aware of the doorbell ringing, and heard footsteps coming down the hall, but nothing prepared her for the sight of the man who marched into her room and stood at the end of her bed looking down on her.

"Mr. Harwood," she gasped.

He pulled a chair up close to the bed and took her hand.

"Listen, Grace. I know you're close to your time, and I can see you're in pain. I've brought a doctor with me. You are going to be all right. But first I want you to do something for me. For both of us. It's important for you and the baby." She looked into his eyes and saw an urgency there. "I want you to marry me." She stared at him, aghast.

"Marry you now? When I'm like this . . . I can't. I just can't."

"Yes, you can. Afterwards, if you want a divorce I'll give it to you. But for now, I've brought a justice of the peace with me. He'll marry us right here and now. Mrs. Murphy can be the witness. Grace, where else are you going to go?"

She stared at him with eyes that were bright with fever. "You don't want to marry me. Not now. People will think . . ."

"I don't care what people think. I care about you, Grace. Please."

It didn't make any sense. But then nothing made any sense. Her head was swimming, her body gripped with pain. She was alone, penniless, an outcast from society, drowning in a sea of poverty, and here was this man, whom she only knew as an employer, throwing her a lifeline. She lay back on the pillow, exhausted.

"If you're sure it's what you want."

"I'm sure," he said.

And so Grace and Mr. Harwood were married before a justice of the peace, with Mrs. Murphy and the doctor as witnesses, and then, five hours later, Grace delivered a healthy, seven-pound baby boy.

# CHAPTER
## ❧ 20 ❧

GRACE didn't develop pneumonia, but she did have a severe chill. The doctor prescribed a medication in addition to hot soups and custards, and, of course, she was to remain in bed. He wanted to bring in a wet nurse, but Grace refused. She was going to nurse her own baby. She looked at the tiny creature in her arms. His face was pink and his head was dusted with gold from a faint little sprouting of downy hair.

"Sure'n he's a beauty, and doesn't he look just like his mother now," exclaimed Mrs. Murphy. Grace could not stem the tears that rolled down her cheeks; she had both hoped and feared he would look like Ian. Her mind was still in a daze as she tried to focus on the events of the last twenty-four hours. She still didn't understand how Mr. Harwood had come to be at Mrs. Murphy's. Mr. Harwood—she had to stop calling him that. His name was Robert—Rob—he'd said. And he was now her husband. She had become Mrs. Robert Harwood, and everyone, Mrs. Murphy included, would assume that this was his child. Why? Why had he insisted on marrying her?

"As soon as you're strong enough I want to bring you home," he told her. "I've already told the servants to prepare a room for you and the baby."

"Have ye picked out his name?" asked Mrs. Murphy. "Is he to be Robert junior?"

"No!" exclaimed Grace in a swift and violent reaction. Then she looked from Mrs. Murphy's startled face to her husband's, which was unreadable. "He is to be called . . . Andrew . . . after his grandfather."

"Of course," said Mr. Harwood smoothly. "Andrew is to be his name."

When Grace was finally well enough to leave, Mr. Harwood brought his carriage round, and mother and baby were carefully installed, well-wrapped in shawls and blankets. He then pressed a generous amount of money in Mrs. Murphy's reluctant hands.

"Sure, 'n 'tis glad I was to be able to help," she said.

"I know, I know, and I appreciate everything," he said.

It seemed to Grace that he had been paying out money ever since he arrived—to the justice of the peace, the doctor, and even to Mrs. Flynn, who arrived too late to do anything.

Grace had never been to Mr. Harwood's home, which was an elegant brownstone uptown on Fifth Avenue. Fifth Avenue, her longed-for destination, and now she was here, but through no efforts of her own. Sometimes it seemed it was all a strange dream and she would wake up back in the cold, ugly tenement room, with the cracked walls, the rusty pipes, and the cockroaches. She shuddered.

"Cold, my dear? We'll soon have you back in bed."

"I'm really fine, Mr.—Rob. I don't need to go to bed."

Once they arrived she was quickly whisked upstairs to her room. Rooms, actually—a sitting room, bedroom, and private bath. She was greeted by an elderly maid, who said her name was Jones, a parlormaid named Rosie, and Miss Maguire, the newly hired nanny, who immediately took charge of little Andrew.

Grace removed her wraps and sank down onto a chaise lounge.

"Would you like a pot of tea, Mrs. Harwood?" asked

Jones, her impassive face showing no surprise at this sudden arrival of a new wife and child.

"Yes, that would be nice," said Grace. "What about Mr. Harwood?"

"I'll ask him if he'd like to join you," she replied, and disappeared leaving Grace alone.

She looked around the room which was decorated in soft pastel shades, thick plush carpets underfoot, and lit on this dreary February day by several alabaster lamps with silk shades.

"If you don't like the decor, we can change it for you."

Mr. Harwood was standing in the doorway. He came into the room, followed by Jones carrying a tray, which she deposited on a small table by the window and then quietly withdrew. Grace's eyes filled with tears.

"Rob, it's all too much. It's too soon . . . I just can't believe all this is happening to me. Why? Why? You didn't have to ask me to marry you. You don't owe me anything."

"Grace, I love you," he said simply. "I fell in love with you that very first day you came to see me—cheeks pink, eyes flashing—to tell me I was being cheated. I'd never met anyone like you before. I knew I had to see more of you. Get to know you better. And the more I got to know you, the more and more I found myself falling in love with you."

"But I've just had another man's child. Surely that will have killed any love you might have had for me."

"You didn't marry him, did you? Or was he already married? No, you don't have to answer if you'd rather not."

She turned her head away. "He's—he's going to marry someone else." *There, I've said it,* thought Grace. *Ian is going to marry Maggie, and I must never, never try to come between them.*

Tears trickled down her cheeks. Her brand-new husband silently handed her a handkerchief. He had nothing but contempt for any man who would use Grace and then abandon her like this, but on the other hand his heart rejoiced to hear that the man *had* abandoned her. Because now she could truly become his. But he knew he had to proceed slowly. She had to get used to being Mrs. Robert Harwood.

For the next few weeks Grace felt as if she were staying at a luxurious hotel. Meals were brought to her on a tray. Little Andrew—bathed, powdered, and dressed in spotless baby clothes—was also brought to her for feeding and cuddling, but then taken away and carefully tucked into his brand-new crib by Nanny Maguire. For a while it was wonderful just to be lazy and let everyone wait on her, but after a while she got restless. As her strength returned she realized that this life of indolence was not for her. She needed to have things to do. She rang for Jones.

"Now that I'm feeling much stronger, Jones, I'd like to see the rest of the house, including the kitchens." Grace knew she had to establish her authority over this household quickly, or she would be forever treated as an outsider. She was sure there was much speculation and gossip about her below stairs, and it was up to her to squelch it.

As she toured the house she realized it needed a woman's touch. The drawing room was dark, the windows smothered by heavy, bottle-green draperies. Also, the morning room, which should have been light and airy, was crammed with heavy furniture. She would talk to Rob this evening. The kitchens were large and, she was pleased to note, spotless. She complimented the cook on the delicious meals, and received a broad smile and knew she had made at least one friend.

"From now on I'd like to take my coffee in the morning room. And Mr. Harwood and I will dine tonight in the dining room." She knew Rob usually had a tray brought to his study. Well, that was all right for a bachelor, but not for a married man.

"Yes, Mrs. Harwood. I'll cook something special for your first night downstairs," said Cook, beaming.

Back upstairs in the dining room, Grace looked around.

"Are there no flowers?" Jones looked at her blankly. "This house needs some flowers to brighten it up. I'll speak to Mr. Harwood about it this evening."

Rob was delighted at her interest.

"You're absolutely right, my dear. Since my late wife passed away, I'm afraid I've been living like a dreary old bachelor. You make any changes you wish. Which brings me to another matter. It is time I introduced you to society. We must start by a notice of Andrew's birth—in *The Times*, I think. We'll simply say Mr. and Mrs. Harwood announce . . . there is no need to give the date of our wedding."

"But Rob, what will people say? There'll be gossip and you'll be hurt by it."

"No, you're the one who'll be hurt, I'm afraid. Society is very hypocritical. You will be the one who is censured, you will be the one who is called names, while I, on the other hand, will be considered the very devil of a fellow. My stock at the club will go up considerably, and I'll be the envy of all the old graybeards settled for eternity in their favorite leather chairs. It's not fair, but it's true." He lifted her hand and kissed it gently. "But don't worry too much. Society also has a very short memory, and when they see how charming you are, all will be forgiven and forgotten. Of course, everyone will assume it is my child. Do you mind?"

"How could I possibly mind? But what about you? You are taking on a mother and child. It's going to change your peaceful way of life."

"I happen to like children; it's one of my hidden virtues." His face clouded for a minute and there was a sadness in his eyes she had never seen before. "I always wanted a family, but when my daughter was born . . . Well, my wife had a very hard time, and the child never developed properly—she died before her second birthday. Helen never recovered. She would never risk another.''

*Oh, poor Rob,* thought Grace. *A loveless marriage and a retarded child.* She resolved then and there to work at the marriage, for Rob's sake. He deserved it. They agreed to have a small reception following the christening.

''Do you have any family you'd like to invite, Grace? Anyone special you want for godmother and godfather? This should be your choice.''

*How kind he is,* she thought. ''Yes, I'd like to have my friend Maisie and her husband as godparents. And I have two young cousins—they live in Paterson. They're not very fashionable, I'm afraid. They work in the mills.'' She looked at him defiantly. ''I used to work in the mills once, too.''

He looked amused. ''But not for long, I'll bet.''

She laughed, ''No, not for long.'' Then she looked at this man she had married. He understood her. Understood her in a way no one else ever had. She took his hand. ''It's all right if I invite Maggie and Jeannie, then?''

''I can't wait to meet them,'' he replied.


Number ten was a house divided. Jeannie and Maggie desperately wanted to go to the christening. Aunt Flora was adamantly opposed.

''Whoever heard of a christening, when there wasna' e'en a proper wedding,'' she said. ''Shameful, that's what it is.''

''But Grace said they had a very quiet wedding, because Mr. Harwood's a widower,'' said Maggie.

''Hmph, was it in the church? Did the minister marry them? I'll guarantee he did not. I always knew Grace would come to a bad end.''

''She's living on Fifth Avenue, that doesna' sound like such a bad end tae me,'' said Jeannie.

''What about Ian, d'ye think he'll want tae go?'' asked Maggie.

"You should know that," said Aunt Flora.

"I didna' ask him," said Maggie shyly. Even though she and Ian were going to be married in June, there were some things they never talked about, and one of them was Grace. She knew Ian had gone into the city to see Grace last year and returned grim and tight-lipped, but he never mentioned her. And while Maggie felt a great lifting of her heart at the thought of her cousin being safely married, as if some intolerable burden had been removed from her shoulders, she still could not bring herself to mention Grace to Ian.

"Well, I asked him, and no, he doesna' want tae go," said Jeannie. "He doesna' have a very high opinion o' Mr. Harwood. Thinks he took advantage o' Grace."

"There's none goin' to take advantage of that one," said Aunt Flora. "The poor auld man probably didna' ha'e a chance."

"How do ye know he's an auld man?" asked Jeannie.

"He's rich isn't he? Probably living in sinful splendor. I'm sure 'tis no place for young girls like you."

"Well, I want to see what he's really like, so I'm goin'," said Jeannie firmly. "And since I canna go into the big city alone, Maggie will have tae come with me. We're Grace's only relatives, and ye should have your relatives there when your firstborn is christened."

Aunt Flora was beginning to recognize that determined glint in Jeannie's eye and knew it was useless to argue. But she had the last word.

"If ye need your good dresses washed and starched, ye'd better see to it yourselves. I've nae time to be fussing with such fripperies."

At the last minute Ian decided to escort them to the city. "You'd never find your way on your own," he said. "I'll drop you off at the house and pick you up later."

"Are ye sure ye dinna want tae come?" whispered Maggie.

"I'm sure," he said. He knew he couldn't face Grace. But even more he knew he couldn't face that man Harwood. Somehow he'd known right from the start that he was going to be bad for Grace. He'd seduced her, no doubt about it. Taking her away, staying at expensive hotels, probably plying her with wine, buying her expensive gifts. He knew Grace loved beautiful things, things he could never afford to give her. That was what had happened, he was sure. Grace didn't love this man. She couldn't, not after . . . He closed his eyes to blot out the memory.

"Ian, you're not listening," exclaimed Jeannie. "What time should we leave?" Ian dragged himself back and tried to pay attention as the two excited girls made their plans.

When they got to New York, Ian hailed a cab, much to Maggie's relief. She knew she would never dare to step into the dreadful traffic that filled the streets. And there were so many streets, all so crowded, so noisy. She trembled at the thought of being alone in such an awful place. Thank heavens for Ian.

"I'll be back here at six o'clock," he said as they stopped in front of an elegant house. "Don't be late."

Maggie watched him go with a sigh, and then turned to face the house that sat back from the street, surrounded by an ornate iron fence. Jeannie was already through the gate, up the steps, and rapping the brass knocker on the huge, carved front door. It swung open almost immediately, and they were faced by a smooth-looking gentleman wearing a starched white shirtfront and black swallowtails. He eyed them suspiciously.

"If you're here to help with the catering, the servants' entrance is around the back." Maggie made to turn away, but Jeannie quickly put her foot over the threshold.

"We're here to attend the christening. We're cousins." He looked at them as they stood holding hands, their white ruffled blouses somewhat wrinkled from the journey, their dark cotton skirts just topping their highly polished boots, and a slight flicker crossed his eyes, but he carefully consulted his list.

"Miss Margaret and Miss Jean McHugh?"

"That's us," exclaimed Jeannie, leaping through the doorway and dragging Maggie with her. "Where's Grace?"

"Mrs. Harwood is upstairs. Jones will show you the way."

Jones eyes them with disapproval but motioned them to follow her. She lumbered up the delicate curved stairway followed by an impatient Jeannie and a thoroughly subdued Maggie, who found herself alternately opening and closing her eyes as she encountered beautiful bouquets of flowers amid alabaster statues of naked men and women. When they reached the landing and came face to face with a huge oil painting of nymphs and satyrs she blushed violently and wanted to run downstairs and back into the street. Aunt Flora was right, Mr. Harwood did live in sinful splendor.

Jones tapped on a door. "Mrs. Harwood, your guests are here." The door was immediately pulled open by a pretty, dark-haired girl, whose cheeks dimpled as she smiled at them.

"Hello, I'm Maisie. I'm the godmother, and you must be the cousins from New Jersey. Which one's Maggie and which one's Jeannie?" They introduced themselves and Maisie gave each a hearty handshake. "We've just got back from the church. Grace is changing her clothes, she'll be out in a minute. She'll be so happy to see you—she's just been on pins and needles all day wondering if you'd come. I'm glad you're here, too. I think everyone else belongs to New York's Four Hundred."

Maggie and Jeannie had no idea who New York's Four Hundred were, but they sounded formidable. They were both quite speechless as they looked around the room. It was not a bedroom, as they had supposed, but a sitting room, all in shades of peach, beige, and creamy white.

The furniture was upholstered in the most exquisite brocade they had ever seen and looked much too fragile to sit on.

"Quite a place isn't it?" said Maisie. "This is Grace's suite. Wait till you see the bathroom; they even have heated racks to hold the towels."

"Do ye live here too?" asked Jeannie.

"Heavens, no. Me and my Joe have a two-room walk-up. We bang on the pipes to get heat and share a bathroom with the other tenants on the floor. Imagine having all this room to yourself! And servants, too. Look, you just pull on a rope," and she pointed to a thick plush bellrope that hung alongside the ornate white fireplace, "and a servant pops up to see what you want." Maggie couldn't restrain a nervous giggle.

"And Mr. Harwood, where is he?"

"Oh, he has his own suite down the hall," explained Maisie. Maggie couldn't believe that Grace and Mr. Harwood would have separate rooms. She always thought being married meant that you slept together. When she got married she wouldn't want Ian sleeping down the hall. A hot burning blush swept over her at such forbidden thoughts, but fortunately no one noticed, for at that moment the door opened and Grace swept into the room.

"Maggie, Jeannie," she rushed over to hug them. "Oh, I'm so glad you're here. Let me look at you. Why you both look so grown-up." Maggie particularly had blossomed. *How pretty she is, thought Grace. I suppose I should congratulate her.* But she couldn't. Not today. She must not think of Ian today.

"Can we see the baby?" asked Maggie. "Or is he asleep?"

"He's in the nursery with Nanny," said Grace. "It's his nap time, but perhaps you can see him later."

"Ye mean he doesna' sleep in wi' you?" asked an incredulous Maggie.

"Oh dear, no. He shares a room with Nanny, but of

course he has his own bassinet, crib, and special bath. You wouldn't believe how much furniture is needed for the little fellow.''

''Who does he look like?'' asked Jeannie. Grace seemed to catch her breath.

''Everyone says he looks like me,'' she said. ''But come, we can't stay here all day, Rob will be waiting for me.''

''Canna we stay up here?'' said Maggie shyly. ''Ye both look sae fine.'' Indeed Grace did look like a princess in a dress of pale lemon silk, with a slight bustle and delicate white embroidery covering the bodice and front panel. Maisie looked equally charming in her one good linen suit, with a white ruffled blouse. Maggie was only too aware of her heavy cotton skirt and black boots.

''I'm nae staying up here,'' declared Jeannie. ''I came tae get a look at this Mr. Harwood, and that's what I'm going tae do. After all, he's now a member of the family is he not?''

''Indeed he is,'' said Grace with a laugh. ''I just hope he meets with your approval. Come on.'' She led the way.

Maisie took Maggie's arm. ''Don't be nervous. They're only people after all. Just because they have money doesn't make them any better than you and me—sometimes quite the opposite. But I've met Rob Harwood, and he seems pretty nice. He's certainly mad about Grace, and she's going to need all the support she can get today. She's a brave girl.''

''Aye, Grace was always brave,'' said Maggie.

Mr. Harwood was waiting for them at the foot of the stairs. Maggie looked at the elegantly dressed man who took Grace by the hand. *But he's so old,* she thought, noting the few threads of gray in his dark hair, and immediately she had a vision of Ian—young, handsome, vital—and mentally shook her head. She would never understand Grace.

''You girls haven't met Mr. Harwood yet, have you?''

said Grace as she introduced them, and Maggie almost fainted when the gentleman in question took her hand and lightly kissed her cheek.

"Hello, cousin Maggie," he said with a smile. "At last I'm getting to meet you. And this must be Jeannie."

"How do ye do, Mr. Harwood," said Jeannie, shaking his hand.

"It's Rob," said Grace.

"Mr. Harwood," said Jeannie firmly. "I hear ye buy our silks and sell them for great sums of money." Maggie gave a little gasp of shock, but Mr. Harwood laughed.

"I certainly try to sell them for great sums of money. It depends how good they are."

"Paterson silks are the finest in the world," said Jeannie.

"And as long as they keep up that standard, young lady, I shall continue to buy them."

"But what about the workers, Mr. Harwood, do ye not think they should get paid some o' that money? Without them ye wouldna' have such fine silk."

He looked at her in amusement. "What have we here, a radical? You're not a member of the I.W.W. are you?"

Jeannie blushed. "Nae, but I dinna think the workers are treated fairly."

"Well, my dear young lady, that's really up to the mill owners. There are some here, would you like me to introduce you to them?"

"Oh, no, no," cried Maggie, pulling Jeannie by her skirt.

Grace laughed. "Rob, don't tease. And Jeannie, this is a special day. You're here to enjoy yourselves. You can challenge the mill owners another time."

They all moved into the crowded drawing room, where Mr. Harwood took Grace by the elbow and steered her around the room, introducing her and accepting congratulations from the curious crowd who had gathered as much to get a glimpse of this mysterious new bride as to celebrate the new son's christening.

Maggie and Jeannie shrank back against the wall, overhearing snatches of gossip that made them most uncomfortable.

"Nothing like producing a bride and son and heir at the same time."

"But they've been secretly married for ages."

"Believe that and you'll believe the moon is made of green cheese."

"Can't say I blame Harwood. That first wife of his was a cold fish if there ever was one."

"Oh, mistress mine where are you roaming . . ." muttered a young man slightly worse for drink. "It's one way to make your lady love settle down."

They were relieved to see Maisie approach them with a tall, thin young man in tow.

"This is my Joe," she said proudly, and they shook hands. Joe was still wearing his best black wool suit, his hair was carefully plastered down, and he wore glasses. When he spoke he betrayed a slight German accent, but he had a nice smile and looked as out of place in that elegant room as the two girls, which endeared him to both of them. Maggie noted that they were carefully avoided by most of the other guests, save one who, mistaking Jeannie for a maid, ordered a glass of champagne. Jeannie rose to the occasion beautifully by beckoning to Jones and relaying the order.

Joe took them under his protection and led them to the buffet table, which was set with magnificent silver serving dishes and strange, exotic foods. Everyone toasted the new arrival with champagne, although both Maggie and Jeannie made a face when they tasted it, and left their glasses almost untouched. At last it was six o'clock and time for them to leave. They said their goodbyes to Maisie and Joe.

"I dinna know what we would have done without ye," said Maggie. "If ye ever get tae Paterson do come and see us." They parted amid promises of future visits, and went in search of Grace and Mr. Harwood to say their farewells.

"Could we not see the wee bairn before we leave?" asked Maggie.

So Grace took them up to the nursery and they tip-toed in, past a prim-faced nanny, to where little Andrew was sleeping; his lashes long against his rosy face, his head dusted with gold.

"Och, he's beautiful. Ye are a lucky girl, Grace," said Maggie.

"Yes, I know," said Grace quietly.

"Maggie, we have tae go, the cab will be waiting for us," said Jeannie. "Ye dinna have tae see us out, Grace." They said their goodbyes and hurried down the stairs.

Grace watched them go before she started back to the reception, when it suddenly struck her. Aunt Flora would never have let them come alone. Who had arranged to have a cab outside? It could only have been Ian. He was here. Just outside the door. She could have gone outside and insisted he come in. Take him upstairs to where . . . She leaned against the doorpost and closed her eyes.

"My dear, you look exhausted." Rob was at her side. "We'll get rid of all these people as soon as we can. You need some rest."

"I'm fine, Rob, really. I was just saying goodbye to Maggie and Jeannie."

"You don't have to look so sad, you'll be seeing them again. They're charming girls." He took her arm and led her back to the crowded drawing room.

Maggie and Jeannie were quiet on the return journey. Ian asked no questions, except to make sure they had eaten.

"Oh, yes, we had lots to eat," said Jeannie. "Some of it tasted funny—verra fishy I thought."

When Ian left to buy their tickets Maggie ventured a comment.

"Maisie's a bonnie lass is she not, and Joe was nice. Mr. Harwood's nice too, I guess, but I didna' like most o' the other people."

"I heard a lot of nasty gossip, but I suppose that's tae be expected," said Jeannie. "It'll die down, after all he *did* marry her."

Maggie looked at her sister. She didn't want to think what she meant by that remark, didn't want to think that about Grace, and was relieved when Ian came back with the tickets and they could go home. Life was much simpler at home in Paterson.

# CHAPTER
## ❧ 21 ❧

JUNE! Maggie could hardly believe it was June. She carefully shut down her loom and checked to see there were no stray threads to cause trouble when it was started up again. That wouldn't be for four whole days, and by that time she would be Mrs. Ian Campbell, wife of the loom fixer. A small thrill ran through her at the thought. Maggie's life at the moment was filled with delightful shivers of joy as the big day approached. The final stitches had been applied to her wedding gown, which Aunt Flora actually volunteered to iron for her. Her veil, a froth of illusion, had been loaned to her by one of the Simonetti girls, and she had acquired a drawer full of lavender-scented linens and towels. What more could a girl ask for?

She heard the sound of clattering feet running up the metal staircase and Jeannie burst into view.

"Come on, Maggie, we're waiting for you downstairs." She followed her sister down the winding staircase to the basement where Jeannie had planned a small going-away party.

"Here comes the bride," called Sneezer. "Make way for the bride."

" 'Ere, luv, sit down on one o' Grace's benches." They were always called Grace's benches—it was her little bit of immortality as far as Potter's Mill was concerned. Maggie sat down and Big Nellie and Moira handed around cups of lemonade.

"An' where's Ian now? Is he off to some bachelor party?"

"No, he's working at the shop. He has a job he has tae get finished before we go away."

"Ian's a hard worker, and a good one too," said Sneezer. "He's going to go far, especially now with such a beautiful bride to inspire him."

Maggie blushed with pleasure. She knew all the men liked and admired Ian. And she knew, too, that she was the envy of most of the girls in the mill. Sometimes she had to pinch herself to make sure she was not dreaming.

She looked around. In addition to Sneezer, Will, Ed, Young Albert and the Simonetti girls, several women who worked with Maggie on the looms, and a few of the carders, had come downstairs to join the throwers for the occasion.

"A toast," said Big Nellie. "I propose a toast to Maggie and her bridegroom-to-be, Ian Campbell."

"To Maggie and Ian," came the chorus.

"And this ain't no ordinary lemonade, let me tell yer," said Will as he raised his cup. Then he looked around suspiciously. "Where's old Anderson?"

"She's upstairs at a meeting with Mr. Whitehead."

"Good, let's 'ope she stays there. Well, as I was saying, this 'ere lemonade's got a good dollop o' gin in it—so you ladies watch yerselves now—we don't want no dancin' on the tables, 'specially you, Nellie."

"Gawd, there ain't a table that'd 'old our Nellie."

" 'Ave to be a pretty darn strong bed to 'old her too," chuckled Will.

"Wot's all this talk about beds?" said Nellie. "You're making the bride blush."

"Bride's supposed ter blush, why else is she called the blushing bride?"

" 'Ow about that, Nellie. When are you going ter be a blushing bride?''

"Never, I don't want no part o' that so-called wedded bliss," said Nellie. "Single blessedness, that's my cup o' tea.''

"Aw, go on, yer don't know wot yer missin'," said Will, emboldened by the gin. "I bet no one's ever told you the facts o' life.''

"Yer don't 'ave ter explain the facts o' life ter me, Will Watson, I been on a farm. I seen a thing or two." She turned to Albert. "You cover yer ears, my lad, this ain't no talk for you to be 'earing." But Albert continued to listen, goggle eyed.

"Oh, yeah, and wot did yer see on the farm, Nellie?'' said Will, winking broadly at the rest of the party.

"I seed that ole' bull ruttin' the cow!" There was a shocked gasp from the girls. "And you can say all yer want about 'ow wonderful it is, but there weren't no bells ringing for that ole' cow, I'll tell yer that," declared Nellie. Poor Maggie was pink to the tips of her ears, but Jeannie laughed.

"Dinna pay any attention to them, Maggie. If ye worked down in this dungeon ye'd get used to all this talk, isna' that so, Moira?''

" 'Tis true, Maggie, but there's no harm in it. If ye had old Anderson breathin' down your neck every day, ye'd need a few laughs. But look, we've got a present for ye.'' Everyone gathered around and the girls produced a large parcel done up in brown paper and a pink ribbon.

"Come on, open it," they urged. With nervous fingers she untied the ribbon and tore off the paper revealing a shimmering rainbow of color.

"Oh, it's beautiful," she exclaimed. "Where did ye get it?''

"And didn't we make it ourselves out o' scraps o' silk that we smuggled out under the old banshee's nose. 'Tis a crazy quilt, ye see, and as fine as any ye'll see in the big houses on Park Avenue or Broadway.'' The quilt was a kaleidoscope of colors that looked at first as if a rainbow had been cut into little pieces and scattered at random, but a closer look saw that there was a pattern to it with colors repeating themselves in the squares, and each square stitched together boldly with fancy, colored thread. To Maggie it was the most magnificent piece of needlework she had ever seen.

"That'll keep you and Ian warm on a cold winter's night," said the irrepressible Will.

"Oh, 'tis the bonniest thing I've ever seen. Thank ye, thank ye all," murmured Maggie, who looked as pretty as a bride should with her pink cheeks, dark curls, and sparkling eyes. Nellie put her arms around her.

"Enjoy it, Maggie, and don't pay no attention to this rough crew. You're marrying a good man, you've nothing to worry about."

# CHAPTER

## ❧ 22 ❧

GRACE was slowly getting used to her new way of life, although at times it still seemed unreal. She did not feel married. Rob had so far made no demands on her. Sometimes she wondered why, and at other times she was relieved, because if she wasn't truly married, then there was still a chance for her and Ian. In her weakest moments she visualized opening the door and finding him standing on the doorstep looking incredibly handsome. She imagined taking him upstairs and showing him the baby. His baby. He'd be overjoyed. He'd take her in his arms and tell her he loved her, that he'd always loved her, and would always love her. Then they'd snatch up little Andrew and run away together. But where would they run to? She sighed.

Then one day in June, Grace received a letter that shattered all those dreams. It was from Jeannie.

Dear Grace,
   I'm writing to tell ye about Maggie's wedding. She was the bonniest bride, and of course Ian was the handsomest bridegroom. They were married last Saturday in Aunt Flora's church by the minister . . .

She laid the letter down and struggled to contain her tears.

"What's wrong, Grace? Not bad news, I hope." said Rob, who was sitting across from her at the breakfast table.

"No, not at all," she said faintly. "It—it's from Jeannie. Maggie got married last Saturday."

"Maggie. That's the pretty little one with the dark curly hair?" Grace nodded. "Well, whoever she married is a very lucky man, I'd say."

"A very lucky man," echoed Grace in a choked voice.

"It's too bad you didn't know about it sooner, my dear, you could have gone." He glanced at his watch, stood up and kissed her on the cheek. It was their morning ritual. "Tell you what. Why don't you invite them over here one day soon?"

"Yes, I'll do that. And now I must go and see to Andrew." She fled the breakfast room, burst into the nursery, and much to Nanny's dismay, gathered the baby into her arms, carried him into her own room and locked the door. Then, her cheek against his soft cheek, her arms around his plump little body, she slowly rocked back and forth, back and forth, and all the hot, bitter tears she had tried to hold in check spilled down her cheeks and splashed onto little Andrew's spotless kimono.

It was shortly after that, that Grace invited Rob into her bed. "I want us to have a real marriage," he had said, "but not until you're ready. I told you when we got married that you could dissolve it if you didn't want to go through with it. But I love you, Grace. I want you for my wife." And so she had finally gone through with it, humbled at Rob's gratitude and grateful for his tenderness.

As for Rob, he was in heaven. He knew he had taken a terrible risk getting Grace to marry him when she was in such dire straits. She could have wanted no part of him, could have left him at any time. But now that she had given herself to him, he knew the marriage was going to

last. Even if Grace didn't love him as he loved her, she
was drawn to him. He had sensed that from the very first
time he had met her. There had been that tingling current
between them. He tried not to speculate on little Andrew's
real father. The man must be both a fool and a cad. For
a while he had lived in fear that the man would show up,
and Grace would take the baby and go with him. That
would have left such a terrible void in his life that he
trembled at the thought. But somehow he knew that danger
had passed. Grace was his, and Andrew was his. His life
was complete.

After what had been almost six months of not doing
much of anything, Grace suddenly found herself bursting
with energy. She wanted to redecorate the house from cel-
lar to attic, including the servants' quarters, which she discovered were poorly furnished and completely unheated.

"Doesn't it get cold up here in the winter?" she asked
Rosie.

"Yes, ma'am, it sure does," replied the little parlormaid, who was showing her around. "We go to bed to
keep warm."

She told Rob about it and he seemed surprised.

"What made you go up there?" he asked. "No one's
ever complained about the rooms before."

"Who's going to complain?" she said. "Most of these
women are glad to have a job, but that doesn't mean they
should freeze to death in the winter."

"To my knowledge no one has ever frozen to death on
Fifth Avenue, my dear," he replied, "but if you think the
heating system needs an overhaul, an overhaul it shall
get." He kissed her lightly on the cheek. "And thank you
for telling me about it, Grace. You've done wonders for
this dull old house." He gestured to the bowls of fresh
flowers, the new delicate lampshades, and the thick wool
rugs in warm, soft colors. He was even getting used to the
new painting that hung over the fireplace. It was by one
of those avant-garde French artists whose brush strokes

were crude but who seemed to be able to capture the sun-light.

They had remained in New York all summer. Rob had suggested renting a summer home in the Hamptons, or on one of the lakes in northern New Jersey, but Grace hadn't wanted to be out there alone. So they had stayed in town, which meant there was very little social life, but again that was fine with Grace. She knew she had to move slowly when it came to being accepted by Rob's friends. Oh, they had been polite to her at the christening and the few times she encountered them, but she was not yet one of them. And she still winced at the memory of Mrs. DeWitt-Kenton and her snobbishness.

The advent of fall brought the social set back into town, and a few invitations started trickling in.

"My dear, your entry into society has now been as-sured. Your grandfather's name has apparently stirred the great man himself," said Rob, fingering a beautiful en-graved invitation.

"Grandfather? I don't understand," said Grace.

"Little Andrew, named for his grandfather."

Grace flushed guiltily. Rob had never questioned her choice of a name but had accepted it willingly. He treated little Andrew as if he were his own child. Indeed it was obvious to the entire household that Rob adored the little boy, which ensured him a place in Grace's heart. But she didn't understand what her grandfather had to do with get-ting accepted into New York society.

"I still don't understand," she said with a puzzled frown.

"Mr. Andrew Carnegie requests the pleasure of our company at a small dinner party . . ." Rob looked up with a grin. "The old boy probably thinks we named the baby in honor of him."

"Oh, Rob, I can't possibly go."

"Don't tell me you've nothing to wear."

"It's not that, you've been more than generous—but Mr.

Carnegie—Rob, he only entertains the cream of New York Society, and I'm a nobody.''

"My dear, we're a nation of nobodies. That's what makes us so interesting. And dangerous. When old Andrew Carnegie, who started life working in a steel mill, can go over to Scotland and buy a castle, well, my dear, that sets the entire House of Lords shaking in their aristocratic boots. 'The old order changeth yielding place to new . . .' We're the new order, Grace, and we should be proud of it.''

The evening at the Carnegie mansion was a great success. Mr. Carnegie was charmed with Grace, especially when he learned she was from Scotland, and she was given the place of honor at the dinner table. Word soon got out and invitations started arriving from other well-known families. Ladies came to the house and presented their calling cards. Now when Grace wheeled little Andrew in the park, as she liked to take him out herself at least twice a week, other young matrons joined her. They chatted casually about the difficulties of finding a good nanny, and keeping junior parlor maids who always seemed to be running off and getting married. Someone suggested contacting the Society for the Training of Indigent Females, but Grace turned away and began fussing with the baby. She wanted no part of that conversation.

But in spite of all her activities in redecorating the house and her social engagements, Grace felt that something was missing from her life. There was a lack of purpose, an absence of challenge. She wished she could still work in the offices of Harwood Associates, but she knew that was impossible. As Mrs. Robert Harwood, she simply could not go to work. Rob did fill her in on some of the details of the business, but it wasn't the same.

Then one morning when she was idly glancing over Rob's old newspaper a small item caught her attention, then absorbed her completely. Potter's Mill was going public. A block of shares were up for sale. It would, in effect, be a partnership. She began to pace the floor. She'd seen the balance sheet at the mill the night she'd worked with Mr. Whitehead. It was a sound investment, but would Rob consider it? He had never become involved with the mill end of it. He bought raw silk and he dealt with the finished goods. This would be something new. She spent the day marshalling her arguments, and after supper that night she presented them to her husband.

He looked at her quizzically. "This isn't the mill you used to work in by any chance, is it?"

"How did you know?"

"Isn't that every worker's dream, to buy the company and fire the boss? Do you intend to fire the boss?" Grace had to admit that the thought of firing Mrs. Anderson was tempting, but she knew she couldn't go in like an avenging angel. Rob laughed. "I can see from your expression that the idea has crossed your mind. Let me look into this for you. I'll talk to my broker." But as the days went by Grace heard no more about buying into Potter's mill. She didn't like to hound Rob, and when she mentioned it he just said his broker was studying the proposal.

In the meantime Christmas was approaching, and she had a feeling that the nursery was going to be turned into a toy store. Mysterious packages were being delivered daily, marked "Do not open until December 25th," and Rob went about humming Christmas carols and looking smug. *How different from last year*, she thought with a shudder.

She was in the nursery watching Andrew while Nanny had a few hours off to go shopping herself. The baby was now creeping and pulling himself up to a standing position, his fat little legs getting stronger every day. *Soon he's going to be walking*, she thought, and tried to picture the two of them in that freezing little room off Mulberry Street, with the bare, splintery floor, and the icy drafts from the ill-fitting window. She could see herself hunched over a sewing machine, struggling to keep them both alive. Just then Rob walked into the room and she flung herself into his arms and kissed him fervently.

"Whoa, am I standing under the mistletoe or something?" He looked at her in amazement.

"We don't need mistletoe, Mr. Harwood—we're married, remember."

"Oh, Grace, I remember it every single minute of every single day," he murmured, burying his face in her hair so that she wouldn't see the tears that sprang into his eyes.

On Christmas morning they exchanged presents. She had bought him a silver-backed brush and comb set, and a little matching one for Andrew. Andrew, as she had suspected, was surrounded by toys—big rubber balls, trains, kiddie cars, and stuffed bears—with Rob down on his hands and knees demonstrating them all to an excited little boy who wasn't sure whether to bang everything like a drum, or try to stuff it into his mouth.

"And this, my dear, is for you," said Rob, as Nanny carried Andrew off for his nap. He handed her a box wrapped in gold paper and tied with a bow. She undid it curiously, stared at the contents for a minute, then gasped. "Oh, Rob, you bought it for me."

"A forty percent interest in Potter's Mill of Paterson, New Jersey. I was planning to get you pearls . . ."

She threw her arms around him. "I'd much rather have this than pearls."

He laughed. "Grace, you're a woman after my own heart. We're cut from the same cloth, you and me. Filthy capitalists, both of us. It isn't a controlling interest, but it is substantial. The shares are in your name, and you're free to hold them or sell them as you see fit."

"Oh, I'm going to hold them," said Grace. "When can I go to my first board meeting?"

# CHAPTER

## ❧ 23 ❧

"It's just a wee gathering o' my friends, Ian,"
said Aunt Flora. "We've been getting together for Hogmanay for years. Ye dinna mind, do ye?"

"No, it's all right with me. How about you, Maggie?"

"It wouldna' be Hogmanay if we didna' have some sort
of party," said Maggie. "Are ye going to bake some hinny
cakes?"

"Aye, we always have hinny cakes," said Aunt Flora.

"But no haggis," said Ian. "I draw the line at haggis."

"Who's coming?" asked Maggie.

"Oh, the usual, Jock and Dora, the McDougals, the
McCraes, that is if his bronchitis is better. Perhaps ye
want to have some young folks over too."

"I did ask Moira, but she can't come. She had to go
home for a few days, her mother's sick," said Maggie,
"but maybe Jeannie would like to invite someone."

"As long as she doesn't bring one o' those Eyetalians,"
said Aunt Flora, pursing her lips. "They probably
wouldna' even know what Hogmanay is."

"Well they know it's New Year's Eve," said Maggie.
"Just think, in a few days 'twill be 1913. We've been in
America two and a half years already."

What a lot had happened in those two and a half years.
She vividly remembered that first night when Aunt Flora

had invited her friends over, the same friends who would
be coming for Hogmanay. She remembered all the talk
about Scotland. She hardly ever thought about Scotland
these days. She remembered Jeannie singing, but mostly
she recalled that breathtaking moment when Grace and Ian
had stepped into the room. She'd fallen in love with Ian
then and there, but he only had eyes for Grace. Maggie
suppressed a little sigh.

They had not seen Grace since the day of the christening, but they had all received lovely presents at Christmas.
A pretty muff for herself and one for Jeannie, slippers for
Aunt Flora, and a fine set of linen handkerchiefs for Ian.
He barely glanced at them, however, and later threw them
carelessly in the back of the drawer, as if to say he would
never use them. Aunt Flora, on the other hand, for all her
disapproval of Grace, had accepted the slippers and wore
them every day. *Grace is still a presence in this house,*
thought Maggie, *but she can no longer come between us
because I'm the one Ian married, I'm the one who is having Ian's baby.*

Every time she thought about the coming baby, Maggie
felt a little leap of joy. Her own wee bairn, hers and Ian's.
She just knew it was going to be a boy. A son. He would
work alongside his father, and when Ian's business grew,
as she knew it would, it would become Campbell and Son.
She could picture the sign over the shop now and her heart
swelled with pride.

When they discovered Maggie was expecting, Ian arranged to take over the house from Aunt Flora. He now
paid the rent, and Aunt Flora, technically, was a boarder.
But Maggie found it hard to think of it as her house, and
her aunt still acted as if she were the landlady, so things
went on pretty much as before. *But when the baby comes,*
thought Maggie, *Ian and I will move downstairs, and
Jeannie can take the attic rooms.* Grace's old room could
become a nursery. For a while Aunt Flora had rented it to
a quiet little man who worked nights for the newspaper,

but he had moved out two months ago and now it was empty.

It was the usual guests who gathered in the parlor for New Year's Eve, or Hogmanay as the Scots called it. Ian had stoked up the pot stove, which sent off a glow of heat, and that, plus the bottle of whiskey he had provided, warmed the little party so that they became quite merry. Even Aunt Flora, while she determinedly sipped her lemon and barley water, joined in the fun. From the kitchen came the tantalizing smell of mutton pies and hinny cakes, which would be consumed once the midnight hour came.

"I propose a toast," said Davie McCrae. "Tae our charmin' hostess, Flora McDonald."

"Tae Flora," they cried in unison.

"An now," continued Davie, who was already slightly tipsy, "let's have a song. How about, "Stop your ticklin' Jock."

"Not in my house," said Aunt Flora. "We'll not have any indecent songs in my house."

"I don't know about the tickling," said Dora, who was sitting next to her husband on the sofa, "but ye've been bobbing up and down like a cork in the ocean all night. What's eatin' ye, Jock?"

"He's got ants in his pants," said Mrs. McCrea with a giggle. "What are ye in such a dinnie about, Jock?"

"You'll see, you'll see," he crowed. "And won't ye be surprised. What time is it, Flora?"

"It's nigh on midnight," she replied. "Time for me tae take my pies out o' the oven." As if to reinforce her statement the clock on the mantel began to chime. Jock was jumping up and down like a hop toad, his face red from the whiskey, his eyes sparkling with mischief, when there was a knock on the door.

"Now you'll see," he exclaimed, hugging himself with glee.

Ian opened the door, with Jock hovering behind him,

and stared in amazement at the tall, thin negro man who stood on the doorstep.

"Elroy! Is anything the matter?"

"That's what Ah wondered, Mr. Campbell. Ah was tole to come here right at midnight, that it was important."

"Well, then come in, man, come in. Dinna stand there shivering," said Jock impatiently.

"Yes, please come in," Ian stood back as the black man stepped cautiously into the room. Jock let out a hoot.

"It's good luck all year," he shouted. "If a dark man crosses the threshold at midnight on Hogmanay, it means good luck all year. How about it Dora, they don't come no darker than him, now do they?" Jock did a little dance around the room, while the women squealed in shocked delight. Maggie stood clasping her hands in embarrassment. She could see the flush of anger spread over Ian's face, while their unexpected guest looked from one to another in bewilderment.

"Ah'm sorry, Mr. Campbell, maybe Ah should go round the back, but he said Ah was to be sure to knock on the front door."

Ian shot a murderous look at Jock, who was wiping his eyes between doubling over with laughter. Then he turned to Elroy.

"I'm sorry, Elroy, there seems to have been some mistake. But now that you're here, come on in the kitchen and have a drink for the New Year."

"Oh, no, Ah couldn't do that."

"Of course you can," said Ian, taking him by the arm and leading him into the kitchen. Aunt Flora was in there taking the mutton pies out of the oven. She gave a little shriek and fled into the parlor, where the others were both praising and scolding Jock for his audacity. But Maggie, who had followed Ian, stayed to watch the two men.

"D'you like whiskey?" asked Ian.

"Ah takes a little bourbon now and then," said Elroy.

"This is Scotch whiskey," said Ian. "Maybe you'd better have some water with it." He poured two glasses and then raised his. "Happy New Year."

"Happy New Year to you, Mr. Campbell." Elroy took a swallow of the Scotch and quickly reached for the water. He refused to sit down, but stood nervously eyeing the back door. A couple of other men came in for a refill and talk soon turned to the mills.

"How's it going in the dye shops, Elroy? You busy?"

"Yessir, we's working full time these days. Don' know what's going to happen iffen there's a strike."

"You think there's going to be a strike?" asked Ian. Jeannie, who had come in for a plate of cakes, joined in when the talk turned to the suggestion of a strike.

"Mr. Simonetti says there's bound to be a strike. He says that's what happened in Italy when they brought in the four looms."

"Och, Angelo's naught but an anarchist. He's against everything," said Davie McCrae.

"Aye, but he's right about the looms. Four looms isn't going to help the workers."

"Why not, twice as many looms means twice as much money."

"That's what they'd like you to think," exclaimed Jeannie. "But wait a few months till they've got their inventories built up, then what do you think the mill owners will do? Lay us off, that's what, so where's the gain?"

"Aye, and when they take us back it'll be at a lower wage," said McDougal.

"If it does come to a strike, what about the dye shops, Elroy? Will they strike too?" asked Ian.

"Ah don' rightly know, Mr. Campbell. The broadsilk workers didn't go out with us when we were striking last year. They kept on making silk and it went to Pennsylvania to be dyed, so we finally had to settle. Of course if the I.W.W. comes in, then we'll strike."

"That bunch o' Bolshevik agitators! What do ye want

wi' the likes o' them?'' demanded Jock, who had also joined the group in the kitchen.

"The International Workers of the World are a fine organization. They don't care if you be black or white, if you're a worker you can join. Ah's got my red card and Ah's proud of it,'' said Elroy firmly. He spoke with a quiet dignity that took them aback. Then he flashed a brilliant smile. "Ah thanks you for the whiskey, but Ah'd better be gettin' home or my wife'll be worried.''

"You're married,'' exclaimed Maggie in surprise.

"Yes Ma'am, and Ah got three chil'en—two boys and mah little girl is jest two years old. I sure hope it won't be no long strike. Well, goodnight Mr. Campbell, Mrs. Campbell. I'll jes' go out the back door here.''

After he left, Aunt Flora forbade any more talk of strikes or work as she passed around the pies while Maggie made a big pot of tea.

But later, when Aunt Flora and Jeannie were in bed and Maggie was putting away the last of the dishes, Ian said, "You know I learned more about Elroy tonight than I have in all the years I've known him, thanks to Jock. Although I could have killed him for pulling such a damn fool stunt.''

"Fancy him being married and having children,'' mused Maggie. "I just never thought of darkies as being married and having families.''

"Maggie, you don't call them darkies, they're negroes. And of course they marry and have families. They're human beings, same as we are.''

"I just never thought of them that way,'' she said. "And I don't like all this talk about a strike, although it won't affect you, will it?'' She looked at him anxiously.

"I don't know. If it comes to a showdown I guess we'll have to go along with the rest of them. But I don't think it will last long, and I'm not going to lose any sleep over it tonight.'' He put his arm around her waist. "Come on, Maggie, let's go to bed.''

# CHAPTER
## ❧ 24 ❧

GRACE'S first meeting with Mr. Potter was not exactly a success. He didn't recognize her, of course. There was no way he could connect this elegant young woman, in her stylish dress, short fur cape, and pale gray kid gloves, with a mill hand in the throwing department of Potter's Mill. But Grace remembered him, small, wizened, wearing, she was sure, the same old-fashioned frock coat, the same gold rimmed pince-nez clipped to his thin nose.

"I didn't realize the shares were to be in Mrs. Harwood's name," he said, peering at the signature on their agreement.

"Not just in her name," said Rob. "They're hers, to do with as she wishes."

"This is most unusual," muttered Potter. "Most unusual. But I presume you will advise her."

*They are discussing me as if I'm not here,* thought Grace. "Mr. Potter," she said sharply. "I'm quite capable of making my own decisions. And I would like to see a statement of the mill's earnings for the last quarter." He glared at her, and she smiled back at him. Rob leaned back and lit his pipe. He was quite enjoying himself.

Mr. Potter reluctantly found the last statement and handed it to Grace.

"These are the figures up until the end of the year. However, there will be significant changes during this coming year."

"What sort of changes?" she asked.

"We expect to double our production." She looked up, interested. Mr. Potter was looking pleased with himself. "We're going to four looms." He turned to Rob. "Up until now the operators have only worked two looms at a time, but there's no reason they can't handle four. All the mills are planning to convert to four looms."

"How do the workers feel about this?" asked Grace.

"What business is it of theirs? They do their job, they get paid. Otherwise they get fired."

"There's talk among the merchants of a possible strike," said Rob. "I've heard that if you go to four looms the weavers are going to walk off the job. And if they go out, all the rest of them will go out too."

"Talk, just talk," said Potter. "The workers can't afford to strike. Besides, they can make more money with four looms. They've got no cause to complain, believe me."

Grace thought about the dingy, smelly basement where Jeannie and Big Nellie toiled day after day. *If I still worked there, I'd probably be leading the strike,* she thought. *But I can't take their side now. It looks as if I've picked a bad time to become part owner of Potter's Mill.*

All over Paterson the topic was four looms. There were some who saw no harm in it. Aunt Flora, for instance.

"Lazy, that's what these mill workers are—lazy. That's the trouble with these young 'uns today, afraid they might have to do a full day's work."

"They're not afraid of work," said Ian. "But these are skilled people. They take pride in what they do, they're not mindless bobbin watchers."

"Thanks for the compliment," said Jeannie, with a

laugh. "But you're right, the mill owners are just exploiting us. Grinding the faces of the poor."

"Och, Jeannie, nae one's grinding your face," said Maggie. "Ye've been spending too much time wi' the Simonettis. Now they're troublemakers."

"No, they're not," said Jeannie hotly. "But they know all about strikes. Mama Simonetti says in Italy they had no money and no food, they had to eat grass."

"Oh, come on Jeannie, no one eats grass," said Ian.

"Just the same, Mama says we should get a goat, for the milk."

"We'll do no such thing," exclaimed Aunt Flora. "Nasty, smelly things goats, and they eat the sheets right off the clothesline. I'll nae have one in my yard."

*It's really my yard*, thought Maggie, *but I'll no argue wi' Aunt Flora over it.*

At Potter's Mill all the throwers were in favor of a strike.

"Sure'n what have we got to lose?" asked Moira.

"Half our pay if we get caught talking about a strike," said Will. They were having their tea break. Moira, who did a wicked imitation of Mrs. Anderson, mimicked her now, squinting her eyes and speaking in a high nasal voice.

"Nellie, I heard ye say the word—s-t-r-i-k-e—one dollar fine. Ye said it again—two dollar fine. Did I hear the words I.W.W.—ten dollar fine. What d'ye mean ye don't make ten dollars? Then ye owe Potter's Mill five dollars—to the workhouse wi' ye."

Heavy footsteps on the iron stairway indicated the arrival of the real Mrs. Anderson and everyone immediately scurried back to work, trying to stifle their laughter. She looked around with a scowl.

"What's going on here?" she asked. A smothered giggle was her reply. She glared at them, the color rising in her sallow face. "Oh, it's a great joke is it? Well if I hear of any more seditious gatherings among this group, you'll all be fired."

"Will ye listen to that now," whispered Moira. "Seditious gatherings it is, and I thought all we were doing was having a cup of tay."

"What's that? What are you saying?" Mrs. Anderson pounced.

"I said, whatever you say, ma'am," said Moira.

"Why isn't that machine running?"

" 'Tis a broken spool we're thinking, and isn't the loom fixer supposed to be here any moment now."

"Nonsense, we can't wait around all day for the loom fixer. It can be run, you just have to adjust the thread every now and then. Now get to work."

What followed was forever indelibly burned into Jeannie's mind as if all her nerves had been seared with a red hot branding iron. Moira set the winding machine running and then leaned forward to adjust the spool. There was a sharp snapping and cracking noise and then a scream—a scream so terrible it rose above the steady clack-clack of the machines, a scream that tore across the room and climbed the walls in desperation, a scream that rose in pitch until it seemed as if all the world was screaming.

"For Christ's sake, switch it off!" Nellie charged past the gaping Mrs. Anderson and stilled the groaning mass of machinery, while Jeannie stood paralyzed, staring at the ever-widening pool of bright red blood that was slowly spreading across the floor. Big Nellie swept up the scissors and quickly freed the few remaining strands of Moira's hair from the spikes, and gathered the semi-conscious girl into her arms. Jeannie grabbed a clean rag to wrap around the torn and bleeding flesh of Moira's head and followed Nellie up the stairway, past the horrified weavers and out onto the street, while in the background she heard Mrs. Anderson's strident voice crying out,

"Back to your looms, all of you, back to your looms."

As they ran through the streets Jeannie had no idea where they were going. There was no hospital that she knew of, but Nellie had a destination in mind and in a few minutes Jeannie found herself standing at the front door of the convent of the Sisters of Charity, pulling desperately at the bell. The door was opened by a small, elderly woman in the black garb of a nun. She took one look at Nellie, and the moaning, bleeding girl in her arms.

"Mother of God," she cried. "Come in, come in. Sister Mary, Sister Ursula, come quick. 'Twas an accident at the mill, was it not? Bring her in here." Two other nuns came hurrying on silent feet across the highly polished floor, and Nellie and Jeannie followed them into a large, airy room containing several beds, most of them occupied by old women.

Nellie laid Moira, who was mercifully unconscious by now, on the bed where one of the nuns had placed a large rubber sheet.

"How bad is it?" asked the elderly nun. "Let's take a look." She made a move to take the blood soaked rag from Moira's head, but Jeannie couldn't bear to look. She turned away, trying to quell the awful sickness that rose in her throat. Almost immediately one of the sisters was at her side, leading her back out into the hallway, where she made her sit down and put her head between her knees.

" 'Tis a terrible shock you've had, my dear. Stay here and I'll fetch you a glass of water." Jeannie sipped the water, but her hand shook so that half of it slopped onto the floor. A few minutes later she was joined by Nellie, tears streaming down her heavyset face as she kept murmuring over and over again.

"All her beautiful hair, gone. All her beautiful hair."

"Is she going to die?" whispered Jeannie.

" 'Tis in the hands of God," said the sister. "Perhaps you'd like to go into the chapel and say a prayer. If you ask Our Lord to watch over your friend I'm sure he will listen to you."

Jeannie looked up in alarm. A Roman Catholic chapel, according to Aunt Flora, was a place to be avoided, a den of iniquity, but she couldn't be rude to these women who in spite of their strange clothes were only trying to be kind. She followed Nellie into the chapel, where she glanced curiously at the statues, one of a lady in a blue cloak, and another, apparently of Jesus, with a heart outside his chest.

There were many small candles flickering around the feet of the statues. A small red lamp hung over the altar and the sisters made a little bob each time they passed in front of it, even Nellie bobbed before she entered the pew, and knelt down murmuring prayers in a tear-choked voice. Jeannie slipped into the end pew and sat down. She could think of no prayer to say, but as she sat there she felt a calm descend on her. *Nellie brought Moira to the right place,* she thought, *if anyone can save her these women can.*

On their way back to the mill, with promises of prayers night and day ringing in their ears, and invitations to visit Moira any time, Jeannie wondered if the mill would pay the sisters.

"Potter's pay for anything!" said Nellie in disgust. "Not if they can weasel out of it."

"But won't there be an inquiry? Mrs. Anderson should never have made Moira start up that machine."

"We know that, but we won't be called on. No, it'll be Mrs. Anderson's version, and she'll say it was Moira's carelessness that caused the accident, and the case will be closed."

"Don't we have any rights at all?" said Jeannie bitterly.

"Sure we do, the right to work twelve hours a day if we can get someone to hire us, the right to spend those days in damp, smelly basements, the right to be on our feet no matter how tired we are, and the right to be fined or fired whenever the boss is in a bad mood."

They had arrived back at the mill by now and the atmosphere was tense. Foremen were pacing the floor making sure everyone stayed at his job, but there were whispered questions as Nellie and Jeannie walked by.

"She's with the nuns," said Nellie, and that seemed to satisfy the shaken workforce.

They clattered down the winding metal stairs to find Mrs. Anderson waiting for them.

"Back to work," she said, "and no talking."

"Don't you even want to know how she is?" demanded Jeannie.

"I can find out when the shift ends. Now get those machines going. We've lost enough time as it is."

Jeannie looked around. Will, Ed, Harry, and Sneezer were bent over their vats—they looked white and ill. Albert was crouched in the corner, his thin shoulders shaking with suppressed sobs. The Simonetti girls were busy at their spools, not daring to look up. With a defiant glance at Mrs. Anderson, Jeannie stood on her tip-toes and shouted at the top of her lungs.

"She's still alive—she's at the convent." The she moved towards her workplace and suddenly came face to face with Moira's machine, idle, broken, stopped by a tangled mass of bloodstained hair. She gave a strangled shriek, turned, and ran. She heard Mrs. Anderson's harsh voice following her up the staircase.

"If you don't finish your shift you'll be docked."

"I don't care if I'm fired," she cried as she rushed out of the building, down the empty streets, her feet pounding on the pavement as she ran and ran, trying to escape that terrible tangled mass of once beautiful auburn hair.


Jeannie visited Moira as often as she could. Sometimes Big Nellie would go with her, and sometimes she went alone. Maggie did not go. Aunt Flora would not let her.

" 'Tis not good for ye, in your condition, tae be seeing such dreadful sights," she said. "Ye must be around pleasant, happy things, then ye'll have a happy baby."

Maggie did not argue with Aunt Flora. She was relieved that she didn't have to go. She knew she couldn't bear to look at the injured girl. She trembled with horror every

time she thought back to that dreadful day, when she had
seen Big Nellie rushing out of the mill with her bloodstained burden. She had been sure Moira was dead. Jeannie said she probably would have died if it hadn't been for
the nuns.

Jeannie knew it was more because of the nuns than Aunt
Flora's concern for Maggie's unborn baby that kept her
sister away. Aunt Flora had a deep distrust of these women
who shut themselves away and supposedly devoted themselves to God. She would have liked to stop Jeannie going
to the convent too, but knew it was a hopeless cause. As
for Jeannie, the more she visited Moira, the more she came
to admire the women who tended her with deft but gentle
hands.

But for all their care Moira did not respond. She lay
perfectly still, her head swathed in bandages, her face
whiter than a sheet, her eyes closed. The sister who kept
watch clicked steadily at a long string of beads that hung
from her waist, and Jeannie knew that they were a way of
praying. She tried to pray, too, but no words would come.
So she just came every evening and sat quietly by the bed,
watching, until at last one day Moira opened her eyes and
smiled weakly.

"Hello, Jeannie," she whispered faintly. Jeannie was
too choked with tears to even speak, but she took her
friend's hand and squeezed it gently.

"Thanks be to God," exclaimed the sister, crossing
herself.

That marked the turning point. The next time Jeannie
came Moira was awake and waiting for her.

"I have a present for ye," said Jeannie. " 'Tis from
Maggie—she made it herself." Moira was delighted with
the pretty pink bedjacket Maggie had knitted for her.
"And look," said Jeannie, "even Aunt Flora sent you
something. A plate of fresh baked scones." Moira gave
the scones to the nuns, and Jeannie smiled to herself as
the sisters received them with thanks and blessings.

"Sure'n it was kind o' your aunt," whispered Moira. "And tell Maggie the bed jacket is beautiful. It is sittin' up now I'll have to be doin'."

"Soon you'll be getting up," said Jeannie.

"But when will I be gettin' back to work? Faith'n I miss ye all. Never thought the day would come that I'd miss Potter's, but I do. Not the auld banshee, but the rest of ye."

Jeannie didn't know how Moira could bear the thought of Potter's, but she recognized her loneliness. She lived alone in a small room. Her mother and father and umpteen brothers and sisters were on a farm way out in a place called Hacketstown. They couldn't even afford to come and visit her, but sent her postcards written in a round, childish hand.

"We miss ye too, Moira. 'Tis not the same without ye."

As the days went by Moira grew stronger. Soon she was sitting up in a chair.

"Have ye heard anything from the mill?" asked Jeannie. "Are they going to pay you while you're sick? 'Twas their fault."

"Them, not a penny will they give me," said Moira scornfully. "And 'tis never their fault. If 'twas lightening struck ye while ye were standing at the loom, 'twould somehow be your fault for standin' there."

"I'm going to write to Mr. Potter. Who's going to pay the sisters? You canna."

" 'Tis saints they are, the sisters, and if ye can't pay they keep ye anyway. Maybe I'll be a nun when I'm better."

"You a nun!" Jeannie gave a hoot.

"And why not? Indeed, they wouldn't even have to cut my hair. Ye know, nuns have to cut off all their hair when they join the convent."

"Oh, Moira." Jeannie's eyes filled with tears.

"Sure'n I was only joking," said Moira. "Tell me now, when are ye going to strike against that auld skinflint?"

"Any day now. Doherty's mill is already out. They told old Henry Doherty that they weren't going to work four looms, no matter how much he threatened them. There's going to be a meeting tonight, and I know they're going to vote to go out with them. If old Potter saw a chance tae make more money off us he'd have us work ten looms. I'd love tae see his face when we all walk off the job."

"I'd like to see the auld banshee's face," said Moira. " 'Twould be worth gettin' out o' a sick bed just to thumb my nose at her. Will ye do it for me, Jeannie?"

"I'll do more than that. We're going to bring them to their knees, just wait and see."

When Jeannie left Moira that day she made up her mind she was going to write to Mr. Potter. He owed it to Moira to pay for her care, but she knew it was useless to send the letter through the offices at the mill; it would never reach him. She had to find his New York office, but how? Perhaps there was a way. Tony was always telling her if ye wanted to find something out go to the library, and if Tony could do it, so could she.

It took a lot of courage for Jeannie to walk into that great building and ask for the librarian, but for Moira she had courage. The lady was very nice and gave her a directory, and that's when she made an astonishing discovery. Potter wasn't the sole owner. He had a partner: Mrs. Robert Harwood of New York City. Grace! Grace was part owner of Potter's Mill, and she'd never told them. Not a word had she said when she'd written to them at Christmas. Well, Grace was in for a surprise now. She'd write to her tonight.

Jeannie hurried home. She couldn't wait to see Aunt Flora's face when she learned that Grace was now part owner of Potter's Mill, and her aunt didn't disappoint her. With a mouth like a prune she declared that Miss High and Mighty would soon find out what it was like to be the boss "when all your workers walked out on ye."

"But we canna go on strike now," exclaimed Maggie. "We canna strike against Grace."

"And why not?" said Ian sharply. "She's no different from any of the other owners. Has she done anything to improve conditions at Potter's? Everyone knows it's the most backward mill in Paterson. I'd go on strike myself if I worked there." They all looked at him in astonishment. Ian had never been enthusiastic about the strike.

"Och, Ian, ye wouldna'." Maggie was shocked. "But you're a loom fixer. They'll nae go out will they?" She sounded anxious.

"They're going to vote on it, but if everyone strikes we may as well go along. There'll be no looms to fix anyway."

"But what about your own looms? Ye'll continue to run them, will ye not?"

"Now, Maggie, you know I can't do that. I can't be a strikebreaker."

"But how will we manage if you're nay working? Ye have bills to pay. What about the baby?" Maggie was frightened, and Ian put his arm around her.

"Don't worry. It'll be over long before the baby comes."

"And when it's over, we'll be twice as well off," said Jeannie. "This strike's going to bring the mill owners to their knees."

"Grace, too?" asked Aunt Flora hopefully.

"Aye, Grace too, if necessary," said Jeannie.

"Hmph, perhaps this strike business is nay sae bad after all."

Jeannie wrote to her cousin that night, telling her about Moira, about Mrs. Anderson insisting she start up the machine—Grace of all people knew what Mrs. Anderson was like—and she described the terrible accident.

. . . They didn't even clean up the blood, but made everyone stay on the job. We're not treated like human beings at all. You should remember how it was—well it's even worse now. That's why we're going on strike. Grace, here's your chance to help us. Listen to our side of the story. . . .

The next morning she walked to the post office before work and mailed the letter herself. Grace had to help. She couldn't side with Potter on this. She'd do something for Moira, and she'd have to listen to the strikers. Why, if she were still at Potter's she'd probably be leading the strike, thought Jeannie, remembering with a smile how Grace outwitted Mrs. Anderson over the benches. Grace would be on their side, even if she was part owner.

# CHAPTER

## ❦ 25 ❦

GRACE was troubled. She read Jeannie's letter for the tenth time, even though it sent chills down her spine. She remembered her own mill experience. She could still see the wicked spikes on the winding reels, and suddenly had a vivid picture of her own beautiful long hair, torn from her head and tangled in a bloody mass around the deadly machine. She felt sick.

"Rob, we must do something for that poor girl." Rob was sympathetic but adamant.

"Right now, Grace, you can't do anything. In the first place you'd have to consult Potter, and you know how he feels. If you so much as mention helping one of the workers now you'll be considered a traitor."

The letter could not have come at a worse time. The workers had issued an ultimatum to the manufacturers, which they had rejected outright. A strike was imminent, and the owners were prepared for a fight, and she was now a mill owner. Any feelings she had towards the workers would have to be firmly squashed.

"I didn't plan on this when I asked you to buy stock in the mill," she said. She had had wonderful dreams of making Potter's a model mill. A place where the workers were treated like human beings. A clean, well lit, open airy workplace, with a decent lunch room with tables and

237

chairs. She had hoped to eliminate the unfair fines, the grueling hours without a break, the ugly washrooms. But now her hands were tied.

"Whatever plans you had, my dear, will have to be set aside until these troubles are over. My advice to you is to put that letter away and forget all about it. What's done is done, and you can't change it."

So Grace reluctantly put Jeannie's letter away in her desk, but she couldn't stop the terrible vision of the mangled girl from haunting her dreams.

February 25th was the day set for the strike and the mill crackled with tension. Mrs. Anderson, grim faced and dressed in solid black, stalked the aisles. Mr. Whitehead paced up and down outside his office nervously removing his glasses, wiping imaginary spots from them, and replacing them. Foremen were lined up alongside the looms. The men and women of the mill, the weavers, carders, twisters, and throwers, stood motionless in front of their machines, but there was a pent-up energy in their stillness that threatened to explode. Except for an occasional whisper no one spoke, but a nod of the head or a raised eyebrow passed the message from worker to worker—today is the day—wait for the signal.

With the seven o'clock whistle the machines leapt into action and the ear-shattering clickety-clack of the looms filled the air. Shuttles flew back and forth with the speed of bullets as the strands of warp and weft came together into shimmering bolts of silken fabric. To Maggie watching her loom they seemed to go faster and faster, faster and faster, back and forth, clickety-clack, clickety-clack, then she saw Mike, the head weaver, step away from his loom and draw out a large pocket watch. He stood in the center of the mill for a few seconds staring intently at the watch face, and at the stroke of eight he thrust his fist into the air and shouted, "NOW!"

With a creak and groan the entire mill shuddered to a

halt and an eerie silence enveloped the building. Men and women laid down their tools, quietly gathered up their coats, and filed out, walking slowly past the speechless and helpless managers.

Jeannie clattered up the old iron staircase and grabbed Maggie by the arm; together they hurried outside where they were met by an unforgettable sight. All up and down the streets of Paterson workers were pouring out of the mills. They thronged together on the roadways and sidewalks, and once they realized they were free from their labors they broke into a great cheer. All that pent-up energy was released. Intoxicated by an unfamiliar sense of power, they joined together, held hands, laughed, sang, and danced in the streets. This was going to be a strike to end all strikes. Before it was over the whole of Paterson would be shut down. Six thousand workers walked off the job that morning and more would follow; the owners would have to give in. And so, the sweet taste of victory on their lips, they rejoiced and linked arms, blocking the streets, and from there surged en masse towards Turn Hall.

"Are you going to join the I.W.W.?" asked Will as they were swirled along by the crowd. "I'm going to sign up today. If anyone can win this strike for us they can. Look what they did for the woollen mills in Worcester."

"Och, Jeannie," whispered Maggie in a worried voice, "I dinna want no part o' the I.W.W. Aunt Flora says they're a bunch o' Bolshies."

"Pay no attention to Aunt Flora," said Jeannie. "Wait till ye hear what Miss Flynn and Mr. Tresca have to say. Then ye'll change your mind."

Jeannie was dying to meet Elizabeth Gurley Flynn and Carlo Tresca, she'd heard so much about them from the Simonettis and the men at the mill. They were the leaders of the famous, or infamous, International Workers of the World. But when Jeannie, Maggie and the others finally reached Turn Hall, they found the place in a turmoil. Flynn and Tresca had been arrested.

''Just for trying to speak. Is this a free country or isn't
it?''

''What were the charges?'' asked Jeannie indignantly.

''Conspiracy, unlawful assembly, and raucously, riot-
ously and tumultuously disturbing the peace,'' said
Sneezer, who'd arrived earlier. ''Now ain't that some
charge.''

''They ain't seen no raucous riotin' yet,'' said Big Nellie, ''but keep this up and they will. Come on, I'm going
to sign up right now.''

Aunt Flora did not approve of the strike. To her there
was something sinful in deliberately not going to work, in
setting yourself up as knowing better than the mill owners.
Pride, that's what it was, the sin that brought down Lucifer. Besides, she was worried. How would Ian pay for the
house if he wasn't working? And what of herself? Aunt
Flora, like many housebound women, did work at home,
picking mostly. It gave her a little spending money and
she was grateful for it. But these young folk were not
grateful for their work. There was even talk of demanding
an eight-hour day, did ye ever hear of such laziness? Aunt
Flora shook her head sadly and wondered what the world
was coming to.

Maggie too was uneasy, especially the next morning
when she realized she didn't have to go to work. Jeannie,
however, was up, dressed, and drinking her tea.

''Where are ye off to?'' asked a sleepy-eyed Maggie.

''To picket, of course,'' said Jeannie. ''We dinna want
scabs taking over our jobs now.''

''Jeannie, ye'll nae use sich filthy words in my kitchen,''
said Aunt Flora, reverting to her thick Scottish brogue.

''There'll be more than bad words if anyone tries to
cross the picket line,'' said Jeannie. ''What about you,
Ian? What are you going to do?''

''I'm off to the shop. I still have some repair work I can

do." He kissed Maggie gently and went in search of Old Mac.

"Oh dear, do I have tae picket too?" said Maggie, who felt it was somehow shameful to walk up and down with picket signs.

"Since you're in such an interesting condition, you're excused," said Jeannie, taking a final gulp of her tea and winding a long woollen muffler around her neck. "Sit down and put your feet up, Maggie. Ye may as well rest now, ye'll be busy enough when the baby comes."

"But it's not due until June," said Maggie.

"Och, we'll be back tae work long before that," cried Jeannie, and she flew out the door letting it slam behind her.

In Paterson the atmosphere was festive. To men and women used to spending long days tied to the machines, the unexpected freedom was a heady experience. Jeannie soon saw Big Nellie and Albert and several girls from upstairs. Nellie had a sign around her neck that said, "ON STRIKE." They were marching up and down in front of the mill chanting.

"Two looms—Eight hours. Two looms—Eight hours."

"Ain't this something," said Will. "Everyone's together—carders, weavers, Eyetalians, Poles. Like those I.W.W. people say, 'One Big Union'."

"Are they still in jail?" asked Jeannie.

"Naw, they couldn't hold them. Them police have met their match with the Wobblies."

But arrests followed arrests. The police, according to the strikers, were in the pockets of the manufacturers, and as the weeks went by, picketer after picketer was carried off to jail.

"Wait till Big Bill gets here," said Sneezer. "Then things will be different." He was referring to Big Bill Haywood, a big, soft spoken, one-eyed giant of a man, who was the leader of the International Workers of the World.

\* \* \*

The mill owners were gathered at the Waldorf-Astoria, and as Grace walked through the wide and plush lobby to the elevator she couldn't help thinking of the rattly iron staircase that led down to the damp and smelly basement of Potter's Mill. She couldn't blame the workers for striking, but she knew such sentiments would not be understood here. She smoothed her gloves and gave a slight tilt to her ostrich-feathered hat. Now she was a mill owner she'd have to act like a mill owner, even if she didn't always think like one. She glanced at Rob, looking elegant as always in his cutaway suit. He wasn't troubled by these spasms of conscience.

They were met by Mr. Potter, who scowled at Grace. "Wouldn't you like to wait here, Mrs. Harwood? Your husband can represent you at the meeting."

"I will represent myself, thank you, Mr. Potter," said Grace. "But my husband will accompany me, so you need not be concerned about my welfare." Her unhappy business partner muttered something under his breath and wrenched open the door.

When she entered the room, dark panelled, with a long, highly polished table in the center surrounded by leather-covered chairs, she instinctively put her hand on her husband's arm. A thin layer of cigar smoke wafted across the room towards her as a row of faces turned to watch her progress, and she realized there were no other women present.

"Afternoon, Harwood," said a tall, heavily whiskered man. "Afternoon, ma'am." He made a slight bow in her direction. "I think you know everyone present."

Grace glanced around her, vaguely recognizing men she had met at the silk merchants dinners. Suddenly, she stiffened with shock. Austin was across the table from her, and by his side sat Uncle Thomas. Austin's eyes widened in astonishment.

Mr. Potter made the introductions. "Mr. DeWitt-Kenton and Mr. Thomas Lindsay are here to represent

Mrs. DeWitt Kenton,'' he said. ''*She* preferred to remain at home.''

''Really,'' said Grace. ''What a shame, perhaps she was not feeling well.'' She acknowledged Austin, whose glance went from her to Rob and back again.

''How do you do, *Mrs. Harwood*.''

The emphasis was slight, but cutting. Well, she didn't care what he thought. Uncle Thomas had been looking at her with a puzzled frown, but now recognition hit him, and he pursed his lips together tightly. She was not going to be easily forgiven by Uncle Thomas. Rob squeezed her arm gently. He knew the DeWitt-Kentons had been involved in the scheme to defraud Harwood Associates, but beyond that he knew nothing of Grace's involvement with them.

The little scene was quickly taken in by Catholina Lambert, however, and he recalled the interesting events that had taken place that night at the castle when Grace had been escorted by young Kenton. But that was her business. He smiled at Grace as he seated himself at the head of the table, but gave no indication that he had met her before.

''Glad you could come, Mrs. Harwood; you, too, Rob. Now, if we can get down to business.'' They took their seats, and one of the men began to relate the latest events in Paterson, including the arrest and subsequent release of Elizabeth Gurley Flynn and Carlo Tresca. It didn't take long to see that these men were not in a generous mood.

''I might consider talking to the workers themselves, but I'm damned if I'm going to sit down with those blasted Wobblies.'' They had stopped apologizing to her for their language and Grace simply ignored it. ''Who invited the I.W.W. to Paterson anyway? They're nothing but a bunch of lying Bolsheviks. Fill the workers heads with nonsense—eight-hour days—that would be the ruination of the industry. But do they see that? They do not. You're as good as the owners, they tell 'em—you should live in a mansion and eat off fine china. Let me tell you, I worked hard for what I've got—and risked my capital—but do they think of that? They do not. They're at the bottom of this whole business, and I think they should lock 'em all in jail and throw away the key.''

"I think they should ship the Italian chap, what's his name, Tresca, back to Italy,'' said Austin. "Let him practice his anarchy over there.'' There was a murmur of agreement.

"That woman is the worst.'' This was Mr. Potter speaking. "Why isn't she home where she belongs? Taking care of her husband and child, instead of gadding about with other men. She's nothing but a . . .'' He glared at Grace then shrugged slightly. "Well, we all know what she is,'' he said, and they all laughed.

"If she were my wife, I'd soon make her behave,'' exclaimed another. "She might not be able to sit down for a week, but she'd stay home.''

Grace shuddered. They complained about the other strike leaders, but there was real venom when they spoke of Elizabeth Flynn. *It's because she's a woman,* thought Grace with a burst of sympathy. *They hate her because she's a woman and she's challenging them.* And suddenly she felt ashamed. If Elizabeth Flynn were here, she'd stand up right now and demand they do something for Moira. *I'm a coward,* she thought with a pang. What had happened to her? She hadn't been afraid to speak up at the mill. Ah, but now she had more to lose. She glanced at Rob and he reached over and touched her hand. He'd warned her before they came: *Remember whose side you're on, Grace. You can't straddle the fence.* She was one of the owners now and she had to try to see things their way. They were not going to listen to the workers' demands. Lambert just about summed it up when he declared, "I have the right to walk through my mill and fire any man I please if I don't like his looks, and by God no one's going to take that right away from me.''

"I agree with you Lina, but this strike isn't going to

last. Once their bellies are empty they'll come crawling back, and let's see what the I.W.W. does then. In the meantime no deals, agreed?''

The vote was unanimous and Grace had to go along. But later that night she took one hundred dollars from her dress allowance, slipped it into a plain white envelope and mailed it to the Sisters of Charity. They could use it for Moira and no one need ever know.

# CHAPTER

## ❧ 26 ❧

THE strike was not over in a few weeks. The presence of the I.W.W. put courage into the hearts of the strikers and fear into the hearts of the owners. Both sides dug in for a long siege. Paterson became a city divided, but as the strike wore on the mayor, the council, the police chief, and the merchants began to side with the owners. The mills stood idle, stores lost business, banks started to call in loans, mortgages were forfeited, and a heavy silence lay over the city.

A program of harrassment began. Gatherings were broken up, picketers arrested, meeting halls closed.

"Look at this," exclaimed Jeannie, who was avidly reading the latest news of the strike. "Bimson's closed down another hall. Soon there'll be no place left for the strikers to meet. That's anti-American, we have the right of assembly. Who does he think he is?"

"He's the Chief of Police, that's who," countered Aunt Flora, who was vigorously stirring a pot of porridge. "And I say good for him. Yon Wobblies are nae American, they're nought but a bunch o' Bolsheviks, and ought tae be run out o' town on a rail."

"Tarred and feathered, too, I suppose," said Jeannie sarcastically. "Well, not everyone around here is against us. We've been invited to Haledon."

"That's nae surprising, the mayor o' Haledon's a Bolshie too."

"No, he's a Socialist," said Ian, but he knew that to Aunt Flora it was the same thing. "I for one don't care where they meet as long as they reach a settlement, and soon."

"Och, Ian, we canna just settle," cried Jeannie. "We've got to win."

"Win." There was a trace of bitterness in Ian's voice. "We've already lost more than we'll ever regain." He looked at Maggie who was washing dishes at the sink, the child within her growing while she herself looked pale and drawn. It frightened him to see how quickly his small savings was disappearing. How was he going to put food on the table and pay the rent? The strike had to end soon.

"There's going tae be a meeting on Sunday at Pietro Botto's place in Haledon. They've got some sort of picnic grove there. Let's all go, it'll be a fine outing."

"Not me," said Aunt Flora. "Ye can go if ye want to. All the speechifying will probably be in Eyetalian anyway."

"Not all," said Jeannie. "Only Mr. Tresca speaks in Italian." She sighed. "He's sae handsome, and I think he's in love with Miss Flynn."

"*Mrs.* Flynn," snapped Aunt Flora. "And she should be home wi' her husband and child instead o' gaddin' about the countryside wi' strange men, Eyetalian ones at that." Then she glanced at Maggie and her expression softened. "But why don't ye go, Ian, and take Maggie. An outing would do her good, she looks sae pale."

" 'Twould be nice," said Maggie. "I hear the Bottos have a grand house and ye can get there by trolley." A house of her own at the end of the trolley line was Maggie's secret dream.

"All right," said Ian, "I guess I can afford the fare."

\* \* \*

It seemed to Maggie when they climbed down from the overcrowded trolley car that everyone in Paterson had decided to come to Haledon. The fields surrounding the Bottos' house were jammed with people. She spotted Big Nellie, Sneezer, and young Albert, and they shouldered their way through the crowd to join them.

"What a mob," said Ian.

"Yes, Bimson should see this," said Nellie. "He's done us a favor, the old fool. We got more people here than would fit in all the halls in Paterson."

"And all the best speakers are here," said Sneezer. "Tresca, Gurley Flynn, and Big Bill Haywood himself." At that moment Elizabeth Gurley Flynn made her way to a small platform built for the occasion. She wore a crisp white blouse, dark skirt, and her beautiful dark hair was pulled back into a low bun. She was young and pretty, and when she spread her arms in an embrace and smiled at the eager crowd they lost their hearts to her, Maggie included. Jeannie, who had given her heart away long ago, sighed with pleasure as Flynn began to speak.

"Let me ask you a question," she said. "The mill owners' wives and daughters wear the finest silks—do you wear silks? Do your wives, mothers, daughters, own one piece of the beautiful silk you make?"

"NO!" roared the crowd.

Jeannie remembered the shimmering green silk scarf that Grace had bought for Aunt Flora that first day they'd gone to Paterson, and how shocked they'd all been. Well, Grace was probably wearing silk right now and the rest of them were wearing frayed and mended cotton. Miss Flynn was right, it wasn't fair.

Gurley Flynn knew how to work the crowd—she had them in the palm of her hand when she finally turned the platform over to Carlo Tresca. Tresca, too, knew his audience, even those who couldn't understand his words felt the excitement of his message, so that when Big Bill finally appeared on the upstairs balcony the crowd went wild. In his gentle voice he spoke of a mill that was cool in the summer, warm in the winter, with big morris chairs so the workers could rest.

Nellie poked Jeannie in the ribs. "Remember what Grace went through to get us a couple of hard benches. Can you see them skinflints giving us morris chairs?" She gave a derisive snort. By now Maggie would have been glad of even a hard bench, she was beginning to feel a little faint.

"Ian," she whispered, "is there anywhere I can sit down for a wee bit?" Ian looked at her anxiously.

"I'm sorry Maggie, I didn't think. Let's see if they have a chair up at the house." Once more they made their way through the crowd towards the house. Ian spoke to a young woman who was on the porch. She beckoned to Maggie, who was leaning on the gate looking very peaked.

"Come on in," she said, "I'll get you a drink of water." Maggie disappeared into the house and Ian waited outside. He could still hear the speakers, could still feel the enthusiasm of the workers, but he had lost his. All he wanted was for the strike to be over so he could get back to work. He had hoped to have a doctor for Maggie's delivery, but if the strike didn't end soon he'd be lucky to get a midwife. And she needed more nourishing food— she needed milk, meat, and eggs, not just carrots and turnips. When she reappeared he suggested they go home.

"Jeannie will be all right, she's with Big Nellie. If we leave now we'll beat the crush." Maggie was just as happy to leave. She hadn't realized how tired she was. Once they were on the trolley she put her head on Ian's shoulder and closed her eyes.

"I shouldn't have brought you here," said Ian. "You're exhausted."

"Nae, I enjoyed it. Och, Ian, ye should see the Bottos' house. They've a fine hallway in the middle, wi' a grand set o' stairs wi' a real carpet runner on them. There's a parlor on the right and a proper dinin' room wi' tables and chairs and a lace cloth and all. D'ye think we'll ever ha'e sich a fine house?''

"We will, Maggie, I promise you. Once this miserable strike is over, I've got a lot of plans." But Maggie was asleep.

"The mill owners want to meet with the small shops," said Ian. "Old Mac thinks I should go." The three of them were on the porch, Maggie in the rocker knitting something small and white, Ian on a chair, and Jeannie perched on the railing.

"Och, Ian, ye canna start to side wi' the owners now," wailed Jeannie, "wi' victory sae near."

"Victory!" said Ian. "People are starving, mortgages are being foreclosed. The McCready family were put out on the street the other day and their neighbors had to take them in. Mac and I are in danger of losing our shop and everything in it, and you talk of victory."

"They canna take away your tools and your looms can they?" said Maggie, looking up from her knitting. She had a fierce interest in the shop. She felt she was part of it. "I dinna understand why ye don't do some small weaving jobs, it would bring in some money."

"And be a strike breaker," said Jeannie scornfully. "Ian wouldna' do that."

"I canna see what good this strike is doing for us, or for anyone for that matter," persisted Maggie. "Are ye going to the meeting then?"

"Might as well, hear what they have to offer."

Jeannie jumped off the railing. "Could I come with ye? I'd like to hear for myself what those bloodsuckers have to say."

"You mean you want to keep an eye on me and make sure I don't sell out," said Ian over Jeannie's protests, but he agreed to let her come.

He watched her as they walked along, her head high, braids flying, a spring to her step and a determined lift to her chin. *This strike means so much to her,* he thought, *but I have Maggie to think about, and the baby. What difference would it make if I did agree to start up my looms. Maybe I could lease them out, at least it would mean some money coming in.*

"Where's this meeting being held?" asked Jeannie.

"Potter's Mill, in the office."

"Good, then I get to face the auld skinflint himself across the table. He's going to get an earful from me."

"Now listen, Jeannie, this is between the owners and the small shops. By rights you shouldn't even be here. In fact, they may put you out when they recognize you."

"Who's going to recognize me? Potter wouldn't know who his workers were if he fell over them. And I don't think old Anderson will be there. But don't worry, I'll be good."

They had reached the mill by now and were being stopped by the pickets. Jeannie explained that this was a meeting of small shop owners.

"And I'm here tae see it's all legal. They're nay going to start settling behind our backs."

"Go on then, Jeannie," said Big Nellie. "I know you'll never give in to them, and if you see old Potter, tell that hard-hearted bag o' bones that he'd better do something for Moira. She'll be leavin' the sisters soon, and not a penny to her name."

Moira was one of the reasons Jeannie was such an ardent striker. The mill had done nothing to help her. Even after she'd written to Grace. *Grace!* Jeannie stopped dead in her tracks.

"Ian," she cried, but she was too late. Ian had already gone inside and joined the other independent weavers in Mr. Whitehead's office. Jeannie raced after him and arrived just as a tall, white-haired man was welcoming them.

"Gentlemen, glad you could come. My name is Carter and this is Mr. Ryle, Mr. Todd . . ." he continued the introductions ". . . and here representing Mr. Potter is his partner, Mrs. Harwood, and we have another charming lady present today, Mrs. DeWitt-Kenton.''

Jeannie had reached Ian's side by now, but he was unaware of her, he had eyes for only one person in the room and that was Grace.

"Why, *Mrs. Harwood*, your friends are here," murmured Mrs. DeWitt-Kenton. "Are they going to serve refreshments?" she added spitefully.

"We're here tae see what the owners have to offer, ma'am," said Jeannie quickly, "but I doubt it will be anything of interest to us."

"Now just a minute, just a minute, gentlemen, and ladies, too," Mr. Carter nodded towards Jeannie. "Suppose we all sit down. Do we have enough chairs?" Chairs were found and the groups sat, mill owners on one side, shop owners on the other. "Now that we're all comfortable, let us begin," he said. "We're not here to exploit our differences, we are here because we share a common interest— silk. Stores in New York are clamoring for silk. If you are willing to weave it, we are willing to pay you for it. It's to everyone's advantage."

"It's nae to the workers' advantage," muttered Jeannie.

"The workers! Can't you see it's their stubbornness that's hurting you?" said Mrs. DeWitt-Kenton. "What does it matter to you people if we go to four looms?"

"That's true," exclaimed a small, grizzled man. "I've only got three looms anyway. Would you provide us with raw silk and guarantee a price for the finished goods?"

"Of course we will," said Mr. Carter smoothly.

"For how long?" said Ian. "What happens when the strike is over?" He stared steadily at Carter. After the first shock of recognition he tried not to look at Grace, but even in that brief moment she had made an indelible impression. She was wearing some sort of blue dress with white collar and cuffs, and a small white straw hat sat atop her upswept red-gold hair. She looked both cool and beautiful. Her cheeks had flushed at the sight of him and then turned very pale. He knew he had probably done the same, and his heartbeat was so loud he felt sure it could be heard across the room as he tried to concentrate on Carter's reply.

"I told you the stores are desperate for silk. There will be more work than you can handle."

"But if ye go to four looms ye'll build up your inventories, then ye'll cut prices and wages, and where will we be then?" cried Jeannie, her good intentions forgotten.

"It won't affect you," said one of the owners, "so what are you worrying about?"

"The workers are our friends and neighbors," said Ian. "We don't want to hurt them."

"What's the difference?" said Mrs. DeWitt-Kenton. "If you don't want to work, there are plenty in Pennsylvania who will, and for less money, too. Isn't that right, Mrs. Harwood? I hear you and Mr. Potter just signed a contract in Scranton."

"Och, Grace, ye didna'," cried Jeannie. "How could ye? Ye'll spend your money in Pennsylvania, but not a penny will ye give to a poor girl who had the hair torn from her head by one o' your broken machines. 'Tis wicked and selfish ye've become just like that old skinflint, Potter—"

"Now just a minute, just a minute," broke in Mr. Carter. "Young woman, how dare you insult Mrs. Harwood. Who are you, anyway? Do you represent one of the shops?"

"Nae, but I represent the workers—"

"Then you have no business being at this meeting. Kindly leave immediately."

Jeannie looked around her desperately.

"Can't ye see they are not concerned about you?" she cried. "They're just worried about putting more money in their own pockets. Admit it, Grace."

But Grace couldn't trust herself to speak. Her fingers locked together, her face pale, she looked imploringly at

Ian. Surely he would understand. She knew Potter had
sent work to Pennsylvania, but she hadn't been consulted.
Potter never consulted her if he could help it. And as for
the poor girl who lost her hair, Grace had sent money to
the convent, but she couldn't say anything here in front
of the others, they'd despise her for it. But now Jeannie
and Ian despised her anyway.

" 'Tis a traitor ye've become, Grace," said Jeannie. "I
never thought I'd live to see the day that my own cousin
turned traitor."

Ian stood up. "Come on, Jeannie, we don't belong here.
I'm sorry, gentlemen, but we'll do no business until the
strike is settled."

There was much scraping of chairs as the shop owners
stood up to leave. Mrs. DeWitt-Kenton looked derisively
at Grace, "It seems that treachery is your stock in trade,
*Mrs. Harwood.*"

Grace escaped from the scornful eye of Mrs. DeWitt-
Kenton and the oppressive atmosphere of the mill as
quickly as she could. Thank heaven Rob had insisted on a
chauffeured carriage to take her back to the ferryboat. She
slipped into it quietly, feeling a surge of guilt as she
watched her erstwhile co-workers, bearing their heavy
picket signs and trudging up and down in the hot sun. If
they recognized her, they gave no sign as the carriage
quickly sped away.

She sank back on the cushioned seat and closed her
eyes, but it didn't help. She kept seeing Ian. Ian sitting
across from her, so close she could have touched him. Oh,
how she wanted to. She'd heard his smothered gasp and
seen the hunger that had leapt into his eyes at the sight of
her. Her own pulse raced at the memory of his lean, strong
face. How handsome he looked, even in his work clothes,
which she guessed he had worn deliberately and with
pride. Ian's pride—oh, what it was costing them.

*Why must we be so far apart?* she thought. What harm

could there be if we saw each other once in a while? But she knew that would not be enough. Ian was the only man she had ever really loved, and sitting in her chauffeur-driven carriage, oblivious to the envious glances that followed her as they sped through the narrow New Jersey streets, Grace lamented Ian's pride.

When they reached the ferry she dismissed the chauffeur and found a seat on the corner of the deck. Ignoring the other passengers she remained by herself, staring heedlessly at the skyline of Manhattan as the boat chugged slowly across the river to where Rob would be waiting for her.

Her mind was still filled with thoughts of Ian as she left the ferryboat but gradually as the other passengers disappeared and she was left standing on the curb, she began to wonder where Rob was. It was then she noticed Jones, their housekeeper, making her way across the street. The woman's nervous manner and pale face already told Grace she had bad news and her heart gave a terrible lurch. *Andrew,* she thought, *it's Andrew.*

But as Jones reached her the woman blurted out, "It's Mr. Harwood, Ma'am. There's been an accident. He's in the hospital."

Grace stared at the woman, torn between relief and anxiety. "What happened?" she cried, clutching her arm.

"His carriage overturned. I don't know how bad he was hurt."

"Where have they taken him?"

"Bellevue, Ma'am. Do you need a cab?"

"Yes, yes. I must go right away."

Jones hailed a hansom cab and helped Grace into it.

"Are you sure you'll be all right, Mrs. Harwood?"

"Yes, don't worry about me. Go home and explain to Nanny, and be sure no one upsets little Andrew. I'll let you know how Mr. Harwood is as soon as I can."

Grace clung to the sides of the carriage as it rattled through the streets. Emotions swept over her in waves—

guilt, relief, and fear of what had happened to Rob. She had to see him, to speak to him, to take his hand. He had been so good to her; he'd been her salvation. He'd given her everything, and how had she repaid him? By dreaming of Ian. "Oh, God," she prayed, "don't let him die. Please don't let him die."

She repeated the prayer as she followed a starched and straight-backed nurse down the long, shiny corridor of the hospital.

"We put Mr. Harwood in a private room as he needs to rest," said the nurse, "so I suggest you don't stay long." She opened the door and stood aside so that Grace could enter. To her immense relief Rob was half-sitting up in the narrow, iron hospital bed. His usually crisp hair was dishevelled, his face had a grayish tinge to it, a large plaster was taped above his eye, and his right arm was in a sling.

"Oh, Rob!" She ran to him.

"Visitors are not permitted to sit on the beds," came a glacial voice from the doorway. "There are chairs provided." Grace dutifully pulled up a hard, wooden chair and waited until the woman had departed. Then she sat on the edge of the bed, took Rob's good hand and held it to her cheek. For a moment she couldn't speak as relief washed over her. He was alive.

"What happened?" she whispered.

"I'm not really sure." His voice sounded weak and quavery. "One minute we were rolling along, the next minute it was all flailing hooves, screams, and the crunch of wood and metal. Next thing I knew I was being wheeled in here."

"What about your arm?"

"Just a dislocated shoulder, and the rest is cuts and bruises. I'll be out of here in no time." He squeezed her hand gently and gave her a faint smile. She felt a tightness in her throat and she couldn't seem to speak. The silence stretched between them. Finally Rob spoke.

"How did the meeting go?"

Grace felt herself flush. "Not too well. The shop owners walked out on us."

She didn't mention Jeannie and she certainly didn't mention Ian—just the thought of him flooded her with guilt. She felt as if she were being punished, but that wasn't fair. If it was a punishment, she was the one who should be lying in the hospital bed, not Rob.

"Let's not worry about the mill, Rob. What about you? How soon will they let you come home? We can hire some nurses if necessary . . ."

"Now wait a minute. I'm not an invalid. I'm a bit sore at the moment, but other than that I'm fine."

However, as he said this he laid back on his pillow, his face drawn and exhausted. He seemed relieved when the nurse returned to tell Grace it was time to leave, but as she stood up he clutched her sleeve.

"The driver got the worst of it, poor devil. See if there's anything we can do for him." He lay back again and his eyes were closing when she bent to kiss him goodbye.

"He needs to sleep," said the nurse not unkindly as Grace followed her back into the corridor. "And the doctor would like a word with you, Mrs. Harwood. His office is at the end of the hall."

The doctor was a short, portly man with a harried look about him, but he welcomed her into his office and seated her in a comfortable chair before he took his place behind his desk.

"I'm afraid this has been quite a shock for you, Mrs. Harwood, but I do assure you that your husband's injuries are not serious. He was fortunate, it could have been much worse."

"Well, I'm relieved to hear that," said Grace.

"However," he continued, tapping the desk nervously with a pencil, "we have uncovered a problem. Mr. Harwood is experiencing a wildly erratic heartbeat. Now it may be entirely due to the shock of the accident, but I fear it is indicative of some permanent damage.''

"You mean Rob has a bad heart?'' exclaimed Grace. "But he's always been the very picture of health.''

"Yes, well, we cannot always go by looks. We are monitoring him closely, but I am recommending complete rest. No strenuous activities, no excitement, nothing to disturb or upset him. If you can guarantee that, Mrs. Harwood, he can probably leave here in a day or two.''

"Of course, I'll do anything you say. I've already suggested we hire some nurses.''

"That would be an excellent idea. We have a register of visiting nurses here in the hospital.''

"Does Rob know this—about his heart, I mean?''

"I think he suspects it, but I intend to talk to him later on today. If he cooperates, then there is a good chance he will improve.''

"And if he doesn't improve?''

The doctor shrugged his shoulders. "It is hard to say, Mrs. Harwood, but we will keep a close watch on him.'' He stood up and extended his hand.

"Thank you for being so frank with me, Doctor,'' said Grace. But as she emerged into the corridor she felt as if she were living through some strange nightmare. The long white corridors, the nurses moving on silent, rubber-soled feet, the reek of disinfectant, what had this to do with Rob? Rob, who had always been so charged with life and energy. He couldn't have a bad heart, he couldn't.

# CHAPTER

## ❧ 27 ❧

PATERSON grew hungry. Soup kitchens were organized and for many that was the only meal of the day. Children were sent away. Jeannie met Big Nellie on the picket line and tears were running down the big woman's face.

"Young Albert's gone," she said, wiping her eyes with the back of her hand. "The whole bunch of 'em got taken in by some farmer in Connecticut. Mind you, it'll do Albert good, all that fresh air and big farmhouse meals, but I'm goin' to miss the runny-nosed little runt." She blew her own vast nose and hoisted her picket sign a little higher, and Jeannie saw once more that in spite of her tough exterior Big Nellie had a heart as soft as a feather bed and just as big. "How about your Eyetalian friends," she added, "did they send their kids away too?"

"No," said Jeannie. "I dinna know how they're managing, but they are. They've been through strikes before in Italy. Mrs. Simonetti told us to get some goats, but of course Aunt Flora wouldna' listen."

"What I can't figure is how the mill owners are holding out. They're losing money every day."

"Not as much as you think," said Jeannie bitterly. "They're sending work to Pennsylvania."

"But what about the small shops?"

"So far they're supporting us, but I dinna know how long it will last. The mill owners are doing their best to get them on their side. Soon they'll have everyone on their side. They've already got the mayor, the police, and all the bigwigs in their pockets. We're the ones who get blamed for everything, but it's the owners who go around stirring up trouble. Look at their so-called 'special police,' nothing but a bunch of goons. They go around beating up the strikers, and then we're the ones who are locked up in jail, like poor Will."

"Or dead, like Mr. Modesto, shot by one o' them specials, and him not even a striker. It just ain't fair, here's Will locked up for walking up and down with a sign around his neck, and the man who shot Mr. Modesto is walking around free. Of course, they say it was an accident, but if we shot one o' the mill owners we'd be strung up, accident or no. And they call themselves Americans." Nellie spat on the sidewalk.

Will spent thirty days in what the workers called "Bimson's Hotel," but when he came out he was still chipper.

"Listen," he told them, "there's going to be some fireworks soon, mark my words. While I was a guest of the county a young fella was brought in, name of Jack Reed. Real high-toned, good clothes, talked real proper, but Big Bill said he was okay. Seems he's some sort of a writer, and he's going to put on a pageant to tell the world about how we're being treated by the mill owners and Paterson's 'finest'."

"Where's he going to hold this pageant?"

"New York, and all the big newspapers will be there. That'll make the mill owners sit up and take notice."

Grace stepped into the small cage-like elevator and pressed the button. It rose slowly and smoothly up past the curved stairway. She had been amazed at how quickly it had been installed. The doctor had suggested it, and it enabled Rob to come downstairs for at least part of the day. In fact, her day now revolved around Rob's time spent downstairs, and she was on her way up to see if he was ready.

He met her on the landing.

"You're looking very smart this morning," she said. Rob was dressed as if he were going to the office, and in a way he was. Grace had arranged to have the office mail delivered to the house, then she and Rob went over it, making decisions, arranging purchases and sales. Grace thoroughly enjoyed these sessions. She felt she was back where she belonged in the world of business and finance. Now she arose eagerly each morning, anticipating new challenges with each new day. It was strange that it had taken Rob's illness to truly bring her back to life.

He kissed her gently on the cheek. "And you, my dear, are looking beautiful, as always."

They took the elevator down to Rob's study and there he seated himself behind his desk. They worked quietly and efficiently, and Grace took notes as Rob carefully explained each transaction. *He's teaching me the business in case anything happens.* She pushed the thought aside with a shiver. When they had completed their session, Grace called Miss Finch and had a messenger come and pick up the papers. Once a week she went into the office where she met with the managerial staff, legal advisers, and Maisie's Joe. She still mentally called him Maisie's Joe, even though he was now their accountant. She seldom saw Maisie, who was living way out in Westchester and was expecting her second baby. Joe was an excellent accountant and Grace knew exactly how Harwood Associates stood financially. Their balance was good, in spite of the strike.

"Of course, I would recommend you sell your shares in the mill once it resumes production," said Joe. His accent was growing fainter each day, and he had long since abandoned his black wool suit. "Paterson has too many labor problems to make it a sound place to invest,'' he added.

Grace had quickly realized that buying into Potter's had been a bad move. Prompted by a burst of vain pride, she had had dreams of turning the mill around, making it a model of labor and management relations, but the strike had squashed that dream, and Mr. Potter's resentment of her made it unlikely she would influence his running of the mill once the strike was over. But Harwood Associates was another matter. Rob had always listened to her suggestions, had treated her as an equal. She was beginning to realize what a remarkable and unusual man he was.

She looked at him fondly as he gathered up the papers on his desk. To the casual observer he still looked like a man in his prime, still gave off an aura of energy and authority, but Grace noticed with a pang the slight tremor in his hands, the occasional shortness of breath, the weariness in his step when he returned to his room to rest, and she sighed. He looked up at her.

''Have you heard the latest attempt by the strikers to drum up sympathy for their cause?'' he asked.

''No, what is it?''

''According to Joe, and he has his ear to the ground, they're planning a pageant. Damn fool idea if you ask me, but they've got themselves mixed up with a bunch of radicals from the village—writers, artists, you know the sort. Anyway they're putting on a pageant in Madison Square Garden.''

''But that must be costing them a fortune,'' exclaimed Grace.

''I told you it was a damn fool idea. And who do they think is going to go and see it? Not the owners and investors, you can be sure of that.''

*I wonder who's going to be in it?* thought Grace. Not Ian, she couldn't picture him play-acting. But perhaps he would go to see it. Yes, she was sure he would go to see it.

\* \* \*

"I'm going to be in the pageant," said Jeannie proudly. "Mr. Reed says we're going to show the world what's happening in Paterson."

"Will ye have tae go to New York?" asked Maggie anxiously.

"Not by yourself!" exclaimed Aunt Flora.

"No, we'll all go there together and practice. Mr. Reed is taking care of everything."

"And who is this Mr. Reed?" said Aunt Flora suspiciously.

"He's a writer. He's got a fine college degree and he knows lots of important people."

"Then what's he doing in Paterson?"

"He came here to write about the strike, and d'ye know what the old fool Bimson did? Had him arrested and thrown in jail. Well, he'll be sorry because now Mr. Reed's going to put on his pageant at Madison Square Garden and everyone will know what's going on—people being arrested, beaten, and killed."

"Och, it's not that bad," said Maggie. "I dinna think ye should get mixed up with this pageant, Jeannie. What do ye think, Ian?"

"I guess there's no harm in it," said Ian. "But I can't see much good coming from it either. It's just a game to these rich people, but it's life and death to us."

"It's going tae raise money for the strikers, Ian, you'll see." Jeannie was elated.

Many of the strikers, however, shared Ian's views, especially those who weren't in it. They were the ones who continued picketing day after day. Hot, tired, and hungry they walked up and down the streets of Paterson, harrassed by the police, ignored by the populace, while those in the pageant were taken into New York, given a good lunch, and brought home again filled with high spirits and enthusiasm. In spite of the doubts and resentments, when the big day came on June 6th Paterson put on a united front, and it seemed as if the whole town turned out for the occasion. They filled the trains and the ferries, and once in New York, lined up eight to ten abreast and marched down the Avenue, waving their red banners and singing strike songs.

But no one was able to go from number ten. Maggie was not feeling well enough, and Aunt Flora wanted no part of it, so Ian, who would have liked to have actually seen the pageant, felt he should stay home with his wife, and had to be content with Jeannie's description.

"Och, Ian, ye should have been there," she told him the next day. She'd been up all night but was still too keyed up to sleep. "The place was packed, almost all the strikers were there. Then when the curtain went up it looked like the whole city of Paterson had been picked up and put on the stage. The audience went wild. The silk mills were lined up in the background, lights shining from their windows. Then the strike was called and the workers came pouring out into the street and the mills went dark." As she talked Jeannie acted out the scene, pacing up and down the kitchen waving an imaginary picket sign. "Then the so-called special police came and started beating up the workers—oh, ye should have heard the crowd boo. Then they showed Mr. Modesto being shot. He died in the arms of his wife—everyone was crying both onstage and in the audience people were sobbing out loud. But the funeral was the best part. Ian, ye should have been there." Jeannie paused to wipe the tears from her own eyes.

"They carried the coffin right down the aisles and everyone threw red carnations on it—soon it was covered with red carnations, the whole place was covered with red carnations. Then Big Bill got up to speak, just as he does at our meetings, and ye could have heard a pin drop, but when he finished his speech the whole crowd got to their feet and cheered. They cheered and cheered, and they sang the Internationale." She danced around the room. "It was the grandest night of my whole life."

But in the end the pageant did more harm than good. The expected monies didn't materialize. Most of the audience were workers and only paid about a dime for admission, the cost of the hall was higher than anyone had figured, and Jack Reed's friend, Mabel Dodge, wound up paying the balance out of her own pocket. The strike wasn't over yet.

Grace was shaken by the pageant. She knew she shouldn't have gone, but it drew her like a magnet. *Perhaps*, whispered a treacherous little voice, *Ian will be there*.

None of the other owners would even think of going.

"Lot of radical nonsense," said one. "Shows they've got nothing better to do with their time than play-acting with a bunch of Bolsheviks."

But Grace went. She dressed in her oldest clothes and bought a ticket at the door. She recognized Jeannie up on the stage, and thought she saw Big Nellie and Sneezer in the audience, but there was no sign of Ian. Oh, well, what would she have done had he been there? She didn't know. But now she knew she didn't want to be recognized. She pulled her hat down a little more and shrank back in her seat. Surely, she told herself as the story unfolded, they don't beat on the workers like that, and surely they aren't so hungry that they had to send the children away. She thought of little Andrew, fat and rosy, who bounced on her bed every morning. Supposing she had to send him away; she couldn't bear it.

In the end, after the funeral procession, when the big man started to speak and everyone stood up and cheered, she slipped away. She hadn't even told Rob she was going, but he had guessed.

"You can't let them get to you, Grace. It's all propaganda, you know."

"Maybe, but if they are hungry, and Maggie's expect-

ing—Jeannie wrote to me about it—well, I am their cousin.
There could be no harm in sending them a food package."

He kissed her gently. "They may send it back—they're
a stubborn bunch those silk workers—but if it will ease
your conscience, my dear, go ahead and send one. Just
don't tell anyone."

"Rob, you're an angel." She threw her arms around
him, then hurried down to the kitchen.

"What do you want me to put in it, Mrs. Harwood?"
asked the cook.

"Everything," said Grace. "Send them everything they
could possibly need."

Ian refused to picket and spent his days trying to find
some extra work. Maggie's time was drawing close and
they needed many things. His own looms stood idle and
there were no repair jobs to be had. He and Mac could
barely pay the rent for the shop, but they'd hang on somehow, even if he had to pawn his father's watch. He'd managed to scrounge some wood and had built a cradle,
working by himself in the empty shop. Maggie spent her
days sewing scraps of linen into a layette, but even that
task seemed to tire her. And as for Aunt Flora, she was
constantly bewailing her meager larder. Ian felt if he never
saw another dish of porridge it would be fine with him.
Their hens had long since stopped laying and been con-
signed to the pot as they could no longer afford to feed
them. They could scarcely afford to feed themselves. That's
why he was shocked to arrive home that evening, empty-
handed and disheartened, to find almost a party going on.
Jock and his wife and the neighbors from across the street
were there. Maggie ran to greet him. For a moment he
thought the strike must be over, but then Maggie started
dragging him into the kitchen.

"Och, Ian, look at this wonderful surprise." A huge,
half-opened crate stood in the middle of the floor. "It's

from Grace. Look Ian; tins of milk, tea, good salmon, even peaches. Och, isn't it wonderful.''

"Wonderful!'' All the humiliations and frustrations of the past weeks welled up inside of him. Grace! Grace and that man Harwood, living in luxury while they starved, and now offering him charity. Well he wouldn't take it. "Get that the hell out of here!'' he shouted. "Do you think I'm going to accept charity from a mill owner? Send it back.'' Maggie recoiled as if he'd struck her.

"Send it back?'' wailed Aunt Flora, clutching a tin of Scottish shortbread. "Ye canna send it back, it's been opened.''

"It's not staying in my house,'' said Ian bitterly. "Jock, Davie, give me a hand. We'll take it down to the Nag's Head and pass it around.''

Aunt Flora fled to her room to hide the shortbread, Maggie was weeping, and the other women looked at each other and quietly crept away. Jock and Davie dragged the crate outside and hoisted it onto Davie's old wagon.

"Okay fellas, do whatever you want with it,'' said Ian, and he returned to face a hysterical Maggie.

"It's because it's from Grace, isn't it,'' she cried. "You don't care that we're starving, but you can't take anything from Grace because you're still in love with her. You've always been in love with her. 'Tis her ye should have married, not me.''

He was stunned. He didn't know what to say. He tried to take her in his arms, but she pushed him away.

"Leave me alone, don't touch me. I hate you. I hate—'' Suddenly she doubled over and clutched her swollen belly. He looked at her in horror. She straightened up and groped her way to a chair, but in a few minutes she was gasping for breath and doubled over again. He ran to the stairs.

"Aunt Flora,'' he yelled. "Come quick, it's Maggie.''

Flora ran down the stairs, and took one look at Maggie who whispered, "I think the baby's coming.''

*Oh, God,* thought Ian, *Not now, please not now.* But Aunt Flora grasped his arm.

"Get the midwife, bring her back immediately. *Then stay out of our way.*" And she pushed him out the door.

He walked the streets. He knew he should have been at Maggie's side, but he couldn't bear to see her pale, stricken face, or look at the tiny wrinkled little creature that had barely the strength to cry.

"You've got a daughter, Ian," said the midwife after what had seemed like an eternity. "A wee little girl. But she's awful puny, I'm afraid, and Maggie's so weak I don't think she's going to have much milk."

"But the baby's going to be all right, isn't she?" He searched her face for an answer but she turned away.

"It's in the hands of God," she said.

He paid her the few dollars he had hidden away for the purpose and went in to see Maggie. She looked exhausted and tears trickled unheeded down her face. *She's half starved,* he thought. *She's been sacrificing herself for me.* "Eat Ian," she'd say. "Ye need your strength. I've nought to do but lay around here all day."

"Our baby's going to die," she whispered. He looked at the tiny bundle that lay in the crook of her arm. The fragile egg-shell head with its dusting of down caused his heart to constrict.

"She's not going to die, Maggie, she's not," he said fiercely. "I'll get you some food—milk, butter, eggs." *Oh God,* he thought, *all the things I wouldn't accept from Grace.*

So he walked the streets, a tumult of emotions. He'd always dreamed of having a son. A fine, strong, handsome little fellow who would one day work alongside of him. Instead, he had a daughter. A tiny, frail, little scrap of humanity, who hovered between life and death. And somehow it was his fault. His own false pride might cost him the life of his child. Pride, the sin that brought down

Lucifer, the root sin, the original sin. He was overwhelmed by guilt. But there was an even greater guilt, one
that he buried deep within his subconscious, one that he
couldn't bear to acknowledge. "Grace," Maggie had said,
"you're still in love with Grace."

He noticed a house standing on a large corner lot where
chickens pecked among the rows of vegetables. He
knocked on the door. The woman who answered looked
tired and drawn, several small children clung to her skirts.

"Will you sell me some of your eggs?" he asked. She
shook her head sadly and pointed to the children.

"Too many mouths," she said. "No can sell." It was
the same everywhere. Too many mouths to feed, not
enough food to feed them with. He stumbled back home,
tired and defeated. Tomorrow he'd have to try again. He
turned the key in the lock and stepped into the small hallway. A heavenly aroma greeted him, and Jeannie flew out
of the kitchen and threw her arms around him.

"Och, Ian, they're going to be all right. Maggie, the
baby, everything's going to be all right." He looked at her
dazedly. She was radiant.

"What's that smell?" he murmured.

"Spaghetti sauce," she looked at his puzzled face. "The
Simonettis are here." She announced it in a tone that indicated the cavalry had arrived. Without further explanation she led him into the kitchen where an equally dazed
Aunt Flora sat at the table watching Mama Simonetti stirring a big pot. Tony was outside plucking a chicken and
various Simonetti daughters were trooping up and down
the stairs. Mama stopped her stirring long enough to clasp
him to her ample bosom and congratulate him on becoming a Papa.

"Maggie, how's Maggie?" he cried.

"She's going to be fine," said Jeannie. "Come and
see." Upstairs he found Maggie sitting up in bed, a large
tray in front of her and a slim, dark-eyed girl urging her
to *"Mangia, mangia."* Another Simonetti daughter was qui-

etly rocking in the corner, the baby—his baby—hungrily nursing at her breast.

"You're all sae kind," said Maggie, wiping away the tears that flowed unchecked but smiling in spite of them.

Later, when Maggie and the baby slept, they all gathered around the kitchen table and Mama ladled out generous portions of pasta and sauce.

"Jeannie, remember I tell you to get a goat," said Mama. "*Bambinos* need milk, mamas need milk. I send milk for little Maggie. Tony you bring, every day."

"How can I repay you?" said Ian.

"Jeannie helpa my girls, now we helpa you. We neighbors, no? Tony, you finish cleaning chicken?"

"*Sì*, Mama, I put it in the icebox."

"Good. Now *Tia* Flora, tomorrow you make big pot chicken soup, give to Maggie. Soon she have lotsa milk for *bambino*."

Ian had to turn away so they wouldn't see the tears in his eyes.

Later that night when everyone had gone, he sat on the side of the bed while Maggie put the baby to her own breast.

"She's going to be fine, Ian. I'm sorry I said all those awful things—I didn't know what I was doing."

He took her hand and squeezed it tight. "I'm sorry I was such a pig-headed fool, Maggie. Forgive me."

She gently wrapped the now contented baby in a shawl and handed her to him.

"Say hello to your little girl, and then put her in the cradle." Ian looked once more at the little face, no longer screwed up in hunger but pink and soft. He examined the tiny fingers and toes, marveling at their perfection.

"She's beautiful, Maggie," he whispered.

"I havena' even got a name for her. I was sae sure I would give ye a son, Ian. Ye dinna mind do ye?"

"Of course not. And her name is Margaret, just like

her mother, but I think we'll call her Meg.'' He gently kissed the tiny head as he laid her in the homemade cradle. Then he turned and took Maggie in his arms and all the angry words were forgotten.

# CHAPTER

## ❧ 28 ❧

"I'm going back to work," said Ian.

"But you canna'," cried Jeannie. "The strike's not over."

"It is as far as I'm concerned, and I'm not the only one. Half the mills are operating, the dye shops are open, and the ribbon workers have settled. I've got Maggie and the baby to think about. The mill owners aren't going to give in, so what's left to strike for? There's no money left in the relief fund."

"Aye," said Aunt Flora. "Where's all that money from the pageant? Lining the pockets o' those rich New Yorkers I'll be bound."

"That's not true," cried Jeannie passionately. " 'Twas not their fault the pageant lost money."

"Oh, no? Then why has that Mr. Reed gone off to Mexico? And that Big Haywood man, where's he? Sailin' off tae Europe."

"He's sick, that's why he had to go away. Miss Flynn told me." Jeannie was near tears. "You dinna understand."

"Och, I understand. These thieving Bolshies, come here and stir up trouble, then when they've taken all your money, off they go to make trouble somewhere else."

"What difference does it make now, Aunt Flora?" said

Maggie. "Ian's going back tae work, and soon he'll be able to start bringin' some silks home for us tae work on, the other doesna' matter."

But it mattered to Jeannie. She had so desperately wanted the strike to be successful, but she knew it was a lost cause as far as the other three were concerned. She left them sitting around the kitchen table and set off on foot to a meeting in Turn Hall. But when she got there the mood was gloomy, and even Gurley Flynn advised them to settle as best they could. She told them the mayor of Haledon had been indicted, so now they had nowhere left to hold their rallies. It was soon obvious to everyone that the I.W.W. were packing up and leaving town.

"It's back to the dungeons for us," said Big Nellie. "But I reckon I'm ready for it."

"Well I'm not," declared Jeannie. "I don't know what I'm going to do, but I'm never going back to Potter's basement."

"Young Albert ain't comin' back either," said Nellie. "Seems 'ee's thrivin' on the farm and they're letting 'im stay there. It just won't be the same. I hear Moira's comin' back, though."

Jeannie, who had been visiting Moira regularly, was distraught at the thought of her friend working once more on the winding machines. She still had nightmares of that terrible day.

"I wish she didn't have to. There must be something else she could do."

"What, for instance? She's gotta live—can't stay with them nuns forever. You've got your aunt and your cousin to watch out for you, but Moira ain't got no one. She's lucky Potter's is taking her back."

"Lucky. The only lucky thing could happen at that mill would be for Potter to drop dead," said Jeannie in disgust. She didn't mention Grace. She had never told any of them that Grace was co-owner. She was too embarrassed. How could Grace have turned against them like that? The only

reason Jeannie could think of was that her husband forced
her into it. But it was still no excuse.

"I reckon the strike did do one thing," said Will, who
had joined them. "They're not going to make us go to
four looms, and that's what it was all about in the first
place."

That was small comfort to Jeannie, who had dreamed
of an eight-hour day, decent wages, and a clean, comfortable workplace. *I won't go back,* she thought, *I'll stay with
the I.W.W.* But when she approached them she found they
didn't have a job for her, either. They were leaving town,
going out west to work with the miners. Jeannie felt abandoned, as did many in Paterson.

There had to be something she could do besides work
in a mill. She'd heard of other groups. There was someone
called Margaret Sanger who talked about birth control,
whatever that was. Then there was Emma Goldman, who
was always writing about equality for women. *Ha! that'll
be the day,* thought Jeannie. She'd read something about
Miss Goldman giving a lecture in New York. Perhaps if
she went in and spoke to her. New York was not so terrifying to her since she'd gone there to take part in the
pageant, but just the same it would be better not to tell
Aunt Flora or Ian, as they definitely wouldn't approve.
Perhaps she could talk Moira into going with her. Maybe
they would both find a job and Moira wouldn't have to go
back to the mill, either. She counted out her money, there
was just about enough for carfare. That was a good sign.

Moira agreed to go with her. This would be her first
venture into the outside world since the accident. She had
finally left the sheltering walls of the convent and was back
in her little room where the sisters had paid the rent for
the next two weeks. After that she was on her own. She
saw no alternative but to go back to the mill, although the
thought filled her with dread. Perhaps something would
come of this trip, but she doubted it. She wound a scarf

around her scarred and battered head and hurried to the station to meet Jeannie.

The sight of Moira's head, now swathed in scarves, still filled Jeannie with rage, and her anger at Mrs. Anderson and the mill owners grew fiercer every day. *I've got to find someplace else to work,* she thought desperately. *If I go back to Potter's I'll be fired before the day's half over.*

They made their way into the city easily. Jeannie now knew the way, but they had some trouble finding the hall where Emma Goldman was speaking, and finally discovered it tucked away on a small side street. Once inside, however, they saw that the place was quite full. There were several men in the audience, many of them wearing little skull caps, their faces covered with bristly black beards, but their overall appearance was more gentle than fierce. The women were mixed—some very plain, with hair pulled severely back from pale faces, while others were fashionably dressed. The two girls worked their way down the aisle, which was lined with grim-faced muscular men, until they reached the front row. A number of people were on the platform, including a heavy, dark-haired woman with round, steel-rimmed glasses, whom Jeannie recognized from the newspaper as Emma Goldman.

"Wait here," she whispered. "I'm going to catch her before she starts to speak." She approached the platform. "Miss Goldman," she called, "I just came from the Paterson strike."

"Ach, a fellow worker. Help her up, help her up." Jeannie found herself hauled up onto the platform just as a tall, thin man stepped forward. He began to speak in a language she didn't understand, until he finally announced Emma Goldman. The plump, matronly looking woman began to speak in that same, strange language, but even though Jeannie couldn't understand a word, could feel the energy that seemed to pour from the speaker. The audience was mesmerized, but somewhere in the back of the hall there was a disturbance, and shouts of "Anarchist," "Murderer," "Assassin," rose above the voice of the speaker. The crowd called out, "Hush, hush," but the shouts grew louder, and suddenly the strong-armed men who had been lounging along the aisles sprang to life, pushed their way to the platform and began arresting everyone in the name of the law.

Jeannie was grasped by rough hands and dragged past a horrified Moira into the street. Here she was shoved into a waiting police wagon along with others from the platform, and carried off into the night. When Moira finally emerged into the street, surrounded by a crowd of hysterical strangers, there was no sign of Jeannie. The crowd surged this way and that, but was finally broken up by the police and disappeared into the surrounding streets and alleyways.

"My friend! I can't find my friend," cried Moira, clinging to a young policeman.

"What's she look like?"

"She's young, wearing a white blouse and black skirt."

"So were half the women in the hall," he said.

"But she was on the platform."

He gave her a sharp look. "Then she's locked up with the rest of them murderin' anarchists, and you'd better get along before you get locked up, too." Moira turned and fled. There was only one thing left to do, go back to Paterson and get help.

She never fully remembered how she got there, but she finally stumbled up the steps of number ten where Maggie and Ian were waiting up and beginning to get very worried about Jeannie.

"Where did she go?" wondered Maggie.

"She said something about finding a job," said Ian. "Don't worry, Jeannie knows how to take care of herself." But they were shocked when they discovered a frantic Moira on the doorstep. She poured out her story: how they went to New York to look for work, and how Jeannie went up to speak to Emma Goldman and was pulled up onto the platform. Then she described the men who began shouting insults.

"An' before we knew what was happening, all them big louts that were loungin' in the aisles began pushing and shoving their way to the platform, where they grabbed everyone and dragged them outside. Sure'n before I could get to her the whole shebang were locked in the paddy-wagon and carted off the devil knows where. Poor Jeannie, they were all babblin' in some strange language, nary a word could I make out."

"Yiddish, probably," exclaimed Ian. "Why in the world did she go and get mixed up with a bunch of Jewish anarchists? Italian ones are bad enough, but Emma Goldman's crowd are bomb throwers."

"Bombs!" cried Maggie in alarm. "Och, if they think she's a bomb thrower she could be locked up forever." She began to cry.

"Nothing's going to happen to Jeannie," said Ian, putting his arm around her. "It was all a mistake. Tomorrow Moira and I'll go and talk to the police. You don't know where they've taken her do you?"

"No, but 'twill probably be in the paper."

"Dinna' let Aunt Flora see it, she'd die of shame," said Maggie. "Moira, ye'd better stay here tonight. Ye can sleep in Jeannie's room." Maggie wiped her eyes. "I canna' bear tae think o' her locked up in some dreadful prison."

"Don't worry, we'll have her out in no time. But we'd better get some sleep so we can get an early start."

They did get an early start, but it didn't do them much good. They were sent from precinct to precinct, no one seemed to know or care very much where the prisoners were being held, until finally, around seven o'clock at night, worried and exhausted, they were given some information.

"Jeannie McHugh." The officer behind the desk consulted a notebook. "She's probably being held at Ellis Island."

"What in the name of all the saints would she be doin' there?" cried Moira. "She's no immigrant."

"Waiting for her deportation hearing along with the rest of the agitators. Send 'em all back where they come from, that's what I say, ungrateful wretches."

"But Jeannie's no agitator," cried Moira. "She's a foine upstandin' citizen."

"If she's a citizen she's got nothing to worry about, has she?"

Ian felt the first real surge of panic. "When is this hearing?" he asked.

"If you want any more information you'll have to go to the immigration authorities. That's all I know." And he closed his notebook.

They were exhausted and depressed when they got back to Paterson.

"Where's Jeannie?" cried Maggie, clutching him and looking around desperately. He told her and she was horrified, as was Aunt Flora.

"Och, Ian, surely they wouldna' send a young girl like Jeannie back tae Scotland all alone."

"If she's to be deported, they don't care if she's alone or not."

Maggie burst into tears. "I'll never see mae sister again. Och, Ian, ye must do something. Jeannie's nae Bolshevik, or whatever it is they think she is. She's nae done anything wrong."

"She was at the wrong place at the wrong time," he said with a sigh. "Maggie, why on earth didn't Jeannie get her citizenship papers when you did?"

"She could see no need for it. She said she already knew all that stuff in the book."

"Well, it looks as if they're going to make an example out of her. Mostly they put these so-called troublemakers in jail for a few weeks, or fine them, but every once in a while the powers-that-be decide to deport a few as a warning to others.''

''Couldn't we be seein' them now, these mighty powers-that-be, and explainin' it all away?'' said Moira. ''Jeannie's no anarchist, 'twas just a job she was looking for.''

''With the Bolsheviks!'' exclaimed Aunt Flora. ''She's gone daft for sure. I knew no good would come of her bein' with those Eyetalians.''

''The Simonettis had nothing to do with this,'' said Ian firmly. ''It's all a mistake, and someone has to go and explain it to the authorities.''

''And who's going tae listen to a couple of country bumpkins from New Jersey?'' said Aunt Flora.

''No one, I'm afraid,'' said Ian. ''But there is someone they'll listen to, much as I hate to ask.''

''Who?'' demanded Aunt Flora. ''Who do you know in New York?''

''Grace,'' he said bitterly. ''Grace and that Harwood man. If money means influence, and it does, then they've got it. And they can damn well use it to help Jeannie.'' From the expression on his face the three women knew there was nothing more to be said, so once more he and Moira made plans to go back to New York the next morning.


The thought of seeing Grace was more disturbing than Ian cared to admit. No matter how much she had hurt him, no matter how angry she had made him, he could never suppress the tingle of excitement that rose inside of him at the mention of her name. He knew he couldn't just walk in on her. There must be some way to get in touch and prepare her for his visit. The mail was too slow and he didn't want to send a telegram. That left the telephone. They didn't have one in the house, and since neither Maggie nor Moira, and certainly not Aunt Flora, would touch the newfangled thing, he had to go himself to the drugstore where finally, with some assistance from a friendly operator, he was put through to the Harwood residence. A maid answered, but eventually Grace came on the line. He recognized the familiar lilt to her voice immediately and it seemed impossible that she was far away in New York—she sounded as if she were right beside him. He wasted no time on small talk, however, but came straight to the point.

"Grace, this is Ian. Jeannie's in trouble and needs help." Grace immediately arranged for him to come and meet with her husband.

"If anyone can help, he can," she said. "He's well known in the city." Ian swallowed his resentment and agreed to a meeting.

Once more, accompanied by Moira, he made his way to the city. He remembered the house from the day of the christening, and since they were expected they were admitted immediately. Moira was wide-eyed with wonder at the lofty entrance hall, the delicate curved stairway, the statues and flowers. They were ushered into the study where they were met by Grace and Mr. Harwood. The two men faced each other across a burled walnut desk. Ian was surprised to note that Grace's husband was not as old as he had pictured him, and it irritated him to discover that the man, although rather pale, was quite good looking.

Harwood extended his hand and Ian had no recourse but to shake it. He quickly introduced Moira, barely glancing at Grace as he did so, and then took the proffered seat.

Moira was speechless. She had forgotten seeing Grace at Lambert's Castle, but she remembered her now. She remembered how she and Ian had danced together, and how upset Maggie had been, but now these two acted as if they barely knew each other.

Grace in turn concentrated her attention on Moira, avoiding Ian's eyes. She smiled at this pretty little Irish lass, inexplicably swathed in immigrant-style head scarves, until Ian's casual remark that Moira had worked with Jeannie at Potter's mill triggered a shocking memory, and suddenly the significance of Moira's scarves hit her like a blow to the stomach. She felt sick. She forced herself to concentrate on Rob's questioning.

"Was Jeannie part of this Goldman organization?" he asked.

"Indade, she'd never set eyes on her till that night," said Moira. "They pulled her up on the platform, but when they all started makin' their speeches, 'twas gibberish. Nary a word could we understand."

"Well, let's see what I can find out," said Harwood, and to Ian's chagrin he casually reached for the telephone standing on his desk and put in a call to the authorities at Ellis Island. After a brief conversation he hung up.

"It looks like the Goldman woman has already been released, but young Jeannie and a couple of others are due for a hearing the day after tomorrow. If we can get an interim injunction we can probably have the charges dropped before the hearing. I'll call Judge Haversham."

Again he picked up the telephone and after a hearty, "Hi Bill, Rob Harwood here," he launched into his story. About three phone calls later everything had been arranged.

"They're going to consider it a case of mistaken identity, and they'll drop all charges. She should be free to go by this afternoon." Ian reflected on their exhausting day yesterday, going from precinct to precinct, while this man, in his well-cut suit, gold cuff links, and stylishly cut curly hair, accomplished everything without leaving the comfort of his home. He felt an upsurge of the old bitterness, but again he had to bury his resentment. He thanked him.

"I guess we'll be off to Ellis Island. Do we need any papers or anything?"

"I don't think so, but just in case . . ." He wrote something on a piece of paper, put it in an envelope, and handed it to Ian. "If you have any problems, give them this." He leaned back in his chair. He looked tired. "Well, now that's settled I'm sure Grace would like to have some news of the family. How is young Maggie?"

"Yes, tell me, did Maggie have her baby yet?" asked Grace.

"We have a little girl," said Ian briefly.

Grace, who found she had been holding her breath, relaxed. A girl.

" 'Tis a foine little babe she is, for all that she was so tiny. But 'tis thriving she is now," said Moira.

Rob beamed. "Our little boy's getting bigger and smarter every day. He's starting to talk, now he says Mama and Dada." Grace thought she was going to faint, but Rob continued. "Grace, why don't you take them up to the nursery and let them meet little Andrew."

"No!" she exclaimed, clutching the edge of the desk for support. Seeing the look of shock and surprise on his face, she quickly tried to explain. "I'm sorry, but he was a little flushed this morning. I'm afraid he may be coming down with a cold." She couldn't look at Ian. Oh, how she wanted to take him up to the nursery. To put Andrew in his arms and say, "Ian, meet your son." But she could never do that.

"I think it's time we were going anyway," said Ian. "Thank you again." He refused Grace's offer of coffee and took Moira's arm. Grace accompanied them to the door and watched them walk away. She felt as if her heart were being rent in two.

When she returned to the study, Rob was already tidying up his papers.

"I'm going up to lie down for a while, my dear. I don't think there's anything urgent here, but if there is you can take care of it." He looked at her and there was sadness in his eyes. "I didn't think little Andrew looked flushed this morning, Grace, but I guess you know best." *He knows*, she thought. *Oh God, he knows*.

"I—I," but she couldn't continue. "I'll come up with you," she said.

"No need, I'll be fine." He took her hand and kissed her. She looked up at him with brimming eyes. *He's so good to me,* she thought. *I don't deserve it.* When she spoke her voice trembled.

"Rob, Andrew couldn't have a better father."

"Thank you, my dear. I love him as I would my own, but you know that."

She stood at the door of the study and watched him walk slowly to the elevator. Then she returned to the desk, put her head down, and wept.

Jeannie sat on her cot. All around her voices rose and fell like waves crashing on the shore. A babel of voices, high pitched, shrill, frightened, and totally incomprehensible, washed over her. The only people she could understand were the guards. *Guards.* The very word sent a shiver down her spine. She was being guarded like a common criminal, but what had she done? What was this crime that was judged so terrible that she, along with the others locked up with her, were to be shipped out of the country? "Back where you came from," said the guard as the gate clashed shut behind them. Most of the women came from Russia. They huddled in the corner, shawls over their heads, clutching some meager possessions with gnarled, work-worn hands. Would she be shipped to Russia, too? A grim flash of humor assailed her—she'd always wanted to travel. *But not like this,* she thought desperately, *not like this.*

She tried to picture herself back in Scotland, but Scotland evoked children playing hopscotch, skipping home from school, or gathering peat for the fire in their little cottages. *That's all in the past,* she thought, *I'm not a child anymore. There's nothing left for me in Scotland.*

The women had been kind to her and had tried talking to her in their broken English. But they spoke of revolution, of tearing down the old ways, of blood running in the streets. She knew these women had seen terrible things, things she had only read about in books. She saw the grief in their eyes, but she couldn't share their anguish. She wasn't part of their revolution. Oh, she rebelled against injustice, but she wasn't a bomb thrower. She wasn't desperate enough for that.

She seemed to have lost all track of time. She wondered what had happened to Moira. Was she locked up somewhere, also? What about Maggie and Ian? If only she'd told them where she was going. She knew they'd be looking for her, but they'd never think to look here. Not on Ellis Island.

A grating in the lock told her the guards were coming. They had brought lunch, a pot of soup and some dark bread. She wasn't hungry. She thought fleetingly of Aunt Flora stirring her morning porridge, of Mama Simonetti's kitchen, warm and redolent with spices, and she fought back her tears. The guards set out the soup, then one of them unfolded a paper from his pocket.

"Which one of you is Jean McHugh?"

"I am." She stood up, her knees trembling.

"Come with me." She was marched, a guard on either side of her, down the same endless, chilly corridors she had walked down on her way in. She heard the same echoing footsteps, the same clash of doors being locked behind her, until she was back in the big room where they'd all assembled after they'd been brought over to the island from the police station. She stood facing an official-looking man who sat behind a large desk. He repeated her name.

"There's an injunction here signed by Judge Haversham. Seems there's been a mistake." He stamped some papers. "You're free to go, Miss McHugh." Jeannie stood rooted to the spot. Her legs refused to move even though the words echoed in her head: *Free, free, free.*

"Jeannie, Jeannie, over here." She spun around and there, behind the barrier, stood Moira and next to her was

Ian. She stumbled towards them, and they hugged wordlessly. Then she took Moira's arm.

"How did ye find me? I though'd I'd never see any of ye again. I was ne'er so frightened in all my life."

"Sure'n we were all over the city lookin' for ye," said Moira. "But 'twas your cousin, Grace, and her foine rich husband who got you out of here."

"Grace!"

"We'll explain later," said Ian. "Come on, let's get out of this place, it gives me the willies." They hurried out and boarded the ferryboat which was docked at a small pier. The great hall of immigrants loomed up behind them, while in front of them lay New York Harbor. They watched the boats steaming up the Hudson, many of them filled with Europe's poorest.

"I remember the day we arrived," said Jeannie. "I didn't want to get off the boat; I wanted to go back to Scotland." She laughed shakily. " 'Tis funny isn't it? These past few days I thought I was going back, and I knew I couldna'. I'm an American now. It's sort of like being married—for better or worse, I've made my choice."

"Then you'd better hurry up and make it legal," said Ian.

"Oh, I will," said Jeannie fervently. "I will."

On the way home they told her all about their excursions to New York, the trek from precinct to precinct, and finally their visit to the Harwoods.

" 'Tis a real important man he must be," said Moira. "He just talked into that telephone thing for a few minutes, and next thing he says you're free to go."

Ian gritted his teeth at the thought of Harwood's casual authority. "I didn't know anyone else who could help us," he said.

"She's still our cousin," said Jeannie, "for all her money."

" 'Tis a grand house they live in," said Moira with a sigh. She was still dazzled by the elegance of the Harwood home, the soft carpets, the beautiful silk draperies, the soft-footed servants. This was a world she had never even dreamed of, and yet Grace, whom she knew once worked in the mill just as she had, moved in it as if she'd been born to wealth. Something stirred in Moira, the beginning of a dream, a desire, a longing for something better. Jeannie was right—there was more to life than Potter's smelly basement.

# CHAPTER
## ❧ 29 ❧

ROB seemed to grow more weary each day. He had never regained his strength following the accident, but it was after Ian's visit that Grace felt him slipping away from her. She tried desperately to reach him, to hold on to him, but it was no use. He spent more and more time with little Andrew. No longer could he race up the stairs as soon as he came home and toss the happy little boy into the air; now he simply sat and watched him play. At night, long after the ritual of hugs and goodnight kisses, he always stole into the nursery to gaze lovingly at the sleeping child, rosy-cheeked and clutching his teddy bear.

The rest of his time was spent in his study going over the books and ledgers. He called Grace in.

"I'm setting up a trust fund for Andrew, the rest will go to you, Grace."

"Rob, there's no need . . . ."

"Yes, there is, my dear. I know this old ticker's getting weaker every day. That's why I've been teaching you the business. I want you to run Harwood Associates. You're perfectly capable of it, don't let them tell you otherwise." He looked at her and smiled, but it was a wistful smile. "Build it up, Grace. Build it up for Andrew."

A few days later, Rob died quietly in his sleep.

Joe and Maisie came as soon as they heard the news.

Joe helped Grace through the intricacies of arranging a funeral. Rob was known and liked throughout the city, and the church was filled with mourners. As she moved slowly up the aisle, clothed in black, a black veil covering her face, Grace recognized many faces. Mr. and Mrs. Lambert and several other mill owners were there, including Mr. Potter. She even saw Austin and Uncle Thomas, although there was no sign of Mrs. DeWitt-Kenton. A number of people had come from Harwood Associates, which had closed for the day as a gesture of respect, and she spotted Miss Finch's high pompadour among them. She even saw Jeannie slip into a pew in back of the church, but no one else came from Paterson.

As Grace stood and listened to the eulogy she tried to imagine life without Rob. His presence had dominated the house—his energy, his enthusiasm, his humor. *I'll never meet another man like him,* she thought. She knew she had lost her best friend and protector, and she mourned him deeply.

When they began the long, slow procession to the cemetery, she saw Maisie and Joe urge Jeannie into the carriage with them. The rest of the ceremony passed her by in a blur, and she was only vaguely conscious of the coffin being lowered into the ground, the prayers, and the scattering of flowers.

Afterwards several people accompanied her back to the house where the servants, red-eyed from weeping, had set up a buffet. In the general crush of people, Grace found herself accepting condolences and offers of help. After a while she began to sense an air of speculation among some of the businessmen present.

"Grace, I'm terribly sorry." It was Austin, hand extended, a faint sympathetic smile on his face, all past disagreements apparently forgotten. She shook his hand. "Mother sends her deepest regrets."

For a moment Grace was tempted to ask if her sciatica was keeping her home, but she resisted the moment.

"Thank you Austin."

"He will be greatly missed in the city." There was an unctuous tone to Austin's voice. "Harwood Associates was one of the most prestigious of silk dealers."

It was on the tip of Grace's tongue to say it would continue to be so, but again she resisted.

"We understand your present distress, Mrs. Harwood," said Uncle Thomas, placing his thin, dry hand limply in hers. "But please do not hesitate to call on either myself or Austin if you feel the need of some advice. We are, after all, part of the same community."

*So now I'm accepted into the community,* thought Grace, *it was not always thus.*

But there were other people to see and speak to, and she quickly moved on leaving Austin and his uncle to their own devices. She wanted desperately to talk to Jeannie, who was standing in the far corner of the room and appeared to be inching towards the door. After stopping to receive offers of sympathy and help from several people, Grace finally caught up with Jeannie. They embraced silently.

"Thank you for coming."

" 'Twas the least I could do. I never did thank Mr. Harwood for saving me from deportation. He was a good man, for all that he was on the side o' the mill owners."

Grace couldn't suppress her smile. Jeannie was Jeannie, she'd never change. "Rob was glad to do it. He always liked you, Jeannie."

"Well, I'm sorry I didna' get to thank him. Ian told me how he arranged everything."

"How is Ian?" said Grace, then she quickly added, "and Maggie?"

"Workin' night and day to try to make up for the time lost during the strike. They send you their love."

Grace felt the tears well up in her eyes and she quickly brushed them away.

"I have tae get back, Grace. I'm working for Ian now.

He's got two looms, you know. I'd hoped I could get some other work, but there was none. I'd rather starve than go back to Potter's.''

Grace again felt a surge of guilt. She'd done nothing to improve conditions at Potter's, and now they were all back working in that same dank, evil basement. But there was no further chance to talk, other people claimed her attention, and she saw Maisie walking her cousin to the door.

At last, when everyone had left except Joe and Maisie, Grace sank gratefully into an armchair.

"Whew, who were all those people?'' asked Maisie.

"Friends, business associates, and co-workers,'' said Grace. "Rob had no family.''

"No family at all!'' exclaimed Maisie, thinking of all her brothers and sisters back in Brooklyn.

"No, his mother died when he was an infant, and then his father died when he was about fourteen. If he had any aunts and uncles they were back in England and he never knew them. He went to work as a messenger boy for a silk merchant when he was about twelve years old and worked his way up.''

"What will happen to the business now?'' wondered Maisie.

"That's up to Grace,'' said Joe. He looked at her speculatively. "A lot of people would like to get their hands on Harwood Associates.''

"I know,'' said Grace. "The vultures are already circling. But I'm not going to sell. Rob wanted me to keep the business going. That's why he taught me how to run it.''

"You were a good pupil,'' said Joe. "I know.''

Joe and Maisie spent the night, but the next morning Maisie had to get back to Westchester.

"Why don't you come and stay with me for a while?'' she said.

"Thanks, Maisie, maybe later on, but there are so many things to attend to here.''

"Well, you know where I am whenever you want to come," Maisie said, giving her friend a tearful hug.

Grace watched them go, and then returned to the study and sat down behind Rob's desk. Suddenly that terrible sense of loneliness that she had been trying to ignore swept over her. She jumped up, ran upstairs, and burst into the nursery. Tomorrow she would face the world of Harwood Associates, today she needed the warm hugs and sticky kisses of little Andrew.

For the next several weeks Grace remained at home. It would have been most improper to have gone out, even on business matters. Most of her time was taken up acknowledging all the expressions of sympathy she had received, but she also continued to have the company mail brought to her just as she had during Rob's illness. She welcomed the work. It was when she had completed her chores and sat down to eat her solitary dinner that loneliness would once more assail her.

After a while she told Cook she would take her meals in the nursery with Andrew. Nanny wasn't too pleased at first, but when she saw that Grace didn't override her nursery rules she relented, and the two women became quite friendly. In fact, Nanny welcomed Grace's presence, for it was here, in the nursery, that Rob's absence was most painful, and Grace took over the difficult task of trying to explain to a bewildered little boy why Daddy wouldn't be coming back. Bedtime was the hardest. She took to rocking him to sleep, cradling his warm, little body in her arms, gently kissing the top of his golden head as she watched his eyes grow sleepier and sleepier, and all the while fervently thanking God for giving him to her.

It was the business that occupied most of her time and gave her the most concern. So much so that she asked for a meeting with Joe, Mr. Withersby, the company lawyer, and Ed Bixby, general manager.

"What is happening?" she asked. "Why aren't we getting the business we've been used to? Are we becoming thought of as a second-rate firm? We always got top quality silk from our Italian source, now I see we've been offered second-run quality. We're going to lose our best customers if this keeps up. Can you explain it, Ed?''

Ed Bixby, a grizzled man in his late fifties, shook his head. ''I placed the usual order, Mrs. Harwood, but I was told the top grade silk had already been spoken for.''

''But why?'' Grace was perplexed.

Bixby looked hopefully at the other two men. ''It's a matter of credit, Grace,'' said Joe.

''But our credit is good. We've always paid our bills on time.''

''Your suppliers are afraid that may not continue. Rob was the very heart of Harwood Associates, and with him gone . . .'' He shrugged slightly. None of them said what was in their minds, that men don't like doing business with a woman, but Grace could see it in their faces. Mr. Witherspoon finally spoke.

''Forgive me, Mrs. Harwood, but I feel I must speak out. Now, if you appointed a man as president things might be different. Do you by any chance have a brother?'' She looked at him in amazement and shook her head. ''Pity. Of course the ideal situation, if you will forgive me again for being so indelicate so soon, the ideal situation would be for you to remarry.''

A chilly silence filled the room.

''Mr. Witherspoon, marriage is the farthest thing from my mind,'' said Grace icily. ''I'd like you all to understand that it was Rob's wish that I take over Harwood Associates, and I intend to do just that. And in order to make it perfectly clear that we are not cutting back, I want you to contact our Italian sources. Who were they, by the way?

''It was the Comte d'Urbano,'' said Mr. Witherspoon, ''one of our oldest accounts.''

''Very well, get in touch with the Comte and cancel the

order for second-grade tram. Tell them we want first-quality silk or none at all. Then send a cablegram to Mr. Kasawaki in Tokyo. We'll buy Japanese silk.'' She saw the look of surprise on all three faces, but she detected approval also. She was not going to let Harwood Associates go under. Rob had worked too hard to build it up. ''And I've decided to visit the office next week. I'd like to reassure the staff that it's going to be business as usual.''

''An excellent idea,'' said Mr. Witherspoon, in his cool dry voice. ''Rumors tend to fly at a time like this, and they can be very damaging.''

The meeting ended amicably, and it was only after they left that Grace had an attack of nerves. Suppose they couldn't get Japanese silk? Suppose her Italian supplier cut her off entirely? She knew that the Comte had a lot of influence. She could see that a rocky road lay ahead of her, but Grace had never been one to run away from a challenge. In fact she enjoyed a good fight. She felt as if she were coming alive again. The terrible numbness was leaving her and her feelings were returning. And then, somewhere in the back of her mind, a little light flickered. She quickly smothered it, but while it was there it illuminated a hitherto unthought of possibility—remarriage.

One of Grace's first tasks when she emerged from the seclusion of her home was to sever her ties with Potter's Mill. Potter was obviously happy to let her go, although it was difficult to see any outward signs of it in his pinched and narrow face, which became even more disapproving when she raised the subject of compensation for Moira.

''Potter's Mill is not responsible for what happened to that unfortunate young woman,'' he said. ''It was her own carelessness that caused the accident.''

''But surely her supervisor should have realized the danger. I think the least we should do is offer some money to the people who took care of her.''

''Mrs. Harwood, if you wish to make a donation to

those Catholic nuns that is up to you. Personally I prefer to have nothing to do with Roman Papists. Heretics, all of them.''

*Those heretics, as you call them, saved Moira's life,* thought Grace, but obviously that was unimportant to Mr. Potter. She was relieved when the papers were finally signed and she was no longer a part of Potter's Mill.

But it still didn't remove her obligation to do something for Moira. She had received a note from Maggie when Rob died, written in a round childish hand, that extended sympathy from herself and Ian and also Moira. So it was to Maggie that she now wrote, suggesting that she or Ian bring Moira in to see her. She could just as easily have written to Jeannie, but she told herself it wasn't a good idea for two young girls to be coming to New York alone, ignoring the fact that she had been entirely alone when she arrived in the city. She knew, of course, that Maggie would never be the one to accompany Moira, and was not surprised when she heard that Ian would bring her in on Saturday.

As she waited for them at Chambers Street she tried to firmly suppress that dangerous tremor of excitement that always rose at the thought of Ian, and when they emerged from the ferry she concentrated her attention on Moira. Grace decided that the first thing Moira needed was a good wig, and she led her to a small shop specializing in hair-pieces.

''Ye mean 'tis no more scarves I'll be needin','' exclaimed Moira. ''But aren't hair pieces awful expensive?''

''This is compensation from the mill,'' said Grace, knowing Moira wouldn't accept charity.

''Well, 'tis only fair, seeing as how they got my hair in the first place, though it wasn't much use to them.''

Grace winced. She didn't know how Moira could speak so lightly of her terrible disfigurement, but Moira knew if she didn't laugh she would cry, so she laughed and saved her tears for her pillow at night.

When they found the shop, Madam Francine's Millinery and Transformations, and explained to the proprietress their need, she suggested they have two wigs made.

"One for every day, and one for special occasions. First of all you need to pick out the shade of hair. I suggest you try to match your own as closely as possible." She eyed Moira's scarves.

"I have no hair left," said Moira, anticipating her next question, "but 'twas a reddish brown color."

"Chestnut. We have several swatches of chestnut. Once you've decided on the color we will have to measure your head." Once more she looked at Moira's wrappings. Grace felt herself growing weak. She didn't want to be there when Moira unwrapped her head.

"Sure'n why don't you and Ian take a stroll while I decide. 'Twill probably take me a month o' Sundays to make up my mind."

Moira didn't want an audience either. Grace looked at Ian and he nodded. He was even more uncomfortable than she was in the confines of this small shop.

"Give us an hour at least," said Madame Francine. "I don't like to rush my customers."

Grace couldn't help recalling the last time she and Ian had walked the streets of Manhattan. Arm in arm they'd explored the city on winged feet, charmed by everything they saw from the East Side tenements to the West Side mansions, and then, afterwards, those same winged feet had let them up to her little flat. She glanced at Ian, his face was thinner, there were hollows in his cheeks, but his chin was still as determined as ever, and his eyes, when he looked at her, still caused her to tremble inside.

"I hear Jeannie is working for you these days." She had to find something to talk about, something safe.

"It's not steady work, I'm afraid. Mac's been able to get us some weaving to do because everyone's backed up, but most of our work is on the looms. Jeannie hates mill work, anyway."

"I wish I could find something for her. I think Moira could probably find a job as a housemaid, but somehow I can't see Jeannie in service."

Ian laughed. "She wouldn't last a week. She'd probably start lecturing about the responsibilities of wealth. I don't know where she gets all her radical ideas, unless it's from her Italian friends. That's what Aunt Flora thinks."

"I'm afraid Aunt Flora was always prejudiced."

"She's had to change her ways some, after all the Simonetti's were very good to us during the strike when Maggie . . ."

He stopped. He didn't want to talk to Grace about Maggie and the baby. He still felt guilty about the package she'd sent, and the terrifying consequences—he could still hear Maggie's accusations. He'd convinced himself those accusations were meaningless, that he no longer felt anything for Grace, but he found he was disturbingly aware of the young woman at his side, striking even in her widows' weeds. He noticed several admiring glances sent her way, although Grace seemed not to notice them.

They walked in silence for a while until she said casually, "Perhaps the next time you come into New York you could bring Jeannie with you." He didn't answer her. He didn't have to. He recognized an invitation when he heard one.

Moira was beaming when they got back to the shop.

"Sure'n you won't know me, Ian, I'm going to look so grand," she said. "But I have to come back next week for a fitting."

"That shouldn't be a a problem," said Grace, smiling. "I'll meet you again, same time, same place."

But when Moira returned the following week for her fitting it was Jeannie who accompanied her, not Ian. Grace was shocked at the bitterness of her disappointment.

"Ian had an emergency repair job," said Jeannie. "He couldna' spare the time. Maggie's helping him in the shop, an' Aunt Flora's taking care o' the bairn, so here I am."

Jeannie had the happy look of a kid let out of school, and Grace swallowed her disappointment. She tried not to think about Maggie and Ian side by side in the shop, and welcomed her cousin.

Jeannie, of course, had no compunction about seeing Moira scarfless, and Grace was forced to stay and watch the fitting, although she had to turn her head away at the sight of Moira's bare, scarred scalp. The wig, however, transformed her once again into a normal, pretty young girl.

"Och, 'tis perfect," exclaimed Jeannie. "No one would ever know 'twas not your own hair."

"Our wigs are the finest and most natural looking in all of New York," said Madame Francine proudly.

"I canna believe that old skinflint is actually paying for this. How did you wring it out of him, Grace?"

"It was the least Potter's could do," murmured Grace, averting her eyes. Jeannie could spot a lie a mile away.

Once the transaction was complete, and Moira was adorned with her new hairpiece, her second wig carefully wrapped in tissue paper and concealed in an elegant hat box, Grace suggested a small celebration.

"How about some ice cream?"

Later, seated over ice cream sundaes that caused Moira's eyes to pop, Grace brought up the possibility of getting Moira a job as a housemaid.

"Sure'n I've lots o' experience cleaning house," she said. "Didn't I hire out every spring to beat the carpets and polish the furniture in some o' the big houses in Hacketstown."

"And you, Jeannie, what would you like to do if you weren't working for Ian?"

"Not clean houses, that's for certain," said Jeannie.

" 'Tis a shame you're not a Catholic," said Moira. " 'Tis a grand nun ye'd make. Ye should have seen her, Mrs. Harwood, she got so she could change my dressings as good as any of the sisters."

"I always liked taking care of people if they were sick or hurt," said Jeannie.

"You should become a nurse," said Grace. Then she looked at her cousin seriously. Why not? She could afford to send Jeannie for nurses' training. She knew the big hospitals had schools attached to them where the girls lived while they were learning the profession. It was considered most respectable these days, ever since women like Clara Barton and Florence Nightingale set the standards. "Would you like that, Jeannie?"

"Och, Grace, ye know I would. But I canna afford to go tae nursing school. And besides, Aunt Flora would never allow it."

"Aunt Flora could be persuaded. And they have scholarships. Let me look into it for you, Jeannie."

It was two happy girls that boarded the ferry boat for Jersey, and even Grace was feeling well pleased. She was sure she could get Jeannie accepted in a nursing program, but she'd have to come in for interviews, and this time Ian would have to come with her. Grace was smiling when she hailed a cab to take her home.

# CHAPTER
## ❧ 30 ❧

IAN brushed the lint from his best suit, adjusted his tie and scowled at himself in the mirror. *Why am I going?* he asked himself. He had been making regular trips into the city, with Moira and then with Jeannie, but now both girls were settled. Moira had a new job with a family on Park Avenue and was in seventh heaven, and Jeannie was registered to begin her nurses' training at St. Vincent's next month. So why was he alone going to New York today? Even as he questioned, he knew by the eager throb of his heartbeat that wild horses would not have kept him away.

Maggie watched him quietly. He stood in front of the little mirror that hung over the chiffonier. He had to stoop a little to look into it. His back was to her, but she could see his face reflected. The same handsome, strong, masculine face that had captured her heart that first night in Aunt Flora's parlor. But he'd only had eyes for Grace. Grace! The knot in her stomach tightened. She wanted to cry out, *Oh, Ian, Ian, don't go. Don't go running to Grace, she'll only hurt you, hurt us. Oh, Ian, please don't go.* Instead she sat quietly pleating the edge of her apron.

"Jeannie's all set wi' her school. What do ye have to go in to New York for?" she asked without looking up.

303

"Grace wants me to take a look at her elevator, it's making a funny noise."

"Elevator!" Maggie's voice rose. "Ye mean in the office?"

"No, she had one installed in the house when her husband took sick."

"Well, what does she need it for now? She's nae sick." Maggie wanted to bite her tongue. She had promised herself she wouldn't say anything bad about Grace, wouldn't scold like a fishwife—but an elevator! It was just an excuse to get Ian to come to her house. Maggie shivered. She'd had this terrible premonition ever since she'd heard that Grace's husband had died. Poor man. She'd liked Mr. Harwood, and as long as he was alive she felt safe. But now Grace was free. *But Ian's not free,* she thought fiercely. *He has a wife and baby, but what does Grace care about that?* Ian, however, was extolling Grace's virtues.

"How could I refuse, Maggie? She's done so much for Moira and Jeannie. And she's all alone over there in New York, she needs someone to help her."

*But not you,* thought Maggie, *not you.* But she didn't say it, she just sighed.

"Do ye have a clean handkerchief? There's some in the top drawer. I ironed them yesterday."

"I have one, thanks." He gave one last flick of the brush to his errant lock of hair, kissed her hastily on the cheek, and hurried from the room. "Don't know what time I'll be back, it depends on the trains."

She heard his feet running down the stairs and she continued to sit, tears slipping down her cheeks. *I've lost him,* she thought miserably. *I thought he was mine, but he's not. She only has to crook her little finger and he's hers. It's not fair. She has everything, and she still wants Ian.* She looked around her little apartment which usually filled her with a quiet joy, but now seemed small and shabby. Ian couldn't even stand up straight to tie his tie.

She looked at little Meg, who was sleeping peacefully

in her crib alongside the bed. Ian had not even glanced at her in his haste, and suddenly she scooped the sleeping baby up into her arms, rubbing her tear-stained cheek against Meg's incredibly soft one, inhaling the sweet, milky, baby smell, rocking back and forth as the words pounded in her head: *Ian and Grace, Ian and Grace, Ian and Grace.* Had it ever really been anything but Ian and Grace?

Grace met him at the ferry.

"It's such a bright, sunny day I thought we could walk for a while."

She slipped her arm through his and they walked. Grace was tall, she matched her step to his, and they walked quickly and in rhythm. People automatically moved aside to let them pass, they were so obviously together, leaning towards each other, seeing but not seeing the great buildings, mansions, and elegant shops that lined their route. Heads high, hands clasped, fingers entwined, warmth flowing from their bodies in radiant waves, they strode along West Broadway to Washington Square and up Fifth Avenue, not growing tired but generating more and more energy as they walked towards their unspoken destination. Each wholly conscious of the other, as hand-in-hand, hip-to-hip, heart-to-heart, barely aware of the ground beneath their feet, they walked the length of the city.

At last, breathless and laughing, cheeks flushed, eyes sparkling, they ran up the steps to the massive front door. Grace leaned against the pillar and fumbled for her key.

"I'm afraid everyone's away," she said lightly. "Nanny has taken little Andrew to Westchester, Maisie is having a birthday party for her little girl."

*And I should really be there,* she thought, but she'd used a business crisis as an excuse. Because today was hers—hers and Ian's. She unlocked the door which swung open easily and they entered the cool marble foyer.

Grace slipped out of her jacket and tossed it carelessly on a bench.

"Would you like a drink?" she asked.

"No, thanks." He already felt drunk, lightheaded, reckless—as if the very air of New York were a bubbling glass of champagne.

"Well, here's the elevator." They got in together and it rose slowly with a slight creaking noise to the second floor.

"Sounds as if the gear drums need some oil," said Ian.

"But it's not dangerous?"

He smiled at her. "No, it's perfectly safe." They opened the gate and stepped out. Grace led the way and Ian followed. He barely noticed the marble statues or the erotic painting above him—his eyes were on Grace, her lithe movements, her shimmering red-gold hair, the curve of her cheek when she glanced back at him. He felt as if he were on fire, burning with desire.

He followed her into her sitting room, with its pale damask furnishings. The door closed behind him and he took her arm, swung her around, and then she was in his arms and he was kissing her. Long, deep, exploring kisses that left her breathless.

"Oh, Ian," she murmured. "I've wanted you for so long, so long."

He picked her up easily and carried her, unprotesting, into the bedroom where he laid her gently on the bed. He was filled with a terrible urgency and began frantically to unbutton her blouse. He slipped his hands inside, gently touching her soft, firm breast. Grace gave a little moan, and as she moved her red-gold hair loosened from its knot and spread over the pillow. His dream, his fantasy, his secret desires were all now within his grasp.

Grace sighed with pleasure and looked up into his grey-green eyes, eyes that were devouring her, and yet, strangely, it was not herself she saw mirrored in those eyes but Maggie. Gentle, sweet, loving Maggie. *Oh, God,* thought Grace, *I can't—I can't do this to Maggie.* She struggled to sit up, to push him away.

"Grace, no, no. I love you, Grace." Ian's voice was low and breathless.

"No, you don't," she whispered in a strangled voice. "It's Maggie you love. Your wife, Maggie."

It was as if she had slapped him hard across the face. He stared at her in shock, and as he did she seemed to fade, and Maggie's gentle face and bouncing dark brown curls swam before his eyes, and suddenly Grace's soft, warm breast seemed to turn cold as marble and he snatched his hand away. He sat up and looked around bemused at the luxury of her bedroom. What was he doing in Grace's bedroom?

"Grace, I'm sorry. I don't know what . . ." His voice trailed off. She turned away so that he wouldn't see the tears in her eyes.

"It's all right, Ian. We're just not cut out for adultery, you and me. I guess we're still intimidated by old John Knox staring down at us in dour disapproval."

She tried to laugh, but it ended in a choking sob. Ian remained in a daze, as if waking up from a dream—a dream that lingered, elusive, insubstantial, fading even as he tried to recapture it.

Grace quickly rebuttoned her blouse and did up her hair. "I'll have someone come in and oil the elevator," she said.

The elevator, of course, that's why he was here. He stood up. Suddenly he wanted nothing more than to escape from the stifling opulence of Grace's room, to escape from the stiff formality of the house. *I don't belong here,* he thought. *I could never belong here.*

"Grace, I have to go now. Maggie will be waiting for me."

She looked at him in panic. *He's slipping away from me,* she thought, *just like Rob. And if he goes now he'll never know that I love him with all my heart. He'll never know that he has a son, that we have a son.* She clutched his arm,

"Ian, don't go yet. I—I have something to tell you."

"Yes."

Her throat felt dry. She couldn't seem to form the words. She kept seeing Maggie, with a baby at her breast—Ian's baby. She gave a sigh that came from the depths of her soul.

"Nothing. It was nothing important."

She followed him downstairs and held open the great front door as he stepped outside, when to her consternation she saw a carriage pull up in front. Her carriage! Nanny had come back early. She leaned weakly against the doorpost and stared in dismay as the carriage door flew open and Andrew came running out and up the steps followed by Nanny.

"Mommy, mommy," he cried, as he hurled himself into her outstretched arms. She held him tight and looked over his head to Ian who was watching them.

"This is your little boy?" he said. Grace nodded, unable to speak. "Handsome little fellow. Looks like you." He took the little boy's hand. "Hi, you take good care of your mommy now." He waved to them casually and strode away. He didn't look back.

Grace stood, holding Andrew in her arms, straining her eyes, until he was out of sight. Andrew was chattering happily about cake and ice cream, and she clung to him, choking back her tears. He was all she had now. All she had in the whole world. She shivered slightly. There was an ache in her heart that she knew would never go away. But she knew she had done the right thing. Ian belonged to Maggie—dear, faithful little Maggie. Grace closed her eyes and thanked God that she had come to her senses.

As the train drew closer and closer to Paterson, Ian felt lighter and lighter of heart. A burden of old pain mixed with guilt had been lifted from him. A spell had been broken. Never again would he be bewitched by Grace. She had her little boy, he was glad of that, but now he had his own life to live. He and Maggie. Now he was free to love Maggie the way she deserved to be loved. Free to live his life the way he wanted to. He looked down at his hands—strong, brown, capable hands. With them he would build a life for Maggie and the baby. They'd get that house at the end of the trolley line, with a yard where Maggie could grow her flowers and vegetables, where little Meg could play. He'd work hard. He was clever. He could build things, fix things, make them work. Intricate difficult machinery was to him an exhilarating challenge. He welcomed it. He'd talk to old Mac tomorrow. They could expand the shop and advertise in the papers. All the mills were rolling again—there was work to be had, lots of it.

Maggie heard his step on the stair and steadied herself. She'd been frozen numb all the hours he'd been gone, trying not to listen to the endless chiming of the clock, trying not to think. Afraid. Afraid in that cold innermost part of her being. But now he was back, running up the stairs, taking them two at a time, bursting in the door. And then she was in his arms. They were laughing, crying, kissing, hugging each other as if they'd been separated for months instead of a few desperate, dangerous hours.

"Maggie, all the way home on the train I've been thinking. We're going to expand the business. We'll have to stay here for a while, but I'll make good, I know I will. Then we'll buy a house, in Haledon if you like."

"Och, Ian, anywhere, as long as we're together," she said, and with a joyous leap of his heart he knew she meant it.

"Where is everyone?" he asked. "Where's the baby?"

"Jeannie took her for a walk, and Aunt Flora's fixing supper. She'll be expecting us down." Ian grinned.

"Let her wait. A husband has a right to be alone with his wife once in a while." Maggie blushed.

"Now, 'tis not even nighttime."

"Who cares? I love you, Maggie, love you, love you, love you." He wanted to bury himself in her soft, warm plumpness.

Together they moved to the big brass bed and it was better than it had ever been before, because now it was Ian and Maggie, Ian and Maggie, Ian and Maggie, with nothing between them but their hot, young desires.

# CHAPTER
## ❧ 31 ❧

AUNT Flora straightened her new straw hat. She certainly didn't want the Simonettis to think she wasn't properly dressed, and who knew how many of her neighbors would be there. She was sure Jock and Dora were going, if only out of curiosity. That's why she was going. A restaurant! She shook her head. Mama Simonetti was opening a restaurant in the old grocery store, and had moved into the flat upstairs. What an extraordinary country America is, she thought, she couldn't picture this happening in Scotland. Of course there were so many Simonettis there'd be no shortage of waiters and waitresses, dishwashers and sweepers, with Mama presiding over the kitchen like a queen over her kingdom. "Catholics," she muttered. "If we're not careful they'll overrun the earth."

Maggie and Ian were waiting for her in the hall. One of the neighboring girls was watching little Meg, and so they had a whole evening to themselves. Maggie's arm was tucked into Ian's as they walked along.

Jeannie was already there and brimming with excitement. "The restaurant won't be officially open until next week. This is sort of a dress rehearsal. They canna sell wine, but ye can bring your own and drink it."

"I'll be wantin' no wine," said Aunt Flora.

"Try some grape juice, then," said Jeannie, " 'Tis delicious." But Aunt Flora's lips were pursed in disapproval even at the thought of an innocent grape.

The store had been repainted and was bright and clean. About ten tables of assorted sizes and shapes were set out and covered with gingham tablecloths. A jar filled with bright red paper flowers sat in the middle of each table. Aunt Flora raised her eyebrows in contempt, but Maggie and Jeannie declared it beautiful. Tony met them, looking very proper in a dark suit with a bow tie. Jeannie began to giggle.

"Don't laugh," he said. "I'm the one who speaks the most English so I have to take care of you. The family can fend for themselves." Jock and Dora were already seated at a table and began waving frantically to Aunt Flora, so Tony seated them all together.

"Which would you like, antipasto or minestrone?"

Jock threw up his hands.

"And what in the devil might auntypaste be, or minny—whatever you said? Beggin' your pardon, Flora, but the way these dagos speak ye canna understand a word they say."

Jeannie felt an angry flush rising on her cheeks, but Tony just winked at her and explained cheerfully,

"Minestrone is a soup made with beef, beans and vegetables, and the antipasto is a tray set out with olives, prosciutto . . ." Jock held up his hand.

"We'd better take the soup. That paste stuff sounds weird tae me."

Even Jock had to admit that the soup was delicious. It was followed by bowls of spaghetti served with thick chunks of homemade crusty bread.

"Hmm," said Dora, "only peasants eat thick bread like this," but she managed to eat several slices. All around them the babble of voices grew higher and higher, as bottles of wine were uncorked. Jock and Dora also grew more cheerful as the meal progressed, possibly because they too were adding something to their grape juice from a flask Jock carried in his pocket.

When the meal was over, Mama was brought out from the kitchen for a round of applause, and she stood beaming, perspiring slightly, her face glowing from the heat of the kitchen. She accepted everyone's thanks, clasped all within reach to her ample bosom and invited everyone upstairs to continue the party. Most of the men immediately disappeared into the kitchen, along with several bottles of wine, but the Scottish contingent dutifully trooped upstairs.

"D'ye want tae go along with the men?" Maggie whispered to Ian.

"Maybe later, right now I want to be with you." He squeezed her hand and she glowed. They sat around the little parlor and soon the singing began. First came the Italian arias, then the Scottish ballads started, with Jock doing his best to outsing the ladies. Tony pulled on Jeannie's arm.

"Come on," he whispered. "Let's leave these old folks. Angelina's got a phonograph in the other room." The two girls, with Ian in tow, followed Tony into the other room.

" 'Allo, Jeannie, you wanna hear some real music?" Angelina was winding up a brand new phonograph with a shiny trumpet. She beamed at the three of them. "I speaka the good English, no?"

"No. I mean, aye," said Maggie.

"Thanka your sister, then," she said. "An' now she go away an' leave us."

"I'm only going to New York. To train to be a nurse," said Jeannie proudly. She still couldn't believe her good fortune. She'd already had her interview with the Mother Superior at St. Vincent's Hospital and had been accepted. A year ago she would have been terrified of working with nuns, but since she'd seen how good they'd been to Moira, she was no longer afraid. She'd had to answer a lot of questions, though, and had been grateful for the Saturdays she'd spent studying with Tony.

"Our cousin Grace arranged it—wasna' that kind of her?" said Maggie.

Jeannie noticed that Maggie and Ian didn't seem to mind talking about Grace any more. Something had changed. *Maybe it's because she's going away,* she thought. Grace was going to Italy, along with little Andrew, his nanny, and a secretary. Going to buy silk, she said. Imagine going off to Italy just like that—first class, too. She told Jeannie she'd been invited to visit a count and countess who lived in some sort of palace. Grace was moving in very high society these days. But Jeannie didn't envy her. She was more than happy to be allowed in Mama Simonetti's kitchen with its rich smells of tomato sauce and garlic. She knew that Maggie and Ian didn't envy Grace, either. They both looked so happy these days, so wrapped up in each other. *It's time for me to move on,* she thought. *Time for them to be alone.*

Suddenly Aunt Flora's voice, high-pitched and wavery, floated in from the other room.

"Speed bonnie boat like a bird on the wing . . ." she sang.

"For heaven's sake close the door," exclaimed Jeannie.

Angelina laughed, "Here, this will be better." She carefully placed the needle on the spinning platter and the tinny voice of the phonograph sang out,

"Come on and hear,
Come on and hear,
Alexander's Rag Time Band. . . ."

Soon they were all laughing and foot stomping. Angelina and Tony pushed back the furniture and started doing something called the Turkey Trot, and the old songs faded into the background as they sang in unison,

"You wanna hear the Swannee River played in Rag Time,
Come on along, come on along,
to Alexander's Rag Time Band.''

Grace stood on deck and watched the lights of Manhattan slip past. Already the gleaming torch of the Statue of Liberty was behind them, and they were heading out to the mysterious blackness of the Atlantic. A cool breeze lifted her hair as she leaned over the rail.

She thought back to the other ship that had brought her to these shores. She shuddered as she recalled the crowded bunks, the heat and the smell. How longingly she had gazed at the tall buildings and fashionable carriages that to her spelled New York, and she recalled her promise to herself: "If I ever travel again it will be first class." Well, she *was* traveling first class, in her own stateroom with adjoining rooms for Nanny and Andrew, and accommodations below for her secretary.

She thought of the letter in her purse—an abject apology from the Comte d'Urbano for even thinking of offering second-grade silk to so prestigious a firm as Harwood Associates, and an invitation, extended from himself and his mother, the Contessa, to Signora Harwood if she would honor them by staying at their humble *palacio* when she was next in Europe.

"Why don't you go," Maisie had urged. "The change will do you good."

"And," added Joe, "it will do no harm to meet your supplier face to face. Rob always tried to do that."

So here she was on the deck of the Lusitania, a wardrobe of new clothes in her steamer trunk, an excited little boy asleep below, two trusted employees to assist her, and a whole new continent to conquer. And for the first time since the terrible day when she had sent Ian back to Maggie, Grace felt a small surge of anticipation, of hope, and yes, even a glimmer of happiness.